JB TURNER

HARD KILL

EXHIBIT A
An Angry Robot imprint
and a member of the Osprey Group

Lace Market House
54-56 High Pavement
Nottingham
NG1 1HW
UK

www.exhibitabooks.com

An Exhibit A paperback original 2014
1

A catalogue record for this book is available
from the British Library.

UK ISBN 978 1 909223 48 6
Ebook ISBN 978 1 909223 50 9

Set in Meridien and Franklin Gothic by Argh! Oxford.

For my mother

ONE

The headlights appeared out of the darkness on the dirt road that led to Jon Reznick's isolated home. He was sitting on his front porch with a mug of strong, black coffee, trying to figure out whether he should reach for his Beretta. He didn't as a rule get visitors to his oceanfront home outside Rockland, Maine. Ever. And certainly not before dawn broke.

He gulped down the rest of his coffee as he was bathed in the harsh headlights of the oncoming cars. The tires crunched the bone-dry earth, rutted by the recent heat wave. The birds in the trees took flight into the inky-black sky and disappeared into the sultry air.

Three vehicles?

The lead car, a black Suburban, pulled up in a cloud of dust. A few moments later the rear passenger door opened.

A man wearing a navy suit, dark tie and black shoes emerged. He walked toward Reznick and flashed a badge. "Special Agent in Charge of Boston, Jimmy Richards," he said. Perspiration beaded his forehead. "Jon Reznick?"

Reznick remained seated. He stared up at the Fed but said nothing.

"Sorry to drop in on you like this. But we need to talk."

Reznick shrugged. "So talk."

"I've been asked to speak to you in person by Assistant Director Martha Meyerstein."

The mention of her name brought the memories flooding back for Reznick. "About what?"

"I think it's better if you come with me."

"Not possible."

"Excuse me?"

"I'm catching a flight down to New York later this morning to visit my daughter."

"That might be a problem. You're required to come with me, sir."

"Required to come with you? I'm not required to do shit."

"Jon..."

"You can call me Reznick or Mr Reznick. Look, Mr Special Agent in Charge, I don't know you and I sure as hell have never met you. You turn up on my property unannounced. So I'd appreciate it if you could leave me alone."

SAC Richards' gaze wandered over the salt-blasted wooden house Reznick's father had built many years ago. He sat down on the porch step beside Reznick and stared toward the three Suburbans. "Here's the thing. You need to come with us, Reznick. She asked specifically for you."

Reznick said nothing.

"She couldn't make it herself. Back-to-back meetings with various intelligence analysts. But she thought it was appropriate for someone to talk to you in person."

Reznick closed his eyes for a moment. His gut reaction was to tell them to take a hike. His trip to New York was something he'd been looking forward to for weeks, not having seen his daughter, who was at boarding school, for nearly four months. He'd paid for the tickets, the fancy hotel room, not to mention Springsteen at Madison Square Garden. So why the hell wasn't he declining the offer? Was it because he wanted to work with Meyerstein again? Was that it? "You need to tell me more."

SAC Richards sighed. "I've only been told what I need to know."

"What exactly do you know?"

"We need to find someone."

"That's it?"

"More or less. It's on a need-to-know basis."

"I'm guessing the FBI doesn't send special agents in charge of Boston all the way up here in a three-car convoy for the sheer hell of it."

"We flew up here, if you must know."

"Who's gone missing?"

"You'll find out soon enough." He looked at his watch. "You need to get your ass into gear. You got five minutes to pack a bag, Reznick. Let's get to it."

Ninety minutes later, after a turbulent flight from Owls Head's small airport, they touched down at Dulles. Three Suburbans were waiting and they drove east. The first tinges of a blood-red sky appeared as the sun peeked over the horizon, throwing long shadows. Reznick and Richards sat in silence throughout the twenty-minute journey. He saw a sign for the town of McLean. Upscale and affluent. They headed down tree-lined streets and past huge mansions with manicured lawns and electronic steel gates.

He couldn't see any street signs, only trees. In the distance, men in black, standing guard against a six-story concrete building. The car slowed at hydraulic steel barriers. Window wound down.

"United States Police," a guard in black wearing shades said, emerging from a guardhouse, walkie-talkie crackling. "What's your business?'

The driver said, "Refer all inquiries to Assistant Director Meyerstein."

"I got you." An individual access badge was handed out to each of the team. "You must wear these at all times."

Reznick and the Feds each clipped on their badge.

The guard handed over a pale blue-colored card to the driver. "This is to enter the facility gate."

The driver nodded and they were waved through, the guards taking a long, hard look at Reznick.

The car headed past the checkpoint to a parking garage at the rear of the building, where a two-man team rechecked the individual access IDs – taking particular time over Reznick's – and escorted them into the lobby.

More security, airport-style scanners. Two large welcome mats with the words "Liberty Crossing."

Reznick knew exactly where they were. It was one of the most secure facilities in the US and housed both the Office of the Director of National Intelligence and its National Counterterrorism Center past the armed guards and the steel barriers. He'd once been told that at least 1,700 federal employees and 1,200 private contractors worked at Liberty Crossing, the nickname for the complex.

An NCC official escorted them to the elevator and rode it to the fourth floor. He led them along a windowless corridor until they got to a glass door, two cameras scanning the entrance.

He punched a long numeric code into the keypad. The doors clicked open and he ushered them inside.

Reznick was taken to a room.

"Take a seat, Mr Reznick," the official said.

Reznick did as he was told and he was left alone. He looked around. White walls, modern prints. Clock on the wall. Washington Post on a small table. He sighed. He hated waiting. Time dragged.

More than twenty minutes later, the official returned.

"They'll see you now."

Reznick got up and followed the man through to open-plan offices. Wooden desks, geometric-patterned gray-and-white carpets. Then it was down a long corridor to another conference room. Gathered round a large oak table were six men and one woman. Meyerstein looked up, as did her right-hand man, Roy Stamper, who Reznick already knew. Plasma screens on the wall. She stood up and shook his hand.

"Glad you agreed to join us," she said.

Reznick was introduced to everyone around the table. They included the head of the FBI's Hostage Rescue Team, a "special advisor" to the Department of Homeland Security, and a raft of high-level security-cleared members of the intelligence community – senior analysts from the CIA, NSA, Pentagon, State Department and Homeland Security. He shook their hands. He knew all about strategic analysts and rated their skills highly. The people who sifted raw data and tried to figure out the big picture, providing people like Meyerstein an understanding of what was known about a threat and what wasn't. But they were also concerned with trying to determine what threats lay over the horizon.

"Take a seat, Jon," she said after the formalities were over.

The only person who wasn't identified was the man sitting to the left of Meyerstein.

Reznick sat down in his seat and looked up at the clock on the wall. 7.03am. "You mind telling me what this is all about?"

The man to the left of Meyerstein cleared his throat. "My name is Lieutenant General Robert J Black; I am employed by the Defense Intelligence Agency, although for the last year I've worked out of an office at the Pentagon. Now that we're all acquainted, let me set out some ground rules."

Black's gaze lingered for a moment on each and every person around the table.

"What I'm about to tell you is not to be discussed and, secondly, is not to be acknowledged. Only the people in this room plus the President know. And that's the way it's going to stay." A few nods round the table. "A senior diplomat – a defense attaché, Dennis O'Grady, who also worked as a national security advisor in a previous administration – didn't show up for a scheduled meeting with me after supposedly meeting with a trusted source of his in Bethesda forty-eight hours ago."

Reznick shifted in his seat. A few round the table scribbled notes.

"Now, I want to make this clear that this is very, very out of character. Seems to have just vanished. O'Grady worked in the Middle East for the best part of twenty years and was special advisor on the Persian Gulf and Southwest Asia for the State Department."

Meyerstein nodded before she interjected, "While Lt General Black will be providing oversight, I will be taking the lead. We've got a fifteen-strong dedicated team working solely on this special access program."

Lt General Black leaned forward and allowed his gaze to wander round the assembled faces. "Assistant Director Meyerstein's word is law. She will report back to me as and when she decides. We want to keep this tight. In-house. But for now, your primary responsibility is to find O'Grady before it is too late."

TWO

When Black gathered up his briefing papers and left the room, Meyerstein cleared her throat and looked around the table at the stern faces.

"At this stage, it is not possible to rule out that this is a terrorist-related incident with an international nexus, so let's bear that in mind." She flipped through some papers in front of her. "First things first: we're on the clock. And I want O'Grady back safe. That is my top priority. The basic investigative legwork has already been started. We're piecing together his movements in the last week, we're speaking to his wife and children and I've ordered bank records and cell phone records to be subpoenaed. I've also ordered a track-and-trace on the cell phone. But so far, nothing. So, we've got a big job on our hands."

The CIA senior intelligence analyst, Larry Verona, said, "Can I play devil's advocate for a moment?" A few puzzled looks. "Is it possible, just possible, that he's simply run off with his mistress?" He shrugged. "Can we rule this out?"

Meyerstein nodded. "O'Grady is a devoted family man. It's a fair point you're raising, Larry, but this angle is not on our or anyone's radar."

Reznick said, "What is the DC police saying to it?"

"As it stands, we're bypassing the DC police on this."

Reznick said nothing. This was no run-of-the-mill disappearance.

"Ordinarily, we would have issued an all-points bulletin within the first four hours of the disappearance, put out flyers. But that was not appropriate in this case. The media would have gotten a hold of it and that's the last thing we need." She turned to Stamper. "OK, Roy, I know it's early days, but what's the latest?"

Stamper picked up a remote control in front of his papers and clicked a switch. A huge color photo appeared on the plasma screens. It showed a fifty-something white man wearing a beige linen suit, face flushed crimson, possibly with the heat, glass of wine in hand. "This was taken only last week. It shows O'Grady at a reception being held by the US embassy in Qatar. The next day he flew back to Washington. Two days ago, O'Grady left the house he shares with his wife and three kids in Chevy Chase and drove to a meet. Never seen again." He looked across at the State Department official. "Can you update us on who he was supposed to be meeting with?"

The State Department official, Lt Col Ed Froch, said, "I believe O'Grady was meeting with a high-placed source, the name or identity of whom only O'Grady knew."

Stamper sighed. "We need that. Can you look into that?"

Froch scribbled on a pad in front. "I'll get on it. But it may take time."

Meyerstein bit her lower lip. "Christ. So we don't have any footage? What about the GPS?"

"He vanished off the grid, his signal, at 10.37am eastern time. And that was that."

Meyerstein stared at Lt Col Froch, who was scribbling some notes, and leaned forward, hands clasped. "I need more details about O'Grady's work. Your area of expertise within the State Department is the Persian Gulf?"

Froch nodded.

"By that you mean Iran?"

Froch said, "There are other countries which we cover but, yes, primarily, our main focus is Iran."

"Now, you say you don't know anything about O'Grady's meet. But I don't buy the fact that the State Department has no clue about this whatsoever."

Froch gave a thin smile. "I said that we don't know the identity of who he was meeting. But we have some intel."

Meyerstein stared at him long and hard. "Look, Lieutenant Colonel Froch, are you being deliberately obstructive?"

Reznick had been wondering the same thing. He didn't like his smartass attitude.

Froch remained cool. "I can assure you that's not the case. In my line of work, we must be very careful what can and can't be shared with the wider intelligence community."

"Let's cut to the chase. Tell me everything you know."

"Well, as far as we can tell, O'Grady was liaising with a Bosnian émigré originally from Sarajevo."

"And that's it?"

Froch said nothing.

"Tell me more about this meet."

"I've put in a few calls to those who knew O'Grady better than I did. Nothing. The trail goes cold."

Meyerstein arched her eyebrows as she leaned back in her seat. "What do you take that to mean?"

"Maybe O'Grady got careless. Maybe he was being followed. We just don't know, as O'Grady had more-or-less autonomy in what he did."

Meyerstein stared across the table at Froch. "Sounds to me like a lack of oversight."

Froch's gaze wandered round those at the table. He made eye contact with each and every one as if trying to gauge their mood. Then he fixed on Meyerstein. "I don't accept that. I think an experienced diplomat who had moved in such circles for so long needed leeway."

"So much so that we don't know who he was seeing and where the hell he was?"

"Like I said, he had leeway."

"You mind trying to explain the connection between Bosnia and O'Grady's area of expertise Iran?"

"The Iranian sphere of influence is always there. Bosnia was the fallout from the fragmentation of the former Yugoslavia. The Serbs were allies of the Russians, so we were sympathetic to the new Bosnian state. The Bosnian Muslims amount to less than half of the population and are deemed among the most secular and liberal in the world. However, they are by and large not Shia, like Iran, but Sunni."

"So where does Iran fit into this?"

"The Shias constitute around seven percent of the Muslim population in Bosnia, about a hundred and sixty-five thousand people. So, while they're the minority, that's a lot of people who could be linked to Iran, to a greater or lesser degree, in some capacity, and perhaps come under their influence."

Meyerstein scribbled some notes and pondered on that for a few moments. "So there may be an Iranian link to this?"

Froch shrugged.

"Take a guess?"

"They can't be ruled out; that's for sure."

Stamper nodded.

Meyerstein looked across at her right-hand man. "Roy, your thoughts?"

"For me, there are echoes of the disappearance and death of defense attaché Thomas Mooney in Cyprus, 2007. If I remember correctly, his body was found a few days after he disappeared."

Froch stared down at the papers in front of him. "But that was deemed to be suicide, wasn't it?"

Meyerstein rubbed her eyes as if seriously sleep deprived. "That was the official line." Her tone was harsh with Froch, almost dismissive. Reznick could feel the tension in the room. She looked across the table at Reznick. "Jon, I'll be looking for insights from you, too."

Reznick nodded and felt all eyes on him.

Froch shook his head and stared across at Meyerstein. "No disrespect, but how can he know anything? This is not his area of expertise."

Reznick stared at Froch. He had met the type before. Arrogant. Full of themselves. He couldn't abide inflated egos.

Meyerstein leaned forward and stared straight at Froch. "Lieutenant Colonel Froch, this is a joint task force and I'm taking the lead. We work together on this. Understood?"

Froch raised his eyebrows but said nothing.

Meyerstein blew out her cheeks. "The question is, where do we go from here? Let's open this up." She looked at the NSA specialist, who was taking notes on his iPad. "Irwin, what do you think?"

Irwin stopped tapping on the tablet and looked up. "We're trawling through millions of calls, emails and instant messages as we speak, looking to get a heads-up. I'm talking real-time, message boards, the lot. We're on it. That's what I've been doing, in case you're wondering."

Meyerstein nodded. "Here's where I'm coming from. I think there's a very real possibility that O'Grady has been kidnapped or worse."

Everyone around the table nodded.

Reznick said, "The Iranians, as most of you'll know, work out of the Pakistan Embassy, as they don't have their own now. That's where I'd start looking."

Meyerstein nodded. "Ed, you want to expand?"

Froch said, "Currently, seventy-four Iranian nationals are accredited to the Interests Section of the Islamic Republic of Iran in Washington, DC."

Meyerstein made a note.

"However, because the United States and Iran don't have diplomatic relations, none of the Iranians have official diplomatic status."

Meyerstein said, "So, their names would not be published in the State Department's Diplomatic List?"

"That's right. They are, in effect, employees of the Iranian Interests Section. While they come under the umbrella of the Pakistan Embassy, they maintain separate offices. The Iranians working there have permanent resident status in the US or are dual nationals, making it difficult to take any action against them. They attend cultural and social events within the Iranian community and maintain close ties to an Islamic Center in Potomac that is financed by a New York-based foundation. They also have an information section that is used for intelligence work. In addition, all staff members of the Interest section hold green cards or US passports, meaning they are free to travel in the United States."

Meyerstein stretched, stifled a yawn and scribbled some more notes. The red light on her Blackberry began to flash and she took a few moments to check it, perhaps an urgent email or message. "Jon, you want to come back?"

"Yeah." Reznick looked across at the NSA specialist. "What's electronic monitoring telling us?"

The NSA guy sighed. "I only have a team of three, right in this building, doing the traffic analysis. Basically, trawling everything that's sent and received or phoned to and from the Iranians, night and day. Encrypted, non-encrypted, language specialists, you name it. Anything flags up and we're on it straight away. We're also tracing all the numbers called in the last forty-eight hours, but it's wrapped up in layers of advanced encryption. It's gonna take time."

Meyerstein said, "Something we don't have."

Reznick said, "This might have nothing to do with the Iranians; I think we've got to be clear on that, too. But we can't rule them out. Perhaps we need to think about getting a team in close, keep tabs on these Iranians. Their houses, hangouts."

Froch said, "Reznick, we've got to remember that they are operating under the auspices of the Pakistani Embassy and have surveillance detection units just as we do. They're not dumb. They know what to look for when it comes to observing those who're watching them."

"So we stay in this room and sit on our hands? Look, we've got to move on this. Round-the-clock surveillance is needed and not relying solely on electronic monitoring."

Froch shook his head. "That's not practical."

Stamper said, "It's a good point Jon's making. The political attachés and military attachés can be a priority."

Froch cleared his throat and sighed. "We have no evidence, as it stands, that Iran is behind this. None at all."

Reznick said, "I've already said that."

Meyerstein said, "We go with surveillance of the Iranians." She looked around at the assembled team. "This is going to be a 24/7 operation until we find O'Grady. We meet up again in less than twelve hours' time at 6am sharp, in this room. And I want to reiterate once again, this is strictly within the team. This investigation doesn't exist to anyone."

When the meeting ended and everyone had filed out, Meyerstein pulled Reznick and Stamper aside. "Follow me."

She led them down a long corridor. Hanging on the wall were black-and-white prints of DC monuments at night and framed extracts from George Washington's speeches. They took the elevator to the top floor and went through a series of keypad entries and into a carpeted corridor toward more doors. Meyerstein swiped a card and they entered a secure area, her office the last on the right.

"This is where I'm based during this investigation," she said, as Reznick and Stamper followed her inside.

It was all muted beige, a dark teak desk and a couple of brown leather sofas and four seats lined up against the wall. A huge TV on the wall showing live CNN coverage of a school in Ohio. At the far end of the large office, a partially open door to a private bathroom.

"Pull up a seat, guys," she said.

Reznick and Stamper complied and sat down.

Meyerstein sat on the edge of her desk and stared at them. "Firstly, Jon, very good to see you. I appreciated your input. Sorry I wasn't able to call you directly, but we're behind the curve and things are moving very quickly."

Reznick said, "I assume you didn't invite me here to make up the numbers."

Meyerstein shook her head, curling some hair behind her right ear. "Not quite. A short while ago, during our meeting in fact, I got an instant message from the FBI encryption guy, Special Agent Scott Liddell. His people have been looking over O'Grady's phone records. And they think they've finally pulled up the last number he called before he disappeared."

Stamper shifted in his seat. "Whose is it?"

Meyerstein said, "Wait just now. It's taken far longer than they expected. Three of the FBI's best computer experts, who are here in this building, believe that there was a sophisticated attempt to try to block anyone getting their hands on the cell phone records of O'Grady. Nobody knows about this apart from them, me and you two."

Reznick looked at Stamper, who was grim-faced. "When you say sophisticated attempt, do you mean electronic jamming?"

"Quite possibly. Jon, I want you to work alongside Roy. I don't know where this investigation will lead us, but I want someone with your – how can I put it – specialist knowledge, as I don't like the look and feel of any of this. I haven't worked with any of those guys round that table, only Roy and you. They were all appointed by the Department of Intelligence.

But I don't know them and I'm not sure who I can really trust. I know you both. I trust you both implicitly. So, I want you to run a parallel investigation separate from the main official investigation, reporting only to me."

Stamper ran his hand through his hair and sighed. "I don't like this, Martha. The whole feel of this. Something's wrong."

Meyerstein nodded.

"But I also don't feel good with the secrecy."

"It's just the way I want it to run. The cell phone number that O'Grady called is owned by a twenty-two year-old resident of Georgetown, Caroline Lieber. Does the name Lieber mean anything to you?"

Stamper shook his head.

"Ms Lieber is the youngest daughter of Jack Lieber, real estate tycoon. You know anything about Jack Lieber?"

Reznick and Stamper both shrugged.

"Jack Lieber is the single biggest donor to the President in New York City. And his daughter, according to this, is a former intern at the White House."

Reznick felt his heart rate hike up a notch. "OK, we've now got something to work with. We need to get into her life big time."

Meyerstein nodded. "Be careful. I've got a bad feeling about this whole thing."

THREE

The morning sun was throwing long shadows across the road as the SUV with Reznick, Stamper and the Feds inside edged along a leafy street in the historic Georgetown area of Washington, DC. The temperature on the dashboard showed it was 95 degrees. Smart townhouses and upscale cars parked on either side, sidewalks bustling with life. They took a right along Volga Place Northwest and pulled up outside an elegant townhouse. An American flag flew from the first floor and fluttered in the light breeze.

Reznick got out first and Stamper followed. Reznick felt the sweat running down his back within seconds of stepping out of the air-conditioned vehicle and into the stifling heat.

"Damn, it's hot," Stamper said. He wiped his brow with the back of his hand and straightened his tie. "OK, let me do the talking. If anyone asks, you're with us."

"Fine with me," Reznick said as they climbed the three steps.

Stamper gave three hard knocks on the door and cleared his throat, looking around as he waited for an answer. "Apparently lives here with three fellow female students from Georgetown."

Reznick nodded but said nothing. He already felt frustrated at the by-the-book approach.

Stamper knocked again, this time five times, and rang the bell repeatedly.

"Who is it?" a tentative female voice said from behind the locked door.

"FBI, ma'am; open up."

"What's it about?"

"Can you let us in, ma'am? We need to speak to Caroline Lieber."

"She's not here."

Stamper rolled his eyes. "Ma'am, can you please open up? We need to speak to you then if she's not here."

"Look, I don't know who you guys are. I'd prefer not to open up the door to strangers."

"We are the FBI, ma'am." He held up his ID to the peephole. "See for yourself."

"Mr Stamper, how can I be sure it's genuine?"

Stamper held up the court papers. "This states that we have the authority to gain entry to this property and interview Ms Lieber or the occupants. This is a court order, ma'am. If you continue to obstruct us, we'll be forced to break down the door to gain entry. So, can you please open up so we can speak to you inside?"

A long delay, until the chain inside could be heard being taken off the latch, the locks turned and the door cracked open. A girl in her late teens with sunken eyes and messy blonde hair pulled her pink dressing-gown cord tight round her waist. It looked like last night's makeup was still on her face, dark shadows under her eyes.

Stamper showed his badge again. "Are you satisfied we're FBI, ma'am?"

The girl studied the badge for a few moments before running a hand through her disheveled hair. "I'm sorry, I didn't want to take any chances. Please come in." She opened the door wide, and Stamper and Reznick went in and followed the girl down the hall to a brightly lit kitchen. "I'm sorry to bother you," Stamper said. "Are you alone here?"

"Yes. Everyone is spending a night with either a friend or a boyfriend."

"Ms Lieber, too?"

The girl shrugged. "I don't know. She might be staying with a friend from class."

"So you don't know for sure?"

The girl nodded. "Look, I don't know much about Caroline. What's this about?"

"Tell me, when's the last time you spoke to Caroline?

"Is she OK?"

"Please answer the question."

"Caroline? I spoke to her yesterday morning."

"Is there anyone she is close to or confides in?"

"She's from New York City, so her real close friends are all based there. She keeps to herself, really."

Stamper smiled. "You mind if we take a look around?"

"Actually, I do."

"Oh, why's that?"

"It's just that... well, the rental lease is in Caroline's name. I just feel it would be better if she was here before you go through the house."

"We have a warrant to search the house, if necessary."

The girl flushed crimson and closed her eyes. "It's just that..."

"Are you all right, miss?" Stamper asked. "Do you feel uncomfortable because we're going to do the search and you're all alone in the house, is that it?"

The girl grimaced. "It's just that... I'd rather you didn't."

The sound of a floorboard creaking upstairs.

Reznick was up the stairs before Stamper could speak. A skinny white guy was heading across the landing toward the bathroom. "Don't move, son!"

The kid froze.

Reznick grabbed the kid by the collar and pulled him downstairs. The kid was trembling, disheveled. "Thought you were alone?" he asked, staring across at the girl.

The girl bit her lower lip. "He's not supposed to be staying over."

Reznick said, "Empty your pockets."

The kid had tears in his eyes as he handed over a cube of hashish in his back pocket.

"Going to flush it away, were you?"

"Man, it's not mine."

Reznick stepped forward. "I'm going to pat you down. You don't have any sharp objects in your pockets, do you?"

"Absolutely not."

"Because if you do, and I get cut, you're gonna be in a shitload of trouble. No syringes or knives?"

"Absolutely not."

"I hope not, for your sake." Reznick patted the angles and emptied out the other pockets. "He's clean."

Stamper pointed through into the lounge. "Let's take a seat through there." The girl and the kid both nodded and they went through, sitting down on a large black leather sofa as Stamper sat down opposite them. Reznick stayed standing, arms folded, by the door. "OK, here's how it's going to work," he said, leaning forward, hands clasped. "You cooperate with us, and we're all gonna get along just fine. Now, first things first, where's Caroline's room?"

The girl said, "First floor on the right."

Reznick headed up there and did a cursory search. The bedroom was tidy and smelled fresh, white roses in a vase by the window. Two small pink teddies sitting atop the white duvet cover on the double bed. His gaze wandered round the room. The large desk had yellow sticky notes plastered all over it with scribbled page numbers of books, probably for essays she had to do. A floor-to-ceiling bookcase with hundreds of books. Jane Austen, Henry James, Plato, biographies of Churchill, George W Bush, Condi Rice and a few from satirist

PJ O'Rourke. He opened up a wardrobe and saw her clothes were neatly hung up and, on the floor, her shoes neatly laid out, a fresh fragrance lingering. He rifled in a bedside cabinet. Silk pants, bras and God knows what. He headed downstairs. "She's a student, right?"

The girl nodded. "Politics, yeah."

"So where's the laptop, iPad and all that jazz?"

The girl bit her lower lip. "Her iPhone is on her day and night, and I know she also has a MacBook Pro up in her room. Did you miss it?"

Reznick shook his head. "It's not there."

"That's weird. It was there yesterday morning when she left, because she asked me to switch it off as she went out the door in a hurry. She said she'd be back sometime this afternoon."

The young man cleared his throat. "Do you mind me asking what this is about?"

Reznick pointed at the kid. "Speak when you are spoken to."

Stamper looked at the girl. "What time did she leave?"

"Just about nine or thereabouts. I think she was running late. It was just before I left for classes."

"When did you return here?"

"I returned alone just after five yesterday."

"Was the computer still there?"

"I don't know; I didn't check."

"So what did you do when you got home?"

"Made some dinner for us, and Matt came round just after nine with a bottle of wine."

Stamper blew out his cheeks and shifted in his seat. "Tell me everything I need to know about Caroline Lieber. Is it normal for her to stay over somewhere with a friend?"

"Now and again, sure."

"Who would she stay with?"

The girl frowned and shrugged. "I don't know. Like I said, I don't think we're that close."

"Now, this is very important. Is there anything over the last forty-eight hours or so that has happened which you thought was strange or Caroline thought was odd? What about any guy she's seeing? A guy from her class? Anything unusual."

The young man ran his hands through his hair. "Look, I don't see what this has got to do with me."

Stamper stared down the kid. "Here's a bit of advice. When the Feds turn up and you get caught with some hash in your possession, you have some explaining to do. Simple possession of a controlled substance comes with a maximum penalty for a first conviction of a hundred and eighty days in jail, not to mention a thousand-dollar fine. However, you shut up and I could forget I saw your little stash. You understand what I'm saying?"

The girl took the boy's hand, tears in her eyes. "We hear what you're saying." She closed her eyes as if racking her brain. "There was a guy."

Stamper nodded.

"Yeah, couple of nights ago, a guy called asking for Caroline. An older-sounding guy."

Stamper shrugged. "A guy called? Called in person? By phone? Did he have a name?"

"I answered the phone. He didn't give a name. He said he wanted to speak to Caroline urgently."

Stamper nodded. "OK..."

"Caroline said that he was an old creep and was pestering her. She told me to tell him she wasn't home. He hung up."

Reznick wondered if this was O'Grady making contact with Lieber. He exchanged a quick glance with Stamper, who nodded, obviously getting the link.

Stamper said, "Did the guy say anything else?"

"He just said it was urgent that Caroline speak to him... he had some information for her."

"Information, huh? What kind of information?"

"He didn't say."

"And the guy didn't give his name?"

"No. I've told you everything." The girl began to sob.

"Can you describe his voice?"

The girl dabbed her eyes. "It was slow, very deliberate, as if he was being careful what he was saying."

Stamper nodded and smiled as if trying to reassure her. "You're really helping us. Just a couple more questions."

The girl sighed.

"Did Caroline ever talk to you about her internship last summer?"

"She did."

"And what did she say?"

"She said it was fourteen-hour days, but it was a fascinating glimpse into that world. Diplomats, politicians, Capitol Hill and all that. She loved it, but she didn't sing it from the rooftops. She asked me not to talk about it with anyone. She was quite discreet."

"I see." Stamper sighed. "Did her parents ever visit here?"

"Never. She went back to New York about once a month, usually a Friday at the end of each month."

"Going back to that laptop. Do you have any idea what happened to it?"

"I have no idea, unless Caroline came back for it during the day. I guess she must have."

The scruffy kid said, "You mentioned something earlier about anything unusual in the last week or so."

Stamper nodded. "You remember anything?"

"I don't know if it means anything, but I remember Caroline was howling and crying a week ago; some guy had just dumped her."

"Some guy. What guy?"

The kid screwed up his face and looked at his girlfriend. "What did she say his name was?"

The girl nodded and blew out her cheeks. "Adam."

The kid nodded. "Yeah, that's the one. Adam had broken up with her."

Stamper cleared his throat. "So this Adam was a boyfriend of hers. You met him?"

The guy shook his head.

The girl sighed. "None of us have. Caroline told us she'd started seeing this guy sometime in the summer. She was happy. But then he dumped her."

Stamper stood up. "Now listen, guys, this is very important that you tell us everything you know. It might be important. We need you to try to really focus on this and remember anything about this guy. Adam, you said."

The kid began to snap his fingers. "She said he wasn't answering her calls at the hospital when she called him."

"A hospital? A hospital here in DC?"

The kid grimaced. "Honestly? I really don't know. That's all I remember."

Stamper nodded and smiled. "I'm going to get some of my team in and have a closer look around Caroline's room and the rest of this house, if that's all right with you."

The girl shrugged. "Not a problem."

Stamper handed her a card and thanked them for their help before he followed Reznick out of the house and into the broiling street.

While a three-man FBI team headed in to carry out a thorough search of the townhouse, Reznick got back into the SUV passenger seat as Stamper slid into the driver's seat, buckled up and put in a call to the senior NSA computer expert assigned to the program. He requested all recurring calls from the home number and Caroline's cell phone to anywhere in the DC area to be analyzed and flagged. Within ten minutes, the NSA guy was back on the phone and it was clear that Caroline Lieber had been making multiple calls to Georgetown Hospital.

"That's got to be our next stop," Reznick said.

Stamper was frowning, deep in thought. He punched in another number. "Hi, Lenny: Roy Stamper. The human resources department of Georgetown University Hospital, I need to know where they are located." A long pause. "Arlington? OK, got that." He ended the call and turned to Reznick. "Human Resources is on Fifteenth Street North, Arlington."

Reznick nodded.

Stamper turned the ignition key and they pulled away. He shook his head. "This whole thing... I don't know."

"What do you mean?"

"Think we're chasing our tail. Can't see how Lieber's ex-boyfriend fits into the disappearance of O'Grady."

"Maybe we are chasing our tail. But we've got to chase down the leads."

Stamper grimaced but said nothing.

His attitude jarred Reznick. "Look, I'm not a Fed, but I would have thought any lead needs to be run down."

Stamper nodded. "Ordinarily, yes, but we're getting further and further away from the core investigation into the disappearance of O'Grady, aren't we?" His tone was strident. Annoyed, even.

Reznick let it go. He could see Stamper thought they were clearly wasting their time with this angle. Maybe they were.

A few minutes later they were heading across the Key Bridge toward Arlington.

Reznick said, "So, how are we gonna go about this?"

"Well, you've got to bear in mind that not everyone is happy to see the FBI when we show up unannounced. And we have to be wary that the hospital doesn't circle the wagons and get defensive if we want to access their records."

Reznick nodded. "Makes sense. What about getting their consent?"

"That's the way I see it. We ask nicely and professionally for a request to see the names of the hospital employees and contractors."

"And if they refuse?"

Stamper turned and gave a rueful smile. "Trust me, they won't."

Ten minutes later, the SUV's GPS guided them to a large glass building with red brick up to the second level, and into the parking garage. A sign listed the blue-chip clients including Advanced Analytical Consulting, Bonneyville Broadcasting, Ricoh Business, Utilities Management Corporation and MedStar, along with some legal firms.

Reznick and Stamper took the elevator to the third floor and headed along a corridor to a reception area.

Stamper flashed his badge and gave his best FBI smile. "Good morning, ma'am. I'm sorry to bother you, but we have urgent business. I'd like to see the vice-president of Human Resources, Ms Wendy Greninger."

The receptionist smiled. "Have you got an appointment?"

Stamper looked at her badge. "Sadly, no, Christine. But that's not usually a problem for us."

Christine gave a tight smile. "Hold on." She buzzed her boss and picked up the phone. "Yes, two gentlemen from the FBI to see you, Ms Greninger." A few nods and she hung up. She pointed to a door opposite. "You're in luck. She is in the training room."

Stamper smiled. "Much obliged, thank you."

The receptionist smiled back and flushed as Reznick gave a polite nod. As they walked toward the training room door, Reznick put his hand on Stamper's shoulder. "Didn't know you could be such a smooth talker, Roy."

Stamper groaned. "Gimme a break, Reznick." He cleared his throat and knocked on the door twice.

A voice from inside shouted, "Come in!"

Stamper opened the door and walked in, Reznick behind. Sitting, working on a laptop, was a woman wearing a smart dark olive suit. She stood up and shook their hands.

Stamper said, "FBI, ma'am; I appreciate you seeing us without any notice."

The woman gave a warm smile. "No problem at all. How can I help you gentlemen?"

Stamper outlined that they were looking for a man called "Adam" who may or may not work at the hospital and they would like access to the hospital records.

"I see," she said. "Can you tell me what this is in connection with?"

"I'm not at liberty to disclose that, Ms Greninger. We hope, with the hospital's cooperation and consent, we can establish a few facts, and we'll be on our way."

Greninger leaned back in her seat and looked up at Stamper. "I take it you're not at liberty to divulge the nature of this investigation?"

"It's serious enough for us to be here unannounced."

Greninger nodded. "I'll run it past our CEO first."

"Excellent, thank you."

Greninger picked up the phone and punched in the number for the CEO and explained the situation. She nodded a few times. The call dragged on for a couple of minutes. Eventually, she said, "Appreciate that," before ending the call. She smiled at Stamper. "You're in luck. Presumably, you want a list of only those named Adam who work at the hospital? In any capacity?"

"Whether it's full-time, medical, janitor, office worker, nurse, we would like a list of all those who work within the hospital and are called Adam, and their addresses and contact numbers."

"We're talking first name, I'd imagine?"

"That's correct."

Greninger got to her feet. "Just wait here for now and I'll see what I can do."

Less than a quarter of an hour later, she returned with a printout and handed it to Stamper.

"There're five Adams employed by us," she said. "All their details are there." She looked at Reznick. "You ex-military?"

Reznick said nothing.

The woman smiled. "I can tell. I served many years back. Military intelligence."

Stamper took the list. "Thank you, Ms Greninger. We appreciate your cooperation."

"If there's anything else you guys need, don't hesitate to contact me."

Stamper said, "One final thing. We'd appreciate if this conversation stayed within these four walls."

Greninger nodded. "That's a given and won't be a problem."

They headed down to the parking garage and got into the car. Stamper quickly scanned the names and punched in a number to one of his team. "Yeah, Josie: Roy here. I've got five names. I want you to run them down." He gave the names. "As soon as possible. Basically, I need the Adam who works at the hospital to fit the profile of boyfriend material for a rich New York girl studying in DC." He nodded. "Exactly. Trawl the cell phone records of all. Keep me informed."

Stamper ended the call and they headed back into DC, stopping off at Billy Martin's Tavern in Georgetown for a brunch of scrambled eggs, hash browns, toast and coffee. After they'd eaten and Stamper had emailed Meyerstein with an update, he looked across at Reznick. "You're looking well, Jon. You recovered from the last time you visited DC?"

Reznick said, "Took a few months, but I'm fine. I've been working out like I used to."

Stamper patted the padding around his stomach. "Could do with some working out myself." He gulped some more coffee and rested his elbows on the table. "Look, I don't want to come down hard on you, Jon. I like you. But you mind me asking why you were invited into this program? I've asked the assistant director and she brushed me aside."

Reznick stared down into his coffee and shrugged. "Probably my winning personality, Roy; what do you think?"

"I didn't mean to say..."

"Look, you wanna know why she asked me to be involved, why don't you ask her again? I guess she had her reasons."

Stamper took some more coffee but said nothing.

"Have we got a problem, Roy?"

"No problem. I just don't like being kept out of the loop."

"Roy, who the hell cares why I was asked? I answered the goddamn call and that was that. We all want the same thing: to find O'Grady and this Caroline Lieber."

"I just don't understand what you can bring to the table."

"Roy, deal with it. And let's move on, or we're going to have a problem."

Stamper sighed long and hard, pinching the bridge of his nose.

Reznick studied his face. The same dark shadows as Meyerstein. Slightly bloodshot eyes. "You OK? You seem on edge."

"Sleep deprivation. There's only so much coffee a man can drink."

Reznick smiled. "Ain't that the truth."

Stamper's cell rang. "Yup." He listened intently for a couple of minutes. Eventually, he spoke. "One long-term sick, one on a sabbatical to India and one... doing what?" He nodded. "One retires next year, aged seventy-five? OK, that leaves...?" He nodded. "Forget the janitor. I'm interested in the doctor. And he's number two on the list? And there are logs of her speaking to his department on multiple occasions, is that right?" A nod. "That's the one. Pull up everything we have on him. Speak soon." He ended the call and blew out his cheeks. "Interesting."

"You got someone?"

"We think so. Lives not more than two minutes from here, in the heart of Georgetown."

FOUR

The road through the woods was deserted as the headlights of Adam Kendrick's SUV strafed the single lane ahead. Lightning bugs all around glanced off his windshield. He looked in his rearview mirror and saw his shadows silhouetted in the car behind him. He was miles from civilization, somewhere off Route 40, in the foothills of the Blue Ridge Mountains in southwest Virginia.

As the miles wore on, he wondered what test they had in store for him.

The headlights behind him flashed. It was the signal that he was to turn right up ahead.

Kendrick spotted a homemade wooden sign with an arrow, and he headed down a dirt road for just over three miles until he came to a clearing. A man with fluorescent nightsticks guided him over to the left beside a clump of trees. He glanced in the rearview mirror and noticed his shadows weren't there.

His stomach knotted as he parked the SUV. Two men dressed in black and sporting submachine guns approached.

"Out the car," one drawled.

Kendrick switched off his engine and got out of the car. The same masked man stepped forward and patted all the angles. Then an electronic wand was run over his body.

"He's clean." The man cocked his head in the direction of a rutted dirt road. "Follow me."

Kendrick did as he was told, flashlights leading the way. Sweat ran down his back, insects buzzing all around. The air was thick, like glue. The smells of the forest. Dead leaves. Bark. Earth. Behind him the sound of heavy footsteps. They walked on for perhaps half a mile until they got to what looked like a heavily camouflaged wooden garden-shed but was most likely a bird blind.

The man opened the door. "After you."

Kendrick did as he was told and stepped inside. Musty smell. A pale blue light was switched on. At the far end of the bird blind was a sniper rifle with a night vision scope resting on a tripod.

The masked man said, "This is your final test."

"I've already aced the long-range sniper tests."

"We know you have. But that was to test accuracy."

Kendrick said nothing, wondering what the man meant.

The man cocked his head in the direction of the rifle and tripod. "It's all set up for you. The weighting, the sights; it's perfect. I double checked it myself."

Kendrick nodded.

"OK, let's do this. Assume position."

Kendrick complied. He laid himself flat on the floor. He used his left hand to support the butt of the rifle.

"We've checked wind speed and we've adjusted the scopes. It's all in place."

Kendrick placed the butt of the stock firmly in the pocket of his right shoulder. Then, with his right hand, he gripped the small of the stock. He placed his index finger on the trigger and planted his elbows on the wooden floor.

He closed his eyes, took a couple of breaths, enabling him to relax as much as possible. Upon opening his eyes, he saw through the pale green night vision for the first time what the scope's crosshairs were aligned to.

His blood ran cold.

A hooded man was tied by ropes to a tree. The rangefinder showed he was 1097 yards away. He watched as the man writhed as he tried to escape. But it was to no avail.

Kendrick's stomach knotted. "What's this?"

The masked man behind him said, "This is your test. Do nothing until I give the order. Do you understand?"

"Understood."

"OK, zero your weapon."

Kendrick said nothing. He adjusted the scope so that the writhing man's head was in the center of his scope's crosshairs. He zoned out as his training kicked in. A sniper had to take into account the myriad factors that could influence a bullet's trajectory: distance to the target, wind direction, wind speed, the angle of the sniper to the target, not to mention the temperature.

He felt calm. Assured. He focused on his breathing. He felt detached.

"Do you know who this man is?"

"Nope."

"His name's O'Grady. Do you want to know why he is the target?"

"No."

"Well, I'm gonna tell you. This man has compromised the operation. That can't be allowed. Do you understand?"

"Absolutely. I understand."

The masked man sighed and cleared his throat. "When you're ready. It must be a head shot."

Kendrick looked through the sights. The man's head was now hung low, as if he knew what awaited him. For a split second, he stared through the night vision sight and tried to imagine the terror the man was feeling underneath the hood. He felt the cold metal on his trigger finger. He aligned the man in his crosshairs. He paused for a few moments.

He knew that military snipers who shoot over three hundred yards invariably aim for the chest. The loss of blood and trauma would inevitably kill the target. But this was to be a headshot, which was usually used close up.

He breathed in slowly. His yoga and meditation techniques kicked in. He peered through the scope and got the hood perfectly within the cross hairs. He was aiming for the "apricot," or the medulla oblongata, the part of the brain that controls involuntary movement at the base of the skull.

He felt the cold steel again on the ball of his finger and squeezed the trigger. The recoil was surprisingly slight. The noise blasted round the hide.

Through the scope, he saw the hooded man's head slump forward.

He saw two masked men emerge from the wooded area to the side of the tree where the man was tied.

Kendrick watched, fascinated, as one took a hunting knife from his belt and cut the rope that held the man to the tree. The body fell forward and the other man unrolled a body bag onto the ground. They began to lift the body into the bag.

"Move away from the rifle," the masked man said.

Kendrick complied and got to his feet.

The masked man got out a cell phone and punched in a number. "Yeah, it's done." He handed the phone to Kendrick. "They want to talk to you."

Kendrick blew out his cheeks. "Yeah."

"You passed."

Kendrick sighed. "What now?"

"The big one."

"You got a timescale?"

"When we know, you'll know."

"When will I hear from you again?"

"Soon."

He was about to respond but the line was already dead.

FIVE

Reznick was crouching in the back of a stifling surveillance van, its air conditioner broken, when Adam Kendrick pulled up outside his Georgetown home in a smart Mercedes convertible.

"Think I got something," he whispered into his lapel microphone.

Kendrick got out of the car, bag slung over his shoulder. He was lean and tall with a strong jawline. Cropped blond hair, tanned complexion. Neck veins bulged. He wore cargo pants, Topsiders and a navy polo shirt. All-American guy. But he also seemed to exude a superior air as he sauntered towards his house. Was this confidence? Arrogance?

Reznick picked up the camera and zoomed in on Kendrick, taking some shots through the glass. He watched as Kendrick walked up the stone stoop and pulled out his keys. Before opening the door, the doctor checked his watch and looked around. His gaze fell on the van Reznick was in.

Reznick froze and held his breath, the only sound his heart beating. It seemed as though Kendrick was staring straight into the van and into the lens of the camera.

Reznick swallowed hard. He had been holding his breath for what seemed like an eternity. Eventually, Kendrick turned around and opened his front door, shutting it behind him with his foot.

Reznick breathed out. "Target inside house." He sent the photos via instant message to Meyerstein. Three minutes later, she called back.

"Our computer analysis shows that this is a perfect match."

"Where do we go from here?"

"Look, I'm going to get Stamper down there in the next few minutes. He can talk to this doctor, find out what he knows. But I want you to just stay in the van and see if he heads off anywhere. We'll check his cell traffic. You OK with that?"

"Fine by me."

She hung up.

Half an hour later, Stamper and his team pulled up in an SUV outside Kendrick's house. He watched as Kendrick answered the door in his bathrobe, still toweling his wet hair, then ushered the Feds inside. A mere fifteen minutes later, Stamper and his men drove off.

His phone rang a short while later. It was Stamper.

"Hey Jon," he said.

"How did you get on?"

"He seemed very relaxed when I was asking questions. Very smart. Very cool. And he didn't seem unduly flustered, even when I asked if he knew the whereabouts of Caroline Lieber."

"Where had he been?"

"Visiting an old friend in southern Virginia, apparently. We'll check it out."

"So, you asked about Caroline Lieber?"

Stamper sighed down the line. "According to him, she occasionally helped out with his homeless outreach medical charity. He said they were never an item, and that was that. No spark there for him. But she had thought there was something serious between them, and he had to get the director of medicine to speak to her directly about phoning him at the hospital."

"So she was just spinning a line to her friends?"

"That's what he's saying."

"Do you believe him?"

"It's hard to say. He said she had once stayed overnight and he slept on the sofa."

"Why did she stay over?"

"Well, according to him, she'd been locked out of her home after an argument with her roommates."

"So he doesn't know where she is?"

"Nothing. We've checked the calls to his registered cell. Nothing. Says he never gave her his cell number. That's why she called the hospital."

Reznick groaned. "Backing up his story."

"I think we're wasting our time with this guy. I've got a couple of things to check out, but the main thrust of the investigation is the Iranians."

"What else do we know about this Lieber girl's movements?"

"The GPS had her on the Georgetown campus. But after that, she just seems to have vanished. Turned up for her classes yesterday morning, and then gone. Nothing."

"What about a forensic search of his home?"

"I just spoke to Assistant Director Meyerstein. She wants you to stay where you are. Just in case."

Reznick sighed. "And all the time, O'Grady's off the grid. The same as Caroline Lieber. What the fuck is going on?"

"Sit tight, Jon, and let's see how this goes. Chances are, though, he has nothing to do with any of this."

The rest of the morning dragged, as the comings and goings of Thirty-eighth Street NW were laid bare for Reznick. He managed to get the air conditioner working, the blast of cold air a welcome relief. Outside in the oppressive heat, it was dog walkers, joggers, deliverymen and the mailman. Kendrick hadn't made a move in hours.

Reznick knocked back a bottle of water and popped a couple of Dexedrine to keep him going. He felt the amphetamines rouse his system, sharpening his antennae. He stared through the one-way window and continued to watch the world go by. The morning gave way to a blazing afternoon, a few more sirens in the distance, as the heat seemed to warp the asphalt and bricks.

The air conditioner was on full and he was relieved to feel the cold air. And all the time, he kept his eyes peeled on the townhouse, long shadows all around.

He wondered if Kendrick had just gone to bed. But he couldn't tell for sure. He could just as likely head out of the house at any moment. Reznick had to stay alert.

He wolfed a cream cheese bagel and he peed in an empty plastic glass container.

The afternoon gave way to early evening, light fading, and still no sign of life from Kendrick.

The day had ended. Jaded men and women, jackets slung over the shoulders, ambled down their street after a day's work, no doubt looking forward to a refreshing shower and a cold drink.

Reznick smelled his armpits and knew he should be doing with the same. The hours without air had stunk up the van with his body odor. His cell rang a couple of times, Meyerstein asking for updates and Stamper trying to raise his spirits with guy talk about cold beers when it was all over.

A lot of people hated the soul-destroying, mind-numbing boredom of surveillance work. Reznick wasn't one of them. He understood that needs must and someone had to stand watch. It would have been the easiest thing in the world just to tag along back to base with Stamper. To switch off, knowing the core investigation was on terrorist groups, not some doctor who was unwittingly under surveillance. But he knew that leads had to be earned.

They didn't just land in your lap.

It was all about putting in the time and, sometimes, maybe, you get a break. But by God, you had to earn it.

The hours, sometimes days, of waiting, hunkered down in thick mud or deep snow up in the mountains of Afghanistan, or in fly-infested ditches smelling of shit in Iraq, now, that was tough. By comparison, this was a breeze.

Reznick stretched out, using a ten-minute warm-up routine he often used. He felt the calf muscles stretch. Darkness fell slowly as time dragged.

Was this guy even working tonight?

He swigged some more water, pissed some more, and ate a stale donut. As a rule, healthy eating was not compatible with surveillance work in his experience. Reznick focused on the door, through the night vision binoculars, green-tinged.

Just before 9pm, Dr Adam Kendrick emerged from his home. He was talking into his cell phone, navy jacket slung over his shoulder. Reznick quickly alerted Meyerstein.

"He's on the move. Heading south on foot."

The radio crackled into life and it was Stamper. "Got him." A couple of minutes later, Stamper's voice came back on. "The subject has entered the hospital. Alone."

Then radio silence.

Reznick remained in the van, still observing the front of the house. His cell phone rang.

"Jon, how's the lonely vigil?" Meyerstein's voice was soft and warm.

Reznick sighed. "You know me. I'm a glutton for punishment."

"Jon, bad news. We've failed to gain a court order granting access to Kendrick's house."

"What?"

"Look, our counsel is appealing the decision, but it doesn't look good. There was a discrepancy in the papers being submitted, and the judge refused to sign."

"You serious?"

"It happens. We've filed new papers, but at the earliest we won't be able to gain access until tomorrow morning."

"That's twelve hours away."

Meyerstein sighed, long and hard. "We think Kendrick is telling the truth. We've checked him out; a more solid citizen you'll not find. Churchgoing, helps out at soup kitchens, set up his own medical charity for veterans, a top Washington surgeon, avoids parties, teetotal. Clean living. Don't see how he fits into this at all."

Reznick was silent. He wondered if he should broach the subject or if he should let her.

"You still there?"

"Twelve goddamn hours? You think there's a chance she's in the house?"

"No, I don't."

Reznick sighed. "What's stopping me getting inside and having a look around?"

"Jon, I couldn't condone that. Besides, what if he returned unannounced?"

"He won't."

"Look, this guy is not a suspect."

"You want to know where I'm at?"

"Sure."

"I think you've got to close this circle. He is a link back to Caroline Lieber. Until we are a hundred percent on this guy, I say I go in and have a look around."

Meyerstein said nothing.

"Get Stamper and his guys to cover my back."

"Sounds great, but..."

"But?"

A long sigh. "This guy is not where it's at."

"You don't know that for sure, do you?"

Meyerstein said nothing for a couple of minutes. Eventually, she spoke. "What if I said we wouldn't stand in your way; how that would that make you feel?

"Then I would say that's all I need to know. Leave it with me."

The decision by Meyerstein to allow Reznick to gain entry to Kendrick's house was unexpected. He wondered if she knew more than she was letting on. It felt good to be doing something. He wanted to find out more about Kendrick.

Reznick's thoughts turned to the task in mind. He hadn't picked a lock in years. He changed in the back of the van and took a couple of minutes to get out of his sweaty jeans and T-shirt, and into the black jeans, T-shirt and baseball cap. He checked his earpiece was still in place. He lifted up the small metal toolbox, checked the coast was clear, and pulled back the sliding door. He strode across the street and headed down the path at the side of the house.

Pushing open the gate, he saw a side door to the property. He switched on a tiny jamming device to disable any alarms or electronic sensors. He then pulled on some plastic shoe covers over his sneakers, so as not to leave any dirt or mess from footprints, and snapped on his gloves.

The distant sound of sirens filled the DC night air. He glanced around. Lights on across the street, but all quiet. No foot traffic. He pressed his ear against the door and closed his eyes. He was listening for the merest sound inside. Perhaps a TV playing low. But there was nothing. Satisfied it was all clear, he reached into the toolbox and pulled out a lockpicking set. He selected the torque tool and pried it into the dead-bolt lock where a normal key would go. He pushed the pick in and out of the dead bolt for a few seconds, careful not to leave any scratch marks. Then he pushed up on the pick so that the pins were depressed. Slowly, and with the merest pressure, he eased down on the pick until he heard the pins disengage from the lock. The lock began to spin and he applied more pressure to the pick so that the rotation was smooth.

Reznick pulled the dead bolt's latch from the door and pushed it down into his pocket. He turned the handle and pushed open the door. Inside, he took out an electronic screwdriver from his toolbox and reassembled the lock, shutting the door quietly.

Reznick's eyes were slowly adjusting to the dark as he headed through a hallway into a kitchen. He could see the glint from a metallic range that looked like it had never been used. He pulled out a penlight from his top pocket. The thin beam of light strafed the black marble floors and granite work surface. Sitting on a dining room table were two large glass bowls of fruit, overflowing with bananas, apples, oranges and pears. He opened a fridge and the light came on. Dozens of bottles of water, carefully aligned. Fresh low-fat milk in three containers. Low fat spread. The freezer contained packets of free-range chicken breast fillets. The guy was something else. Talk about a health freak, Reznick thought. He shut the fridge and opened a cupboard. Rows and rows of neatly arranged protein shake mixes alongside rows of bags of basmati rice.

He padded through to the living room. It smelled of beeswax polish. Perhaps a hint of sandalwood. He pointed the penlight around the room. Large-screen TV on the wall, photos of the doctor at his graduation. Pictures of him with friends and family, eating out, wearing blue scrubs, unsmiling behind a mask. The sofas were caramel colored, matching the walls.

He headed upstairs. The penlight showed the way. Two bedrooms. The master bedroom had expensive-looking hardwood flooring. His gaze wandered around the room. Gold-leaf framed photos of Kendrick in dark blue Yale rowing colors, his lean torso honed to perfection, muscle definition on triceps.

Reznick went over towards a huge clothes closet and pulled back the doors, and a small light went on. A line of sharp suits. He checked a couple of labels. Hugo Boss, Paul Smith, Armani, Versace. Expensive. On the closet floor, arranged in neat rows, were polished shoes. He opened some closet drawers. Neatly pressed and folded Thomas Pink shirts. Another drawer contained Ralph Lauren polo shirts.

It was like something out of GQ magazine.

Reznick was a jeans and T-shirt sort of guy. Worrying about the cut of a suit always appeared to him to be the height of pointlessness. He pressed on across the master bedroom and into an en suite shower with expensive shaving gels, aftershaves, carefully arranged razors, moisturizers and soft white towels monogrammed with the initials AK in gold thread on each one.

What was all that about? Initials on your towels?

The word narcissistic came to mind.

The more he thought of it, the more he couldn't help thinking that this was the most ordered life of a single male he'd ever seen. Fanatical in tidiness. Almost Gesthaltesque. But then again, maybe the guy just liked things just-so.

He had known several Delta guys over the year that lived such fastidious lives. Their homes were order throughout. And anything that encroached on that perfection had to be dealt with.

He checked the bathroom. It looked like something out of a pristine show house. Never used. A pleasant lemon fragrance.

He went through to the guest bedroom. Another show house. Wheat-colored cushions perfectly placed on the white cotton duvet cover.

Then it was down a hardwood hall and into a small study. A large desk with a leather blotting pad in the middle, crisp white paper on it, and a row of three Mont Blanc fountain pens in a neat row, side by side. No laptop. A dictionary and Webster's Thesaurus.

He shone the penlight on a wall and he saw Kendrick's framed Yale degree. He pointed the penlight around the rest of the room. On an opposite wall, black-and-white photos of DC monuments at night.

Wooden blinds shut tight. A third wall housed a huge bookcase packed tight with all sorts of books. Medical tomes. Anatomy, biology, psychology. Political biographies. George W Bush. Colin Powell. Economic tomes of Milton Friedman. He looked closer. Works of fiction: Faulkner, James and Hemingway. American greats. Very traditional.

In the far corner of the room, a filing cabinet.

Reznick took out his knife from his pocket and managed to open the lock within a couple of seconds. He opened up the top drawer. Arranged in alphabetical order was everything from IRS letters to utility bills, mortgage contracts, photocopies of references he'd given for medical staff. All up to date. But filed meticulously, like everything else in his life.

He went out onto the landing and shone the penlight at his watch. He'd been in the house for less than fifteen minutes. Reznick pointed the light toward the ceiling and saw a hatch for the attic. He reached up and turned a brass handle and attic ladders unfolded. Penlight between his teeth, he climbed up. The light bathed the darkness of the attic. Around a dozen hand-labeled wooden crates of memorabilia.

He climbed in and rummaged around. Old photos of Kendrick as a child, friends at school, boxes with tattered old baseball gloves, worn bats, the smell of worn leather. Old baseball trophies won as a child, rowing trophies while at Andover School and then at Yale. Boxing pictures. Pictures of boxing trophies. His mind flashed back to his own childhood. He was an amateur boxer himself and a school champion. He remembered once getting punched stupid by a kid from Bangor but he had knocked him unconscious with a single punch, despite the boy wearing protective head pads. He felt sick afterward but his father simply patted him on the back, wiped the blood from his face with a cold towel and drove them back home.

The sound of a distant car alarm snapped Reznick out of his brief reverie. He rummaged in a few more crates. Framed certificates from the Red Cross for his humanitarian work. Working in a soup kitchen in one of the projects. Pictures of him as a boy, perhaps ten or eleven, wrapped up against the snow, holding his parents' hands.

Perhaps Stamper was right and this was a wild goose chase.

He looked again at the image and he thought back to his own childhood, helping his dad clear the snow from his driveway and around the neighborhood in Rockland.

Reznick took one last look around and climbed from the attic, shoved up the metal ladders through the attic hole and shut and locked the hatch.

The earpiece crackled into life. "How long you gonna be, Jon?" The voice of Stamper.

Reznick sighed, the penlight strafing down toward the ground floor. "Not long."

"You found anything so far?"

"Nothing to write home about."

Stamper said nothing.

"I'll be out of here in a few minutes. I'm just wanting to check downstairs to make sure I didn't miss anything."

"Yeah, I got that. Don't hang around too long. Over."

The house returned to silence. He headed downstairs and back into the living room. A final look. Nothing. Outside on the street, he heard voices raised. A couple having an argument.

Reznick went through to the kitchen. The calendar on the wall listed various charity lunches, meetings with hospital benefactors and other such stuff. At the far end of the kitchen was a door that led through to a utility room. Washing machine, huge refrigerator humming away, blue light on. On the floor, a small Persian-style rug.

He bent down and lifted the rug.

A hatch. The house had a basement.

He turned the hatch and shone the tiny light down into the dark space. Free weights, a rowing machine, punching bags, medicine balls, treadmill. The guy had a fully equipped gym in his basement.

Reznick climbed down the stairs, the penlight clenched between his teeth. Descending carefully, step by step. The smells of stale sweat and leather. He shone the light around the bare walls. Day-by-day fitness charts. Serious weights lifted at what time and on what day. Time spent on the rowing machine. Strokes per minute. Heart rate monitored throughout. Beats per minute.

This was the gym of a fitness fanatic. Push-ups, pull-ups, squat-thrusts per minute, time spent punching the bags, circuit training.

The light shone on a ledge with a framed picture of a letter. Reznick edged closer. A letter from a mother in the Anacostia neighborhood of DC, whose son had been run over by a hit-and-run driver, had multiple internal injuries and was fighting for his life, but following extensive surgery made a full recovery. She expressed herself "profoundly grateful for your life-saving work, Dr Kendrick."

He paused for a moment, thinking of his daughter. The agony a parent goes through; he understood.

Reznick stared at the letter and it all came back. He wondered if Kendrick used it to remind himself each and every day why he had got into medicine in the first place. He started to look at the guy not as a fastidious workout freak, but as a clean-living doctor. For the first time, he felt bad for invading his space.

The earpiece crackled into life. "Jon, get the hell out of there."

"What? I haven't finished yet."

"You have now. Kendrick has just left the hospital on foot."

"You kidding me? He's only been gone a little while."

"Get out of there! Now!"

Reznick climbed up the stairs and out of the basement, shutting the hatch. He re-laid the carpet exactly how it had been, picked up his toolkit and headed out the door. He quietly opened the side door, glad he'd already reassembled the lock. He shut the door to the lock position, pulled out the trusty pick and locked it again from the outside. Finally, he switched off the jamming device, reactivating the electronics and alarms.

Reznick's heart was beating fast as he headed down the path and across the street, baseball cap pulled low. He climbed back into the van and locked the door.

His earpiece crackled into life. "He's walking down the street now," Stamper said.

Reznick peered through the surveillance van window as Kendrick approached his home.

"Jon, you still there?" It was Stamper.

"Yeah, I'm out of there; don't worry."

A long sigh.

"Why the hell's he back so soon?"

"No idea. Just glad you made it out in time."

Reznick wiped the sweat from his brow as Kendrick entered his home. "There's nothing untoward in the house I could see. Guy likes to keep fit. I didn't get time to check out the garage."

"No sign of Caroline Lieber, O'Grady or anything to incriminate Kendrick in their disappearances?"

"Absolutely not." A light went on in Kendrick's downstairs lounge. "But something doesn't feel quite right."

"What do you mean?"

"I think there's a lot more to this guy than meets the eye."

SIX

It was just after 2am and Reznick was gulping another strong coffee inside the van when he spotted Kendrick emerge from his home. He peered through the binoculars and watched as the rugged doctor, wearing dark jeans and white polo shirt and loafers, climbed into his metallic silver Mercedes convertible, which was parked outside.

"He's on the move, folks!" he whispered, afraid of too much noise from inside the van.

Stamper's voice came over the radio. "Yeah, copy that. We're gonna swing by and you can jump in with us. We'll get one of my guys to take away the van."

Reznick sighed. "Hurry the fuck up," he said, as Kendrick drove away.

A few moments later, a Suburban pulled up. Reznick climbed out of the van and got in the back seat beside Stamper.

"You smell like shit," he said.

Reznick grinned. "Bet you say that to all the boys, huh?"

Stamper shook his head and chewed gum. "Gimme a break, will you?"

The Suburban sped off through the near-deserted streets of downtown DC in pursuit of Kendrick.

Reznick said, "You any idea where he's going?"

"He's not on the hospital rotation for a couple of weeks. Last-minute vacation, apparently."

The driver said, "He's headed northeast. There he is!"

Reznick craned his neck and saw the Mercedes up ahead. "Yeah, I see it."

Stamper took out his radio. "Looks like our guy is getting on I-95 North."

Reznick said, "We're getting too close. Back off."

Stamper turned and looked at Reznick. "We've been doing this for a long time, Reznick."

Reznick said nothing.

A silence opened up as they followed from about one hundred yards back. Ten minutes into the journey, Stamper said, "I don't understand how he fits into this. I don't get it."

Reznick nodded. "What do we know about him?"

"Privileged background, private school. Yale. Star student. All that. I don't think he fits anything we're interested in."

Reznick said, "He has a link to Caroline Lieber. And she has dropped off the radar. I don't believe in coincidences. There is a connection." He looked ahead and saw they were three cars behind Kendrick's car. "What else do we know about Dr Adam Kendrick?"

"Like I said, not a lot. He looks pretty solid. Brilliant surgeon, incredibly bright, top of his class at medical school, humanitarian work. Even founded a medical charity for veterans in DC. Hospital chief executive has told us, strictly confidentially, that he is a dedicated surgeon and loved by his patients. Although he did say he was a bit aloof at times and didn't seem to forge close relationships with other staff."

"What else do we know?"

"Well, we've been trawling his bank accounts, and it's healthy, as you can imagine. He's got $1.8 million in stocks. Apple, Intel, Google, blue-chip technology stocks, mostly."

"What else?"

"He pays his taxes."

"Relationships?"

"Not a great mixer. His secretary said he was scrupulously polite, never flirtatious with female staff. And she never heard him talking about girls or girlfriends."

"What about his parents?"

"Dead, but they were wealthy and solid suburbanites. Father was a lawyer."

"What about donations? Political leanings?"

"None. Worked around the world for the Red Cross after he graduated. Active humanitarian, I guess. But all in all, a very private man."

Reznick stayed silent. He wondered if this told the whole story. He'd known people who on the surface led an exemplary life. But peel back the layers of façade, and no one really knows what a person is like, deep down.

Stamper leaned towards the driver. "Where's he going?"

"GPS shows he's still headed north. Baltimore, perhaps."

They hung back as Kendrick pulled up at an all-night gas station on the outskirts of Baltimore. A visit to the bathroom, and then back in his car, still headed northeast. They passed the city, its lights in the distance. Long silences punctuated the journey. Past Wilmington and into New Jersey. And then Cherry Hill and Trenton.

They saw signs for New York.

Stamper punched in a number. "Martha, we're about forty minutes out of Manhattan. Has he got any connections in New York?" He shook his head. "OK. So what do you reckon? We just watch and wait?" He nodded. "You got it?"

Union City and then down to a crawl before the tollbooths at the Lincoln Tunnel. The first tinges of dawn had lightened the sky as they emerged from the tunnel and headed through the snarling midtown Manhattan early-morning traffic. The driver yawned, as did Stamper. Skyscrapers towered over them as they took a right on West 42nd Street, a left on Third Avenue before a right on East 57th Street. Left on Sutton Place and up York Avenue and then down tree-lined East 63rd Street.

The driver slowed down. "Lenox Hill, prime Manhattan." More than a hundred yards ahead, Kendrick pulled into a space outside a fancy townhouse. He then used a fob to lock his car and walked up to the front door, pressing the entry-phone buzzer. He waited for a few moments. A balding middle-aged man with two young kids opened the door. Kendrick flung his arms out wide, picked up the kids and gave them a big hug.

Stamper peered through powerful binoculars. "He pressed apartment five. Who lives there?"

A short while later, a text came through on his phone.

"William T Rhodes, medical director of Lenox Hill Hospital." He sighed. "Rhodes has two kids. Amy and Alexander. They are the godchildren of Dr Adam Kendrick."

The driver groaned.

Stamper fed the information back to Meyerstein. "Goddamn family friend, that's what he is. Visiting them on his first day of his vacation. Just great."

Reznick stared towards the townhouse as the traffic crawled along the tree-lined street.

Stamper looked at Reznick and sighed. "What do you think?"

"About what?"

"This journey up here. Kendrick. Wild goose chase, is it not?"

"Maybe."

"You don't seem too sure."

"Something about this guy; I don't know."

"What don't you know? You've been in his house, for God's sake. The guy's just a hardworking guy who spends time with his godchildren. What's wrong with that?"

"Nothing wrong with that. Nothing at all. But there's something about him..."

"You kidding me? Is that all we've got? There's something about him?"

Reznick sighed. "I'm no psychologist, but he appears to have no flaws. None at all. He's a high achiever. Brilliant doctor. A single man. Saves kids' lives. You can understand why an impressionable student like Caroline Lieber would fall for him. And he's still a connection."

"We've got nothing. No Islamic connection to this guy. No anything connection. This is a dead end."

SEVEN

FBI Assistant Director Martha Meyerstein was sitting alone in a conference room within the Department of National Intelligence HQ monitoring real-time events on her laptop. She felt frustrated knowing they were no nearer to finding O'Grady or even tracing Lieber. All the time knowing there were vague indications that national security could be compromised. The more she thought of how little her team had achieved, the more she was beginning to doubt herself. She pushed those thoughts aside.

Outside the door, she heard heavy footsteps approaching, a man's voice talking softly. Two hard knocks at the door and General Black walked into the room. He wore a dark navy suit, shiny black shoes, crisp white shirt and blue silk tie. He nodded across to Meyerstein as he ended the call, putting his cell phone into an inside jacket pocket.

Meyerstein smiled as he pulled up a chair and sat down beside her.

"We got a problem. I've got an appointment at the White House later today. And they're looking for answers."

"I'm sure they are. Look, General, this is proving more elusive than I'd imagined."

"I can't see any progress."

Meyerstein sighed. Her brief dealings with General Black had been edgy affairs. He was irascible and prone to mood swings.

But to be fair, he seemed to be like that with everyone he met.

Black leaned back in his seat and sighed. "I got a call just after six this morning from O'Grady's wife. State Department gave her my number if she needed to talk about anything at any time. And, as you can imagine, she was very tearful. She was desperate to know if we've made any progress. And you know what stuck in my throat?"

Meyerstein said nothing.

"All I could tell her was that we're doing everything we can to find her husband."

Meyerstein shook her head. "He seems to have vanished into thin air."

"How the hell is that possible?"

"The analysis so far is mixed. Some of my guys are talking about O'Grady having some sort of breakdown, others talking about an affair that's gone wrong, while others are talking more geopolitical."

"What do you think?"

"If you're asking me for my assessment, it would be that this is linked to O'Grady's area of expertise. Namely, Iran."

"We don't know for sure; is that what you're saying?" His tone was condescending.

Meyerstein shifted in her seat. "That's exactly what I'm saying."

Black pinched the bridge of his nose. "I suppose there is the possibility, as some of your strategic analysts are indicating, that he has just gone missing, and that this is nothing to do with the nature of his job."

"Like I said, I'm ruling nothing out."

Black stared down at the desk for a few moments as if lost in thought before he looked across at her. "Heard you had a lead regarding Caroline Lieber."

"Maybe." She wanted to keep some of her cards close to her chest.

Black looked across at Meyerstein. "You wanna tell me more?"

Meyerstein spent the next quarter of an hour updating the general on all developments.

Black sighed and shook his head. "So, on the one hand, you believe this may be pointing to Iran, but, at the same time, you're bringing the name of this doctor, an eminent surgeon, not a closet Islamist. Do you believe this doctor is a closet Islamist; is that seriously what you're saying?"

"No. There is no indication at all, sir, that Kendrick is in any way an Islamist."

"Has your team run Kendrick's name through TIDE?"

Black was referring to a classified database of known and suspected terrorists – the Terrorist Identities Datamart Environment. "Yes we have, and he's not there. But we are chasing down each and every lead, and that goes for Adam Kendrick."

Black nodded. "You don't need me to tell you, but I think it's important to emphasize we don't want to get too fixated with some peripheral figure, especially if it takes critical resources from the main thrust."

"I couldn't agree more. I'm reviewing the Kendrick lead and thinking about pulling our guys off him."

"OK. Let's get back to O'Grady. Lieber, an intern at the White House, is the last person he calls. What's the connection?"

Meyerstein said, "Their paths crossed at the White House, we're led to believe. But no sign of any relationship."

"What I'm getting at is this. O'Grady, in his position as a White House advisor and intelligence expert, was in and out of the Situation Room more often than the President. Ms Lieber was, I'm told by a couple of people in the Secret Service, also in the Situation Room at the same time as O'Grady. He took her under his wing, so to speak."

"I think it was old-style courtesy, according to the reports I've read. He was like that with all interns. He had a natural rapport with people. Probably why he excelled at diplomacy."

Black stayed silent.

"I take it that you think otherwise."

"The fact both are missing points to a link," Black said. "It's possible that this is something more personal than an intelligence crisis. Could it be the case that they were compromised by a foreign intelligence service?"

Meyerstein blew out her cheeks. "It's possible. I have counterintelligence looking into this aspect. But as it stands, I don't see it. Here's what we know. A senior US diplomat, a defense attaché, goes missing, not turning up for a planning meeting. We've checked medical history and there's no history of mental illness, either with him or his family. And he's a family man. No affairs."

"But what the hell did he call Caroline Lieber about? Are we overlooking the fact that it might have been something more than mentoring?"

"I'm not sure I buy it."

"Let's get back to this doctor... Dr Adam Kendrick... for a moment. I'm trying to get my head round how exactly he fits into this. It seems like we're way off base with this."

Meyerstein felt a wave of exhaustion wash over her. She didn't let it show. Years of practice. "We're trying to figure out the same thing. He may be just an innocent who, purely by association, is dredged up in this investigation."

"What I can't understand is why we've still got this guy under surveillance when everything is pointing to an Iranian link. I mean, three teams heading up to New York? Isn't that overkill?"

Meyerstein sighed. "It appears he had an admirer in Caroline Lieber. It appears they weren't an item for long, although she seemed a bit more keen. But like I said, I'm keeping that under review. If it doesn't go anywhere, they'll be pulled out."

Black steepled his fingers in front of his mouth. "When I speak to the President and his national security advisor, they're gonna want answers." His tone was colder. "And as it stands, I'm not going to be able to give him anything concrete. No leads. Nothing."

"We've gone over O'Grady's house, interviewed everyone who's connected with his life, analyzed his calls, texts, but nothing seems out of the ordinary apart from his call to Caroline Lieber."

"Martha, I like you very much. But I'm very frustrated that we have made no progress."

Meyerstein stayed silent. She shifted in her seat.

"I'm also concerned that this former Delta operator is part of this. Frankly, I don't understand the need for him."

Meyerstein didn't say anything. She now knew the real reason for the general's impromptu meeting.

"I want him off this case."

Meyerstein stared at Black. "I'm sorry, General, I can't do that."

Black let out a long sigh and leaned back in his seat.

"We're busting our guts on this. I have people who haven't slept in forty-eight hours. I know Reznick can help us."

"What about the Iranian Interests Section at the Pakistan Embassy?"

"Round-the-clock electronic and physical surveillance. As are wives, friends, etc. It's a major drain on resources."

"Beef up your numbers. Do whatever it takes. I'm going to give you forty-eight hours to get them back. But I want Reznick off the case."

"And if I don't?"

General Black got to his feet and stared down at her. "Let's hope for your sake that it doesn't get to that stage."

EIGHT

The Lowell Hotel on Manhattan's East 63rd Street was where Reznick and the rest of the Kendrick surveillance team had decamped to freshen up in an eighth-floor suite. It was just over seventy yards away on the opposite side of the street from the townhouse where Kendrick was visiting, a separate FBI surveillance unit keeping watch. It had felt good to take a long, hot shower and put on fresh clothes, sourced by the hotel management, including new boxer shorts, jeans and a pale blue linen shirt.

"You feel better?" Stamper said, pointing to room-service burger and fries.

Reznick nodded and began to wolf down the food. "I could get used to this life. Is this how the Feds slum it?"

Stamper rolled his eyes. "You kidding me?"

"So, what's the latest?" he said, wiping the tomato relish off his chin with a napkin.

"We've activated the microphone on his Blackberry. The whole conversation is being recorded."

"What's he saying to his surgeon friend?"

Stamper sighed, hands on hips. "Talking about his work, his love of rowing, asking about his godchildren, saying nice things to them."

"Nothing bad?"

"Absolutely not. The only thing of note is Kendrick was

told about an opening at Lenox Hill Hospital and asked if he was interested."

"What did he say?"

"Said he'd think about it. But he thought it was too early in his career. He wanted to gain another couple of years' experience with his trauma team in DC."

Reznick said nothing, shaking his head.

"What is it?"

"We're going nowhere fast with this guy."

"He's not our guy, that's why."

Reznick sighed. He was never comfortable with such certainties.

"You don't think so?"

"It's too early to say."

"There's nothing, and I mean absolutely nothing, that we have found or that this guy has said which is anything other than perfect. Not a word out of place."

"Doesn't that strike you as strange?"

Stamper shrugged. "Oh come on, you gotta be kidding me. This guy is just a clean-living single guy. The raw intel is pointing to Iran."

"Answer me this. Don't you think it's strange there was no laptop in his home? Nothing at all. I would've thought a highly-educated professional guy would need a computer to write up notes, email friends; you know what I'm talking about."

Stamper raised his eyebrows. "Maybe."

"Do you have a laptop at home?"

"Sure."

Reznick nodded. "So do I. So does every goddamn person I know. So where the hell is his?"

"Well, he could email from his Blackberry. Perhaps he's got an iPad; I don't know."

"Well, if he has, where the hell is it? Did you ask him about that?"

"There was no need to," Stamper said in a defensive tone.

"Look, I don't mean to bust your balls over this, but it is an anomaly. It's also interesting that Caroline Lieber has gone missing."

Stamper ran a hand through his hair. "Look..."

The radio crackled into life, cutting Stamper short in midsentence. It was the surveillance car outside the townhouse, farther down the street.

"Our boy's on the move," a female voice said on the radio.

A few minutes later, Reznick and Stamper were inside a new SUV being driven uptown.

Stamper said into his cell phone, "He's heading north through Manhattan. We're heading across the Harlem River into the Bronx. But we have three cars on it. I'll keep you posted."

Reznick craned his neck and looked at the traffic bunching up ahead. He caught sight of Kendrick's convertible doing a steady fifty-five. "A drive in the sun after driving all night. This guy sleeps less than me."

Stamper bit his lower lip. "Like I said, I think we're wasting our time."

Reznick said nothing.

"Bruckner Expressway, heading north. Where's he taking us?"

It wasn't long before the landscape turned industrial. Then it was down to a crawl in a low-income neighborhood. Abandoned cars, boarded-up shops and houses. Graffiti scrawled on tenements.

"Where the hell is this?" Reznick asked.

The driver turned round. "Hunts Point. I used to work in New York. Know the area. It's wall-to-wall garbage. Better than it used to be. But the place is d-i-s-e-a-s-e-d."

Reznick stared out at the urban decay. Living, existing and dying in a few dilapidated squares miles. He remembered it was the same area an old Delta buddy was brought up in. Charles "Tiny" Burns. He couldn't wait to get out and vowed he would never return.

They headed past the commercial and industrial areas that were still intact. A huge food distribution center, wastewater treatment plants, freight-rail terminals and waste-processing sites.

Stamper stared out of the window. "It's a place Adam Kendrick isn't likely to be dropping in to, that's for sure."

They headed along the expressway, through the Bronx, the views still brutal. A hopeless wasteland.

Eventually, they were driving through the working-class Baychester section of the Bronx.

They crossed the Hutchinson River parallel to the railroad tracks and it all changed. The grey and concrete gave way to the lush greenery of the suburbs. A golf course on the left, water on the right.

The driver said, "He's taken exit 15. He's now making a left onto Boston Post Road."

The car slowed down at a red stop light. A few moments later, it turned to green and they followed Kendrick when he turned left onto Pelhamdale Avenue.

The driver said, "Seems to be heading for Pelham."

Reznick said, "What's in Pelham worth talking about?"

The driver said, "Commuterville. First stop in Westchester. Really nice place. Great schools. Guy that wrote Primary Colors lives here. Read that one time."

Stamper snapping his fingers as if to remember. "What's his name... Joe Klein?"

The driver nodded. "Yeah, Joe Klein. Worked for Clinton."

Reznick peered up ahead. "So, where exactly is Kendrick headed? I don't get it."

The driver said, "OK, he's made a right onto Shore Road." He kept up a running commentary. "Now a left into the Travers Island entrance."

Up ahead, a huge whitewashed building, terracotta roof. Beyond that, Long Island Sound, water glistening in the summer sun.

Stamper checked the coordinates on his cell phone. "New York Athletic Club. Very ritzy. Wonder who the doctor's planning to meet here."

Reznick said, "Who's monitoring his cell phone to pick up any conversations?"

A navy Suburban pulled up in the club's parking lot. "They are. If there was anything, they'd let us know. We've got a feed coming back to us. Switch it on, Josh. We can monitor it ourselves."

The driver leaned over and flicked a switch on the dashboard. Stamper spoke into his radio. "Jerry, can you get two of your guys to do a recon? Find out where he is, eyeball and report."

Jerry said, "Yeah, got that, Roy."

Reznick said nothing. He had wanted to do that very thing. But Stamper had operational control of the surveillance operation. Reznick figured the last thing Stamper or any of the Feds needed was him griping about what he should or shouldn't do. Instead, he just sat in the back seat, eyes on the entrance to the upscale building.

A few moments later, Jerry's voice. "Roy, he's headed to the nearby boathouse."

Reznick nodded. "The guy is a very keen rower. Got some fancy rowing equipment in his basement."

Stamper nodded. "Jerry, is he with anyone?"

A crackly voice. "Negative, Roy."

"Your guys able to get into position to get a picture? I don't want us all to be milling around."

"I'll get on it."

Fifteen minutes later, a message on Stamper's iPhone. He opened it up. Shaky HD-quality footage of a tall man, wearing a Lycra rowing outfit, Yale baseball cap and wraparound shades, white teeth clenched, pulling hard in the sleek single scull.

Stamper shook his head and clenched his fist. "What a waste of time. He's out there enjoying a beautiful summer's day, and we're fucking around, with O'Grady and Lieber still missing."

It was late afternoon, the sky burnt orange and shadows long, when Kendrick emerged from the clubhouse after an early dinner. He wore shades, hair neatly combed and gelled, and sported knee-length shorts, a navy polo shirt and loafers. He climbed back into his car and sped off, unaware he was being watched.

Stamper groaned. "Goddamn, it's Ralph Lauren."

Reznick sat in silence.

Stamper called Meyerstein and gave her the update. He listened and nodded and ended the call. He didn't say a word for a few moments before he let out a long sigh. "Goddamn."

"What is it?" Reznick asked.

Stamper sighed long and hard. "Fuck."

"What?"

"They've just fished the partial remains of a body out of the Everglades."

"And?"

"They got a head. That's all. They're sure it's O'Grady. Bullet through an eye socket."

Reznick said, "Did someone dump him there?"

"Forensics is speculating that the body was thrown in; a gator ripped it to pieces, only the head remaining. Then, when it became swollen with water, floated to the surface."

"Motherfucker."

"Who found him?"

"Airboat captain."

Reznick stared out of the window and closed his eyes. "Goddamn!"

"Meyerstein is ordering us all back down to DC."

"And what about Kendrick? We just forget about him?"

"He's clean. He's a preppy surgeon. He's never even had a traffic ticket in his life."

Reznick stared out of the window as the deathly pallor of the Bronx sped by. He turned to Stamper. "Can I speak to Assistant Director Meyerstein, please?"

"Look, Jon, the decision's been made. Now is not the right time to speak to her, trust me."

"Can I speak to her?"

"It's not a good idea."

"Can I speak to her?"

Stamper sighed and eventually relented and punched in her number. "Reznick wants a word." A brief pause. "I'll pass him over." He handed the cell to Reznick.

Reznick got right to the point. "I think it's too early to cut and run on this guy."

"There's nothing on this guy, Jon. I want everyone back to DC. I've pulled the plug on Kendrick."

"I think you're being hasty."

"Why are you getting so worked up about this guy?"

"I don't know is the answer. I just feel something. Right down in my guts. It's gnawing away at me. Something about him is not quite right."

"Like what?"

"His laptop, for one. Do you know any urban professional that does not have a laptop, desktop or whatever in their house?"

"Maybe he's a technophobe."

"Maybe."

"We're scanning all his electronic communications. He has an email address and communicates via his iPhone. Sometimes he instant-messages with his Blackberry."

"And it's all fine? What do we know about this guy? I mean, really?"

"We know a lot about him. He's got a nice job, drives a nice car, and a girl who's gone missing had a thing for him.

He teaches at Georgetown Medical School. Probably crossed paths over a coffee on campus."

"But we don't know for sure, do we?"

"We don't have anything to keep us in New York."

Reznick sighed. "What do I have to do to convince you not to give up surveillance on this guy?"

"The decision has been made. I want everyone either back in DC or down in Florida this evening. I've got wall-to-wall meetings over the next six hours. I don't need any hassle."

Reznick closed his eyes for a moment, racking his brain for the right words to say. "There's something about the guy setting alarm bells ringing in my head. I don't think we should let him out of our sight. And I don't think electronic surveillance can cover all the bases."

"I've made my position clear, Jon."

"If you want your team back, great, get them back. But I want to stay. I'll do it on my own."

A long silence opened up between them. Eventually, Meyerstein spoke. "Jon, I don't need this just now." Her tone was icy.

"No one needs to know. Just leave me behind; what do you say?"

A long silence. "Put Stamper on."

Reznick handed the phone to Stamper.

"Yeah, Stamper here, Martha." He nodded a few times, as the glass towers of Manhattan glistened in the sun up ahead. "OK, you got it." He ended the call and turned to face Reznick. "We're gonna follow him into town. And we will drop you off at the Lowell. We've paid for the room up until noon tomorrow. I'll speak to the manager and let him know that you will be based in the hotel until then."

"And after that?"

"After that? Who the hell knows?"

NINE

The afternoon's rowing under a blazing sun on Long Island Sound had left Adam Kendrick in a good place. He felt exhilarated and even more focused. The exertion and cardiovascular workout had pushed him to the max, releasing the endorphins he craved. A calmness washed over him as he ate a delicious dinner in the second-floor dining room at the luxuriously appointed East 63rd Street townhouse with his friends and godchildren, Amy and Alexander. Steaks, lobster, a glass or two of French wine – which he politely declined – and Chopin music in the background.

As he listened to the gentle murmur of polite conversation, his thoughts turned to his recent trip to the woods.

He figured they were testing him to see if he could carry out the cold-blooded killing of a complete stranger. He thought it was all rather easy.

The men in the masks didn't faze him. The technical skill to carry out the thousand-yard headshot was beyond most mere mortals. He could see that they indeed had it all figured out. But he liked the fact that they made him prove how committed he was to the task in hand. How single-minded. How unyielding under psychological pressure.

The sound of his friend William yawning snapped him out of his reverie.

Kendrick smiled. "Long day?"

William rolled his panda-like eyes, patted his small belly and gave a weary shrug. "Same old, Adam. You know how it is."

Kendrick nodded. "Indeed. I'll be turning in early tonight, I'm afraid. I'm beat."

Sandra looked at Kendrick with a mixture of concern and close attention that he liked. It reminded him of the way in which his own mother fussed over his father when he returned home from the office. It was old fashioned. But it was nice. "Probably too much sun, Adam."

Kendrick smiled. "More likely not enough sleep, to be precise."

"You guys need to ease up some days." She looked across at her husband and smiled. "William, what was I saying only last night?"

William shrugged. "What can I say? It's medicine, and it's not a nine-to-five gig, right, Adam?"

Kendrick nodded sagely. "I was in Melbourne for a trauma conference a couple of weeks ago, and I still think I'm jet-lagged. But what can you do?"

Sandra rolled her eyes. "You guys, you're going to die of a heart attack if you're not careful. Did William tell you about his raised blood pressure levels? Only found out during a routine checkup."

Kendrick looked across at William. "Really. How long's it been like that?"

"Couple of months."

"What have you been given?"

"Perindopril, eight milligrams."

"Has that fixed it?"

"We're OK now."

Sandra said, "But let that be a wake-up call for you too, Adam. Sometimes you've got to smell the roses. Kick back."

"Which was precisely why I was rowing. A real tonic, getting back on the water."

Kendrick was tempted to use tiredness as an excuse for an early night. Sorely tempted, but he remained suitably engaged and attentive as Sandra talked about the importance of getting the children into the right school. He listened as she talked about whether Dalton was right for her ten year-old son, or if it should be his father's alma mater, Phillips Exeter. He had learned his listening skills from his mother, who paid attention for hours at a time as his father talked about his day. That was training enough for anyone. He remembered watching as his mother reached over the dinner table and patted the back of his father's hand as he talked about some of the difficult people he had to deal with.

He sometimes practiced in his bedroom when alone, mimicking his mother's mannerisms to try to catch that emotional bonding she so effortlessly achieved. People said that when his mother paid you attention it felt as though you were the most important person in the world. He'd studied the way her eyes showed concern. How she'd listened to his father's woes. He'd quickly realized that it was important to engage and feign empathy. And this skill had developed and embedded itself over the years within his psyche, so much so that it was now second nature.

"Uncle Adam?" Kendrick was snapped out of his reverie when Alexander piped up from the far end of the table. "What do you think is the best school for me?"

Kendrick scrunched up his face as if deep in thought and then looked first at the boy's father, and then the mother. He smiled across at the boy. "I know you're going to go to the best school, which is just right for you. I know your mother and father will have put a lot of thought into that. And I can tell you for nothing, you're going to do just great. But remember, whichever school you got to, you've still got to apply yourself and work very, very hard."

Alexander beamed at his parents and looked across at Kendrick. "What was your school like, Uncle Adam?"

Kendrick dabbed his mouth with his napkin and laid it out on his lap. "My school," he said, a tad theatrically for his own liking, "was very strict, but it was a great place to learn." He didn't say that he thought most of his teachers were second raters and bone idle, despite Andover being a leading school.

"My dad said you were top of the class and won a full scholarship to Yale? Is that right?"

Kendrick averted his gaze for a moment, trying to appear modest. "Work hard, just like your dad does, each and every day, and do your best, and you'll do just fine."

"My dad says he'd love to have you work beside him here in New York."

Kendrick turned and smiled across at his old friend, William Rhodes. "I've got a lot to learn to be as smart as your dad, I can tell you."

William Rhodes Sr beamed with pride and raised his glass. "To my good friend and brilliant doctor Adam Kendrick, who, God willing, will one day come and work in the greatest city in the world."

Laughs and smiles all around.

The rest of the dinner was good humored, although Sandra did belabor the point about education. She talked of Dalton's "rich educational pedigree" but said she felt as if she was in a "terrible quandary" as to which school to send her children to. Then Sandra regaled him with her shopping trips down Madison Avenue.

Eventually, he politely excused himself from the dinner table of his old mentor and his family, explaining that he had an early start. They were understanding, and he got a peck on the cheek from Sandra and a buddy pat on the back from William. He headed to his room, quietly locking the door, relieved to be in his own company again.

He switched off the lamps and lay back on his bed as warm air billowed through the curtains, the noise and bustle and horns and sirens of Manhattan infecting his frame of mind. He'd learned to like William and Sandra and their two children. William had taken him under his wing and taught him how to be a great doctor when he was a resident. And William remained a useful contact for him. He was the embodiment of the New York medical establishment. He had influential friends. But he could only tolerate three, maybe four visits per year with the family.

His thoughts shifted to what lay ahead.

The more he thought about it, the more he wanted the hour to arrive. He knew, however, that patience and the predetermined routine that had been laid out in meticulous detail by his handler were vital to ensure he got to his final destination.

The whole operation had been concealed behind layers of protection. It was quite brilliant.

The priority was the mission.

He would not fail.

He thought of his father on his deathbed, eyes shining, as he awaited his fate. Kendrick remembered feeling nothing, but feigning grief. "Dad, I love you. I'll always love you. And I will never fail you. Never." He'd felt it was the right thing to say.

His father and mother had watched him ascend the medical career ladder. He remembered the graduation as if yesterday, his father's starched white shirt and impeccable navy suit and matching tie, his inscrutable demeanor visible from the Yale graduation stage.

The sound of a blaring horn outside snapped Kendrick out of his thoughts. It had been more than an hour and a half since the meal. He got up and, as he had done for the last eighteen months at this time of day, did sit-ups, push-ups, and squat-thrusts, before he showered in his en suite bathroom. After brushing his teeth, he drank a huge glass of cool water.

Wrapped in a huge fluffy towel, he lay down on his bed, put the earbuds of his iPod carefully in and switched on his meditation exercises. Soothing sounds of the sea. At first, he let his mind wander. The thoughts of the day flashed by as Mozart's Requiem played. The burning sun on his skin. The tightening of his muscles. The fatigue. He let them go, as he'd been trained to do.

He absorbed the music as the sounds of the ocean washed over him.

The precursor to his fugue state.

He felt himself begin to disassociate.

Cleansing. Soothing. Cooling. Every ripple of water, every wave crashing onto the shore.

Then a voice, a reassuring voice in the background, calm and clear.

"Your day is ending. Enjoy this moment. You are free. Let the sound smother you."

He listened carefully. He felt the music soar as he fell deeper into a dark, black ocean. Floating out, billions of stars shimmering.

Deeper and deeper into his dark embrace.

He thought he could hear a distant sound. A beat. A beat behind the waves. Another beat. Electronic. Cold. Hard. Repetitive. It quickened. Almost imperceptibly at first. Then he felt the beat begin to grow within the waves.

He was listening to the sounds envelop him.

And the beat thudded hard, into every fiber. The roar of the ocean as the beat pounded out. The lush beauty of the beat and the waves and calm.

Then the beat slowed down, breathing softer, gentler.

The water was still washing over his mind.

He felt himself suspended in time. In darkness, he was calm.

The silence opened up. Then the beat returned, like a metronome.

Forty-nine beats per minute.

"Let it heal you. Let it become you."

The sounds got louder. Colors emerged, White, blue, green and red. He began to see a big moon. More lights. Flashing. He dived deep into them.

He let the colors envelop him.

The silence was back. He lay in silence.

Then he fell into one last darkness.

When he awoke, he sat bolt upright, struggling to remember where he was, iPod still playing. His iPhone was vibrating on the bedside table. It was 7.08am.

Kendrick rubbed the sleep out of his eyes and picked up the smartphone. "Yeah."

"Morning. How are you today? Did you sleep well?"

"Indeed. Very well."

"Remember, you're playing a part. Never let your mask slip."

"I hear you."

"We're getting close now. Real close to the day."

"The day can't come soon enough."

"All in good time, my friend. Stay safe."

Then the line went dead.

TEN

Reznick yawned as the first pink glints of the new day reflected off the windows of the East Side townhouse diagonally opposite, but still no sign of Kendrick. He was hunkered down in a second-floor room of the Lowell. Stamper had arranged a change of room so that Reznick could carry on the surveillance operation on his own. He was beginning to wonder if he shouldn't have taken up Meyerstein's offer to be assigned to watch over the Iranians.

He went through to the bathroom and splashed some cold water on his face and popped a Dexedrine.

He was alert. Ready for a new day.

A knock at the door, and room service arrived to serve his order of strong black coffee, freshly squeezed orange juice, scrambled eggs and rye toast. The sight and smells of the fresh food made Reznick feel famished, and he wolfed it down in seconds.

Just after 9am, the black townhouse door opened.

Kendrick stepped out with two smiling kids, presumably his surgeon friend's children. The kids were dressed in shorts, T-shirts and baseball caps, carrying a soccer ball under each arm. He wore a light gray tracksuit. Reznick watched as he bent down and tied his sneakers' laces, and did some stretching, before he laughed and joked with them as they headed west.

"OK, doc, where we going today?" Was this going to be another runaround?

Reznick sighed. He wondered if he had been foolhardy asking to do this. And for the first time, he began to seriously consider pulling the plug and heading back to DC. But something deep within him pushed those thoughts to one side.

He had asked to stay, so stay he would.

He headed downstairs to the Lowell's lobby and was greeted with a cheery "Morning, sir" from the day-shift concierge, who opened the front door for him. He pulled Reznick aside.

"Sir, I need to inform you that your room is available to you for another twenty-four hours, if you wish."

"It is? Who told you that?"

"I was told by the general manager to pass on that message to you. I believe that everything has been taken care of."

Reznick smiled. "Who took care of it?"

"All I know is it's taken care of, sir."

Reznick nodded. It had to be Meyerstein. She was giving him more time. He admired the way she worked. She was playing it cute. He could only imagine the pressure she had to be under to find O'Grady.

He donned his shades, not wishing to dwell on the thoughts for too long. He headed west along East 63rd Street, past the Leonori apartment building and across Madison until he reached Fifth Avenue. Traffic fumes and dirt kicked up from the passing vehicles. The oppressive noise of roadwork, drilling and the drone of cars, FedEx vans, garbage trucks, cabs and delivery trucks as they crawled along the East Side. In the distance, the sound of sirens from cop cars. It was an assault on the senses, no matter how often he visited.

He turned and looked across the street and saw Kendrick and the kids, a couple of blocks ahead, disappear from sight on the crowded summer sidewalks.

Reznick jaywalked across Fifth Avenue and eventually spotted Kendrick escorting the kids into the park at East 60th Street. He quickened the pace. They disappeared into the crowds. He couldn't see them for nearly a minute before he again caught sight of Kendrick. He was walking with the kids by the pond, high-fiving with them, occasionally picking them up and goofing around with them.

Reznick slowed down as Kendrick headed round the path, clearly enjoying the kids' company. He saw him enjoying the hot morning sun, fresh air and exercise. He saw him cross the stone Gapstow Bridge, which arched over the northernmost part of the pond, stopped for a few seconds, pointing out to the children the views of the huge skyscrapers dominating the vista.

He kept his distance, as Kendrick was lost in the moment. Kendrick walked the kids to a wide grassy area and set them up for a game of soccer.

Reznick hung back and sat down on a park bench that was out of the direct line of sight. He sat for the next hour and surreptitiously watched Kendrick kicking a ball about with the kids. He got up and walked towards an ice cream vendor and bought a cone. He stared across at the huge skyscrapers towering over Fifth Avenue. His mind flashed to the Towers falling. He imagined his wife's last moments. The images were seared into him.

The sound of raucous laughter from a crowd of frat boys laughing and joking snapped him out of his reverie.

Reznick glanced back towards Kendrick, who was signaling to the kids to wind up the game. They quickly gathered everything up, including baseball caps, and headed off. He walked slowly in their direction, mindful to keep out of their front and peripheral vision. He followed them over the 65th Street transverse road, past some huge trees and toward Sheep Meadow. Scores of people were already kicking balls around on the lush grass, playing baseball, lying in the sun, doing yoga.

He stopped around a hundred yards or so away, shielded from the sun by some huge oaks.

Reznick sat down on a bench and watched as Kendrick hugged the bedraggled kids and hauled them towards the Loeb Boathouse. They boated for an hour, Kendrick showing off his rowing skills as the sun sparkled on the water. The more he watched them, Reznick began to realize he really was wasting his time. The guy was clearly very fond of his godchildren. He watched as Kendrick and the kids retreated inside the boathouse restaurant for an hour-long lunch.

At 2pm, after hours of playing in the park and lunch, Kendrick and the kids walked all the way home. They looked utterly exhausted, the girl on his back, the boy walking hand in hand with him.

Reznick held back and watched Kendrick and the kids head into the townhouse. He felt this was going to be another wasted day. Reznick took the opportunity to have a shower and drink a couple of bottles of still Voss from the minibar. Then he ordered room service: a club sandwich, fries and a large Coke.

Feeling refreshed and rejuvenated, he took up position at the window of the room.

The rest of the afternoon dragged as the traffic crawled along East 63rd Street. Limos, yellow cabs, Bentleys and garbage trucks. On the sidewalk, nannies and mothers and frazzled young fathers pushed their kids and babies around in strollers, headed toward the park, while liveried doormen stood under apartment awnings, shielding themselves from the fierce afternoon heat.

Then, just at 5.55pm, the far side of the street in shade, Kendrick appeared in a white T-shirt, dark jeans and loafers, a small rucksack on his back.

"OK, where you taking me now, doc?"

Reznick took the stairs and was heading out through the lobby within twenty seconds. The air was thick with humidity and traffic fumes. His shirt was stuck to his back within seconds in the steam-bath conditions.

He walked a block and a half along East 63rd Street and turned left down Fifth Avenue. He stopped at a vendor cart and bought a hot dog as Kendrick crossed toward the park.

Reznick ate as he walked. He entered the park and walked by the pond again as he had done in the morning. Walking the exact same route. He observed Kendrick from more than two hundred yards back, as the park was quieter than earlier. He watched as Kendrick sat down on a park bench by the pond, bag at his side, and watched model boats being raced by two kids. The sky was on fire, the tops of trees tinged with gold and reds. The doctor sat and stared as if transfixed. Maybe enjoying the tranquility of the scene. He glanced at his watch.

Reznick was sitting on a fence, finishing off his hot dog, mostly shielded by the leaves of the huge beech trees.

Kendrick glanced at his watch again and opened up his bag. He pulled out a large camera and in a very deliberate and professional manner, began to take pictures of the pond. He then walked over and took some pictures of Gapstow Bridge. He wrapped the camera strap round his wrist and walked a few yards before snapping pictures of the bridge again.

Reznick had a good line of sight on Kendrick, but Kendrick in turn would find it nearly impossible to spot him, concealed by the lush summer foliage and overhanging branches, shrouded by leaves, all around the path.

The minutes ticked by.

Couples arm in arm, standing on the bridge, as Kendrick ambled onto it. He leaned his camera on the stone bridge, facing due south, and took pictures of the Manhattan skyline. He shielded his eyes from the sun and pointed his camera due west, and took some more.

Kendrick looked at his watch again, and then looked toward the iconic skyline, known the world over. Then he took out his cell phone and stared at it for a few moments.

Was he picking up a message?

Something about Kendrick bugged Reznick. He didn't know what.

Reznick finished the hot dog and wiped his mouth. He threw the napkin into a trash can. Shafts of early-evening sun peeked through the greenery, burnt orange light hitting the bridge.

Kendrick was still on the bridge. He checked his watch yet again. Reznick also looked at his watch. Precisely 18.22. Kendrick lifted his camera as the sun glanced off the lens, and pointed it due south toward the Plaza. Then he lowered the camera, before repeating it two more times in quick succession, in all three times.

On the surface, it looked like a keen photographer taking shots of Manhattan.

Look deeper.

Reznick was beginning to perceive Kendrick's movements in a different light. Was it possible that it was a signal?

Out of the corner of his eye, Reznick watched Kendrick head over the bridge. He hung back for a minute and looked for any signs of accomplices, shadows or countersurveillance heading in Kendrick's direction.

Nothing.

Reznick crossed over the bridge and followed Kendrick deeper into the park. The same route as the morning. Skirting Sheep Meadow. Then out at 65th Street. He watched from a distance as the doctor flagged down a cab.

Reznick did the same. "Stay with the cab four cars ahead," he said as they headed downtown.

The Hispanic driver shrugged and glanced in the rearview mirror. "Who you following, man?"

"Keep your eyes on the traffic."

The cab crawled through early-evening Manhattan traffic. Ten minutes later, it pulled up at Grand Central Station, Reznick's cab drawing up slowly a hundred yards back.

Reznick paid the fare as Kendrick headed into the cavernous rail terminal. Thousands of early-evening commuters jostling as they headed for their trains, while hundreds more caught a bite to eat in the numerous restaurants or coffee shops. The place was heaving. Seething. Security blared over the speaker system alerting commuters not to leave their bags.

He lost sight of Kendrick for a few moments. He scanned his surroundings and eventually caught sight of him climbing the stone stairs to the East Balcony, which housed an Apple Store. It was all glass and metal. Scores of mostly affluent young people and New York professionals scouring the iPads, MacBook Pros and shiny iPhones laid out on beautiful tables. He could almost see the love in their eyes as they held the devices.

He pretended to play with an iPad mini. Out of the corner of his eye, he heard Kendrick asking questions of a female staff member about iCloud specs on the device.

Kendrick listened patiently for a few minutes as Reznick hung around, back to him, about fifteen yards away at another table.

He saw Kendrick's reflection in an iPad mini he was playing with. It was a good way to watch him without being overt.

The conversation ended and Reznick hung around the table, still playing with the device. Eventually, Kendrick left and headed back down the stairs to the concourse.

Reznick watched as Kendrick headed down East 42nd Street and disappeared into the Capital Grille in the iconic Chrysler building, a Midtown landmark. Reznick walked on past the location and headed farther down 42nd Street. He stopped and took out his cell, pretending to make a call. He nodded as if listening, gave the occasional "yup" and stood around as the crowds surged by him. He waited fully twenty minutes before he turned around and headed into the Grille.

It had a clubby atmosphere. It was all dark mahogany with a classy air and red leather seats.

A maîitre d' approached, but Reznick indicated he wasn't eating and was ushered to the bar, where he ordered a club soda. He looked around and eventually saw Kendrick sitting alone at a booth. He was tucking into a steak, cornbread and fries.

Reznick glanced up at the TV, showing the Weather Channel, tracking a hurricane heading up from the Caribbean, due to hit the Carolinas in seventy-two hours.

The man two chairs up from him was shaking his head. "It's gonna be a big one," he said. "Real nasty mother."

Reznick nodded as he sipped his drink and waited. His gaze wandered round the restaurant. He caught Kendrick paying for his meal with a charge card. The bespectacled black waitress nodded politely as she swiped his card and handed over a receipt.

After his meal, Kendrick went to the bathroom before leaving the Grille.

Reznick finished his drink and went outside. He was just in time to see Kendrick climb into a cab and head uptown. Thirty seconds later, he caught a cab and managed to follow the cab all the way up Fifth Avenue, where Kendrick got out at the glass-fronted Apple Store.

He waited a couple of minutes before he headed in, and went down the stairs into the Zen-like calm of a geek's wet dream; iPads, iPhones and MacBooks arranged on pristine ash tables, shiny and clean.

Reznick watched as Kendrick checked out the latest iPhone. He spent a quarter of an hour with the assistant discussing the smartphone. He wondered why he hadn't bought the same phone at the Grand Central Apple Store. He pushed those thoughts to one side as he watched Kendrick buy a brand-new phone before heading back up Fifth Avenue and along East 63rd Street to the townhouse of his friend.

Reznick was back at his room at the Lowell when his cell vibrated in his pocket. He checked the caller display and saw it was Meyerstein.

"Hi, how's it going?" she asked.

Reznick sighed. "Not much to give you."

"Any developments?"

Reznick took the next few minutes to outline the comings and goings of Kendrick in New York.

"Jon, I've got to be honest: all the analysis is pointing to the fact that this lead doesn't amount to anything."

Reznick said nothing as he stared at the unrelenting East Side traffic outside his window.

"Jon, I'm going to level with you. Black wants you off this investigation."

"Why?"

"Why? Well, he doesn't think you belong on the program."

"What about you?"

"What about me?"

"Do you think I belong on the program?"

"It was me that requested you be part of the team. I don't cut and run."

"What about the general? Isn't that going to piss him off?"

"Leave me to worry about him. Until then, you stay put in New York."

"What about the analysis?"

A long silence opened up before she spoke. "I can't say any more at this stage."

Then the line went dead.

ELEVEN

Reznick was floating on a river of darkness, unable to breathe. The sky was inky black. He sensed he was not alone. The smell of rotting garbage drifted over him. He tasted dust. Then blood. A humid breeze was blowing through, helping to cool the fever. The sound of screaming. Yells. More screams. Gunshots. Then sirens blaring.

He bolted upright, heart pounding. He looked around. Semidarkness. He was still fully clothed beside the second-floor window of the Lowell. He took a few moments to get his bearings, nightmares of Mogadishu still coursing through his brain.

"Damn." He'd blacked out with exhaustion.

Reznick got up, went across to the bathroom and splashed cold water on his face. His watch showed it was 3.25am. He went across to the minibar and opened a bottle of chilled Evian water. Then he went across the room and looked out of the window. Only a few cars around.

The townhouse was in darkness.

He did some stretching exercises and felt better. More focused.

The minutes dragged as he sat in darkness, keeping watch. Just when he was thinking of calling room service for an early-morning breakfast, a yellow cab pulled up directly outside the townhouse further down the street. He checked his watch. It was 4.01am.

"OK, what've we got here?"

A couple of minutes later, Kendrick emerged from the townhouse, jogged the steps and slid into the backseat of the cab. It pulled away and headed in the direction of Fifth Avenue. Reznick got downstairs in seconds and hailed a passing taxi.

"Where to, buddy?" the overweight driver asked as Reznick sat down in the back seat, leaning forward, scanning ahead for Kendrick's cab.

Reznick thought he spotted it disappearing out of sight.

"Fifth Avenue, step on it."

The driver shrugged. "You're not a crazy husband following his girl?"

Reznick handed the man a fifty-dollar bill. "You wanna step on it?"

The driver nodded. "Whatever you say, my friend."

Reznick spotted the cab with the torn Bloomberg sticker in a rear window turning onto East 62nd Street. The streets were quieter. Doormen were hosing down sidewalks outside upscale East Side apartments. "Hang a left."

The driver nodded as they trailed the cab, fifty yards back.

Reznick sat in silence and wondered where Kendrick would be going at that ungodly hour.

They headed downtown on the FDR. Past the UN building. Past Bellevue Hospital, where he had visited a Delta buddy of his, Craig Lansley, who'd lost his mind after one too many tours of Iraq. He remembered the noise as he walked along the Bellevue corridors and Lansley staring back at him, unable to comprehend who it was who was visiting. Reznick's memories were of a fit, funny and smart tough guy. But what he saw, in the flesh, was a broken-down man whose eyes were dead, tears streaming down, shaking, hugging his body as if for comfort.

A dozen blocks later, they were headed along Avenue C and down Loisaida Avenue. Bars, clubs, late-night booze hounds on the prowl, cops at intersections keeping watch, crowds of college kids roaming the streets. Brownstones, graffiti spray-painted onto shop fronts and doorways.

His mind flashed back to his first date with his late wife. McSorley's Ale House on East 7th Street, a few blocks from where he was just now. The smoky atmosphere. The noise. The laughter. Having to stand close to Elisabeth to be heard. The smell of her perfume. The memories flooded his mind.

"You been down here before?" the driver said, snapping him out of his thoughts.

"No."

"Let me tell you, it's not as bad as it used to be. Yuppies have replaced the yippies. Hipsters and frat boys. But it still has its moments, no question."

Reznick stared out at the crowd of young Hispanic men harassing a couple of middle-aged white men walking hand in hand.

"When I think back to the 1970s or 1980s, it was like fucking Beirut. Scary place. Junkies, homeless, squatters, mental degenerates."

Reznick said nothing.

"But there are still a few crazies around."

"Is that so?"

"A few blocks from here, not that long ago, some fuckhead got gunned down outside the Sin Sin Club. Big fight. I saw it all. I was a witness. They don't tell people all about the freaks, fruits and junkies who still crawl around after dark, especially around the projects along the East River. Avenue D. D for death. You still gotta be careful, man."

Reznick looked out and saw two cops leaning against cruisers, sipping coffee.

The cab driver didn't let up. "Yeah, Alphabet City."

"What's that?"

"It's what they call Avenue A, B, C and D. I remember a time when the cab didn't go east of Avenue A. It was nuts.

Dealers. Dopeheads. Crackheads would stab you as soon as look at you, way back in the 1980s. It was dangerous. I was there when the city was on its knees. It was shit, let me tell you."

Reznick nodded but said nothing.

"So who's in the cab ahead?"

"Just drive."

The cab driver nodded in his rearview mirror and headed past a crowd of boozed-up college boys – some wearing NYU T-shirts – outside a late-night tavern. The cab cut down East 7th Street, hung a right and then a left along tree-lined St Mark's Place.

Some kids were drinking from bottles on a tenement stoop. Some hanging around street corners with friends. It was a warm summer night.

Kendrick's cab pulled up outside Yaffa Café's dark-green-and-white-striped canopy and Kendrick got out.

Reznick said, "Keep going. Drop me off in a couple of blocks."

The driver nodded and dropped him off outside Paul's Da Burger Joint on Second Avenue. He handed over another fifty-dollar bill. "That cover it for you?"

The driver grinned. "Damn right it does. Have a good night. And stay safe."

Reznick watched the cab turn along Second Avenue before he headed back along St Mark's Place. He passed a neon-lit cocktail bar, a drunk sitting on the sidewalk, as people walked on by. Then past a half-empty sidewalk bar, some girls laughing raucously inside. He passed Jules' Bistro as a cop car crawled along First Avenue giving him the eye, windows down. Up ahead he saw the sign for Yaffa.

A few people were sitting and eating on the outside patio, but Kendrick wasn't one of them.

Reznick headed inside. The crowd was mostly young. Talking loudly was the order of the day. The smell of garlic and

Mediterranean heavy in the air. The Beatles song "I'm Down" was playing loud. He looked around. The place was kitsch and retro and very packed. Flock wallpaper from a bygone era. Eastern vibe. Weird artifacts. Low lighting. A picture of Jim Morrison. A Buddha draped in yellow beads, holding a banana. But Reznick couldn't see Kendrick.

He walked through the restaurant and saw it led to a garden bedecked in lights hanging from trees, kids drinking and smoking all around.

Reznick hung back behind the door and saw Kendrick was sitting by himself, talking into his shiny new iPhone, coffee on the table.

Reznick headed back inside and sat down alone at a zebra-and-leopard-print booth. He ordered a double-shot Americano. An Eastern European runner brought it to his table within minutes.

His line of sight was good, seeing everyone entering and leaving the bar. He sipped his seriously strong coffee. It felt good as the caffeine kicked in.

Revived.

He checked his watch. Twenty minutes had passed by. It was 4.42am. His gaze wandered round the room, trying to appear disinterested. Everyone was very much into their groups and cliques, chatting, buzzing and drinking.

Time dragged. He nursed his coffee and listened to conversations. The price of a room on Avenue A, relationships with unsuitable boyfriends, nightmare bosses.

He finished his coffee and went to the bathroom. A couple of minutes later, he peered through the doorway into the garden. Kendrick was reading a magazine, his phone on the table beside him.

Reznick got back to his table and took out his wallet. He wondered if he should stay put, order another coffee, or if he should wait across the street for Kendrick to leave.

Out of the corner of his eye, he saw Kendrick walk through the bar and leave. He stared ahead through the window veiled by Buddha beads and statues and saw Kendrick head down St Mark's. He was headed east.

Reznick left a twenty-dollar bill on the table, waited a few moments and headed out onto the street.

As he left Yaffa, up ahead Kendrick crossed over to the other side of the road before turning right along Avenue A. Reznick hung back. Satisfied he was out of sight, he pressed on past the bars and metal-shuttered shop fronts scrawled with garish graffiti.

Kendrick crossed over Avenue A at the Sidewalk Café and headed down East 6th Street.

Reznick crossed over to the opposite sidewalk. He wondered what the hell the young doctor was doing in the middle of the night, heading down deep into Alphabet City. The area didn't seem like a natural haunt for a clean-cut, high-flying DC trauma surgeon.

He headed past Eastern Bloc, a crowd of guys drinking some wine and deep in conversation. Then over Avenue B and past some more late-night drinkers sitting at tables outside Horus Cafe.

He felt wired as he walked on by. Deeper and deeper into the East Village. His senses switched on.

He hung back as Kendrick crossed over at some lights on Avenue C and headed along East 6th Street. More residential. A vacant lot. More graffiti scrawled on buildings and trash cans.

Then past a deli and across Avenue D. Lilian Wald housing projects towered across the east side of the street. But Kendrick turned right.

Reznick crossed over Avenue D to the opposite sidewalk and stole a glance at Kendrick, who had stopped outside a nondescript brick building with a black door. He pressed a buzzer and stood waiting. The number above the door was 45-51.

Reznick hung back as a woman opened the door and hugged Kendrick before ushering him inside.

Reznick kept moving. He crossed back over Avenue D, headed down to East 2nd Street and turned down Avenue C into a filthy bodega. He bought an energy drink, a couple of candy bars, a gray Yankees mesh baseball cap and a loose-fitting black T-shirt. He ditched his shirt in the shop's trash can, pulled on the T-shirt, pulled his cap down low and walked back to Avenue D.

Same person, different look.

He sat down on a bench in the shadow of one of the housing projects, in line of sight of the brick building Kendrick had entered.

Reznick drank his energy drink and wolfed his candy bars. He took out his cell and looked up the address on his phone. It pulled up Bowery Mission Transitional Center.

Fuck. What was going on?

He mulled on that as a couple of tough-looking Puerto Rican kids walked past with pit bulls on a piece of rope, each giving him the cold eye.

"Yo, faggot, what the fuck you looking at?" the smaller of the two said.

Reznick stared them out.

The kid and his friend tried to look tough for a moment but they crossed over the street, pulling the snarling dogs behind them.

Reznick hung around for thirty minutes. He decided to go for a stroll parallel to the homeless center. The black door was firmly locked, but there were a couple of lights on in the ground floor.

He walked round the block and headed further back down Avenue D. He passed a panhandler huddled in a liquor store doorway under a pile of blankets. Farther north up Avenue D, the soaring smokestacks of Con Edison's huge plant billowing into the pre-dawn air. He headed past the hostel, the sound of a loud TV from an open second-floor window.

Then to the end of the block, bought a New York Daily News from a newsstand that was just setting up and crossed over at the lights.

The sun peeked through the smokestacks and he sat down on a bench in front of the huge Jacob Riis housing projects.

He flicked through the paper as traffic picked up. Sidewalks were busier, early-morning workers on their way to the daily grind. A cop car cruised the main drag before edging up one of the adjoining streets. The sound of metal shutters being opened.

Out of the corner of his eye, the panhandler shuffled into sight, bottle of Night Train in his hand. He took a closer look. The man was white, dirty, wild blue eyes, bare feet bleeding.

The man sat down at the end of the bench, humming a show tune. He turned to face Reznick. "Where you from?"

Reznick sighed. It was the last thing he needed, to engage some broken panhandler. But he knew that to ignore him would be to attract the ire of the man. "Just visiting friends nearby."

He pointed at Reznick. "There's no such things as friends. Not here. Not now. Not ever. Not in this goddamn fucking stinking city."

Reznick said nothing.

The man glugged back some wine. "I don't want to go anymore. You ever feel like that?"

Reznick nodded. "Yes, I do."

The man nodded and closed his eyes, bottle still clasped in his filthy hand.

For the next two hours, as the panhandler slept on the bench, Reznick alternated between walking around the block and taking up different vantage points farther down the avenue. He was starting to wonder how long he'd be waiting for when the red door opened at the homeless shelter.

Reznick watched as he sat on a bench farther down the street from the panhandler, but with good line of sight. He waited a few moments as Kendrick headed off north along Avenue D. He got up and crossed over Avenue D, picking up Kendrick's tail. The sidewalks were starting to get busier. He passed a Latino street vendor selling raspberry slushies from his cart, cigarette hanging from his mouth. A cop was on a corner, leaning against his cruiser, watching the world go by. The place was coming to life as dawn broke.

He caught sight of Kendrick as he turned left at a deli mini market and headed left down East 10th Street. He crossed over and walked on the opposite sidewalk.

He locked on to Kendrick. Farther up the street, on the opposite side, Kendrick crossed over Avenue C, passed a liquor store, and continued down East 10th Street.

He watched as Kendrick crossed over and turned right down Avenue B. Reznick crossed over to the opposite sidewalk. Two women jogging, iPhone buds in, sweating profusely.

Then Kendrick crossed over Avenue B – the same side as Reznick – before he headed past a nail salon and down East 11th Street.

Reznick turned down the same street, as Kendrick walked past a dozen men standing in a soup-kitchen line and disappeared inside the building. He stole a glance as he walked on the opposite side of the street and saw a sign for the Father's Heart Ministry Center. He kept on moving until he reached a deli fifty yards farther down the end of the street. It was situated beside a glass business whose blue-paint exterior had been scrawled in Day-Glo graffiti. At the building opposite, a Puerto Rican flag fluttered from a second-floor window. He bought a bottle of water. He took a few refreshing gulps, needing the hydration after walking in the high humidity. Then he went outside and sat on the steps of the shop.

He stared back down the opposite side of the street at the line of poor bastards gathering for breakfast. Handed a ticket and ushered in by cheery young volunteers.

His thoughts turned to Kendrick.

Three hours at a homeless shelter and now a soup kitchen. The guy was either Gandhi or this was an elaborate cover. But if it was a cover, what was the purpose?

It seemed on the surface as if the good doctor was doing his bit. Giving something back.

The thought depressed Reznick. It would mean that he was wasting his time, tailing a good guy.

Reznick drank the rest of the water, walked round the block and parked himself in a new position on a bench outside the 11B Express pizza restaurant, diagonally opposite the ministry, on the corner of Avenue B. Partially obscured from view by the leaves of a huge broad-leafed tree, Reznick flicked through his newspaper. A steady stream of down-on-their-luck guys lining up for free food.

Time dragged.

He checked his watch. He walked the block. He bought a coffee at the deli.

Just before 10am, Kendrick emerged onto the sidewalk, talking into his cell phone. He walked up East 11th Street and caught a taxi at Avenue A.

It was five minutes before Reznick got a cab, and he'd finally lost Kendrick.

A short while later, in the cab heading back to Lenox Hill, his cell rang. He didn't recognize the number.

"Yeah, who's this?"

"It's Meyerstein."

Reznick kept his voice low. "Hi, any signs of progress?"

"Nothing so far, Jon. Look, I'm going to be straight with you. I'm very tempted to do what everyone is telling me to do and haul you out of New York."

Reznick sighed.

"Look, that's nearly two days and nothing, am I right? The general, besides threatening to haul me off the program, is at a loss to understand this obsession with Kendrick."

"I'll tell you why. There's something about this guy. His actions are..."

"What?"

The cab hit a pothole and Reznick was jolted in the back seat. "He got up and headed down to a homeless shelter on Avenue D, in the East Village. Then he headed across to a soup kitchen."

"And? Are you saying that's the sum of what you've got?"

"Look, I'm not buying this Mother Theresa crock of shit. It does not wash."

"Jon, this is a good guy. There are good people in the world."

"My gut instinct says that we need to keep an eye on him."

A long sigh from Meyerstein. "Jon, listen to me. We have checked into this guy's background. We have gone over it. And there's nothing to arouse suspicion. And what you say about helping out at homeless shelters and soup kitchens tallies with him working in Malawi for Unicef and Haiti. He helped out down in New Orleans after Katrina. He's worked on vaccination programs for the World Health Organization. Jon, the guy's never had a ticket in his life. He is clean."

The cab crawled through Midtown East traffic. "I think we're missing something. What about the trip into the East Village in the middle of the night? The buying of a new phone?"

"The buying of a new phone? Gimme a break. What if you're just plain wrong?"

"What if I'm not? I'm telling you, there's a piece of the jigsaw that will pull this all together. But we're still missing it. Not connecting the dots. I need to know for sure that this guy is legitimate."

Meyerstein sighed.

"I am convinced we're missing something from his past. You've told me about the trips abroad. Are they accurate records?"

"Jon, I think you're reaching."

"Way I see it, we've made no breakthrough. He is the only link, no matter how tenuous, to Lieber and therefore O'Grady. I don't think we can dismiss him so readily."

"The problem is, Jon, no one on my team sees Kendrick as part of the jigsaw. Nothing about his past gives us any cause for concern. Counterterrorism did a separate trawl with the NSA, and it came back clean. You want me to go on? You're out on a limb."

Reznick said nothing. It wouldn't have been the first time in his career.

"Are you still there, Jon?"

"Are we monitoring the new phone? Do we even have the number? And let's not forget the very expensive Mercedes."

"What are you getting at? It's not illegal to have a nice car."

"The guy is putting in some hours at a soup kitchen and a homeless shelter, while driving around in a car which could feed one hundred thousand people. Does that strike you as out of place?"

"People do their bit in different ways."

"Then there is another scenario. Is it possible that these trips around town are a cover?"

"A cover for what?"

"Is he using a cutout?"

Meyerstein went quiet.

"Is he using an intermediary to pass or receive information?"

"I know what the hell a cutout is."

"Well, if he is, the cutout is based in the East Village. Look, I'm telling you, we need to start connecting the dots with this guy."

The silence on the phone was deafening.

TWELVE

The conversation with Reznick bothered Meyerstein. It added to the lingering suspicions she herself was having about the DC surgeon. She hadn't shared her thoughts with anyone on her team, not even Reznick. Her analysis was showing that Kendrick was clean. But the doubts Reznick had voiced mirrored her own, and they had begun to gnaw away at her.

She chewed over what Reznick had said. It was true that Kendrick did have a connection to Lieber, albeit only a couple of light dates, by all accounts. However, his behavior for someone who was supposed to be on vacation, out and about on his own in New York at all hours of the night, visiting restaurants, buying a new phone, soup kitchens, homeless shelters in the East Village, did seem quite eccentric.

She pushed those thoughts to the side. She had had a brutal twenty-four hours without sleep, and what lay ahead was wall-to-wall meetings with counterterrorism experts, foreign policy experts, Iranian strategic analysts working on the big picture at the CIA, and video conferencing with State Department staff who had worked with O'Grady.

Her focus was still fixed on who was responsible for O'Grady's kidnapping and murder, which in turn would answer any questions on national security.

She was beginning to feel the strain. A couple of times as she pored over and discussed a briefing with her team in the middle of the night, she had felt slightly breathless. Was she stressed? She felt the pressure building. It was pressing in on her chest. It was becoming tangible.

The weight of expectations was immense. So many people looked to her for direction and for answers. And sometimes she didn't have any answers, just more questions. She remembered what her father had once said.

Sometimes, you have days that are so long, and so hard, that it seems like it'll never end. On days like that, you don't retreat. You dig in. You remain in control. You don't waver. And it will eventually, I promise you, subside.

The hacking cough of an NSA systems expert snapped her out of her reverie. Meyerstein looked over to the four guys monitoring data traffic and analyzing online intelligence, eyes scanning their monitors.

The more she learned, the more it was clear Iran was in the picture. The current consensus was that a rogue state was using disaffected former Eastern Bloc special ops around the world. The Chechen link was being explored too, the Boston bombing still raw in everyone's memory.

She had learned that several former Russian special ops guys had been apprehended in the last six months in hot spots around the world. Libya, Somalia, Syria. FBI counterterrorism teams had arrested two. Were there others? Is this who had ordered O'Grady murdered? And if so, why?

Meyerstein walked over to the team of senior strategic analysts who looked at threats, vulnerabilities and gaps in the special access program's knowledge. They sifted raw information from numerous sources and brought it all together. "Any further forward, Leon?" she asked the senior NSA egghead.

He turned round and rubbed his tired eyes, probably checking his computer for too long. "Chechen link is firming up. Still early days, though."

Meyerstein went back to her office on the top floor and into the private en suite bathroom. She looked at herself in the mirror. Dark shadows under her eyes despite wearing concealer. She used the Touche Éclat pen-brush under her eyes and applied fresh makeup. Feeling fresher, she got behind her desk.

She leaned back in her seat and stared at the screensaver of her children. She missed them so bad it hurt. She wanted the cuddles and the laughter. Skyping them wasn't the same. She pushed those thoughts aside and turned them to the early-morning telephone call with Reznick. Part of her wished he was with her to talk things over.

Meyerstein punched in the number for Roy Stamper, her trusted deputy, working in an office with his team two floors below. A man whose counsel she valued.

"Shut the door, Roy," she said when he arrived.

Stamper sank into a leather chair opposite and stretched out his arms and legs. He looked exhausted.

"O'Grady dead. Caroline Lieber still missing, not a trace. We're nowhere with this, Roy. Absolutely nowhere. What are your thoughts? And don't sugarcoat it."

Stamper sighed. "There is a link between O'Grady and Lieber. The call tells us that. Counterintelligence is telling us Iran is in the picture, what with O'Grady's area of expertise."

Meyerstein leaned back in her seat. She relayed the latest snippets of information Reznick had told her about Kendrick. "He thinks we need to focus some more on our DC doctor. I'm wondering... What if... What if there is a chance, a chance, that Reznick's right and there is a connection with Kendrick? What if there is a thread which we are missing?"

"Not one shred of intel on that, Martha. Look, I'm going to level with you. I think Reznick is wrong. We've checked Kendrick out. It's not possible that he's connected."

Meyerstein smiled.

"What?"

"What you just said... I remember what my father used to say when I said something was not possible. He would always turn it around and say, 'Are you saying it is impossible?' And when I would say, 'No, it's not impossible, just highly improbable,' he just smiled at me and said, 'Ah, well, that's a different thing, isn't it?' So, it's highly improbable Kendrick has anything to do with this. But it's not impossible, right?"

Stamper stared at her. "Can I be blunt?"

Meyerstein shrugged.

"I'm not too sure having Reznick on this team is a good move. Don't get me wrong; I like the guy. But he's making us take our eyes off the ball."

"Roy, let me ask you this. Have we really dug down into Kendrick's past? I mean, really gotten beneath the surface? I read some analysis from one of the best behavioral analysts we have; did you see that?"

Stamper nodded. "Malone? I thought that was a bit sketchy, part psychobabble part pop psychology. It was all over the place."

"I agree, he can be out there, but he indicates there are personality traits he finds interesting in Kendrick. He thinks we shouldn't ignore him completely."

"What, and that's it? That's what we're going on? This is all we have? Reznick and Malone? Gimme a break."

Meyerstein sighed. "Roy, I don't feel like I know this guy. I want you to set up a dedicated team to analyze all data on dates and times abroad against what we have and recheck everything. Friends, family, lovers, acquaintances. Are we missing something, that's all I'm asking?"

"You got to be kidding me."

"Do I look like I'm kidding?"

Stamper said nothing.

"I want us into every area of his life on a minute basis. Childhood. Education. College. Work. Top to bottom. I want to see documentary proof of each stage of his life, where he was and under what authority. I want pictures of him. But what I also want is a trawl of all foreign intelligence on Kendrick. Do they have anything on him that we don't? Any nugget."

Stamper blew out his cheeks. "I can't believe what I'm hearing."

"What the hell is that supposed to mean?"

"I think we're wasting our time, that's all."

"Maybe we are. Yes, you might very well be right. But I want to seal up every aspect of the investigation. I also want Kendrick's new cell phone number with all calls and messages microanalyzed by the NSA. I also want to know about his old phone. And the one before that. Is he running more than one phone?"

"Martha, I've got to say, I think you're taking a big risk with this."

Meyerstein leaned forward and fixed his gaze. "That's for me to worry about. Now, listen, I've fed the tidbits Reznick gave us into our system. He said Kendrick visited a place called the Yaffa Café just before 5am today, then the Bowery homeless shelter on Avenue D and a soup kitchen on East 11th Street. Find the volunteers and all those who work there and have worked there in the past two years...I want us to drill down into this guy and what he's all about."

"I don't understand your thinking on this."

Meyerstein felt anger tighten her stomach. "Roy, don't sweat it. I'll take the flack."

Stamper let out a long sigh. "I'm sorry, Martha, to appear so negative, but Reznick is barking up the wrong tree. The only thread holding it together is that O'Grady called Lieber shortly before they both disappeared, and Lieber was infatuated with a DC doctor. It doesn't stand up to the most basic bit of scrutiny."

"Look, the only thing we have got to lose is manpower."

"This is a dumb call, Martha; that's all I'm saying. I can't remember any dumb calls in all the time we've worked together. But this comes into that category."

Meyerstein leaned back in her seat. She seethed at Stamper but kept her cool on the surface. "Have you forgotten, Roy, that I am an assistant director of the Federal Bureau of Investigations, and I'm heading up this special access program? I won't have my judgment questioned by subordinates."

Stamper shifted in his seat but said nothing.

"I've got to say, Roy, I thought I knew you better than that."

Stamper cleared his throat. "Look, I think we're all under pressure on this. But I think it's important that we can be frank with each other, Martha. I'm not the only one that thinks Reznick has no place in the team and is questioning why the hell we are even listening to him."

Meyerstein felt her throat tighten.

"Martha, the analysis is clear. On the ground, we're looking for Eastern Bloc mercs, not some candy-ass doctor. You're giving too much credence to what Reznick is saying."

"That's enough! I've heard your gripes but, you know what, Roy? I'm going to ignore them. Someone is working on the ground, probably at the behest of the Iranians or other proxies."

"So where the hell does Kendrick fit into that?"

"I don't know. He might not fit into it. But I need to be sure."

Stamper shook his head, looking dismayed. "Look, I didn't want to say this, but I'm going to."

"Spit it out."

"The guys on the team are busting their guts on this, and they don't like their boss, one of the most senior agents in the FBI, being made to look a fool, over a has-been Delta."

Meyerstein bristled at the criticism. She'd always had a thin skin. She knew it. And it showed. Her father let criticism roll off his back. He laughed it off. But she never could. "In what way, precisely, am I being made to look a fool?"

Stamper said nothing. His silence said it all.

"I don't give a damn what people think. Jon Reznick was brought in to augment the capabilities of my team. He offers something else."

"Like what?"

"He isn't afraid to go out on a limb. He doesn't take the safe path. He tells it like it is."

"And that's just what I'm doing. Martha, what if he's wrong? How are you going to explain how you wasted hundreds of man-hours on the say-so of Reznick? It seems the guy is answerable to no one."

"He's answerable to me."

"So why didn't he listen when you ordered us back to Washington?"

Meyerstein remained silent.

"What is it about this guy?"

"Do not call Jon Reznick into question."

Stamper said nothing.

"Now, you listen to me, Roy, we have worked together in harmony, as a team, for as long as I can remember. And I will not be spoken to like this by you or anyone. So, here's how it's going to work. Do you want to be taken off this investigation and shipped back to HQ?"

It was Stamper's turn to flare. "I don't believe this!"

"Because that's what's going to happen if I hear one more word of insubordination. And that goes for anyone. You got a problem with that?"

Stamper shook his head.

"OK. You stay here and connect the goddamn dots. Updates, analysis feeds, I want it sent to me in real time."

"Where are you going?"

"I'm going to New York. I'm going to find out for myself what the hell is going on."

Stamper sat in silence, staring at the floor.

"When you come to lead such an investigation, you can make whatever call you like. But while I'm in charge, we're going to do this my way."

THIRTEEN

It was late in the evening when Reznick's cell phone began to vibrate as he hunkered down in his darkened room at The Lowell. He checked the caller display and saw a number he didn't recognize.

Reznick sighed and answered. "Yeah, who's this?"

"Jon Reznick," a woman's voice said, "you're to make your way to the Fairfax at East 69th Street and Third Avenue." Her accent was unmistakable New York. "The entrance is across from the Trump Palace, so you can't miss it. Dispose of your cell. Tell the guy at reception to buzz apartment 89 and say it's Jake Smith. You got it?"

"Who the hell is this?"

"FBI Special Agent in Charge, New York special operations, Margaret O'Halloran. It'll all become clear."

The line went dead.

Reznick wondered if the call was legitimate. He mulled on that for a few moments and decided it was. Time to move. He pulled out the SIM card from his cell and flushed it down the toilet, disposing of the battery in the lobby trash on his way out of the hotel. He headed the six blocks to the Fairfax, a pre-war brown brick building. A limestone base, metal awning. He walked through the doors and into a spacious wood-paneled lobby.

The guy on reception wore a dark suit and tie and was smiling. "Can I help you, sir?"

"Jake Smith. I'm visiting number 89."

"Very good, sir." He picked up the phone and punched in a number. "Reception here, sir. Mr Smith for you." A long pause. "Very good, sir. I'll send him up."

The guy pointed to the elevators. "Eighth floor. Right at the end of the corridor, sir."

Reznick rode the elevator to eight and headed right along the carpeted corridor. Modernist prints on the wall. He knocked on the door. A few moments later, a heavyset man in a dark gray suit ushered him inside. He stepped in. It was oak floors and high ceilings. He followed the man down a hallway and up some wrought-iron stairs. It was a duplex. On the next level, it all became clear.

Whitewashed walls, a large-screen TV on one wall. It was a spacious open-plan living area, like a converted loft. The smell of coffee permeated the room. Leather sofa on one side of the huge space. Farther down the room, sitting at a table, was FBI Assistant Director Martha Meyerstein, a cell phone and MacBook Pro in front of her. Sitting at the other end was a middle-aged guy with a goatee, Ramones T-shirt and jeans and sneakers, tapping away with one hand on an iPad.

"Good evening, Jon," she said.

Reznick wondered what was going on. He pulled out a chair and sat down.

She pointed to the man at the opposite end of the table. "Dr Henry Malone. Behavioral analyst with the FBI."

Malone nodded, face impassive.

Reznick nodded back. "You mind me asking what's going on?"

"What's going on, Jon, is that I've decided to have a closer look at Kendrick."

Reznick smiled. "You kidding me?"

She pointed at Malone. "No. I'll explain in a few moments. As of this moment, this will be your base in New York, along with four other members of a surveillance team attached to this program. Electronic monitoring has been set up in the bedroom."

"What is this place?"

"It's a safe house, of sorts. Used to be the FBI HQ in New York until 1980, when it was converted into apartments. We decided to keep a couple of apartments to use for special operations."

He looked around. "Interesting."

"The walls are soundproofed, anti-jamming equipment and countersurveillance equipment are in place, so the place is clean."

Reznick sighed. "So, where are we going with this?"

"I'm staying in an apartment down the hall while Kendrick is in town. But I want to see for myself where he goes and what we have."

Reznick stifled a yawn.

Meyerstein looked him over. "You look like shit, by the way, Jon."

"I feel like shit too, for what it's worth."

Meyerstein smiled. "Look, I appreciate what you've done."

Reznick nodded and held her gaze.

Meyerstein looked away first. "OK, so what's Kendrick been up to today?"

"Hasn't been out of the house. Though no one's watching him now."

Meyerstein nodded. "We've got that covered."

"So, you mind me asking what got you interested in Kendrick again?"

"You. And Dr Malone."

"So you wanna enlighten me?"

Meyerstein sighed. "We need to get a breakthrough soon. I got a call from a counterterrorism specialist assigned to the team. He said something interesting. There was chatter on some Jihad internet boards, encrypted, pointing to New York. Talking about something 'special.'"

Reznick went across to the window, stared at the towering Trump building across from the Fairfax, his back to Meyerstein. "We all know New York is everyone's top target. Economic power of Wall Street, media empires, the symbolism of Manhattan, all that stuff. Nothing new about that."

"Kendrick is in New York. The link to O'Grady via his former girlfriend is there."

Reznick turned and faced Meyerstein. "What else? I assume you're doing some digging on this guy."

"As we speak. I've ordered a comprehensive review of all material we have on him. We've also spoken to Caroline Lieber's parents, and they have never heard her mention his name. So he means nothing to them."

"When this group was brought together, you said its objective was to find O'Grady and Lieber. Well, O'Grady's been found. Dead. And Lieber's still missing. Now you're talking about something going down in New York. And Kendrick's in the middle of this. I know it."

"We're rolling with this, Reznick. Bearing in mind O'Grady's work."

"So who's leading?"

"I'm leading." Meyerstein ran a hand through her hair and sighed. "Let's talk some more about Kendrick. Firstly, just so you know, every behavior analyst who is working on this program thinks we're wasting our time with Kendrick – that is, apart from Henry."

Malone looked up from his iPad. "Yeah?"

Meyerstein said, "Henry, you want to explain to Jon where we are and how you fit into this?"

Malone nodded. "I head up the Behavioral Analysis Unit 1 focusing on counterterrorism and threat assessment. And I specialize in anticipated or active crisis situations."

Reznick nodded.

"OK, I've got to be honest; they all think I'm heading in the wrong direction wishing to look closer into Kendrick."

Reznick said, "So what's got you interested in Kendrick?"

"A few aspects that have piqued my interest. Firstly, I was receiving Kendrick's college and hospital assessments. He clearly was a brilliant student and resident. But when it came to what he was like as a person, common phrases that were used were surface to a fault, glib, cocky and very arrogant. Strong words for professionals to use about a brilliant student and doctor."

Meyerstein sighed. "OK, I'm starting to get a picture in my head of this guy, but I need more than that. He has, after all, a clean record, impeccable credentials; there is no trace or indication of anything untoward in his life. No sign of extremism of any sort."

Malone smiled. "In my work, we are trying to assess psychological constructs, you know, like cognitive and emotional functioning. The technical term, if you are interested, is psychometrics."

Meyerstein said, "Yeah, but I'm interested in how this relates to Kendrick."

Malone sighed. "There's a book I always found fascinating."

"And what's that?"

"The Art of War by Sun Tzu."

Meyerstein shrugged. "I'm more a Patricia Cornwell fan myself."

Malone cleared his throat. "What you said reminded me of a line. Subtle and insubstantial, the expert leaves no trace; divinely mysterious, he is inaudible. Thus he is master of his enemy's fate."

Meyerstein nodded. "What are you saying? Are you saying Kendrick fits that description?"

"Perhaps. Know what Sun Tzu also said?"

Meyerstein shook her head.

"All warfare is based on deception."

"I think you might be looking into this too much."

Malone bit his lower lip and looked at Reznick. "Maybe not. OK, here's where we are, Jon. It was me who persuaded the assistant director to focus more on Kendrick."

Reznick said, "Why?"

Malone leaned forward, hands clasped tight. "Most research into the relationship between psychopathology and terrorism, if indeed that's what we're dealing with here, shows that mental disorders or illnesses are not typically critical factors. Although that doesn't rule them out entirely. But recently, research has shown that it can be much more valuable to focus on vulnerabilities. The three most common vulnerabilities would be a need for identity, a need for belonging, and a perceived injustice or humiliation they suffered."

Meyerstein shrugged. "He seems, on the surface, to have a very privileged background."

"On the surface, maybe," said Malone. "But I think he meets two out of the three criteria. A need for identity and a need for belonging. The charity work or God Complex, call it what you will. Add this to his ego and you have a very interesting case. And you begin to see a picture."

Reznick stayed quiet.

"On the surface, all is well. But something intrigued me about him after you described the inside of his house."

"What was so interesting about that?"

"Three things. Firstly, the fastidiousness. Nothing out of place. It was ordered to a meticulous degree. A man who..."

Meyerstein interrupted, her patience wearing thin. "That's a big leap, from being OCD to being a terrorist suspect."

"It's important to build up as full a picture as possible. It shows a type of personality. Obsessive-compulsive disorder is an anxiety disorder. People have repeated thoughts, feelings, obsessions, or behaviors that make them compulsive."

Meyerstein said nothing.

"The second aspect is that, according to recent research, modern terrorists are far more likely to be highly educated and come from wealthy backgrounds. This guy is, to all intents and purposes, a potential cleanskin. Kendrick is highly intelligent, rational, can be dispassionate to ensure he can focus on the job in hand – namely, surgery. But, along with indications of Kendrick being superficial, glib, all surface, I believe there is a narcissistic element to his personality."

Reznick said, "Narcissistic? In what way?"

"His fixation with self, an identity wanting to belong. I'm talking of the pictures of him in his basement gym, with a boy he had saved. Jon mentioned in a note the monogrammed towels in his bathroom. And it reminded me of a case I'd worked on in the 1990s."

Reznick shrugged. "Which one?"

"Does the name Eric Robert Rudolph ring a bell?"

Meyerstein nodded. "The Olympic Park Bomber. A classic American lone-wolf terrorist. Set off the Atlanta bomb back in 1996."

"The very one. Narcissism was part of his psychological makeup, among a host of other things. With Kendrick, that may be part of his story."

Meyerstein pinched the bridge of her nose as if tired. "So, where the hell does some glib and arrogant doc with OCD and narcissistic tendencies fit into the plan?"

Malone said, "Look, I'm not saying this guy is the one. However, he certainly needs further investigation. But that will take time."

"Something we don't have."

Reznick sighed. "Another point that is easy to overlook. He's been mobile. And that not only makes surveillance difficult, but it also allows him to flush out his tail."

Meyerstein said, "Hence why you stay out of sight from now on."

Reznick looked at Malone. "Getting back to Kendrick, when will you have a full profile?"

Malone blew out his cheeks. "Like I said, it's early days. I must stress we shouldn't get ahead of ourselves. I remember the early profiles of Rudolph were wide of the mark, so we should be wary of drawing too much from the threads we've got so far."

Meyerstein shook her head and smiled. "I think you're being modest, Henry. You gave the most accurate profile before we caught the son of a bitch, as far as I can remember."

"The first thing I was always taught is keep all avenues open. The first goddamn thing."

A member of Meyerstein's team shouted from the monitoring room, "Hey, he's on the move! He's carrying a bike, wearing cycling gear."

They all went through to the room and watched the real-time images from the van parked farther down East 63rd Street, observing the townhouse.

Meyerstein said, "OK, I want motorbike courier surveillance activated."

The next hour was spent watching Kendrick cycling through the streets of Manhattan, weaving in and out of traffic. Midtown, downtown and then East Village.

The footage showed him padlocking his bike on metal railings outside the soup kitchen on East 11th Street. More covert footage showed inside the soup kitchen. Kendrick serving out big bowls of soup to men seated at long tables. He wore hygienic plastic gloves like the rest of the volunteers.

Meyerstein punched a number into her cell phone. "Roy, it's Martha. Are you watching the footage from the East Village?" She nodded. "Yeah, it looks like around a dozen young men and women and four or five middle-aged volunteers, helping out. I'm still waiting to find out who's on the list. But also at the homeless shelter. Get it ASAP."

Reznick stared at the shaky footage showing Kendrick on the screen. "Who the hell are you?"

FOURTEEN

The sour breath and the smell of urine were making Kendrick feel queasy. He was twenty minutes into a ninety-minute stint at the East Village soup kitchen. Time dragged. He looked down at the drugged-up black panhandler. Pathetic. He was wearing a stained Obama T-shirt and filthy pants.

Kendrick kneeled down and checked the man's blood pressure before pulling back his eyelids. No response. The man's brown eyes were glassy, pupils small. He held his breath so he wouldn't inhale the noxious chemicals circulating in the man's system, and gently shook the man's shoulder. "Michael, are you there?" He was glad he had his surgical gloves on.

The man's eyes rolled round his head as he tried to speak, but only a low moan emanated.

"Michael, you're at the soup kitchen on East 11th Street." He raised his voice. "Do you understand?"

Michael's sad eyes opened and began to focus as he came to. "I ain't got nowhere." His speech was slurred. "Got kicked out of the fucking Baruch. You believe that? I've been kicked out of shithole central." He began to laugh, exposing surprisingly good white teeth. "Obama sure as hell won't be living in the Baruch tonight. One thing we've got in common, right?"

Kendrick nodded politely, his empathetic mask on show for the world to see. "No, I don't suppose he will."

The man closed his eyes and tears spilled down his face. He began to hum the tune to "The Lord is my Shepherd."

Kendrick stroked the man's cheek and smiled. "We'll take care of you, Michael," he said as he helped Michael over to a chair.

His mind flashed back to his suburban teenage years. He remembered his father looking at a man in the same predicament in a soup kitchen line organized by his church. Kendrick thought the whole set-up was phony. He couldn't give a damn for the downtrodden or those that had fallen on hard times. Darwin was right. It was the survival of the fittest. The smartest and toughest would inherit the earth. The meek would inherit absolutely nothing. His father, by contrast, cared passionately about those less fortunate. He blamed society for people's ills and not the people themselves. He never apportioned blame. It was his Christian faith.

Kendrick made sure Michael was safely on the seat. "I'll bring you over some nice soup."

Michael looked up at Kendrick, tears still streaming down his face. "The Lord as my witness, I will find the strength."

For a split second, Kendrick wanted to take a gun, press it to the man's head and blow his brains out, putting him out of his misery. That's what people did to lame and crippled dogs. They put them out of their misery. "I'm sure you will, Charles."

Kendrick's cell phone began to vibrate in his top pocket, and he moved across to a quiet corner to take the call, facing a wall.

"I wanted to let you know," the familiar voice said, "we're on track with preparations."

"When will I know the final details?"

"When we know, you'll know. Leave us to worry about that. You're doing great. How do you feel?"

"Alive. I want to do this."

"We know."

The line went dead.

Kendrick stood staring at his cell phone for a few moments. He felt wired. This was real. He breathed in deep and let it out slowly. He breathed in deep again.

"Who was that?"

Kendrick spun round and saw Michael staring at him, stoned grin on his face. "I..."

"You got a secret girlfriend, is that what it is? I knew it!"

Kendrick managed a grin. "You know how it is."

He winked conspiratorially. "I heard what you said. I want to do this. Wanna do what? You leading a secret life, huh?"

Kendrick stared into Michael's dark eyes. His stomach knotted tight. He realized he would have to call this in and get it taken care of. "I'm sorry, I don't follow."

Michael leaned in close to Kendrick and flung his arm around his shoulder like a long-lost college friend. "Your secret's safe with me, man," he whispered, the sour breath impossible to escape.

Kendrick felt revulsion and a dark anger begin to consume him. He stared into Michael's stupid eyes for what seemed an eternity. But he kept his emotions in check.

His thoughts turned to what awaited the panhandler.

And slowly, the anger began to dissipate, a sense of calm and wellbeing washing over him.

Michael was as good as dead.

FIFTEEN

Just after six in the morning, in a bedroom in the upper part of the duplex apartment within the Fairfax on the East Side, Jon Reznick was woken by a burly Fed on the early shift. "Hey Jon, we got lattes and cappuccinos delivered up from Starbucks," he said. "What do you like?"

Reznick rubbed his eyes and groaned as he came to. He looked through into the apartment living area and saw Malone tapping on his laptop. "Latte for me."

The Fed smiled as he handed him a Starbucks cup.

Reznick pulled off the lid and sipped the piping hot coffee. The caffeine jolt from the espresso was just what he needed. "Damn, that's nice."

The Fed left him alone to get ready, shutting the door behind him. He pulled on a pair of jeans, T-shirt and sneakers, and headed through into the improvised intelligence hub with his coffee.

Reznick sat down on a sofa and looked over at Malone. "So, what's the latest on Kendrick?"

Malone leaned back in his seat, biting his lower lip. "Good morning, Mr Reznick. After an hour or so at the soup kitchen, another trip to the Yaffa Café. He feels comfortable there."

Reznick said nothing.

Malone was handed a coffee. He took a sip. "Thanks. Here's the thing. This café is like a hipster haunt, alternative culture

HQ, in the East Village, has been since before it became more gentrified. But his profile doesn't fit it at all."

"What about the lists of those working at the café, photos, that kind of thing? Has that been checked?"

"Yeah, the assistant director has just sent over photos and bios of those working in the last eighteen months. A team is trawling them now."

Reznick sipped some more hot coffee. "So, what angle are you working on now?"

"I'm looking at this from a physiological point of view, as well as the psychological perspective. From what you've reported back, and going on what I've seen in the last twenty-four hours, this guy is not getting his sleep. He might be getting some during the day, but with two kids in that apartment, it won't be the quietest."

Reznick said, "Is he speeding?"

Malone nodded. "Could be."

"What else?"

Malone sighed. "I got a statement from an old college friend. He said Kendrick let slip one day that his father beat him as a child if he flunked a test. He said he couldn't wait to get away from home."

Reznick said nothing.

"By all accounts, he was a model student. He knuckled down, did the work, but wasn't the most sociable. Very private."

A knock at the door. The burly Fed answered and let Meyerstein in. She had a huge tote bag in one hand and a Styrofoam cup of steaming coffee in the other.

"Morning, boys," she said. She sat down at the table, pulling her iPad out of the bag and placing it alongside the coffee cup. "Three hundred and twenty-four separate photos and bios. Soup kitchen, Yaffa Café, steakhouse waiters and cooks, and also volunteers and employees at the homeless shelter. Three have been flagged as having skipped bail on drug charges, two for outstanding speeding tickets, but all the rest are upstanding citizens. On the surface, no red flags. But we're working on it."

Reznick headed into the living area. "You mind if I have a look?"

Meyerstein pushed the iPad towards Reznick and clicked on a file. "Be my guest."

Reznick pulled up the gallery of color photos and short bios of everyone employed by or linked to the establishments. He clicked on the first photo of those volunteering at the soup kitchen. A fresh-faced young white woman. Her name was Candice Olsen. A nineteen year-old political science major at Columbia. She had volunteered every weekend for the last year since she moved to New York from Cleveland. He scrolled down. The second volunteer he scanned was a twenty-two year-old art student from Brooklyn, Leroy Burnett.

Meyerstein said, "What are you looking for?"

Reznick gulped the rest of his coffee. "I don't know. Just like looking, I guess. No harm, right?"

Meyerstein shook her head. "You're an obsessive, Jon; do you know that?"

Reznick grinned and looked across at Malone. "Is that a psychiatric disorder?"

Malone raised his eyebrows, deadpan. "Oh yeah."

Reznick stifled a yawn. He was restless. He didn't want to just sit about and twiddle his thumbs. Even during his Delta days, the waiting was the worst. Waiting for the green light. Waiting for the go-ahead. Always waiting. He couldn't stand that. He'd much rather be doing something.

He switched his attention back to the photos on the iPad. Over the next couple of hours, he scrolled through the pictures and bios as Meyerstein videoconferenced in the next room and Malone researched more on Kendrick's background and upbringing.

He rubbed his eyes as he scrolled down on the iPad to the Yaffa Café employees, past and present. They were mostly young, predominantly in their early twenties. Quite a few were earning extra money while they studied at Cooper Union, a private college specializing in architecture, art and engineering, or at NYU, with dormitories for undergraduates in and around the Village.

Reznick yawned.

Malone said, "You need to get more sleep, Jon, for chrissakes. You look like shit."

"I'm fine."

"You can't be fine. You had four hours sleep last night, and none in the previous forty-eight hours. You're gonna have a heart attack."

Maybe Malone was right. He didn't even know why he was scanning the photos. What was the point?

The last photos were of staff employed at the Capital Grille restaurant. Sous-chefs, dishwashers, dining room manager, cold station cooks, bartenders, waiters, waitresses.

His mind was beginning to wander when he pulled up the photograph of a very pretty young black woman. Joan Wilson. Her hair was straight and long, makeup subtle, and she wore tortoiseshell-framed spectacles.

The face looked familiar. Very familiar.

Something about the face made him stop and stare.

His mind flashed back to the night Kendrick was served at the Grille, as Reznick ate at the bar, watching the Weather Channel on the TV. He remembered the black waitress nodding politely as she took Kendrick's card and returning with a receipt. He looked at the last picture, of a young Hispanic dishwasher.

He scrolled back to the picture and biography of Wilson. The face was familiar and was stuck in his head. He wondered if that was because he'd seen her in the flesh. Maybe that's what it was.

"Pretty girl," Meyerstein said, looking over his shoulder.

Reznick shrugged. "Yeah. She served Kendrick in the Grille when I was there."

Meyerstein sat down with her coffee. But almost immediately, her cell phone rang and she got up again and went back into the adjacent room to take the call.

Reznick stared at the photo. His gaze lingered on the brown skin, dark eyes and gentle smile. The face definitely looked familiar.

He scrolled back to the top and started looking at all the faces again. Then he came across the reason why she looked familiar.

A twenty-something black girl named Stephanie Young, who worked at Yaffa – hair tied back, dimple on the chin and wearing no makeup and no glasses, dark brown eyes, yet was the double of Joan Wilson.

He scrolled back down to the photo of Joan Wilson, made up, hair down on her shoulders. More attractive. Glasses, which made her look older. He clicked on the image to make it bigger.

A dimple on the chin.

Reznick showed Malone and they compared the pictures.

Malone said, "How weird is that?"

"They could be the same person."

Malone winced. "I don't know; the girl in the restaurant looks a bit older, more mature, different eyes."

Meyerstein had ended her call.

Malone called Meyerstein over. "Come and have a look at this. Are we talking one and the same?"

Meyerstein studied the two pictures for nearly two minutes, side by side. She said nothing, her gaze fixed on one image, then the one beside it. "Son of a bitch."

"You think it's the same picture?"

Meyerstein tilted her head slightly, as if looking at the face from a different angle. "I think we need to feed this into NGI."

Reznick said, "What's NGI?"

Meyerstein stared at the screen. "NGI? Next Generation Identification."

Malone interjected. "The FBI's most sophisticated facial recognition software. Basically, it can distinguish between twins, and the 3D face captures take us way beyond two-dimensional mug shots. It's also got some interesting face-aging elements."

Meyerstein punched a number into her cell phone. "Hey, Roy, pull up the mug shots of Joan Wilson and Stephanie Young. You got them?" She waited a few moments. "Yeah, that's them. Run them over to NGI, will you, and get back to me ASAP." She ended the call and stared again at the images.

Twenty minutes later, her cell phone rang.

Meyerstein answered after one ring. "Talk to me, Roy." She nodded. "Get on it. Don't pull her in just now. Let's just do some more digging. Find out who she is and what she's all about. And when we do, get a 24/7 surveillance wraparound for her." She ended the call and looked first at Malone, then Reznick. "The photos are a hundred percent match. Without a shadow of doubt."

Malone leaned back in his seat and blew out his cheeks. "This just got a helluva lot more interesting."

Meyerstein stayed silent as she studied the images.

A few minutes later, her cell phone rang again, and she switched to speaker so everyone could hear.

"Yeah, Roy?" she said, pinching the bridge of her nose.

Stamper sighed. "We're looking over the CCTV footage in the steakhouse on 42nd Street. I'm sending it over. Take a look for yourself."

Meyerstein ended the call and opened up the image on her iPad. They scanned the enhanced footage as the woman handed the bill to Kendrick on a silver tray and left. He picked it up and looked over it for a few moments. He smiled as he took a ten-dollar bill out of his pocket and slid it under his plate. He then placed his credit card on the plate. The waitress returned with a card machine and put Kendrick's card through the system. A moment later, she returned it with a receipt and smiled. She took the money from under the plate, slipped it into her pants pocket and walked away to the next table. "She seemed to know there was money, despite it being covered," Meyerstein said.

Reznick folded his arms. "She's the cutout."

Meyerstein screwed up her face. "I don't think you can say that at this stage."

"I just did. Who the hell is she?"

Meyerstein leaned back in her seat and closed her eyes.

"What if she is a cutout and a cleanskin?" said Reznick. "Someone who doesn't arouse suspicion."

Meyerstein sat up and stared again at the pictures. She had attended a briefing three weeks ago from a high-ranking FBI intelligence expert. He used the phrase cleanskin. He warned that those not on the radar, who didn't fit the profile, were a major headache. He said that cleanskins who weren't on any watchlists had carte blanche in a free and open society. "You remember Richard Reid?"

Reznick nodded. "The would-be shoe bomber?"

"Yeah. Not on anyone's radar."

Reznick rubbed his eyes, feeling tired.

Meyerstein looked at her watch. "In approximately fifteen minutes, I'm videoconferencing with the team back at McLean for the latest briefing. I'm sure we're going to get a fix on who this young woman is. She might be an illegal, using a false identity."

Reznick said, "She is one person who is made up completely differently in two different environments. Hair different. Makeup different. Glasses, no glasses. Is she wearing contacts? If so, why not always wear contacts?"

"Tired eyes?"

"Maybe."

Meyerstein's cell phone rang, and again she switched it to speaker mode. "Yeah, Roy, talk to me."

Stamper cleared his throat. "Our investigation is still ongoing into this woman, but I wanted to flag something."

"What is it?"

"The social security numbers have something in common."

"What?"

"They are both genuine numbers assigned to two women, neither of whom is the woman in the picture."

"I don't follow."

"I just got off the phone with the Social Security Administration. It does not invalidate or destroy original social security numbers when a new social security number is assigned."

"And?"

"Two separate women, victims of domestic violence, white women, one in Ohio, the other Kansas. And they both changed their names and were assigned new social security numbers. But their old numbers, these two separate numbers, are being used by the woman in this picture."

Meyerstein stared at the screen and ran her hand through her hair. "So who the hell is this woman?"

"That's the thing. We just don't know."

SIXTEEN

A few minutes later, Meyerstein was hooked up to videoconference with McLean. A tiny green light at the corner of the screen signaled she was on. The stern faces of Ed Froch of the State Department and Lt General Black were staring back at her as they hunched over a conference room table, papers in front of them.

Meyerstein sighed. "Gentlemen, you'll have had time to see the update we've sent through. It's more than a coincidence, her working in two places Kendrick has visited. Special Agent Stamper will draft an affidavit justifying the need for the search warrant. It may take time. But I think we need to close down this line of investigation and identify who this young woman is. It might be nothing, but we're not exactly inundated with strong leads."

Froch said, "I'm a State Department guy, Martha. My knowledge is with foreign policy, terrorist threats. Do you mind if I play devil's advocate for a moment?"

Meyerstein shook her head. "Go right ahead."

"Might she not be a scam artist or illegal who bought the numbers on the street? It happens."

"Perhaps."

"Our focus is on O'Grady. The doctor and this woman and the Lieber woman, if they are connected, do not appear to be anything more than a distraction from the main event."

Meyerstein said, "I don't disagree entirely with what you say, but, where I'm sitting, a thread from Caroline Lieber to Dr Kendrick and to this woman is emerging. She could be a cutout."

Froch blew out his cheeks and looked at the general, who rubbed his eyes as if exhausted. "I understand we've now got round-the-clock surveillance on Kendrick again, is that correct?"

"That's correct."

"Let me get this straight. This girl, whose real name we don't know, has got a job in a Midtown steakhouse and a second job at some coffee shop in the East Village, and is using old social security numbers. You say she may be a cutout. If so, why don't we haul her in right now and find out exactly who she is?"

Meyerstein shook her head. "I've run this past my team. These guys are drawn from our Counterterrorism Division. I handpicked them from the International Terrorism Operations Section II. They focus on non-al Qaeda threats including the Iranians, Hezbollah, Syria, and Palestinian rejectionist groups. But they all say that we should watch and wait. It's better to observe and gather more data and, when we get the search warrant, examine her apartment and place some listening bugs. With regards to identifying the woman, we are hoping to get a DNA sample or fingerprint from her apartment."

Black sighed long and hard. "I'm with Ed. I just don't see where this New York angle is heading, Martha. The doctor is clean. And she just might be a patsy scam artist."

"That's a pretty sophisticated scam, if you don't mind me saying, sir."

Black stared back at the screen. "Martha, it happens. I feel like we're losing focus. And we're wasting precious time. You want to know what the President's national security advisor said to me before I came into this conference?"

Meyerstein shook her head and said nothing.

"He described it as farcical, chasing after some surgeon, tracking him to some soup kitchen and homeless shelter. He thinks we've got it wildly wrong. And you know what else he said?"

Meyerstein bristled at the criticism. She cleared her throat as she composed herself. "What?"

"He wondered if I should hand over the reins to one of your colleagues within the Bureau. Someone with a counterterrorism background."

"As I explained earlier, my team consists of counterterrorism experts, critical incident specialists, CIA, Homeland Security; we're working on numerous levels, night and day."

Black sighed. "The national security advisor also questioned your judgment."

"The national security adviser in question, sir, is an academic bed wetter. He thinks because he teaches at Brown on international security and he has the President's ear that he can run an operation like this. Well, you know what? He's wrong."

Black cleared his throat. "That may be." His voice had an edge to it. "But the national security adviser is concerned that Jon Reznick is on the team. The same concerns I've raised directly with you."

Meyerstein leaned forward. "Now, listen here. I'm not going to take any lessons in procedure, Lieutenant General, with respect, sir, from some academic who has never investigated anything apart from chasing down students whose dissertations are a week overdue. And Ed, until the State Department gets a grip and comes up with any rationale or explanation as to why O'Grady contacted Caroline Lieber, I respectfully ask for you guys to stop the blame game. Do not try pointing the finger at a member of my team."

Froch shifted in his seat and his cheeks flushed red. "Look, you've said yourself we're no further forward than we were three days ago when O'Grady went missing. And now we're hearing about some young woman who served Kendrick in a steakhouse and might be using false ID? I mean, gimme a break."

Meyerstein inwardly seethed at the criticism. "It's not the fact that it is a false ID; it's the level of sophistication needed to obtain old social security numbers and the names of women, victims of domestic violence who have assumed new IDs. Standing alone, that information might not raise a red flag. But we need to run down this lead and see where it takes us."

Froch said, "How about the Iranian Interests section? Isn't that where the focus should be?"

Meyerstein nodded. "That is where the main focus of our investigation is and will remain. We have that covered. Our teams are all reporting countersurveillance techniques being used. These are no dummies."

Froch steepled his fingers and turned to face Black. "I don't feel comfortable with Reznick being part of this. If this gets out, it'll be a mess."

Black nodded. "Martha, I expected his role to be more peripheral. Instead, reports reached me that he was conducting a one-man surveillance operation in the Upper East Side, no backup, no plan, just him and this doctor. That needs to stop. And I say again, I don't want him on the team."

Meyerstein sighed. "I appreciate your concerns, and I'll make sure in future that there will be no more one-man operations. But I would say that without his surveillance we wouldn't know what we know now."

Froch stared back at her on the screen.

She felt his withering look and shifted in her seat. She felt exhausted. The last few days had taken their toll on her. She was being touted as a candidate to be the first female director of the FBI. But she ignored all the internal political chatters about who was up or down within the FBI. She was more interested in digging down into an investigation, bringing the bad guys down, than in schmoozing with colleagues after work. She drove herself hard. But she knew that she was gaining a reputation for taking risks, having previously used Reznick to work outside the rules. She had to be careful.

Meyerstein stared back at Froch and the others. She wasn't fazed. She didn't scare easy. And she certainly wasn't intimidated by the guys staring back at her. She ran a hand through her hair. "So, any more questions?" she asked.

Froch leaned forward. "We're nowhere with this. I for one think Reznick should not be on this team. I don't see what he brings to the table."

Black nodded. "And you know my views on Reznick."

Meyerstein cleared her throat. She went quiet for a few moments before she spoke. "I don't want distractions within my team. Everyone has to be pulling in the same direction. OK, I hear what you're saying. If you can leave it with me, I'll get back to you during our update meeting later today."

Froch looked at Black, who was nodding. "Appreciate that, Martha."

Then the link to Froch and Black went dead.

SEVENTEEN

Reznick was drinking his sixth coffee of the day and listening to the FBI's behavioral scientist, Malone, talk about his work on compiling the Olympic Park Bomber profile, when Meyerstein interrupted.

"Jon, I need to talk in private," she said, heading for the door.

Reznick finished his coffee and followed her out of the room.

"Central Park OK?" she said, as they headed down the hall and into the elevator.

"Fine by me." He punched the button for the ground floor and waited. "You mind telling me what this is about?"

"Not here."

They headed out along East 69th Street. The din from the traffic was like an assault on the senses. They crossed Fifth Avenue and into the park, the noise subsiding. Flush-faced joggers and the smell of their sweat and suntan lotion as they passed. Young mothers and fathers with strollers. He felt sweat run down his back in the sauna humidity as they walked.

Reznick sensed that things weren't right with Meyerstein. She looked wired. Pupils like pinpricks. The more he thought about it, the more he realized the suffocating strain she had to be under. He could dip in and out of assignments as he saw fit. But she couldn't walk away if she wanted to.

"You OK?"

"Why do you ask?"

"I can almost touch the tension coming from you."

Meyerstein said, "That bad, huh?"

Reznick smiled.

"As it happens, yes, I am feeling tense. I'm getting it from all sides. Look, I've always been frank with you, Jon. What I say doesn't go any further; I'm sure you realize that."

Reznick nodded and squinted against the sun. He put on his shades. "You wanna tell me what's troubling you?"

"What's troubling me is that I'm coming under pressure to ditch you from my team."

Reznick looked away and remained silent.

"Look, I just finished a videoconference with senior members of the team, and the consensus was that you weren't the sort of guy they wanted on the team."

"Who's they?"

"General Black and Froch."

"What about Roy?"

"Roy? Roy likes you. But he doesn't think you should be on the team."

"I see."

"Lieutenant General Black is also coming under pressure from the national security advisor to replace me."

Reznick shook his head. "Replace you? Why the hell?"

"This is no longer a kidnapping or even murder; it's moved way beyond that. There's the possibility of an emerging threat to national security. And the national security advisor is none too happy at the perceived lack of progress."

Reznick stopped and wiped the sweat from his brow with the back of his hand. "Look, I'm not going to be an impediment. If the powers that be deem that I'm not needed, so be it. I'll walk. And I'll be gone."

"And that's it?"

"Yeah, if that's what you want."

Meyerstein sighed. "It's not what I want."

"Look, I answered the call. You wanted me on the team. Fine. But if I'm causing some problems for you, then that's also fine. There'll be no hard feelings, trust me."

"Jon, the problem is, your mere presence has upset people. They don't like it when guys like you are brought in."

Reznick sat down on a bench and Meyerstein joined him. He leaned forward, hands clasped. "Is this about me tracking Kendrick on my own?"

"It's part of the problem. Firstly, no one, apart from you, Malone and maybe me, seems to think Kendrick is in any way linked to this investigation. Secondly, they absolutely did not like the fact that you were operating without any oversight. And thirdly, they think that by focusing energy, time and resources on Kendrick, we're denying extra resources to the emerging threat."

Reznick said, "What do you think?"

"My counterterrorism people say, while he doesn't fit the bill as it stands, they think it's too early to pull the plug."

"Watch and wait, right?"

Meyerstein nodded.

"That's the way I see it. Look, these guys that want me gone, that's fine. Not a problem. But if they are contradicting what your counterterrorism team is saying, then you've got a problem."

"I'm well aware of that."

"These things take time. It would be crazy to ditch the investigation into Kendrick and this woman."

Meyerstein rubbed her eyes. "But we have nothing."

"Watch and wait. Keep your nerve. Cover all your bases."

"I don't know. Maybe they're right. Maybe I'm not thinking straight. I don't know..."

They were in the shade of huge overhanging beech trees, and Reznick was grateful for the respite from the sun's rays. He looked at Meyerstein. Her hair and lightly applied makeup were still intact. He was sweating but she looked cool and fresh.

Reznick said, "Bullshit. You're leaving no stone unturned. Stiffs from the Pentagon see things in black and white. In the real world, the bad guy never wears a T-shirt proclaiming he's the bad guy."

Meyerstein sighed. "You still think Kendrick is worth pursuing, don't you?"

"I think it's right to keep our options open. What's the worst that can happen? It will cost you only money, not lives."

Meyerstein said nothing.

"Malone's taking a keen interest in Kendrick."

Meyerstein nodded. "The problem is that he is the only one."

"You rate him?"

"Very much. Malone is intuitive. He seems to have a sixth sense at times. Top of his class at Quantico. A bit unorthodox."

"How do you mean?"

"He's not a team player. He prefers to work on his own. But his success rate is the best. He takes chances. And he is not constrained by conventional wisdom, no matter how convincing."

"Do you trust his judgment?"

Meyerstein went quiet for a few moments. "Yes, I do."

"Well, let's watch and wait. I know Malone is building up quite a picture of Kendrick – childhood, education, upbringing – and trying to bring it all together."

Meyerstein sighed. "Malone was the deciding factor for me to get surveillance back onto Kendrick. And his decision was based, as he'll have told you, partly on the narcissistic elements he sees in Kendrick. But Kendrick is a long shot. The problem is I don't like being blind. I'd rather be accused of overreacting than of not reacting quickly enough. But sometimes, you can't win."

Reznick's gaze wandered round. Dog walkers, cyclists, people talking into cell phones, the smell of hot dogs from a nearby kiosk. "Look, if you want me off your team, don't sweat it. I'll be gone. It's business. I realize that."

She rubbed her eyes. She didn't seem herself. "I don't know, Jon. Maybe I'm not reading this right. Maybe I'm just being stubborn like my father."

"Maybe you are. What's wrong with being stubborn, for chrissakes? Where I come from, my background, that's a badge of honor."

Meyerstein cracked a smile. "Thanks. Come on, let's walk." Reznick got to his feet and they headed farther into the park.

"My father once gave me a bit of advice when I was starting out. He's a lawyer. And I still remember his words."

Reznick turned to look at Meyerstein.

"Be wary of those who offer certainty. There is no such thing as certainty, unless you're talking about death and taxes."

Reznick smiled. "Smart man."

"Every senior member of the team believes Kendrick is irrelevant to this investigation. When I raised the possibility that the young woman may be a cutout, they didn't buy it. In fact, they dismissed it. But when I hear people talking with such certainty, that concerns me. It means that a particular avenue is being dismissed without assembling the facts before us. For chrissakes, we don't even know the woman's real name. She could be anyone. And that bothers me."

Reznick said nothing. The sound of a plane high up in the flawless blue New York sky. He looked up at the white vapor trail. His mind flashed back. The planes flying into the Towers. The explosion. The Towers collapsing. The dust cloud engulfing everyone within. His late wife, Elisabeth.

"You OK?" Meyerstein asked, snapping him out of his reverie.

Reznick's heart was racing. He inhaled deeply to control his breathing.

"You look a bit distracted."

"Just thinking back."

Meyerstein gave a sympathetic smile. "Elisabeth?"

"It's been a long time since I've been in New York. Her folks lived not far from here. They brought Lauren to the park as often as they could. They brought her up."

Meyerstein smiled and ran her hand through her hair. "Sorry, I forgot. How is Lauren?"

"Still at that fancy school in upstate New York. Costs me a small fortune."

Meyerstein smiled.

"Lauren loved Central Park. Beth used to take her here during school vacations. And Lauren would sometimes write me letters as she got older, telling me what she'd been up to that week."

Meyerstein nodded. Her eyes were glassy. "What about your kids?"

"I hardly see them these days. It's not for want of trying. But needs must, I guess."

Reznick saw there was a ring on her finger. "What about your husband?"

"The divorce came through. He's now officially shacked up with a twenty-one year-old student of his. Last time we spoke, he had the audacity to complain that his girlfriend had flown all the way to California to the Coachella rock festival to see Kanye West with her friends."

"Why the ring?"

Meyerstein looked at her wedding ring and bit her lower lip. "I have no idea." She cleared her throat as if embarrassed at showing emotion. "But my ex-husband is the least of my problems. We need to make a breakthrough soon..." Her cell phone rang and Meyerstein rolled her eyes. "Gimme a goddamn break, will you?" She took the call. Nodded a few times, then ended the call.

"Who was that?"

"Surveillance unit. The waitress who uses the false names is on the move. She's just emerged from her apartment in the East Village. A second surveillance team will pick you up at the Fairfax in fifteen minutes."

"You saying I'm still on the team?"

"That's exactly what I'm saying."

EIGHTEEN

When Meyerstein got back to the Fairfax, feeling in a stronger frame of mind after speaking to Reznick, she was immediately on the phone to Roy Stamper.

"Roy, how far on are we with the search warrant?"

Stamper sighed. "Martha, we got another problem."

Meyerstein had had her fill. "All you seem to be doing, Roy, is coming to me with problems. I need answers."

"Are you wanting to hear this or not?"

"You can cut that attitude right now. Who the hell do you think you're talking to?" Her patience with her colleague she'd known for years since their first days at Quantico was wearing thin.

Stamper sighed. "Look, I'm sorry. Here's where we're at. We drafted an affidavit justifying the need for a search warrant and sent it to the assistant attorney, who in turn drafted the search warrant. It was a real quick turnaround. But Judge Donald McCoy is refusing to sign."

"Are you kidding me?"

"Sadly not."

"On what grounds?"

"He said there weren't enough facts to give probable cause linking this woman to any national threat."

"Gimme a break, will you?"

"Wondering if we shouldn't just go warrantless. Patriot

Act allows search warrants to be issued without showing probable cause."

Meyerstein groaned. "Damn."

"What do you think?"

"I think you're forgetting the Mayfield case."

It was Stamper's turn to groan. Meyerstein was referring to an infamous FBI warrantless case when Portland attorney Brandon Mayfield, a Muslim convert, was mistakenly linked to the 2004 Madrid train bombings.

She remembered the case well. It was deemed that two provisions were unconstitutional. And the court ruled that evidence obtained through a Fourth Amendment violation is generally not admissible during a defendant's criminal trial.

Meyerstein's father had made her memorize all the amendments of the Constitution as a little girl, including the Fourth.

The right of the people to be secure in their persons, houses, papers, and effects, against unreasonable searches and seizures, shall not be violated, and no Warrants shall issue, but upon probable cause, supported by Oath or affirmation, and particularly describing the place to be searched, and the persons or things to be seized.

Stamper sighed. "Damn, of course. You want me to try another judge?"

Meyerstein blew out her cheeks. She looked across at Malone, who was tapping away on his laptop. "Wasting our time."

"What about the Foreign Intelligence Surveillance Court?"

Meyerstein closed her eyes for a moment. The Court oversaw top-secret requests for surveillance on suspected foreign intelligence agents. But since 2013, when it was leaked to the media that the court approved a top-secret warrant ordering Verizon to provide all call detail records to be sent to the NSA, it had been very difficult to get their approval without delays or modifications to the warrant. "Not an option in this climate."

"So I assume we just continue the surveillance of this woman?"

"Absolutely. Until we know who this woman is, we tail her."

He let out a long sigh. "Sure." He went quiet for a few moments. "You OK? You don't sound like yourself."

"No, I'm not OK. But thanks for asking." A long silence opened up between them as Meyerstein mulled things over, her mind racing. "We're missing something, Roy," she said. "We just aren't there."

Meyerstein ended the call. She sat down and closed her eyes. She wondered if she had lost a sense of perspective. She ran through the options. Option one: they watch and wait. Option two: send in an FBI search team who could undertake a sweep of the apartment. Option three: send in Reznick. He could do the same as the search team, but if his cover was blown he was just breaking into an apartment. He would give a false ID, and Stamper could get him out.

She punched in the number for the head of the surveillance team half a block from the woman's apartment in the East Village.

"Ramon, it's Assistant Director Martha Meyerstein."

"Ma'am, you looking for an update?"

"Very quick."

"She's been out for twenty-seven minutes. Mobile surveillance says she has just entered the Capital Grille."

"What do we know about her apartment?"

"It's a brownstone on East 7th Street, just down the block from Tompkins Square Park. It's a walk-up, three flights. No neighbors on the same floor, so that's a plus. But it has video security."

"Damn."

"Don't worry about that. We got an electronics guy with us who can shut that off if required."

"Fine, do it right now. Jon Reznick will go in. I want you to be his eyes and ears. If she returns unexpectedly, that kind of thing."

Ramon sighed. "You want Reznick to go in?"

"I'll take the heat. Get him kitted out."

"What's the legal authority?"

"I'm giving you the authority. Have you got a problem with that?"

"No, ma'am."

"Hand me over to Reznick." A few moments of silence before Reznick came on the line.

Reznick said, "Hi, how's it going?"

Meyerstein sighed. "Jon, I want a clean search, just by you. Nothing disturbed. We need an ID on this woman. Ramon will give you an ultraviolet light scanner to pick up latent prints. You know how to work it?"

Reznick cleared his throat. "Not a problem."

"Be careful. No one can know you've been in the apartment."

"You don't have to explain."

"You have fifteen minutes. Not a minute more."

NINETEEN

The cover for Reznick was as a visiting friend from college. It was August in New York, the air like glue, the heat almost palpable and East Village sidewalks buzzing with people as the midday sun took hold.

He sat crouched in the back of the van half a block away, awaiting instructions in his earpiece. He wore a dark baseball cap with no logo, navy jeans and a dark blue polo shirt, a backpack slung over his shoulder. Inside were forensic gloves, disposable shoe covers alongside the crime-scene light-source equipment, bump keys, encrypted iPad, camera, tweezers and plastic evidence bags.

"OK, Jon," a voice said in his earpiece, "you're good to go. Nice and easy."

Reznick took in a deep breath and stepped out of the van, carefully locking the door behind him. Then he walked fifty yards or so and up to the entrance. He punched a preset code into the video entry pad and the door clicked open. He had been told that the surveillance camera used inside had been deactivated remotely, giving him a clear run. He got inside, glad to be out of the broiling sun, and walked up the three flights of stone stairs.

He knocked at the door to apartment 7 and waited. Silence. He examined the lock. It was a basic double-cylinder dead bolt, as he'd been told. He knocked again. No answer.

Reznick pressed his earpiece firmly into place and unzipped his backpack. He slipped on the shoe covers and snapped on his latex gloves. Then he took out a bundle of bump keys, a favorite tool of the trade. He remembered a CIA instructor had gone over basic tradecraft with regard to black-bag jobs and showed how the bump key manipulated the lock tumblers, allowing a covert entry to a property. It never failed.

He checked the lock again and picked the bump key that would fit. Taking great care, he carefully inserted it into the lock. A soft click and he turned the handle.

A long hallway, whitewashed walls, modern art, dark hardwood floors.

He stepped inside and shut the door. "That's me inside," he said.

Ramon said, "Nice and careful, Jon. We want to keep it as it is."

"Yeah, I got that memo."

Down the hallway and right into a loft-style lounge, two beige sofas, bookcases filled with books on two walls. Plasma TV on one wall. Glass table in the center with neat piles of art history books and Vogue back copies. Madonna biography. African art on one wall.

Off a door at the far end of the room was a tiny kitchenette. A stainless steel refrigerator and freezer, small oven and two cupboards. Dirty dishes strewn on the white oak worktop. He picked up a used glass, ideal for a set of prints.

Reznick opened up the bag and pulled out the alternate light source. It looked like a home projector. He ran the fan before he switched on the power. The Luma-Lite had a high-intensity arc tube. It detected blood, semen, fingerprints and trace evidence.

He put on his orange-tinted glasses and began scanning the glass. Almost immediately, the blue light picked up fingerprints.

"Bingo," he said.

The image was wirelessly downloaded to the accompanying iPad for analysis by the Feds. He did the same on the stainless steel kettle, once again picking up numerous fingerprints. Scanned and downloaded.

He packed the equipment away and headed through to the small bathroom, painted aqua blue, with navy and white mosaic tiling throughout and a shower in the corner. He noticed a hairbrush beside a small mirror. He tweezered a hair sample into a plastic evidence bag and packed it in a side pocket of the bag he was carrying.

Then he went from room to room, photographing the layout, the books, the artwork, family pictures. It would all build up a profile of the woman who lived there.

Finally, he got to the bedroom, which doubled as a study. A Dell desktop computer on a small work desk was switched on.

Reznick hooked up a USB cable to his laptop and then connected it to an external hard drive. The screen came to life and he downloaded all the files in less than two minutes. He disconnected the cable.

"How you doing, Jon?"

"One minute and I'll be out of here," he said, packing the external hard drive and the cable into the heavy bag. He searched the wardrobe and rifled in the chest of drawers. Nothing of note.

Reznick took one final look round the apartment. And then he left, relocking the door, no one any the wiser.

He checked his watch. It had taken him just eleven minutes to complete the black-bag operation.

TWENTY

Meyerstein was staring at a mug shot of a haggard young black woman on her laptop when Reznick returned.

"Very good work, Jon," she said. "We got a match."

Reznick leaned forward and studied the woman's face. "Jeez, has she had a face transplant?"

"Funny. This is Chantelle McGovern, aged twenty-eight. A former drug addict and dealer. The Integrated Automated Fingerprint Identification System confirms the match."

Reznick shook his head. "What's her story now?"

"She is now a political science student at NYU. Five years ago, aged twenty-three, she pleaded no contest to felony heroin possession with intent to sell. Police found more than thirteen thousand dollars' worth of drugs in her rented car during a traffic stop in Queens. But she's been clean since."

Reznick stared at the picture. "Clean from drugs, maybe. But still a felon?"

Meyerstein signaled across to one of her team. "Jimmy, where are we with the full picture on McGovern? How long has she been living in the East Village? How is she affording the tuition?"

Jimmy looked up from his computer screen. He looked as though he hadn't slept in days, dark circles around his eyes. He was one of Meyerstein's trusted technology experts, and she knew he would push himself to the edge to get what the Fed strategic analysts needed. "I'm on it, ma'am."

"I also want computer analysis back to me ASAP." She turned to Reznick. "Roy is also working this from a different angle. Will have something to go on soon. I know it."

They didn't have to wait long. Ten minutes later, Roy Stamper was on the line. Meyerstein switched it to speaker mode. "Chantelle's place of birth is down as New York City on her student records. But we've checked. That's not correct."

Meyerstein shook her head. "And?"

"Wait for the kicker. She was born in Chicago. Her brother was a major league gangbanger and dirtbag."

"Roy, get to the goddamn point."

"Get this. He spent the best part of ten years in Stateville Correctional Center in Illinois for armed robbery. He's slipped off the radar in the last couple of years since he got out. No one knows where he is. But we have evidence that he converted to... are you ready for this?"

"Roy, get to the goddamn point!"

"He converted to Islam. Now goes by the name Jamal Ali."

The news sent a buzz of excitement around the room. It was the first possible break.

Meyerstein looked across at Reznick, who was deep in thought, brow furrowed.

"She is the cutout," he said.

Meyerstein looked across at Malone. "What are you thinking, Dr Malone?'

Malone was biting the end of his pen. "A picture could be emerging, Martha. We still have nothing on Kendrick. But this obscure connection to this woman – in two separate places – and now her brother. We might be on to something."

Reznick said, "How long will we have to wait on computer analysis of McGovern's laptop?"

Jimmy interrupted. "That'll take time. Initial analysis shows it is heavily encrypted. We believe there are hundreds, maybe thousands of photos, documents, correspondence, perhaps diaries. And we'll have to check for embedded data. Stenograph experts are looking through what we've got as we speak."

Reznick shrugged. "A Muslim connection, huh?"

Meyerstein closed her eyes for a moment. "My instincts are telling me not to get too carried away."

"Where does this leave us?"

"We need to know more about Chantelle. Her time in jail is important. Vulnerable. Impressionable. Angry. All very potent combinations. And with an Islamic convert brother, a picture is emerging."

Reznick said, "You think she's a convert?"

"Could be."

"No sign of headscarves or anything like that."

Meyerstein sighed. "Please."

Reznick said, "We need to locate the brother. And fast."

Meyerstein's cell phone rang. She saw the caller ID of General Black and got up and went through to a small windowless room she had been using as an office. She shut the door and sat down, AC growling low in the background. She closed her eyes. She knew what was coming.

"I want to see you now," he said. "Face to face. Right now."

"Robert, I've got a hundred and one things to deal with."

"I want to see you now. Face to face."

Meyerstein closed her eyes. She knew what was coming.

"I think you know why I want to speak to you, Martha. This is out of hand. And you're breaking the law."

"Under the Patriot Act, sir..."

"I don't want to hear about Patriot Acts. This is serious. And I want answers."

"Robert, I'm in New York. I need to be here. We have a developing situation."

"Not any more, you don't. I want you back here by the end of the day."

"Sir, with respect, that's not going to happen. I am in New York and we've just had the first break. So I sure as hell won't be walking away."

Black went quiet for a few moments. "Martha, I can't always protect you from those above me. I'm talking the National Security Council, people like that."

"Robert, trust me. I know what I'm doing here. We could have a cutout. I need to chase this down."

Black sighed long and hard. "I don't like the methods you've employed."

"The judge refused to sign and I didn't want to risk a warrantless search. This was a third way."

"An illegal way, Martha."

"Sir, that's the call I made. And it's the call I will stand by."

"Martha, you've crossed the line. I'm going to consider whether you should be leading this investigation or if this should be handed over to someone else."

Meyerstein felt more isolated than she'd ever felt working for the FBI. She was starting to wonder where and if the investigation would ever end. But the more she thought of it, she more she knew that she had to do things on her terms. "Sir, do what you have to do. I've got work to do."

Then she ended the call.

"Son of a bitch," she said, and walked out of the office and back to the table where Reznick and Malone were hunched over a laptop, reading a file on Chantelle's brother.

Reznick looked up at her and smiled. "Someone bustin' your ass?"

"We live to fight another day."

Norris, one of the Feds in the surveillance monitoring room adjacent, shouted through, "Ma'am, she's back in the East Village."

"Back home?"

"Nearby. Come and have a look."

Meyerstein and Reznick crowded round Norris' screen. They watched Chantelle enter a laundromat and pick up a bag of laundry as she smiled and struck up a conversation with a middle-aged man wearing traditional Muslim dress. "Coin-operated laundromat," she said. "Where exactly is this?"

Norris said, "At the corner of First Avenue and East 11th Street, ma'am."

"Who runs it; who owns it?"

"Pulled it up already. One-man operation. Owned by a Mohammed Akhtar. Originally from Bangladesh in the early 1970s."

Meyerstein clicked her fingers excitedly. "Get the surveillance team to split up. Two on Chantelle and two on Mr Akhtar."

"I'm on it." Norris picked up a headset and cleared his throat, before he repeated the message. He turned to Meyerstein. "You're gonna love this."

Meyerstein said, "Love what?"

"Guys, team two, give me diagonal line of sight from the laundromat. What you showed me two minutes ago."

Meyerstein watched the camera pan round a busy intersection and then zoom in on a redbrick building directly on the diagonally opposite corner. She read the words on the sign. "Islamic Council of America. You gotta be kidding me."

"It's one of the few mosques down in Lower Manhattan. Akhtar attends this mosque. He lives above the laundromat with his wife and five kids."

"Is he clean?"

"As far as we can see."

"This changes everything, people. I want team two on him round the clock. I want to know who he meets up with, where he goes, what he has for dinner."

Reznick leaned in closer. "It's perfect cover. She drops off laundry, she picks up laundry. How easy would that be for messages to be exchanged? No need to worry about electronic surveillance. It's old-school tradecraft."

Meyerstein sighed. "Let's not get ahead of ourselves, Jon."

"This is a clear Islamic connection."

"But there's a difference between Islamic and Islamists."

"Nuance was never my thing," Reznick said.

Meyerstein turned to Norris. "We need to feed this into counterterrorism for an urgent review of what we have."

Norris nodded. "On it."

Everyone's attention returned to the real-time footage of the laundromat front. Meyerstein shook her head. "Is she still in there?"

Just as Norris was about to answer, the door opened and Chantelle McGovern emerged, wearing shades and carrying a bag of laundry. The surveillance switched to footage from team one, who tailed her back to her East Village apartment.

Meyerstein turned and looked at Reznick. "What do you think?"

"I think we need to wake the fuck up and smell the coffee."

An hour later, as Meyerstein was reviewing new intelligence analysis from her team on Chantelle McGovern, the FBI's most senior counterterrorism official assigned to the special access program besides Meyerstein – Assistant Director Sam Chisholm – was on the speakerphone. "Martha, we're getting up to speed with what you've got, and we've done some preliminary analysis."

"So where we at, Sam?"

"There are enough elements here to seriously concern us. I think the watch-and-wait was the right call. But I think there is something here."

"What?"

"It could be a clandestine cell structure. The problem is how Kendrick fits into this. We just don't get him. He's not on our radar."

"What about Chantelle McGovern or her brother, Jamal?"

"That's interesting. I've got people trying to find out where this guy Jamal is. But nothing. The last known address was in DC and that was three years ago. Since then? Nothing. As for Chantelle? Just what we know already. Nothing new."

"Sam, what have you got on this mosque?"

"Well, this Akhtar guy we know about. He is a long-standing senior member of this mosque. We have a source in there. This is Friday so, after evening prayers, they'll head to an apartment down in one of the projects along the East River for Koran discussions and study."

Meyerstein sighed. "Yeah, I bet. OK, we need more from your source, Sam. I need to know about everything and everyone linked to this Akhtar and Chantelle. We need to integrate our two efforts. Let's hook up our teams for this. I'll oversee operations. I'll send Reznick to meet up with you."

A long silence opened up between them. Meyerstein was wondering what Chisholm was going to say. "Martha, can you take us off speaker?"

Meyerstein picked up the receiver and pressed the button to mute the speakerphone. "OK, just me and you, Sam. What's on your mind?"

"It's General Black."

"What about him?"

"He's been checking up on you, Martha. Wanting to know what progress there is. He's particularly interested in Reznick."

"Is that right?"

"I've also had two calls from people I trust saying he's digging around. Martha, you need to watch your back."

Meyerstein felt her stomach tighten. "Sam, thanks for the heads-up. I owe you one."

Meyerstein ended the call and took a few moments to let the information sink in. She sometimes wondered who the enemy was. It was tough enough to oversee a secret investigation on multiple levels that involved six separate government agencies. But for Black to be going behind her back like that was inexcusable. Her father had warned her about people like that. He said they existed in all walks of life. The thing to do, he counseled her when he had run into a similar problem at the FBI nearly six years earlier, was to face down the other person. Show she would not be cowed or threatened, no matter what.

Her mind switched tracks.

Was it possible that Black wanted Meyerstein to know that he was checking up on her?

Meyerstein closed her eyes and sighed.

Reznick said, "Problem?"

Meyerstein turned and looked at him, shaking her head. "Nothing I can't handle."

TWENTY-ONE

The sky was darkening as the SUV headed down East 10th Street and turned right on the FDR. Reznick sat in the back and stared out at the redbrick Riis housing projects that towered over the area. FBI Counterterrorism Division chief Sam Chisholm sat up front, radio crackling in the background. It had been less than forty-eight hours since Reznick had followed the DC surgeon down to this nearly forgotten part of the East Village. The projects on Avenue D were ugly, no getting away from it. And they seemed like a stark reminder of the crime-ridden 1970s and 1980s, when this part of Manhattan was not synonymous with hipster haunts, cool bars and bistros.

His thoughts switched to the surveillance operation. Things were moving apace, and they were on to something.

He stared out at the projects as they passed by. The nineteen high-rise buildings housed nearly four and a half thousand residents across the neighborhood and went on as far as the eye could see. The residents looked down on graffiti-scrawled playgrounds and ballfields. Mostly poor, working class, predominantly Hispanic and African-American. Gang problems, guns and violence still part and parcel of daily life.

Three separate surveillance crews were working the area that night, all focused on Akhtar. Reznick's job was just as an extra pair of eyes and ears.

Chisholm pressed his earpiece in tight. "Our guy is heading towards one of the houses on East 6th Street. Mobile surveillance is on him. He's on foot and walking there with two other guys from the mosque."

Reznick stared at the passing rust-colored brick projects. "Interesting part of town. You were saying this used to be a lot worse?"

Chisholm said, "Trust me, a lot worse. I used to work undercover when I was here twenty years ago. Crazy days."

"Who did you work for?"

"DEA." He pointed to a passing courtyard beside a side entrance. "Friend of mine, a cop. Crack dealer gunned him down just over there."

Reznick said nothing.

They turned onto East 6th Street and pulled in outside a side entrance to one of the Riis houses.

Chisholm pointed diagonally opposite to a green door to another Riis house, across the street. "That's the one. Third floor."

Reznick focused. "So what do we know?"

"Well, it seems like every Friday evening, after sunset prayers, a handful of the regulars at the mosque, including Akhtar, pop in here. We have a guy on the inside. He's wired up. Lets us see if it's just a Koran class or something we need to worry about."

"How long till they turn up?"

"Prayers finish around 8.30pm. It's a twenty-minute walk so should be here just before nine."

Reznick was listening to the surveillance team set up in an empty apartment directly opposite the target's home.

A man's voice said, "They're all there. Heading up the street now, Akhtar and usual bearded friends from the mosque. Our man is already inside. Sit back and enjoy the show, guys."

They watched the shaky surveillance footage as the trio buzzed the entry phone beside the green door and went inside. A few moments later, real-time images appeared on Chisholm's iPad showing the group hugging each other. Then tea was served by an elderly man.

The strains of as-salaam alaikum filled the vehicle.

Reznick sat and listened. He knew the words meant "peace be upon you" although it was in everyday use just a hello. For a few moments, the voices took him back to Afghanistan. Talking to illiterate village elders in the mountainous tribal areas. The taste of rancid tea that was passed around and had to be drunk. The smell of stinking goats and flies round shit.

The sound of one of the Muslims on the iPad laughing uproariously snapped Reznick back to the present. The men under surveillance were now sitting cross-legged on the floor in a circle as tea was served.

For the next hour, the men talked of money worries, decadence in America, the influence of alcohol and its availability on young Muslims, the drugs in the community, the outsiders who flooded the East Village each Friday and Saturday night, flocking to bars and clubs and spreading what they called the godless hell into each and every one of their lives.

Reznick couldn't help but wonder, if they were so unhappy living in a Western country, why they didn't head to a place more in keeping with their religion.

He pondered on that as the meeting came to an end, and Chisholm instructed the driver to pull away and park on First Avenue, with line of sight to the laundromat. "The guys in the apartment are the same crowd every week. Same talk. But it never goes any further."

Reznick nodded.

A short while later, a car dropped Akhtar off, who waved goodbye to his friends and headed upstairs to his apartment over the shop.

Chisholm sighed. "Got a feeling that's it for another night."
He was right. A couple more lights went on upstairs, and less than an hour later all the lights were off and the apartment was in darkness.

The hours dragged. A backup night shift surveillance vehicle pulled in one hundred yards up the street.

"Time to refuel," Chisholm ordered the driver over to Sunny & Annie's, a 24/7 corner deli on Avenue B at 6th Street, one block from Tompkins Park. Reznick and the Feds tucked into beef and grilled chicken sandwiches, Vietnamese soup and huge Styrofoam cups of coffee.

Just before 2am, as they sat in the back of the van having scoffed the food and soup, drinking the dregs of the strong coffee, a crowd of around a dozen Hispanic teenagers, nearly a block away on the opposite side of the street, was a young white guy. They rained down punches and kicks as he lay helpless on the ground, and ran off with his cell phone and wallet. It was over in seconds. No one stopped to help.

Chisholm shook his head. "What a fucking sewer."

Reznick sat and stared down the road toward the poor kid writhing on the sidewalk, only yards from a neon-lit bar. He was just a guy, heading home after a night out. Now he was another casualty of the street.

The team drove back to First Avenue and resumed their position near the laundromat.

Shortly after 5am, a light above the laundromat went on. An hour later, Akhtar emerged onto the street. He headed across to the mosque and opened it up. A light went on inside.

The night shadows disappeared like ghosts as the first shards of orange light splashed on the streets. Just after 6.30 am, men began to arrive at the mosque for the Salat al-Ishraq post-sunrise morning prayer. Dropped off in cabs and cars, by friends and family.

The sidewalks began to become busier. The hustle and dirt and grime of a blazing summer day, kicked up by passing trucks and cars on First Avenue. The driver cranked up the AC a notch. The cool air felt good.

After early-morning prayers, the worshippers went their separate ways. Some handshakes and hugs.

Just before eight, Akhtar emerged, locking up the mosque, before he turned and walked down East 6th Street.

The driver said, "Where's he headed now?"

Chisholm yawned and leaned forward and tapped the driver on the shoulder. "Just stay where we are, and let team one cover him." He held a radio to his mouth. "Team one, do you copy? It's over to you."

The driver nodded. "Got it."

Ten minutes later, a voice crackled on the radio, "FDR, heading east, past the Riis houses."

Chisholm said, "Wonder if he's heading back to the same apartment as last night."

But he wasn't. Five minutes later, the voice said, "OK, he's headed into the Baruch Houses at the corner of Delancey Street. They overlook the Williamsburg Bridge."

Reznick said, "How far's that?"

Chisholm said, "Couple of miles, give or take. Lower East Side." He spoke into the radio. "Keep on his tail."

"Yeah, I got that. Stand by."

Chisholm shook his head. "The Baruch Houses. More goddamn projects. Man, what can you say?" He tapped the driver on the shoulder. "Let's drive over there, and park up on Delancey."

The driver nodded and pulled away from First Avenue and along the FDR. In the distance, the giant steel shadow of the Williamsburg Bridge loomed large over the neighborhood, the grim, crime-ridden red-brick Baruch public housing, almost identical to the Riis projects.

Chisholm punched in a number on his cell. "Karen, it's Sam. Baruch housing project at the corner of the FDR and Delancey. I need to know if there are cameras either inside or outside any of these high-rises." A brief pause. "Shit. OK, thanks." Chisholm shook his head as the driver cut right onto Delancey and pulled into a parking space with line of sight to a side entrance door. "Not one damn camera for seventeen separate Baruch high-rises. Not one."

Reznick watched a middle-aged Hispanic woman pushing a stroller, chatting on a cell. Her hair was unkempt, and her skirt and T-shirt looked as though they hadn't been washed in weeks. He wondered what chance the baby had in life, growing up in such a desolate and dangerous place. "You got one of our guys inside just now?"

The radio crackled into life. "We have no number for the high-rise, been ripped off, but Jeff is in. He's identified it as having 'boyz' in black spray paint across the blue door. And he's on eleven."

Chisholm nodded and spoke into the radio. "Copy that."

"So is your surveillance guy a Fed?"

"One of the best. Jeff Morales. Tough, smart; you'd like him. I think he used to be in the Marines too, same as you. He's perfect for the East Village or the Lower East Side."

The minutes dragged and no word from Morales. Chisholm tapped on his cell's plastic casing. Reznick stared at the graffiti-scrawled blue door of the side entrance of the Baruch high-rise, beside some trees and welcome green space. He wondered if Morales was in an elevator, unable to talk or relay where the target had gone.

Reznick's mind was racing. He wondered if something had gone wrong. Why was it taking him so long to respond?

Chisholm bit his lower lip. "Where the hell is he?"

A voice from the team one surveillance said, "Stand by."

Time seemed to slow down.

Chisholm began to grind his teeth and shake his foot. "It's taking too long. It doesn't feel right."

Reznick turned to Chisholm. "Let me go in and have a look."

Chisholm nodded. "You packing?"

"Yup."

"Just be careful."

Reznick headed across to the entrance door and found it was open, despite having a controlled entry system. Inside, graffiti was all over the walls. The smell of piss and bleach and old booze and smoke. Even the hallway ceiling had a black blotch of graffiti, burned into the concrete.

The voice of Chisholm in his earpiece. "You OK, Jon?"

"I'm fine. I'm taking the stairs."

Before he entered the stairwell, the elevator lights showed that it was making its way down from the eleventh floor. Ten. Then nine. It stopped at nine. Then eight. Seven.

His senses were all switched on.

He positioned himself in an alcove so whoever came out of the elevator wouldn't see him.

Six. Five. Four. Three. Two. One.

The elevator pinged but the door didn't open. Reznick waited a moment. Nothing. He walked over and pressed the button. Nothing. He pulled a penknife out of his rear pocket and tried to pry the doors open. Again, nothing.

Reznick headed up the stairs. The sound of the soft rubber soles of his Rockports as he climbed the stone steps to the first floor was perfect, virtually noise-free. His breathing quickened as he climbed higher. Step by step. He reached the third floor and saw that the elevator was still stuck on eleven or, maybe more likely, was just broken.

The light in the stairwell was bad. The smell musty, damp and smoky, cigarette butts and trash strewn everywhere. Graffiti scrawled on doors. Lower East Side Boys. Baruch Boyz.

The names of girls, phone numbers for "girlz."

The sound of hip-hop from an apartment along the hall. Higher and higher he climbed. He was on seven, heading up to eight.

Onto the landing at eight and two tough-looking Hispanic kids were smoking, hats at an angle, pants down low.

"Yo, whitey, you got a lightey?" The kid grinned like an imbecile and stepped in front of Reznick.

Reznick reached into his back pocket as if to give them a light. Instead, he pulled out a 9mm Beretta from his waistband and pressed it to the kid's forehead. "No, I haven't got a fucking light."

The kid's eyes were wide. "Man, I don't want no trouble."

"Disappear, you dumb fuck."

The kids scrambled downstairs.

Reznick headed up to the ninth. It was deathly quiet. More graffiti on doors and walls, expletives too many to consider. It was up to ten and then toward eleven.

Each step, senses switched on. Edging closer. But closer to what?

He was in the zone. Something wasn't right.

The silence was bad.

He sensed Morales was in trouble. He turned onto the landing for eleven. His brain sent the signal but it short-circuited for a split second.

Lying sprawled on the floor inside the elevator door was a Hispanic man, blood pouring from a wound to the neck. It was Morales.

Reznick shouted into his lapel microphone, "Man down, immediate assistance on eleven!" He rushed over to Morales and checked his pulse. Weak but still alive. He ripped off his shirt and pressed it against the fallen Fed's neck.

Morales tried to open his eyes as blood seeped from his wound onto his light blue shirt, the top of which had turned dark red.

"Don't move, man," Reznick said. "We're gonna get you out of here."

Morales opened his mouth to speak. The words came out. "N.... Ni...."

"What is it?"

"Nine." The word came out gargled, thick with blood. "Ninth floor. White door. I tried to escape. Black guy. He's the..."

The sound of scraping of feet interrupted them. Then the high-speed scrambling downstairs of someone who'd emerged from an apartment.

"I need help, eleventh floor!"

Chisholm's voice. "We're coming in, Jon."

Reznick squeezed Morales's hands. "Help's on the way." He didn't want to leave. "I gotta go, man."

Morales managed to nod, eyes glassy. He was getting cold. "Hang in there."

Reznick turned and sprinted downstairs, two steps at a time. "I'm coming down, Chisholm. Suspect may be heading your way. Get a paramedic up to the eleventh! Right fucking now!"

The sound of a gunshot. Shouting. Screaming. The smashing of glass.

Reznick careered down onto the first floor landing. He got to the ground floor and carefully swept the area with his 9mm. He turned and saw the body of a burly undercover surveillance guy from team one lying motionless beside an exit door, blood pouring from a neck wound.

Reznick didn't have to check. He knew the guy was dead.

Reznick ran out of the building just in time to see a black guy running toward the thundering traffic on the FDR, out of sight of Chisholm's team.

His lungs were burning as he ran, sinews nearly snapping as he gave chase.

The black kid was about fifty yards ahead of Reznick. He wore dark clothing. He turned around and saw Reznick gaining ground.

He hurdled concrete barriers and ran onto the freeway, cars screeching to a halt or swerving to avoid him. He climbed over a fence and was on the East River bike path. Reznick's mind was racing as fast as his heart. He had to catch the guy before he disappeared for good. He hurdled the metal divider and narrowly avoided being hit by oncoming, snarling traffic. Under the Williamsburg Bridge and hurtling towards the smokestacks in the distance. Baruch projects loomed large on the other side of the busy freeway.

He was now thirty yards behind.

Up ahead, on a green metal pedestrian bridge that spanned the FDR, four Feds were heading towards the bike path, blocking off an escape route for the guy.

They had him.

Reznick was closing in. The guy glanced back at Reznick. Desperation in his eyes. He knew Reznick was going to catch him. Ten yards. Heart pumping blood.

Suddenly the guy darted off to his right, vaulted back over the fence and ran straight toward an oncoming truck.

The screeching of tires, blaring horns and screaming from bystanders as the man was crushed under the wheels of the massive truck.

TWENTY-TWO

The seconds that followed seemed like a lifetime to Reznick. Everything seemed to slow down as if he was unable to wake up from a bad dream. The horrified faces of motorists, snarled-up lines of cars, the truck driver being sick on his knees beside the mangled, twisted and partially limbless body of the black guy still under the wheels of his truck at an angle. Blood trickling down the freeway.

Reznick vaulted over the fence onto the road and crawled underneath the truck. The smell of warm blood, gasoline and oil. He was within touching distance of the mangled body and rifled through the pockets of his pants. He pulled out a wallet from the back pocket and looked inside. Driver's license. A Walter Irving. Date of birth May 4th, 1981.

When he crawled back out, blood on his hands, a passing young white jogger screamed.

Reznick vaulted back over the fence and headed back to the surveillance van. He held his lapel mike to his mouth. "Chisholm, he's dead. Got an ID of a Walter Irving, thirty-one years old."

Chisholm sighed. "What the fuck happened?"

"I found Morales on eleven. Heard the guy make a run for it and went after him. Where's Akhtar?"

"We got him. Hiding in an apartment on the ninth."

"How's Morales?"

"Touch and go. Special Agent Tim Mallory from team one didn't make it."

"Fuck."

"You better get the hell out of there before the news choppers catch you on the scene. We'll take it from here."

Less than an hour later, Reznick was back at the Fairfax and had showered and changed into new clothes. The blood-soaked clothes he'd been wearing had been bagged for forensics.

When he went through to the hub of the apartment, filled with laptops and huge screens, Meyerstein was pacing the room on the phone. "Call me back when you have anything, Roy. We're on the right track."

She ended the call and stood, hands on hips.

"What the hell happened out there?" she asked.

Reznick went through the story again.

"What a fuck-up."

"It is what it is."

Meyerstein said nothing, eyes hooded. She looked like she was close to physical collapse. But she also had a determination etched on her face he hadn't seen before.

"Look, I know we lost a man and Morales is fighting for his life. These things happen."

"Don't you think I know that? Both I knew. Good men." She sighed. "We're hoping Morales pulls through."

Reznick slumped on a chair, head in hands. "Goddamn..."

"I think we're all hurting."

Reznick looked up. "A guy like Morales doesn't want sympathy. He'd want us to hunt down these bastards."

Meyerstein sighed and ran a hand through her hair. "I know that."

"OK, tell me about this guy that was living on the ninth floor."

"We've got a laptop, which we're analyzing as we speak."

"What about Akhtar?"

"Not a word. He wants a lawyer. That's all he has said. No explanation of why he was at the apartment. Was that man a friend? What was that man's real name?"

Reznick nodded. "We're peeling this back."

"We have nothing. We have a dead black guy who had a false name, a laundromat Muslim and..." Her cell phone rang. She listened to the call, expressionless. She screwed up her face. "Are we sure about that?" She nodded. "Good work. But I don't want any delays. Get it to me ASAP."

She ended the call.

Reznick said, "Who was that?"

"Forensics lab. Fingerprints were taken at the scene. They could have a result in less than an hour." She shook her head. "This is just a mess."

Reznick sighed. "There was a link, and it had to be chased down."

"Couldn't he have been taken down before he reached the freeway?"

"I didn't foresee the fuck running straight into oncoming traffic."

Meyerstein closed her eyes. "Tell me about Morales."

"Knife wounds to the throat. Close-range."

Meyerstein stared back at him, glassy eyed. There was a haunted quality to her look as if the whole investigation was bearing down on her. Morales fighting for his life seemed to have been the final straw. "He has a wife and five kids. His superior has just visited them in Brooklyn to give them the news. You can only imagine what they're going through."

Reznick said nothing.

"Doesn't end there. His wife collapsed and is now in hospital. Five kids are being looked after by social workers."

Reznick blew out his cheeks and shook his head.

"Just doing his job." She was holding a pen. Then threw it down on the table. "Just doing his goddamn job!"

"Take it easy."

"No, I won't take it easy, Jon. He is a highly decorated special agent. I know him. I worked with him shortly after I joined the Bureau. He was always there when the deal went down. Always."

Half an hour later, her cell phone rang and she answered on the third ring. "Meyerstein; talk to me." She nodded a few times. "Are we certain? I mean one hundred percent certain?" Meyerstein ended the call and blew out her cheeks. "We got something. The lab has a preliminary result. It's not conclusive at this stage, as they still have to do more tests. But they think it's a high probability it's who we're looking for."

Reznick shrugged. "Who is he?"

"You were right, Jon. You were right all along."

"Who?"

"Jamal Ali. The older brother of Chantelle McGovern."

A buzz spread round the room. Meyerstein clapped her hands together and brought the room to order. "People!" she said, raising her voice. "Time to refocus. There are clear Islamic links, but still nothing to tie Kendrick in. So, let's recap what we have. O'Grady. Lieber. Kendrick. Then McGovern, Akhtar and Jamal."

Reznick looked at her.

"What's their game? Christ, we must be missing something."

Reznick was handed a fresh coffee by Malone. "Thanks. What's your take on this, Malone? You've gone all quiet."

Malone sat down at his desk, sipped some coffee and leaned back in his seat. "I'm interested in this thread from Kendrick to McGovern to Akhtar and Jamal."

Meyerstein said, "Give me some odds on what you know."

Malone blew out his cheeks. "I'm not a betting man, as you know. But if I was, I'd say that the odds are we have a sleeper cell, and perhaps O'Grady woke them up, either by accident or design."

Meyerstein said, "We need Akhtar to talk."

Reznick moved to her side. "Let me try."

Meyerstein was tempted. "We're in New York, not Guantanamo, Jon. Let's bring in his wife and two eldest sons. See if that shakes him up." She looked across at Malone. "What do you think?"

Malone nodded. "Depends on the state of the mind of the individual. Sometimes if the detainee believes their loved ones are under duress or suffering, they will tell us what we want to know."

Meyerstein said, "Yeah, I'm well aware of that, Malone," she snapped.

Reznick said, "What about McGovern? We need to bring her in? Confront her with Jamal's death?"

Meyerstein ran a hand through her hair. "Let's not rush things. She's won't know about Jamal or that we have Akhtar. We have a media blackout on this. Let's see what her next move is."

Malone smiled. "Makes good sense."

Meyerstein sighed and looked at her watch. "Look, I need to bring everyone back at the Department of Intelligence, including General Black, up to speed. Jon, I want you to sit in on this."

Reznick shrugged. "Fair enough."

They went through to the adjoining room, sat down in front of the huge screen as Meyerstein tapped in the encrypted videoconference code to link with the team in McLean. She outlined the recent developments in a cool and rational manner. They listened. This time, there were no threats to take her off the investigation. An Islamic link was emerging. The big problem remained Kendrick.

General Black didn't mention Reznick's presence at all, but he belabored the point about Kendrick. "On what we have so far," he said, "it could strictly be a coincidence that Kendrick had contact with this McGovern."

Meyerstein avoided responding to the general's concerns. "Gentlemen, we have work to do. I will update you at 1800 hours. Thank you." As she was disconnecting the videoconference call, the desk phone rang. She switched it to speaker mode.

"Martha, it's Roy. It's all happening."

Meyerstein gulped the last of a cold coffee and grimaced. "What's up, Roy?"

"Something's cooking."

"Tell, for chrissakes." She looked at Reznick and shrugged as if she was used to Stamper being long-winded.

"I've just been told by the team looking into Kendrick's history, personal and employment, that there is, in their words, 'a discrepancy.'"

"What kind of discrepancy?"

"All I know is that the timelines don't appear to be accurate."

"In what way?"

Stamper let out a long sigh. "That's all I know. They're piecing it together. But it's his time working at the Red Cross that does not tally. Perhaps it's an administrative error, perhaps a wrong date given by him; we just don't know."

"When will they be able to confirm?"

"They're working flat-out on this."

"How long?"

"Honestly? I have no idea."

"I'm updating General Black and the rest of the team at 1800 hours, Roy. So I want to know everything there is to know about this discrepancy by 1730 hours at the latest. Understood?"

There was no response. Stamper had already hung up.

TWENTY-THREE

It was dark and the air was like a steam bath as Kendrick stood on the Gapstow Bridge in Central Park, wearing a backpack. He was partially concealed by the canopy of leaves from the overhanging trees beside the pond. He took a few moments to drink in the scene. The lights from the New York skyscrapers towering in the distance. He marveled at the city. The apex where America met the world. It felt great to be cloaked in a pleasing darkness in the beating heart of America. The park was still busy, summer strollers, night joggers, tourists and people taking photographs of their friends with their cell phones.

Kendrick took off his backpack and reached in for his night-vision Nikon camera sporting a huge paparazzi-sized telephoto lens. He took off the lens cap and pressed his eye against the viewfinder, focusing on a high floor terrace at the Plaza. He brought it into sharp focus. The infrared camera showed up two loungers, a dark wooden table bathed in a warm light from the penthouse, no curtain or blinds to block the view. Inside, he could make out the edge of a white sofa, flowers in a vase on a bookshelf. He couldn't believe his luck. This was a perfect spot. Would this be the one?

The more he thought of what lay ahead, the more a raw energy surged through his body like an electric current. Something primeval.

He thought of the headlines to come. He could see his name in bold black print. He could see his picture. They would remember him. But more than that, they would remember what he stood for.

He carefully replaced the lens cap and put the camera back in his backpack, slung it over his shoulder and walked off deeper into the park. He sensed people were watching him. But nothing more than that. He hadn't actually seen any tails. He'd been too careful.

His cell rang.

"Your first trip to the drop zone awaits."

"Are we all set?"

"It's all been taken care of. We just want you to go there, acquaint yourself with the surroundings and people." A silence opened up for a few moments. "How are you enjoying Central Park?"

Kendrick smelled the cut grass and the moisture in the air. The blossoms from the trees. And the smell of hot dogs, drifting across the park. "Not a city in the world like it. What a place."

"It just feels so right, doesn't it? You're a very lucky man."

Kendrick took a deep breath and felt his heart swell with pride. "I know."

"Some of your backup team had some useful target practice with that panhandler from the East Village. He won't be clogging up any more soup kitchens."

Kendrick smiled but said nothing.

A long silence opened up. "OK, this is the one word you need in the drop zone."

"Shoot."

"The city of your birth."

Washington. "Got it."

"We're going to keep mixing things up but will reach you whichever way we have to."

Kendrick smiled and looked back at the lights of the Plaza in the distance. He knew what that meant. "Whatever it takes, I will not fail you. I will not fail America."

"We're counting on it. Till the next time, my friend. Stay safe."

TWENTY-FOUR

Reznick was floating on a black sea, inky sky overhead. He heard ringing and he wondered where it was coming from. He opened his eyes and realized he was in the Fairfax, and it was dark outside. The ringing had stopped. He sat up in bed and heard voices outside his room. Meyerstein was talking in hushed tones. But there was also the gruff voice of counterterrorism expert Sam Chisholm, his voice slightly raised.

He splashed cold water on his face, cleaned his teeth, showered and shaved and pulled on a clean seat of clothes the Feds had provided. Chinos, black v-neck T-shirt and his Rockport shoes. He put on his watch. It showed 10.42pm.

He went through to the main room that was adjacent to his sleeping quarters and poured himself a coffee.

Chisholm nodded across at him. "Hey, Jon, how you doing?"

"Felt better. What's the latest?"

Chisholm looked across at Meyerstein, who was sitting beside Malone, eyes scanning her laptop. Then he stared at Reznick. "What happened this morning has changed a lot of our thinking."

"In what way?"

"Our guys are working round the clock on this. And we're beginning to see a threat. O'Grady's call to Caroline Lieber, her disappearance, and her friendship with Kendrick. We just couldn't figure it out. But after what happened earlier, things are becoming a bit clearer."

"You wanna explain?"

Chisholm scratched his clean-shaven chin and looked across at Meyerstein. "Am I OK to give this out?"

Meyerstein nodded. "Jon is part of this team."

Chisholm pulled up a seat and sat down. "Kendrick was assigned as a junior doctor in April 1992, shortly after the UN's establishment of what was then known as the Department of Humanitarian Affairs. He worked in Rwanda, Albania, Angola, Burundi, Eritrea, Sudan, you name it. The guy is considered to be a great humanitarian as well as a brilliant surgeon and doctor. Saved children's limbs. Saved countless lives. We have plenty of photographic and documentary evidence to back up that he was there at the time he said."

"So where's the problem?"

"This is where it gets interesting. We've checked the United Nations' records of their field staff, and there's a three-month assignment where he was in Somalia from June to August 1995."

Reznick said, "That's impossible. The UN withdrew in March 1995. I know all about Somalia."

Chisholm nodded. "We've spoken to Franz Topping, a senior official within the Department of Humanitarian Affairs, and he insists there definitely was not a UN presence in Somalia. But this contradicts the field record of Dr Janice Sanderson, from Ithaca in upstate New York, who was working for a Christian medical charity. Her records state that Kendrick was working in Mogadishu. He was mentioned in her diary. Here's the kicker. Guess what? Sanderson was killed in a car crash three months ago."

Reznick rubbed the top of his head. "So either Kendrick or a third party wants to hide three months of his life. We need to know why."

Chisholm nodded. "We're still working through the records of the other humanitarian agencies. It's a lot more fragmented. Less computer records, so that's causing a problem."

Reznick said, "But it's this three months we need to be concentrating on. Can we rule out that he was in a training camp somewhere?"

Chisholm stared across at Reznick. "We can't rule out anything at this stage."

Meyerstein looked up from her computer. "Sam, what's the latest on Kendrick's movements?"

Chisholm leaned over and checked a nearby laptop. "Surveillance team two has him back in the park. Alone. Taking pictures."

Reznick said, "At this time of night? Same place?"

Chisholm nodded. "Same route he took when you were watching him."

"The exact same?"

"The exact same."

Reznick shook his head. "Consider this. The main object of surveillance is to check a possible target for security measures, vulnerabilities. Is this what's going on here?"

Chisholm nodded. "Perhaps."

Reznick said, "Are we talking a high-profile target or target in the park? A spectacular?"

Meyerstein rolled her eyes. "Complete supposition, Jon."

"So what's your take on what he's up to and who he's linked to?"

Meyerstein was leafing through some papers. She leaned back in her seat and sighed. "I've got some analysis that we're working on. It's pretty raw. But it's showing that perhaps Kendrick is sympathetic to the aims of some of our homegrown militias. Extreme libertarians. Anti-government hardliners. Perhaps in the Timothy McVeigh mold."

Reznick blew out his cheeks. "McVeigh? Christ. He was a whackjob."

Malone leaned back in his seat and cleared his throat. "McVeigh, huh? Interesting."

Chisholm shook his head. "Gimme a break. He was a cold-blooded bastard. Oklahoma bomb killed a hundred and sixty-eight people, including children on the second-floor day-care center. More than eight hundred injured. Nothing interesting about that."

"Hey, keep it down. I'm not disputing that. But I studied McVeigh at close quarters. Psychologically, he was not insane. Not by any means. I can remember he had an IQ of 126."

Chisholm said, "I don't give a shit what his IQ was."

Malone said, "Neither do I. Tell me, Sam, have you ever read The Third Terrorist by Jayna Davis?"

"Yeah, and it's bullshit."

"The author said McVeigh and one of his accomplices, a guy by the name of Nichols, had significant ties to an Islamic terror group."

"She's wrong."

Malone shrugged. "Maybe. But we can't rule such thinking out when we're compiling where Kendrick fits in."

Chisholm said, "We can feed that into our analysis, but I don't see that theory getting beyond first base. I think the book didn't give credible sources for this information that there was a Middle Eastern connection to Oklahoma."

Reznick said nothing.

Malone shook his head. "Check it out. The book calls into question why the FBI turned a blind eye to eyewitness testimony that suggested McVeigh had a Middle Eastern accomplice. Twenty-two eyewitnesses gave written affidavits confirming there was a third terrorist. A guy called Hussain Hashem Al-Hussaini, an Iraqi soldier in the first Gulf War. All the eyewitnesses say that this Iraqi accompanied McVeigh to the federal building."

Meyerstein interrupted. "Malone, I've got to stop you there. I know the case very well. Investigation didn't back that up."

Malone said, "Terrorism makes for strange bedfellows. Unforeseen alliances are not uncommon. Even in prison, the Mexican Mafia and Aryan Brotherhood have a loose alliance against their common enemies. Outside, the Tijuana Cartel operates in alliance with the Aryan Brotherhood at various levels."

Chisholm sighed. "I think we're getting a bit off base. The thing that strikes me most about Kendrick is that he is lily white. He has no criminal history and no obvious links to Islamic terrorist groups or militias. He just does not fit the profile."

Reznick cut in. "We need to know where he was for those three months."

Meyerstein shook her head. "We'll chase that down, but I feel like we're going round in circles. And I always come back to the same thing. How is it that the State Department doesn't know anything about why O'Grady was contacting Caroline Lieber? Surely they had to have something."

Chisholm nodded. "Something wrong there. To me, the State Department is withholding information."

Meyerstein sighed. "It's frustrating, I know. I know from personal experience how one agency jealously guards the very intel they should be sharing the most freely. But unless we get access to their files, it's on a need-to-know basis."

"That's dangerous."

"I know. Look, Froch isn't the most cooperative, I'll give you that. But I guess that comes with the territory." She caught Reznick's eye. "What's wrong, Jon? You've gone quiet on me."

Reznick said, "What about the apartment at the Baruch houses? Our dead Muslim friend."

Chisholm shook his head. "We've sent in forensics and specialist search teams. They've scanned every inch of the apartment, drilled through walls, partitions, pulled off crown molding, lifted the tiles, and checked in all dead space. Not a goddamn thing."

Reznick, "What about Akhtar's place in the East Village?"

Chisholm said, "We've had to rehouse the wife and kids, but same again; we've drawn a blank."

Meyerstein said, "Which leaves a deep search of Chantelle McGovern's place. We've only had a fifteen-minute sweep of the place. And we're still waiting for the computer analysis to come through."

Chisholm stifled a yawn. Dark shadows under his eyes.

Meyerstein looked across at Chisholm, curling some hair behind her ear. "What do you think? McGovern's apartment. We go in again. But this time we go over it inch by inch."

Chisholm grimaced. "Tough call. If she's involved, I doubt there would be anything there."

Meyerstein looked across at Reznick. "What do you think, Jon?"

"Off site, that would make sense."

Meyerstein closed her eyes. "We could do with having Morales here."

Chisholm put his hand on Meyerstein's shoulder. "Looks like he's going to pull through, Martha."

Reznick said, "How the hell did they know Morales was in the building?"

Chisholm said, "Maybe they got spooked. No knife found. Akhtar's taking the fifth."

A voice shouted through from the adjoining room, "OK, we got something. He's out of the park and he's hopped in a cab. We're on him."

Meyerstein rubbed her hands together. "OK, where to now, Dr Kendrick?"

A short while later, surveillance footage showed him getting out of a yellow taxi and buzzing a door on East 81st Street. "Where is this? Locale?"

A short pause. A young systems expert checking the computers said, "Neighborhood Coalition for Shelter facility.

It houses sixty-five formerly homeless men and women, most of whom are mentally ill."

Meyerstein sighed. "Shit. OK, I want a list of all volunteers, past and present, over the last eighteen months. And also the names of the homeless who stayed there."

Chisholm rubbed his eyes. "Goddamn, what is this guy playing at? I mean, what the hell is all this bouncing around shelters and soup kitchens at this time of night?" He put on a headset, adjusting the microphone in front of his mouth. "Surveillance, we need a female inside the facility. Agent Ferez. Get her made up as a panhandler ASAP. I want her in there and see what we've got."

The rest of the night was spent scanning the surveillance footage coming from inside the East 81st hostel. It was high definition quality. Reznick and the rest of the team monitored the screens as Kendrick talked with the undercover Fed about her alcohol use and asked when the last time she'd used the facility was. He was attentive. It was like a master class in compassion.

As the hours passed, Malone grabbed a nap on the sofa. Reznick, Chisholm and Meyerstein drank strong coffee after strong coffee. Reznick went to the bathroom and popped a Dexedrine. The chemicals hit his system.

Time dragged some more.

Just after four, the FBI surveillance operative Special Agent Ferez was sent on her way, with hot soup, sandwiches and a few dollars, and asked to come back the following night when they would have a spare bed.

The first shafts of light began to break through. Reznick thought it strange to think that, less than twenty blocks away, Kendrick was oblivious to the sophisticated surveillance operation that was tracking him.

What was he really up to?

His motives seemed, on the surface, selfless. Reaching out to the poor and the dispossessed. But was that really the story? Was that what was really happening? Where was he for those three months? And if he wasn't there at the behest of the UN, who was he working for?

The voice of a surveillance operative snapped Reznick out of his thoughts.

"Hold on," the operative said, "who's this? Check this out. We got movement out front of the facility."

Reznick and the others checked the screens that showed the real-time footage. A figure, clearly female, with tight, dark trousers, dark vest, hair tied back, and dark glasses even though it was dark.

Reznick peered at the screen. "Is this a volunteer?"

Then the woman turned, as if spooked, and stared straight up into the camera, unaware she was being watched.

The woman took off her glasses. Reznick thought she looked familiar. The face. He knew it.

Meyerstein said, "You gotta be kidding me."

It was Chantelle McGovern.

TWENTY-FIVE

Just after 6am, Meyerstein was ready for a three-way secure videoconference with the three most senior members of the special access program. She had managed to snatch three hours of uninterrupted sleep and, after a shower, fresh clothes and applying new make-up, she was served a strong Americano and croissant. She scarfed them down and felt immeasurably better. She got a rushed five-minute briefing from an exhausted-looking Chisholm, who hadn't slept, and got to the tiny, windowless videoconference room in the Fairfax and sat down. She punched in the encryption code, sipped her hot coffee and stared back at the stern faces of Lt General Black, who was in McLean, and Lt Col Froch, who was on the eighth floor of the State Department office in New York, directly opposite the UN.

Over the next ten minutes, she gave a situation update. When she had finished, she stared back at the faces on the screen in front of her. "Bottom line, gentlemen, our analysis is pointing to Kendrick being linked in some way. Otherwise, the statistical chances of him going to the same East Side homeless shelter as McGovern in addition to being served by her at a Midtown steakhouse and East Village restaurant are too ludicrous to contemplate. That is three separate locations. And that is in addition to her brother, Jamal, an Islamist convert, being holed up in one of the Baruch projects on the Lower East Side."

Black leaned back in his seat and shrugged. She could tell he was not convinced. "You have not given one iota of evidence to show that he is in any way linked to anything. I accept that it is a coincidence, but there is no forensic proof linking him with anything."

Meyerstein sighed. She hadn't expected to be dismissed so readily.

Froch cleared his throat. "Can I jump in here?"

Meyerstein said, "Sure, Ed."

"I've got to say, I feel uneasy when people talk about a person – in this case Kendrick – being 'linked' in some way. In what way is he linked, other than these bizarre coincidences? I'm not ruling out the possibility, but come on..."

Meyerstein leaned forward, hands clasped, as she felt the anger rise within her. "Counterterrorism strategic analysts, military intelligence and behavioral analysts all conclude unequivocally that Kendrick is far more likely to be involved than not. We're talking probability. And it's more probable than not that he is involved."

Froch said, "Involved in what?"

"At this stage? We just don't know."

"Oh, come on, Assistant Director, that's not gonna wash. We believe someone may be involved in something we don't know anything about? Is that what you're telling me?"

Meyerstein kept her anger in check. "Ed, we are building a picture. It takes time."

Black said, "O'Grady is dead, Martha. Lieber is still missing. These are concrete facts. And we can't keep this from the media forever."

Meyerstein said, "I know exactly where we stand. Look, we are getting closer to this. The analysis favors our focus on Kendrick and Chantelle McGovern. We are peeling it back."

Black said, "What about the Iranians?"

"We have them covered. There is nothing, chatter or movement, to indicate anything in the offing."

"Let's be honest, Martha. We have been playing catch up since the get-go. And to make matters worse, consider this. I was informed that, last night, the parents of Caroline Lieber met with the President, begging him to allow them to make a public appeal, to see if someone out there knows anything. They're beside themselves. They believe that is the only way."

Meyerstein sighed. "I can't begin to imagine what they're going through. But the feeling is that if we open this up, and let the newspapers, blogs, Twitter, Fox, Bill O'Reilly and God knows who chew over whether there is some kind of link between O'Grady and his murder and the disappearance of a young intern, there will be wider consequences. If there are sleeper cells in place, which we believe there are, there is a very real chance they may activate their plans immediately. As it stands, we believe they may be nearing the endgame although not there yet."

Black shook his head. "Caroline Lieber's parents are very influential in this administration. They are donors. Major donors. And they are not the sort of people who are going to be browbeaten by any politician, even the President. I think we've got to expect them to go public on this, from what I'm hearing, in the next twenty-four hours."

Meyerstein said nothing. Her mind raced ahead, thinking of the fallout for the investigation.

Froch said, "OK, let's just all back up for a few moments. If I can make a suggestion here, I'd like to talk this over, face to face, with the assistant director and offer the services of the State Department, or at least outline some diplomatic channels I think we can use to reach out to the Liebers to give us some more time. What I have in mind might just give us the extra space we need to make the breakthrough. Because, as it stands, if the Liebers decide to go public, then there will be no place to hide, and it'll sure as hell turn into a media firestorm when they find out about O'Grady and a link to their missing daughter."

Meyerstein could see the logic. "I'm all for that, Ed. As you know, I'm in New York. You wanna meet up this morning?"

"I've got a meeting with the Secretary of State at 8am. How does 9.30 sound?"

Meyerstein nodded. "I'll be there."

Black was also nodding. "Let's keep this tight. I want a goddamn breakthrough. And I want it real quick."

The New York office of the State Department was housed in a monolithic twenty-six-story concrete tower across the street from the UN in Midtown. It housed the US mission to the UN, where hundreds of diplomats and support staff worked behind thirty-inch concrete walls and no windows on the first seven floors, specially designed to withstand explosives-laden truck bombs on First Avenue.

Meyerstein was dropped outside a side entrance on 45th Street at 9.26am. "I won't be long, twenty minutes max," she told Chisholm, who was sitting up front beside the driver, talking to one of his team on his cell phone. She turned to Reznick, who was sitting in the back seat. "Let's see what Froch has to say. Wish me luck."

Reznick stared at her long and hard before he smiled. "Good luck."

She strode up to the entrance, flashed her ID at the armed guard and was ushered inside to go through security. She walked through metal detectors and was searched by a poker-faced female guard.

"She's clean," the woman said. "Sorry, ma'am, but it's the same for everyone."

Meyerstein looked at the woman and smiled. "Not a problem."

She rode the elevator alone to the eighth floor and was escorted through a maze of corridors to Froch's office by an attractive twenty-something female intern.

Froch was sitting behind his desk, leafing through some papers. He stood up and pointed to the chair opposite. He blew out his cheeks as Meyerstein sat down. "One minute early. You want a coffee?"

Meyerstein said, "Good morning, Ed. Black coffee, please."

The intern left the room to make the coffee. Froch made small talk. The high humidity, plans for vacations. When the intern returned, she placed the coffee on the desk, in front of Meyerstein. "Ma'am," she said.

Meyerstein said, "Thanks for that." She sipped some coffee, enjoying the caffeine taking hold. She was so tired.

Froch said, "Gillian, can you shut the door behind you? Make sure I'm not disturbed."

The door shut and Froch let out a long sigh.

"Thanks for making it at such short notice." He leaned forward and steepled his fingers. "Firstly, I want to say that any State Department involvement does not impinge on your role as leading this investigation. I was briefing the secretary of state and she is being kept in the loop, as you can understand."

Meyerstein nodded. "I would expect nothing less."

"There are one or two people within the State Department who say this should be led by Counterterrorism. But the feeling is that you have that base amply covered with Sam Chisholm being on board."

Meyerstein smiled but said nothing.

"Here's where I'm at. I've already dispatched an old family friend of the Liebers to calm the waters. He heads up the State Department's Office of Global Intergovernmental Affairs."

"Charlie Stanton?"

"The very man. He's known the Liebers for over thirty years. He'll be asking for seventy-two hours' grace."

Meyerstein sighed. "You kidding me? Ed, I need more time."
"That's all that's on the table. Charlie believes we can get that seventy-two hours. Nothing more." Meyerstein shook her head. But she knew it was a take-it-or-leave-it. Not up for discussion. She was tempted to fire off a volley of criticism in his direction on how unforthcoming they had been with regard to O'Grady, his undefined role within the State Department and who he had or hadn't been in contact with. But she knew, from long experience, it was better to try to be constructive, or at least appear to be.

Froch averted his eyes from her direct gaze. "The State Department's intelligence bureau and our counterterrorism people are studying the developments closely. They're pretty smart."

Meyerstein knew that was correct. She only had to think back to the National Intelligence Estimate of 2002 before the Iraq War on whether Saddam possessed weapons of mass destruction. They were about the only intelligence agency who emerged with any credit, primarily because of their dissent. "They're very nuanced. I like that."

Froch gave a thin smile. "I'll pass that on. We pride ourselves on the rigor of our reports and the quality of our staff."

Meyerstein said, "So, has Stanton spoken to the Liebers?"

"Not yet. He's due to meet them around midday. We don't think there will be a problem. But we are on the clock now."

Meyerstein rubbed her eyes. She reached over and picked up her coffee, gulping down the rest. The caffeine had hit the mark. "I appreciate your help. And trust me, we need every bit of help we can get."

Froch's desk phone rang and a red light lit up. "I must take that. President's national security advisor."

Meyerstein nodded and got up from her chair. "Let me know as soon as you hear from Stanton."

"Count on it."

Meyerstein left Froch's office and felt a migraine come on. She headed to a bathroom and popped a couple of Advil, washed them down with a small bottle of Evian she had in her bag. She looked at her reflection in the mirror. Shadows under the eyes. She applied some fresh Touché Éclat. Then she touched up her lipstick.

She closed her eyes for a few moments, hoping the pain would subside. So many things going through her head, it wasn't real. Analysis, counterterrorism briefings, Reznick's presence on the team, pressure from Black, missing the kids. The more she thought of it, the more she knew she needed a vacation when it was all over.

The door opened behind her. Standing there was a fresh-faced, dark-haired woman. Her high cheekbones and peachy complexion made Meyerstein envious as she put away the pen-brush concealer.

The woman gave a thin smile and approached the mirror. She took a small bottle of perfume from her bag. Then she turned to Meyerstein and sprayed the cold spray into her left ear.

"What the..." was all Meyerstein managed to say before the words didn't come.

"Take care now," the woman said as Meyerstein collapsed to the floor, struggling for breath, the woman staring down at her, smiling.

Then she was swallowed up in a spiral of darkness.

TWENTY-SIX

Reznick checked his watch as he sat in the back of the SUV parked on 45th Street outside the Uganda House. Skyscrapers towering, shading the street. He glanced at the clock on the dashboard. It showed 10.45."

"What's taking her so long?" he said to the driver. "She's been away for over an hour."

The Fed just shrugged, eyes dead in the mirror. "Relax."

Reznick felt his foot tapping. He had never been good at just waiting. "Wasn't she supposed to be in for just twenty minutes?"

The Fed nodded. "It happens. Meetings run over all the time."

That was true, Reznick thought. But Froch didn't seem like the sort of person who allowed meetings to run over. Stickler for detail. A small-print kind of guy.

The waiting went on. He looked at his watch at least a dozen times in the space of fifteen minutes. And still nothing.

He wondered what was keeping her. Neither the FBI driver nor Chisholm sitting in the front seat seemed unduly bothered.

Reznick leaned forward and tapped Chisholm on the shoulder. "That's way over an hour she's been gone. Is that normal?"

Chisholm was checking his emails on his Blackberry. He turned round and grimaced, eyes still focused on his smartphone. "No idea, Jon."

"Look, do you wanna at least send her a message asking her how long she'll be?"

"I don't think that's a great idea."

"Why not?"

"Well, if she's in a meeting with Froch and some of his State Department buddies, you can rest assured she won't want to be disturbed by us, asking her where the hell she is. I know Martha. Have for a long time. And she does not like being disturbed in meetings."

Reznick sighed. "She had a twenty-minute meeting, Sam. She's now been gone a while."

"You need to get out more, Jon. Here in the real world, meetings run over all the time. It's a pain in the ass. But we roll with it."

Reznick sat back in the rear seat and remained unconvinced. She had said earlier that she wouldn't be too long. But here they were, an hour and a half later, and still she was inside.

He pondered on that. He had always been a stickler for timekeeping, especially back in his Delta days. If you were given forty-five minutes to do a task, it meant forty-five minutes max. Not a second more. A night run for thirty miles over rough terrain had to be completed in less than twelve hours. And on and on it went. He was obsessive about the time. It kept him focused. But anything that ran over jarred with him.

He liked order. Precision.

The minutes dragged. He checked his watch some more.

"11.15, Sam," he said. "She's been gone an hour and forty minutes."

"What do you want me to do? She's an FBI assistant director. I can't just go marching into the goddamn office and ask what the hell is taking her so long."

Reznick tried to keep his natural aggression in check. "Can't you at least call Froch's assistant or secretary? Ask how long she'll be?"

Chisholm shook his head and smiled. "You're wound up too tight, Jon; do you know that?"

Reznick said nothing.

Chisholm shrugged. "OK OK, I'll deal with it," he said, and punched in a number. "Hi, sorry to bother you; this is Sam Chisholm of the FBI." A long silence. "Yes, counterterrorism. Thank you. Can you put me through to Ed Froch's secretary?" A silence opened up for a few moments. "Are you sure? I'm sorry, how long ago? Are you positive?" He nodded and closed his eyes before ending the call.

Reznick leaned forward. "So, where the hell is she?"

"She left more than an hour ago."

"What?"

Chisholm punched in another number. He waited for a few moments and left a voice message. "Martha, it's Sam. Where the hell are you? They said your meeting finished way before ten. It's now 11.17am and no sign of you." He ended the call.

Reznick said, "We need to get up there."

Chisholm gritted his teeth. "Fuck is going on?"

Chisholm and Reznick got out the SUV and rushed through the security door. They were patted down and given temporary passes to enter the building. They rode the elevator with two security guards to the eighth floor and headed straight to Froch's office.

The secretary let them in, as Froch was on the phone. He hung up immediately.

Froch said, "I've just been alerted that Assistant Director Meyerstein isn't with you," he said. "So where the hell is she?"

Chisholm ran his hand through his hair. "Shit."

"I've just ordered the security cameras to be reviewed. Something's not right."

Reznick said, "No fucking kidding." He began to pace back and forth. "Did she say where she was going?"

"I assumed she was heading back to base."

Froch's desk phone rang and he picked up on the first ring. "Yes?" He nodded. "On this floor? Put the building on lockdown. Right now!" He hung up. "Security says the footage shows she went into the restroom on this floor. No sign of her since then." Reznick said, "Fuck!"

He ran out of the office with the security guard in tow and headed back down a corridor in the direction of the sign that indicated female restrooms. He barged inside and it appeared empty. But he saw one door partially shut. He spread-eagled himself on the floor and saw legs and shoes: Meyerstein crumpled in a heap.

"End stall!" Reznick shouted at the guard. "Call 911! Now!"

He pushed back the door with his left hand and kneeled down. He gently cupped his left hand behind her head and felt the pulse on her neck with his right hand. "Very faint, but alive." He touched her cheek. It was getting cold. Clammy. Lips were turning blue. Then he spotted some crystalline residue in her hair.

He pushed back the hair from her head and saw the same residue on her earlobe. It reminded him of a hit by the Israelis on a Palestinian terrorist on the West Bank.

He turned to the guards. "Seal this place off! Don't let anyone out of this building, do you understand?"

The guard nodded and passed on the instructions on his radio.

Reznick turned his attention back to Meyerstein. "Stay with me, Martha!" He tapped her cheek, trying to rouse her, and began to shake her. He turned to face the guard. "Where the hell are the paramedics!"

A few moments later Chisholm came in with a female paramedic, who began to take Meyerstein's pulse.

"Not good... Very faint. Is this an overdose?"

Reznick pointed out the drug residue. "Someone got to her."

The paramedic said, "With what?"

"Opiate, almost certainly. Try for fentanyl."

"How do you know?"

"Just do it! Naloxone, you got it?"

The paramedic nodded. "I'm on it!"

Reznick turned again to Chisholm and cocked his head. "Let's go."

"We can't just leave her."

"She's in medical hands. Leave two of your team with her. We need to act fast."

Two Feds were called up to stay with Meyerstein as the paramedic fought to revive her. Then Reznick and Chisholm headed down to the building's security room, which contained banks of monitors covering entrances and exits.

The head of security pointed to a freeze-framed image of a young woman, perhaps in her late twenties, wearing a dark pantsuit, long brown hair, State Department ID hanging round her neck. "We've checked. This woman entered the small bathroom, just after Assistant Director Meyerstein entered. She left twenty-two seconds later. Precisely."

Reznick stared at the woman. High cheekbones, white, fresh face with dark, deep-set eyes. He leaned closer, trying to read the nametag. "Zoom in on the name tag!"

The head of security did as he was told. The nametag read "Sacha Hall." He punched the name into his computer and it came up blank. "There is no Sacha Hall with State Department accreditation."

"So how the hell did she gain entry to this building?"

The man flushed a dark crimson. "We're checking it out."

Reznick stared at the man. "When did she leave this building?"

The man clicked a button on the laptop, and it brought up another image showing the woman leaving the main entrance at 10.05am.

Chisholm said, "I need those images."

"I'm sorry; I'm going to have to run it past..."

Chisholm pointed at the man, inches away from his face. "You get those images to my guy right fucking now! You got it?"

The man nodded, visibly shaking. "Yes, sir."

"OK." Chisholm handed him an FBI business card with an email address on it. "Send them to Andrew Livingston, FBI Counterterrorism. Right now. But send them secure. Do you understand what that means?"

The security guy just nodded. "Encrypted, yes. You got it." He keyed in the email address and sent it across. "Consider it done."

Chisholm turned to Reznick. "What a fucking mess."

"Tell me about it."

They headed out of the building and into the waiting SUV, then Chisholm's cell phone rang. He answered and listened. "Hold on." He covered the mouthpiece and looked at Reznick. "That's Livingston. He's got a match with our mystery girl. Facial recognition has just made a hundred percent match at Grand Central's food court. They've been tracking her via security cameras. There's a shadow with her. A big guy, jeans, shades, Yankees hat."

Reznick tapped the driver on the shoulder. "Let's move it!"

Chisholm ended the call as the car sped on through the Midtown East traffic until it pulled up outside Grand Central. Reznick and Chisholm headed through the soaring beaux arts main concourse. They careered down to the food court, knocking people out of the way, scanning faces, trying to block out the announcements, earpieces relaying the command and control from Livingston. "She is on the move, headed for the platform. Yeah, she is on Track 3 on the 42nd Street Shuttle."

Reznick sprinted down a ramp to the platform, only to see the train pulling away. "Damn."

Livingston's voice in his ear. "Reznick, next train will be along in thirty seconds from Track 1."

Reznick and Chisholm headed across from the Track 3 platform to the waiting train. The time dragged. A minute. Then two minutes passed. "Fuck is going on?" he said, frustrated at the delay.

Chisholm called Livingston and ordered the lockdown of Times Square station – less than a mile away – so no one could exit. Eventually, nearly five long minutes later, the 42nd Street Shuttle thundered away from the station into the tunnel.

A minute later, they were there.

Reznick and Chisholm squeezed off along with hundreds of others. Bustling and shoving and moaning into the Times Square station. Down badly lit corridors, down more stairs, avoiding street kids and homeless musicians, until they got to one of the lower platforms. "Where the hell has she gone?"

Livingston's voice said in the earpiece, "We got her. She's on the 7 platform."

Reznick saw a sign and sprinted for it, careering down more stairs. The roar and rumble of a train careering through. He descended onto the platform, scanning the faces. He spotted her. She turned and stared straight at him.

Reznick moved toward her.

The huge man appeared from the crowd behind her, eyeballed Reznick, and calmly pressed a gun against the back of the woman's head. He stared at Reznick with cold eyes and shot her dead. The noise was like an explosion in the confined space. Panic ensued. Blood and brain matter splattered everywhere. Crowds screamed. The sea of people parted.

It was then that time seemed to stop for Reznick. Shocked faces. Blood. The screaming. He was in the moment.

Reznick drew his 9mm and aimed at the man, but the target had already made his move.

The gun was already in the man's mouth, his fierce eyes locked onto Reznick.

Then the man calmly blew his brains out on the platform, the back of his head exploding in an eruption of blood.

TWENTY-SEVEN

Reznick somehow managed to block out the noise, chaos and screaming that followed as people scattered amid the carnage. He felt detached. Part training, part instinct. His mind seemed to have split away from what he had just witnessed. He began to think rationally. He got a Fed's iPhone and zoomed in, photographing both faces.

Reznick stood above the man's body as blood pooled and congealed around his shoes. He was surprised that the front of the man's face was remarkably intact. But the woman's face was a different matter, a gaping hole where half of her face had been.

He stared at the two faces for a few moments. The woman's face was virtually unrecognizable, torn to shreds by the bullet, but he had already seen her Slavic features on the surveillance footage. Her mouth was slightly open, as if aware only for a split second that she was about to die. The man looked Russian, perhaps Slavic too, pieces of flesh, fragments of bone and brain matter all over the platform. Eyes pale blue, still open.

He wondered what ideology drove the man to kill the woman and take his own life. What did he want to hide? What was worth dying for?

Reznick saw Chisholm out of his peripheral vision but didn't let on. He bent down and rummaged in the man's pockets. Nothing. Inside the woman's jacket pocket there was an iPhone. He put it in his pocket and disappeared into the fleeing crowds, with Chisholm and two Feds who'd joined him, before anyone could ask any questions.

His mind raced as he stepped out of the enclosed cauldron, noise and confusion and into the steam-bath humidity on street level, the car horns and neon advertising of Times Square. Hundreds of people all around, cop cars pulling up everywhere. Chisholm's driver hailed them from an SUV, and Reznick, Chisholm and the two Feds climbed in.

Safely inside, Reznick handed Chisholm the woman's iPhone. "This is her phone. We need to download everything on it. Let's get back to the Fairfax."

The driver hit the gas and they sped away.

Chisholm held the cell phone gingerly and dropped it into a plastic evidence bag. "What the hell happened?"

Reznick breathed out long and hard as Midtown Manhattan flew by. "They eyeballed us. The guy shot the woman first. Then he shot himself. You wanna tell me what's going on?"

Chisholm's face drained of color as he stared at the phone. "We're using facial recognition to try to establish who they were."

"And?"

"We believe they may be Russians."

"Working on whose orders? The Russians I know don't shoot at each other. I think you need to look at that again. Is this Boston all over again? Are we talking Chechens?"

"Distinct possibility. We're working this from all angles."

"What's the latest on Meyerstein?"

"Not good. She's unconscious. On a ventilator. Doctors believe it's an offshoot of China White, a form of fentanyl. Two hundred times more potent than morphine. Russian mob's very involved in the importation of the drug."

Reznick put his head in his hands. "Fuck."

Chisholm held up his hands as if to pacify him. "Take it easy, Jon."

"Look, Chisholm, they might be Russian, they might even be Russian mob, but why the hell would he kill the woman and then kill himself? They don't want us to get below the surface. We're talking ideology."

Chisholm closed his eyes for a moment. "Here's another problem we're facing. Who the hell would target Meyerstein? Counterterrorism thinks we might be compromised in some way."

"Communications?"

"Should be impossible, but... it can't be ruled out."

Reznick stared at the heat-laden streets as they headed uptown. "How the hell did they get to her?"

"Too early to say."

Chisholm's phone rang. "Yes, sir. We got the female's phone. Computer forensics will already have copied over the contents of this phone and we'll have the analysis within the hour. You'll have the results as soon as I get them. Sir, I'm well aware of that." He nodded a few times before he handed it to Reznick. "General Black wants to talk to you."

Reznick looked at the phone.

"Don't worry; it's encrypted."

Reznick cleared his throat and took the phone. "Sir."

"I just heard about the assistant director. This is quite outrageous."

"Indeed it is, sir."

He let out a long sigh. "Jon, your photos of the two dead guys will be very helpful. Save us a lot of grief with the NYPD. We are strictly in-house on this. And that's the way it's going to stay."

"What the hell is going on, sir?"

A long sigh. "You know as well as I do, Jon, nothing is straightforward in our world. We could be dealing with a terrorist cell, Russian Mafia, who knows? Take your pick."

"Sir, with respect, how the hell could someone get to an FBI assistant director in broad daylight, within a secure complex?

This is an inside job, isn't it? Someone wanted to derail this investigation. Throw us off the scent."

"There's a lot of questions we need answered, Jon. And whoever is behind this will be taken care of. But as of now, as I've just told Sam, I'm taking charge of this program. Now, I know there were one or two objections about your inclusion in the team, and I was one of the objectors, but I want you to know that I want you to stay on the team. That is, if you want to. If you want to walk away and get back to your life, I understand. Your call."

Reznick sighed long and hard. "I don't do walking away; you should know that. I want to help you find out who did this."

"Very well. So, what's your take on this?"

"We have definitely been compromised; that's goddamn obvious. My question would be, who knew Assistant Director Meyerstein was heading to Froch's office?"

"Half a dozen people directly but then another half a dozen who'd get to know by association."

"The key players would be me, you, Chisholm, Froch and Stamper."

"The person would need to know her every move well in advance to plan this."

A silence opened up before Black spoke. "Go on."

Reznick looked at Chisholm, who was receiving a real-time update on his iPad. The car hit a pothole and the suspension shuddered. "It happened on Froch's patch. He was the last person to see her. It happened only yards from his office."

"I've know Ed Froch for two decades. He's beyond reproach."

"Check his phone records. Check his home phone records. Check the dead woman's phone."

"Jon, Froch is connected to very powerful people within the Administration. We can't go pointing the finger."

"I'm not asking you or anyone to point the finger at him. We need to do some checking."

"I suppose I could call him up... videoconference."

"Assume the worst, sir. If we call ahead, he has prior warning, if he has been compromised."

"And if he's not been compromised?"

"Then we're only being thorough."

"Jon, this isn't how we work."

"Sir, we need to speak to him and he needs to answer some questions."

"Jon, he would never harm the assistant director."

"We don't know that."

"You're saying we give him no prior warning and just turn up at his office?"

"You got it."

A sigh and then a grunt. "Pass me over to Sam, will you, Jon?"

Reznick did as he was told.

Chisholm took the phone, nodded twice and ended the call. He leaned forward and the driver turned around. "Straight back to Froch's office."

Fifteen minutes later, they were back outside the State Department's New York office. Heavy police presence. The exits were covered.

Chisholm and Reznick rode the elevator to Froch's office. Cops and forensics milling around the restroom. Down a carpeted corridor and toward the outer office, where his secretary looked up. "I need to speak to your boss."

"He's not here."

Reznick said, "Where the hell is he?"

"I don't know."

"What do you mean, you don't know?"

The young woman flushed pink. "He left the office ten minutes ago and didn't say where he was going."

TWENTY-EIGHT

The heat was almost unbearable as Kendrick pounded the paved track around Central Park's reservoir. He felt the spray, whipped up by the gusts of wind from the choppy water, cool him as the temperatures climbed into the nineties. He wondered how long it would be until the day. He mused on that as he passed red-faced joggers as they pushed themselves in the stifling New York heat.

The thought of what lay ahead sparked a new endorphin rush.

He ran on and looked across the water toward the iconic Manhattan skyline in the distance. The sky pale blue, only a few wisps of white cloud drifting through.

He was in the zone. He was in the right city at the right time. It was all coming together.

The voice of his mentor on the tape ran through his head. He was playing it three or four times a day now. Everything was becoming clearer. More focused, as they said it would.

It was remarkable to think that he was going to be remembered. That's what his father had wanted for him. His name would live for a thousand years. Infamy. Echoing down the years like a dark whisper.

Satisfied with the workout, Kendrick slowed down and stood beside the steel fence that surrounded the reservoir. He stretched out his legs, feeling his calf muscles tighten.

He felt himself cocooned in the afterglow of exertion, sweat dripping down his neck.

He closed his eyes, listening to his breathing, as the runners pounded past him.

He loved that moment. Being still.

His cell phone vibrated on his belt, snapping him out of his relaxed state of mind.

Kendrick pressed the phone to his ear.

"We got a new location," the familiar voice said.

Kendrick got up and leaned against the fence. "At this late hour?"

"It's all in hand."

"Why the change?"

"It's still in New York."

"Who changed the plans?"

"That was beyond our control."

Kendrick went quiet for a few moments as he mulled over the change. He liked order. He liked visualizing what he was about to do. Now that wasn't possible. "Not ideal."

The man said nothing.

"When will I know the venue?"

"All in good time."

"And my wingman?"

"He's watching your every move. We got you covered. You're going to have a clear run."

Kendrick afforded himself a smile at a passing beautiful jogger, and she smiled back. "This is going to happen, right?"

"It gonna happen because you're going to make it happen."

Kendrick detected a slight tension in the man's voice as if he wasn't telling the whole story. "What about an exact date and time?"

"The date is still the same. The time is changing. We'll let you know."

Kendrick said nothing.

"One final thing."

"What?"

"It won't just be the main event at the venue."

Kendrick's stomach knotted. "The wife?"

"You'll get a clear shot at both."

Kendrick closed his eyes and could see the whole scenario unfold in his head as the line went dead.

TWENTY-NINE

It was nearly dark when the Feds, with Reznick in tow, pulled up outside Terminal 4 of JFK International Airport. It had been less than an hour since plainclothes Feds at the airport had seen the FBI circular that was sent out to law enforcement agencies with Froch's details. Facial recognition software running on surveillance cameras had pulled up a perfect match. And they had alerted Chisholm that the missing NSA official had been spotted. But Chisholm had instructed them that under no circumstances were they to approach Froch unless he boarded a flight.

Reznick knew that was the smart thing to do. The last thing they needed was for airport Feds, outside of the secret program, to haul Froch in for questioning. They had to bring him in and let Chisholm's guys interrogate him.

They were ushered through the arrivals hall by the Feds and onto Concourse B, past a myriad of shops: a chocolate shop, duty-free, Panda Express, Peet's, Shake Shack and a Travelex currency exchange.

Finally, they headed toward the gates.

Reznick spotted him in a line at gate B20, talking into his cell phone. He turned to Chisholm. "How do you want to work this?"

Chisholm stared across at Froch as the line slowly moved forward. "We do not want a scene. The last thing we need is for passengers to be pulling out their goddamn iPhones and filming us taking him down. We want to do this slow and quiet."

Reznick said, "What about Customs?"

Chisholm shook his head. "The less they know, the better. OK, approach him, nice and gentle, and explain that he needs to come with you. If necessary, make something up."

"And if he says go to hell?"

"Then haul his ass out of the line. The last thing the FBI needs is for me to be filmed dragging some NSA guy out of an airport line."

"Got you." Reznick turned and walked across the concourse and straight up to Froch. He stood in front of him and smelled liquor on his breath, sensing looks from the other passengers. "Sir, you need to come with me." His voice was low.

Froch flushed a dark red and took a few moments to speak. "What's going on? Why are you here?"

"Your wife, sir."

"My wife? What about her?"

"I'll explain on the way over there."

Froch went quiet for a few moments as if mulling over his options. "Is she OK?"

"I'll explain on the way over. You need to come with me now, sir."

"And if I don't?"

Reznick inched closer to him, eyeballing him hard. "Don't make this more awkward than it has to be."

Froch visibly blanched. "I see."

Reznick cocked his head in the direction of Chisholm and the other Feds. "OK, now we're clear, let's get a move on."

Froch stood still for a few moments before he sighed long and hard. He then headed over towards Chisholm, shadowed by Reznick. He was frisked by the Feds, his cell phone confiscated, and led away to the waiting car. He didn't say a word in the twenty-five-minute car journey as he sat sandwiched between Reznick and a rookie Fed.

Fifteen minutes later, he saw a sign for Brooklyn and then a ramp.

Reznick looked out of the window and wondered where they were headed. It looked sketchy. The area was post-industrial, junkyards and auto-body shops standing like rusting reminders of the area's past.

The car headed toward an unmarked red-brick building and into a rear parking lot, screeching to a halt.

Froch was taken out of the car by the rookie Fed and the driver and led into the building, cameras strafing the steel door. Reznick and Chisholm followed behind.

Inside, it was a different world. Gleaming steel, countless large-screen TVs, Al Jazeera, Arab TV stations, BBC World, CNN and Fox being watched by terrorist-threat language experts with headphones, some reading classified intelligence briefings. In an adjacent room, plainclothes men and women were poring over Farsi, Arabic and Pashto jihadist chat rooms, translating tons of audio recordings.

Froch was taken on ahead to an interview room.

Reznick pulled Chisholm aside beside a water cooler. "What the hell is this place?"

"The Feds have an arrangement with the NYPD. Their counterterrorism guys run this. We stripped it out and reconfigured a few things."

"So is this run as a separate FBI New York field office?"

"We're in New York, and yes, it is an FBI office of sorts, but this runs strictly parallel to both the FBI and NYPD. We use it for high-value targets we pick up in Manhattan. Need-to-know investigations."

Reznick could see what he was getting at. "I see. You run special counterterrorism operations in and around New York, answerable to who exactly?"

"You think too much, Jon."

Chisholm popped out of the room for a few moments with two Styrofoam cups of coffee. "Get this down you, Jon. You must be running on empty too."

Reznick nodded. "Tell me about it." He took a gulp. It was strong and hot.

Chisholm sipped his coffee. "Follow me." He turned and walked toward the far end of the room and the keypad-operated doors, Reznick in tow, both carrying their coffees. He punched in a code and the doors clicked open. They headed along a long corridor and entered a tiny room with one large window through which they could see Froch sitting, head bowed, drinking a cup of tea.

Reznick stared through the two-way mirror. He watched as Froch tapped his feet as if agitated and looked through the glass. He wondered what part Froch had played, if any, in Meyerstein fighting for her life. He felt helpless knowing that the FBI would use their own interrogation techniques on Froch, and certainly nothing enhanced.

He turned to Chisholm. "So what's the lowdown on Mr Froch?"

"We're working on the assumption that he may have been compromised. If so, we need to know in what way and by whom." Chisholm sighed. "The problem is we have nothing. We're chasing shadows. They're fucking with us."

"Who is 'they'? Do we know who those two dead Russians are yet?"

"All we know is that they entered this country on Russian tourist visas."

"There's someone behind them, Sam. They're not just Russians. This has echoes of Boston. I'm talking Chechens."

"We're working with the Russians, trying to connect the dots."

Reznick cleared his throat as he stared through at Froch, picking at his fingernails. "We're also forgetting something."

"What?"

"Kendrick. How does he fit into this? And what about that goddamn Jamal from Chicago?"

Chisholm looked through the glass as Froch leaned back in his chair, arms folded and eyes closed. "We're checking the Russians to see if there is a security or military background. We've got search warrants for an apartment in Queens and a suburban house in DC."

Reznick shook his head. "They might be Russian. But this sure as hell isn't the sort of operation sanctioned by Moscow."

Chisholm said nothing.

"What about Meyerstein? You think Froch knew anything about that?"

"For his sake, I hope not." He stared through the glass. "Look at the poor bastard. How the hell did it come to that?"

"I'm convinced, and this is just me talking, that someone got to him. Pure and simple. Either that or he's lost his goddamn mind."

Within the first few moments of the interview beginning, Reznick could see through the glass that Froch was going to talk frankly and freely. He talked incessantly. He had been blackmailed. It began, he said, with a trip to MIT to recruit talented math and computer graduates to work for the NSA.

Reznick wondered where this was going. He watched as Chisholm nodded empathetically, occasionally took notes and listened carefully.

It wasn't long before Froch had his head in his hands. He began to cry. He had been staying at the Mandarin Oriental in Boston afterwards, he explained. His drinks had been spiked. He had sex with two different women. Prostitutes, he was told later. He passed out. He remembered half waking and looking up as his picture was being taken, and seeing lights from a video camera.

It was a lost weekend.

He flew back home to his quiet life in McLean, to his wife and family. Life went on as normal for months. He thought that he would never hear any more about it. But then he received a phone call to his home one evening, from them, just hours after the special access program had been set up. The red flags were all there. But he was too frightened to tell anyone.

The phone calls continued. It escalated to threatening his wife, family and friends. His carefully ordered life was going to fall apart if he didn't do as he was told.

Reznick stared through the glass. He felt sorry for Froch. But everyone knew the rules. Never succumb. Never put American national security at risk. Tell your superiors. No matter what you've done. There can be a fix.

He listened as Froch begged Chisholm not to tell his wife. Chisholm retorted, "Your wife is the least of your problems".

Chisholm turned the screw. He wanted to know if Froch had received any kickbacks and from whom. Froch said absolutely not. Chisholm said, "We are going to scour every bank account in your name, your wife's name, you kids' names, your mother's name and every goddamn relation in the world. We will check your cell phone records, home telephone records, office phone records, and we will get to the bottom of this, so if you want to stand a chance, you better spill the beans."

Froch shook his head. He said he hadn't received money. He was frightened for his family and his career, not to mention his reputation getting trashed in the press.

"Why didn't you alert your superiors at the State Department?

Froch bowed his head low. "I'm in the church. I believe in God. My family. What sort of man would I have been made to look like then?"

Chisholm rubbed his face as Froch began to cry again. He stopped for a coffee break and joined Reznick in the observation room.

"What do you think, Jon?"

"Hard to say. What about a polygraph?"

"That's next. You know what all this reminded me of?"

Reznick shook his head.

"The book by Dulles, The Craft of Intelligence. He said that honey traps, bar girls and all that were classic moves, favored by the Russians. And such lures were sent to trap him."

Reznick stared through the glass as the sobs from Froch got louder. "Russian tactics, absolutely. But as I've said, there's something more at work here."

"Well, whatever the purpose, the end result is that two of the senior members of the special access program, Meyerstein and Froch, are both now not on the team investigating the disappearance of O'Grady."

Reznick said, "They're sending us a message."

"And what's that?"

"We know who you are. We know what you're doing. We can get to you. I'm telling you, these guys are something else."

Chisholm went quiet for a few moments. "The whole thing – O'Grady, Lieber, Meyerstein and now this Froch business – it's like a slow-burn nightmare. You think you're getting close to something, and it disappears."

"You know as well as I do, we need to refocus this investigation."

"Jon, gimme a break. We're working round the clock. Scores of FBI, Homeland Security specialists, NSC, counterterrorism specialists desperately trying to figure this out."

Reznick stared through the glass. "Either wittingly or unwittingly, that fuck in that room has endangered the life of Assistant Director Meyerstein and threatened the integrity of this investigation. I want to rip him to shreds."

Chisholm sighed. "He's weak and he should've seen the signs. But he could have made it OK by just reaching out to someone in the State Department and saying what had happened. It would never have gone this far."

"What about his bank accounts?"

"We're checking that."

Reznick shook his head. "To think that a few hours after he sat down around that table with Meyerstein, he was selling her down the river."

"Froch was compromised many months ago, he said. So this operation is a long-term thing. And the planning would've gone on for at least a year before it started."

"Which brings us back to Caroline Lieber and Kendrick."

It was Chisholm's turn to sigh. "The Liebers will go to the press and try to publicize their daughter's disappearance."

Reznick said, "Can you blame them?"

"No, I don't blame them. Not in the least."

"Got any theories as to what happened to her?"

Chisholm shook his head and said nothing.

Reznick said, "We're missing something, Sam."

Chisholm's phone rang. He rolled his eyes as he pulled his Blackberry out of his pocket. "Yeah." He nodded. "Three cars on him, cell phone tracking, everything we have." He pressed the red button and ended the call.

"What's up?"

"Our guy's on the move."

"Kendrick?"

"Yup. Picked up his car and he's heading out of the city." He bit his lower lip, a red light blinking on his phone. He scanned the encrypted messages, sent through the FBI-customized BlackBerry Messenger system. He pressed the button and opened up the message, eyes quickly scanning the words. "There's a girl."

The words were spoken as if in a trance.

"Who?" Reznick asked.

"Stamper and his team have discovered that Kendrick had a girlfriend before Lieber. Hilary Stapleton."

"Why the hell has this taken so long?"

Chisholm ignored Reznick and stared at the message on the screen. "Jesus H Christ."

"What is it?"

"Says here she's in a psychiatric unit in Baltimore."

THIRTY

The twelve-bed unit was located on the fourth floor of the Johns Hopkins Hospital campus in East Baltimore. Reznick and Chisholm were led down tiled corridors, then through locked doors, before they reached the office of the director, Ron D Franklin. The receptionist knocked on the door and they entered. The smell of old leather from the books that lined the oak-paneled walls. Impressive-looking medical certificates in gold-leaf frames.

Franklin was waiting for them. He introduced himself, shook their hands and sat down behind his desk, leaning back in his seat. He was in his mid-sixties, tall and slim with wispy white hair. His shirtsleeves were rolled up as if he was ready for business.

He waited until Reznick and Chisholm pulled up a seat opposite before he spoke. "I believe you're interested in talking to one of our patients."

Chisholm sat down and cleared his throat. "That's correct, Dr Franklin."

"Do you mind me asking the nature of this visit?"

"It concerns a major investigation. Counterterrorism."

Franklin furrowed his brow for a few minutes as if deep in thought. "I'm ultimately in charge of the medical care of all those within the inpatient unit. Patient confidentiality is paramount, so unless she consents there's nothing I can do."

Chisholm shifted in his seat. "Dr Franklin, I'd ask you to bear in mind that we have already applied for an order requesting access to her records, section 215 under the Patriot Act, and this has been approved." He pulled out the signed paperwork and handed it over to Franklin.

Franklin glanced at it and paused for a brief moment. "How very thorough."

Chisholm said nothing to the barbed comment.

"So what do you want to know?"

"We want to know more about Miss Stapleton and why she's being kept within the Mood Disorders Center."

Franklin let out a long sigh. "Bipolar disorder. Self-harm. Then a mental breakdown."

"How long's she been here?"

The doctor pursed his lips and sighed. "Three months, give or take a few days. She was a high flier. Then she crashed."

"What line of work?"

"Hedge funds. High pressure."

"What about a boyfriend?"

"Interestingly, just after she was admitted, she talked about her boyfriend." He flicked open a file on his desk. "Adam Kendrick. She mentioned that he was seeing another woman. She also mentioned that she thought she was being followed. That could've been paranoia. Calls to her office, telling her to be careful, to stay away from her boyfriend. People watching her. Who knows?"

Chisholm nodded. "Did she know the person or people who were calling?"

"No. All she said was that it was a man's voice. An American. But we believe she was suffering from hallucinations. Voices in her head."

When was she diagnosed with bipolar disorder?"

"When she was twenty-one. But she was a functioning bipolar. She would work manically for four days without sleep and then crash. But hallucinations started earlier this year. She said her boyfriend was lacing joints she was smoking with PCP."

Chisholm sighed. "So the boyfriend is slipping PCP into a joint. She starts to get hallucinations. Then she crashes and is sent here."

"Right. She said the hallucinations were off-the-scale frightening. She talked about a strange taste in the joints she was smoking."

Chisholm allowed a long silence to open up before he spoke. "We really need to speak to Miss Stapleton, if that's all right with you."

"We asked her earlier, and she said she had no problem with that. I would ask that you please bear in mind that her mind wanders, she is prone to flights of fancy, her moods can be dark, but also, by sharp contrast, she can go manic. Very excitable. Chatty."

"How is she just now?"

The doctor arched his thick eyebrows and smiled. "Go and see for yourself."

The room was all beige with gentle watercolors on the wall, two terracotta sofas and a coffee table in the middle. Hilary Stapleton was standing with her back to them, staring out of the window, dragging hard on a cigarette. She didn't turn around when Chisholm and Reznick were ushered in by a nurse.

"FBI to see you, Hilary; you OK with that, honey?"

Stapleton turned round and beamed a wide smile at the nurse. She was very attractive even without any makeup. "Thanks." She wore faded jeans, a tight-fitting pink T-shirt and sneakers.

The nurse smiled. "I'll be waiting outside, Hilary," she said before shutting the door behind her.

"You wanna take a seat guys?" she said, pointing to the sofa nearest the door.

Chisholm nodded and they sat down.

Stapleton remained standing. "First goddamn visitors I've had; you believe that shit?"

Chisholm smiled empathically. "I'm sorry to hear that, Hilary."

"You have no idea. I'm going out of my mind." She closed her eyes and laughed. "Do you know how that feels, huh?" Tears filled her eyes.

Chisholm shook his head as Reznick stared back at her. She seemed to Reznick to be ricocheting between depression and mania, unsure where the mood was going to take her.

Stapleton sat down on the sofa opposite and leaned forward, crushing the cigarette into a glass ashtray. She looked at them long and hard for a few minutes. "I'm sorry."

Reznick said, "You've nothing to be sorry for, Hilary."

The tears filled her eyes again. "Thank you. I like it when people are nice to me. It's just that..." The words fell away and she looked up and smiled. Her mood was changing by the second.

Chisholm leaned forward, hands clasped. "Hilary, we very much appreciate you seeing us. My name is Sam Chisholm; I'm from the FBI. And this is a colleague of mine."

Hilary smiled. "Nice to meet you both."

"Now," Chisholm said, quickly clearing his throat, "we just want to chat with you. We don't want to write anything down and make you feel uncomfortable."

Her face relaxed. "I don't like it when people write things down when I'm here. It's like they're judging me. They don't know me."

Chisholm smiled. "Absolutely, Hilary. OK. We've got a few questions about a guy you know."

"What guy?"

"Hilary, what can you tell me about Adam Kendrick?"

She closed her eyes for a moment, as if composing herself. Then she began to bite her lower lip. "Why do you want to know about him?"

"It's nothing major. We're just trying to find out a little bit about him."

Stapleton stood up. She was rigid. Staring straight ahead. "I'm going to need more information," she whispered.

Chisholm nodded and let out a soft sigh. "What do you want to know, Hilary?"

"Do you think he still loves me?"

"I'm sure he does, Hilary." She nodded. "Let's sit down, Hilary, and tell me about him."

Hilary sat down slowly, crossing her legs. "Things were great at the start. He was attentive. Caring. I was in love." She stared off into the middle distance. "But there were differences."

Chisholm nodded. "What kind of differences?"

"I like music, I like to dance, have fun, drink, smoke pot, have a good time; you know what I'm talking about?"

Reznick nodded. "Sure."

"He didn't like my friends. He liked sports. He ran ninety miles a week sometimes. He rowed. He was down in his basement gym at all hours of the night. He meditated. I mean, for chrissakes, I'm open-minded, but that's fucking nuts, right?"

Chisholm smiled. "So, you had different lifestyles. Did he take drugs of any sort?"

"Absolutely not. Categorically fucking not. He hated me smoking. He'd put me out in his back garden, like a dog, in all weather, while I smoked myself crazy."

"How did you meet?"

"My sister lives in DC. I visited and we went out to a few clubs. I was stoned and slipped on the floor and fell onto a broken glass." She pulled up her T-shirt and showed a scar across the top of her breasts.

Reznick and Chisholm averted their gazes.

"When I went to the hospital, I was covered in blood, and then I met Adam."

Chisholm nodded. "And you hit it off?"

"I liked that he was so kind. I wanted to see him. I wanted more than that, to be honest. I think I'm a nymphomaniac, but I've still to be diagnosed for that."

Reznick struggled not to laugh.

Chisholm cleared his throat. "OK, Hilary, so, you wanted to see him again?"

"Yeah, so I started phoning him, and eventually he agreed to see me for a coffee. We talked. I had taken my Xanax, so I was OK."

"And it grew from there?"

"Slowly. Very slowly. I was working eighty hours a week on Wall Street, and by the time the weekend came, to see Adam, I was exhausted. But when I saw him I felt alive. Full of energy."

Chisholm pinched the bridge of his nose. "Can you tell me what he was like to be around?"

Stapleton shook another cigarette out of the pack that had been lying on the table and lit up. She inhaled deep into her lungs and blew the smoke away from them. "What can I tell you? He was nice and gentle. I think he was trying, at least in the beginning, to save me from myself."

Chisholm nodded but said nothing.

"He hooked me up with a therapist he knew. I didn't like him, but I persevered, because Adam wanted it for me so much. He really did. But then it all kinda, I don't know, started to change."

Reznick said, "What started to change?"

"Him. At least I think it was him. He started paying less attention to me. He seemed very cut off, all of a sudden."

"When did this start?"

"Earlier this year. I was convinced he was seeing another girl."

"And was he?"

Stapleton rolled her eyes. "He's a guy... I don't know, maybe. It was hard to figure it out. I kept on asking him if he was happy, but he didn't want to talk about things. Not even his work, which he used to like doing. He really had a mission to save people. I don't know; this is probably not making much sense, right?"

Chisholm said, "Was there one trigger for you guys breaking up?"

"It all started, I guess, when he came back from a trip."

"A trip where?"

"I don't know. He just said he went on a trip to find himself for a week."

"Go on."

"When he came back, well, about a week after he came back, I thought I was being followed."

"Followed by whom?"

"I had an apartment in Battery Park, and I reported a prowler around my block, a man acting suspiciously, as if he was checking on me, spying on me."

"Did you report this to the police?"

"Yes I did. NYPD. Check it out if you don't believe me."

Chisholm reached forward across the table and patted the back of her hand. "We absolutely believe you, Hilary."

Stapleton dragged again on the cigarette and watched the plumes of smoke fill the room. "I looked out of my window a few times and was convinced I saw people photographing me."

"Hilary, I don't want you to take this the wrong way, but was this just paranoia on your part?"

"No. This was plain as day. It was a man. Sometimes in the shadows. I didn't like it. The police thought I was a crazy lady."

Chisholm smiled. "The doctor said you've been doing PCP. Couldn't this have led to paranoia?"

"I'm telling you, I didn't take PCP. You've got to believe me. It was Adam. He laced the joint. I know it."

"Why would he do that, Hilary?"

Stapleton went quiet for a few moments, a look of uncertainty crossing her fine features. "I think he was playing games with me. I think he's a monster."

Reznick smiled empathetically at Stapleton and then exchanged a knowing glance with Chisholm. Chisholm got up and went over to Stapleton and sat down beside her, taking her hand.

"Hilary," Chisholm said, "we need to know all about Dr Kendrick."

"When I look back now, I can see that I was a toy for him to play with and then throw away. I think he arranged for me to be watched, to be followed so that I would become paranoid. Maybe to keep an eye on me; I don't know for sure. Then the PCP to finish me off. My breakdown, and now I'm here." Stapleton laughed, tears filling her eyes, before she leaned forward and stubbed out the cigarette in the glass ashtray. "No one believes me. Everyone thinks I'm a crazy loon who is trying to blame someone else for her problems. But believe me, Adam isn't the kind doctor type he makes himself out to be. There's something so dark and scary about him, I feel I don't ever want to fall asleep. I'm telling you, I get afraid even thinking about him."

"OK, Hilary, anytime you want, you just say, and we can stop this interview if it gets too upsetting."

Stapleton stood up and walked to the window. "Within twenty-four hours of arriving here, I was self-harming." She pulled up her jeans and showed cuts to her shin and back of her calf. "I was losing my grip on reality. I needed to try to feel something. I felt the knife go into my skin. It felt good. For the first time in a long time, I felt at peace."

Chisholm nodded. "I think you've been through a helluva lot. And I'm glad you're getting the help you need here."

Stapleton stood up and walked to the window. "Feel like I'm

in a fucking zoo. Fat-assed nurses talking about art therapy, cognitive therapy bullshit; I mean, gimme a break, I just need some quiet. Is that asking too much?"

"No, it is not."

"Thank you. Thank God somebody gets that. Since when has it been wrong for an American, in America, to want to shut the door on the world and just be left alone?"

Chisholm smiled and nodded along. "That's not wrong. I know where you're coming from. Every single day of my life, I want to shut the door on the world. I mean, who needs that shit?"

Stapleton flung back her head and laughed. "You guys are fun. Wasn't it Sartre who said hell was other people?"

Reznick smiled but said nothing.

She ran a hand through her hair. "I always envisioned the Feds to be real cold bastards. You're not so bad."

Chisholm said, "You kidding me? Just ask my kids; I'm as soft as they get, trust me."

Stapleton got a faraway look and tears filled her eyes. She had changed. There was sadness in her eyes. "Always envisioned having kids. You know, cuddling up to them, being with them, nurturing them."

"It's not too late."

"I had visions of Adam and myself, me a stay-at-home mom, baking bread with my daughter, or son, take your pick... yeah, baking bread, that would've been nice."

"Did you ever talk to Adam about this?"

Stapleton turned and looked out of the window. "I saw, certainly in the early days of knowing Adam, a gentleness that I'd never encountered in a guy before. The way he looked at kids or expectant moms. He talked a lot about how America seemed to have lost its way. Its ideals had gone. It was all about the family, he would say. And I thought he would make a great father."

Chisholm nodded. "Did he ever talk about his friends or family? Did you ever meet them?"

"Never."

"What about old girlfriends? College buddies, that kind of thing?"

Stapleton turned and stared across the room at Chisholm. "Why do you want to know that?"

"We're just trying to build up a picture."

"Of who?"

Reznick said, "We need to know more about Adam."

"Is that right? But you've not answered my question. Why do you want to know about any old girlfriends?"

Reznick leaned forward and smiled. "What we're looking for is very important to us, and we're hoping you can fill in any gaps in our knowledge. You've been very helpful so far."

Stapleton smiled and walked back to the table and shook another cigarette out of the pack before lighting up. "You're not telling me the full story, are you?"

Reznick said nothing as the room filled with tobacco smoke.

Chisholm's expression changed. "Look, Hilary, if you can't help us any further, that's fine; we'll be on our way."

Hilary held up her hand as if to stop them. "I never said I can't help you. I want to help you. If you need this information, for whatever reason, fine."

Chisholm said, "So were there any old girlfriends that you knew of?"

"I asked him about that once. He said there was a girl a long time ago, in the 1990s. He sometimes called out a name in his sleep. He would sometimes wake up in a cold sweat, panting hard, in the middle of a nightmare. I don't know." She screwed up her eyes. "I think she had a foreign-sounding name. Russian."

Chisholm tried to appear disinterested, scratching his chin. "Russian, eh?"

"Yup."

"Did he talk about this girl?"

"Only the once. They were planning to get engaged but she died. He wouldn't elaborate. But I could sense a sadness there."

"What about a name; can you remember the girl's name?"

"Kristina, I think."

THIRTY-ONE

A couple of hours later, Reznick and Chisholm were around the conference table at the Department of Intelligence for a real-time video link with the rest of the special access group. General Black took the chair as they hooked in with the Pentagon and three White House national security special advisers.

Black took off his spectacles, shrugged and gazed around at those at the table and on the video link. "Hard to know where to start." He looked back across at the huge screens showing the interested and tense-looking faces at the Pentagon and in the Situation Room at the White House. "If it's OK with you guys, I'll let Sam Chisholm give the update." A few nods.

A Pentagon intelligence specialist called James McCormack said, "That's fine. Go right ahead, Sam."

Black leaned back in his seat and nodded in the direction of Chisholm.

Chisholm blew out his cheeks and looked at the screen, glancing quickly at the notes in front of him. "OK, people, anyone want to add anything, jump in. Here's what I know." Over the next fifteen minutes, he outlined the revelations about Kendrick's previous girlfriend Hilary Stapleton and the possibility Kendrick's girlfriend before her was a Russian called Kristina. They listened in rapt silence, all taking notes. When he had finished, he opened it up.

General Black looked across at Reznick. "What are we missing here, Jon? I've got FBI counterterrorism, the NSA, the CIA, Homeland Security and every goddamn expert at the Pentagon scratching their heads on this." He glanced at the screens. "Jon is part of our team and has been working closely on this from day one."

A few nods.

Reznick said, "I'm thinking a cell. Government backing."

A few murmurs from those at the White House Situation Room.

Black said, "What about Kendrick? I think it would be fair to say that there are some within the intelligence community who are not as convinced on Kendrick as you are."

Reznick shrugged. "Well, there are strong indications of loose Islamic connections – perhaps cutouts – to Kendrick. Why is that? Who knows? Let's chase down the leads; that's what I would do. Was there a former Russian girlfriend? Also, what about the missing three months?"

General Black rubbed his eyes and looked across at Stamper. "Are we still waiting for details of Kendrick's past?"

"Yes, we are. We're still filling in the blanks."

Reznick said, "Roy, what's taking so long?"

Stamper's gaze fixed on Reznick, who returned the look. "The FBI has allocated major resources to this investigation, and Kendrick is not the only avenue we are pursuing."

Reznick said, "Didn't Assistant Director Meyerstein ask for this forty-eight hours ago?"

A long silence. "Yes, she did. As I said, we're still working on it. Do you know how many aid agencies and government agencies provide medical assistance during natural disasters, wars, what have you?"

Reznick shook his head.

"Hundreds. And we're checking and rechecking incomplete records as far back as the last couple of decades to see where Kendrick fits into this."

Reznick sighed.

"You don't look satisfied with the answer, Reznick."

"I'm not."

Stamper's face flushed. "Look, I don't take orders from you, Reznick. Are you clear on that?"

"This is not about you, Roy. This is about this goddamn investigation. It's about the disappearance and murder of O'Grady. It's about a critically injured FBI special agent, Morales, a dead Islamic convert originally from Chicago, his goddamn sister in the East Village. It's about a missing intern. It's about who took down your boss in broad daylight. And it's about trying to piece this jigsaw together. You want me to go on?"

"Who the hell do you think you are, coming in here, telling me what I should or shouldn't be doing?"

General Black held up his hand to restore order. "OK, let's take this down a notch." He looked across at Stamper, who had now flushed a bright red. "It is true that you don't answer to Jon Reznick. But he was only asking a simple question. He is part of this team in an advisory role."

Stamper shook his head, his lip curling in a sneer. "In answer to your question, we should get something within the next twenty-four hours. There's a hole in Kendrick's timeline in the 1990s, a period of three months spent away from the hospital in the US. Once we know that, I can give the group what it's looking for."

Reznick nodded. "Appreciate that."

An awkward silence followed amid rustling of papers.

General Black said, "Let's move on. Roy, that's the last I want to hear of this. Jon is part of this team."

Stamper closed his eyes for a few moments. "Look, I'm sorry about that. It's just that this is very close to home. It's rattled us all." He looked across at Reznick. "We're chasing down the leads on Kendrick, I can assure you, Jon. As soon as I get something, you'll be the first to know."

Reznick said, "As General Black says, let's move on."

General Black nodded and looked over at Chisholm. "OK, Sam, what else is on the go?"

Chisholm said, "The question we keep coming back to is how Kendrick fits into this. So Jon's right to maintain focus on this guy. There are links."

Black said, "What links? It's so sketchy."

"We can't pin him down, I grant you. But a couple of our people have noticed some chatter on some hardcore extreme-right white militia blogs, too. New York has been mentioned. Encrypted messages about bombing a synagogue on the Upper East Side. They might be cranks. But we can't rule them out being linked to Kendrick."

"You kidding me?"

"No. Three separate hidden messages on militia boards. Oregon, Wyoming and Michigan. 'Our time will come,' 'our time is nigh,' seem to be the phrases appearing, posted from here in America, but all untraceable so far. Talking about Jewish blood flowing down Fifth Avenue."

Black said nothing.

"They're using similar phrases. In addition, quotes from the Bible, apocalyptic messages written, we believe, by the same person or people."

Black said, "They're communicating with each other? Signaling what?"

"A couple of the groups, American Resistance and American Front, have some fringe elements, and we're monitoring what they're doing."

A hand from the Pentagon feed. "Can I jump in, General Black?"

"Sure."

"Lt Colonel Jack Anderson; I can confirm that Fort Meade has highlighted numerous channels going through several militias as well. We're working closely with Sam's team to track them down."

General Black said, "As it stands, we have Islamists, militia, a DC surgeon coming into our field of vision. It doesn't take an expert to see that something is not adding up."

Chisholm piped up. "You're forgetting the Russians. What the hell are they doing? I just don't get it."

Reznick said, "I think they're proxies. Would they be dumb enough to use militias or Islamists to further their cause?"

The Pentagon guy put up his hand. "When it comes to Moscow, you can never rule anything in or out. You want me to remind you of Anna Chapman and those nice Russians living as American suburbanites? That was deep cover."

General Black nodded. "Everyone round this table knows the Russians like to play the long game."

The Pentagon guy nodded. "The Russians, in the case of Chapman, had carefully integrated into their American lives. Eleven were arrested with the Russian intelligence service pulling the strings. False names and backgrounds, including stealing the ID of a dead Canadian. That was very well thought out. A few lived under their real names, but this was a Moscow operation. They controlled it."

General Black interjected, "OK, so we've got some level of Russian involvement. That is very worrying. But what is the motive? What is their rationale?"

The Pentagon guy said, "I'll tell you what. This is a new cold war. They're wanting to get us off balance. Islamists, militias, maybe they are the proxies. But the fingerprints of Moscow cannot be erased."

General Black said, "Look, I think we're going round in circles. The question that I don't think we've really addressed is, what is the endgame for whoever is pulling the strings? Is there a target? Is there a mission?"

The Pentagon guy spoke first. "As has been suggested before, the 9/11 timeline is looming large. We've got a lot of people in New York on that day."

Reznick said, "Like who?"

Chisholm said, "The commander in chief himself, no less. But we have no indications as to who or what the target is."

A silence opened up for a few minutes.

The Pentagon guy spoke first. "We're wondering if this Kendrick was turned while overseas."

General Black pinched the bridge of his nose. "Sam, what is the FBI saying to this?"

Chisholm flicked through some briefing papers before looking across the table at Black. "We concur with the 9/11 timeline analysis. The problem is Kendrick. We just can't get a handle on where he fits in. Does he have a hatred for the US government? Has he been radicalized? Ethiopia? Venezuela? Is he on the Moscow payroll? He has worked in the Third World: Nicaragua, across Latin America, Venezuela."

The Pentagon official put up his hand again. "That's very interesting, what Sam is saying. However, these countries change. Take Ethiopia. Russians disengaged. Ethiopian People's Revolutionary Democratic Front is now in power, which we back."

Chisholm nodded. "What I'm saying is we can't rule anything in or out. Kendrick was in Ethiopia in the 1990s when the Russians were still on the ground. The presence was there. We're also looking at Iranian intelligence to see if they are driving this whole thing, using former Soviet networks to carry out an operation, but as it stands, nothing concrete."

The discussion went round in circles for the best part of an hour. Reznick listened as some wanted to stress the Iranians, whilst others pointed at the influence of Russia, or perhaps disaffected KGB aligned to powerful oligarchs, or Islamists in the West.

Reznick waited until everyone had had their say before he spoke up. "Perhaps it might be more helpful to strip away the geopolitical stuff and get down to the street level, to see what is happening."

General Black shrugged. "You wanna explain, Jon?"

"I mean, let's think back to the fundamentals of what we know. Let's start with McGovern. I believe she was a cutout for this operation. And here's what I think. Take it or leave it; doesn't matter to me." He leaned forward and looked around at those at the table before snatching a glance at those watching on the screen. "Kendrick is a white Muslim convert."

A look of strained faces up on the screen and around the table.

Chisholm blew out his cheeks. "It is possible... Is it likely? I'm not so sure."

General Black looked across at the Pentagon guy. "What are your people saying?"

"We've still to complete analysis on this, but this is a strictly minority view. Three out of fifteen strategic intelligence analysts say that may be the driver for this. But we can't rule it out."

Stamper shook his head. "Sorry, guys, I'm not buying that. Are you seriously telling me that this guy is not only a Muslim convert – which he seems to have done without anyone else noticing, including every imam on our payroll and every FBI informant at every goddamn mosque in America – but that he is a direct threat to this country?"

Reznick said, "I once read that there are more than seventy-five thousand white and Hispanic Muslim converts in the US."

Stamper said, "It's a long shot. I mean a stretch. No proof."

"We have Jamal Ali dead and Akhtar under arrest, both linked to Chantelle McGovern. She in turn is spotted at the same restaurants as Kendrick. So what's happening with her? What's she all about? Another long shot coincidence? I don't think so."

The red light on Chisholm's Blackberry – sitting on the table in front of him– began flashing. He picked it up and scanned the message.

General Black said, "Any updates for us, Sam?"

Chisholm stared at the message for a few moments before he looked across at Black. "That was the fingerprint guy at Port Mortuary in Delaware. There's been a development with regard to identifying the two Russians."

THIRTY-TWO

The military mortuary in Delaware was run under the auspices of the Department of Defense and was one of the biggest in the world. Low buildings with swathes of tinted glass. Reznick had visited once before when a Delta buddy was killed in Iraq. The mother wanted him to be there to ensure everything was just so. He'd never felt so empty in his life. He remembered when the boy, because that's what he had been, arrived in the aluminum transfer case, packed in ice inside a large refrigerator, along with a dozen other soldiers who had been killed on duty.

Port Mortuary, officially called the Charles C Carson Center for Mortuary Affairs, was where they brought the men and women killed on 9/11 at the Pentagon for processing. His own wife, who died on 9/11, had been turned to dust. No body for him. No closure.

His mind flashed back to the wailing of relatives as their dead loved ones arrived home from Iraq. Mothers and fathers sobbing, hugging each other for comfort. The crying echoing around the building as they waited.

Reznick was on edge as he followed Chisholm. They were ushered through an atrium with plants and a fountain. A motto on the stone wall read, "Dignity, Honor and Respect" above a commemoration of those soldiers who had fallen in wars and terrorist attacks in modern US history.

The list seemed to go on forever. Vietnam: 21,693 deceased... Mass Suicide, People's Temple Cultists in Guyana: 913 deceased... Terrorist Bombing of Marine Headquarters in Beirut, Lebanon: 237 deceased... Operation Iraqi Freedom: 3,431 dead or missing in action.

He looked at two doors, one labeled "Counseling" and the other "Meditation." He wondered which one a bereaved family was to choose. They were led down a series of corridors until they got to the director's office. The door was open.

James Mulcahy was standing stern-faced. He was tall, barrel-chested, cropped hair shaved to the bone. He wore a navy polo shirt and cargo pants. He stepped forward and shook their hands. "I believe one of our fingerprint specialists has already been in touch," he said.

Chisholm nodded.

Mulcahy shut the door behind them before sitting down behind his large mahogany desk. "Look, I'm really sorry about this, but I'm afraid this journey has been a bit premature. Take a seat, guys."

Reznick and Chisholm sat down as Mulcahy adjusted the gold-framed picture of his family on his desk.

Chisholm shrugged. "I'm sorry, I don't follow."

Mulcahy sighed, huge hands spread out on his desk. "The fingerprint specialist who is one of your guys is quite new here. By new, I mean wet behind the ears. A matter of days. He doesn't understand the protocols that exist. These protocols ensure that each and every process is done logically, with regard to the needs of the dead soldier's families taking precedence over everything."

Chisholm scratched the back of his head, obviously getting frustrated. "Of course, I appreciate there are protocols; that's only right. But I was told there had been an important development in the identification of the two bodies brought in from New York. It's vitally importantly that they are identified as soon as possible."

Mulcahy's gaze fixed on Reznick for a few moments. Reznick met his gaze and Mulcahy looked away. "Firstly, like I said, the fingerprint guy should not have contacted you directly. Secondly, the autopsies haven't even been started."

"Hang on, are you kidding me? They've been here for nearly forty-eight hours."

"I appreciate that. But we have other priorities. A planeload of dead Marines, thirteen to be precise. Blown up by a rogue Afghan army officer. That takes precedence, I'm afraid."

Chisholm leaned forward, forearms resting on his thighs. "Listen, I need these bodies identified. You can do it now."

Mulcahy sighed. "I don't think you understand how it works. We don't have to answer to the FBI. We answer to the parents and loved ones of the brave men and women who serve this country. The procedures are very detailed."

"Listen again. We are running a sensitive investigation that has implications for national security. And we need to find out about the two dead bodies which were brought in here."

"They'll be dealt with like all the dead bodies which arrive here. They carry the 'believed to be' status, meaning identity can be confirmed only here."

Reznick knew from bitter personal experience that all dead soldiers returned to Dover were tagged "believed to be" until their identity could be confirmed officially after a series of exhaustive forensic tests.

Chisholm said, "I appreciate that, but..."

"I don't know if you do. The fingerprints will have to be examined, dental and full-body x-rays, DNA samples taken. Only then can the body on the table officially be given a name and formally identified."

Chisholm shrugged. "I hear what you're saying. But I want to speak to your fingerprint guy about what he knows."

"Look, he jumped the gun. I can't just go bumping two

unknown dead bodies up ahead of our guys because you are running some investigation."

"Are you fucking kidding me? Are you saying we've come all this way...?"

Reznick shifted in his seat, glad Chisholm had shown his displeasure.

Mulcahy put up his hand. "I run this place, not you. Do you understand?"

Chisholm said, "You want me to go above your head on this? Do you want me to call up the Office of Special Counsel and report what you're saying? Do you want them to know that you are hampering a critical investigation which has, as I'll say again, national security implications?"

Mulcahy leaned forward. "Don't threaten me. I answer to the US Air Force and the Department of Defense. We do things our way, with respect."

Chisholm took a moment to compose himself. "Maybe I'm not making myself clear. While I understand that the autopsies have not been done, I would nevertheless like to speak to the fingerprint specialist who contacted us about developments. Now, I don't think that's asking too much, is it?"

Mulcahy leaned back in his seat and shook his head. "Look, I deal with a lot of requests, from pathologists to anthropologists, forensic photographers, and Air Force Office of Special Investigation, all wanting priority access or information there and then, and it's just not possible. What you're asking for flies in the face of what we do. All I can say is that I'm sorry you've had a wasted journey, but as soon as we're in a position to conduct the full autopsies, including fingerprint analysis, and have the results, we will let your team know." He fixed his gaze on Reznick. "It's protocol. First, last, everything."

Reznick sighed and slowly stood up. He stared down at Mulcahy. "Fuck your protocol, you desk jockey. We need to speak to your fingerprint guy. Right fucking now."

A sneer crossed Mulcahy's large face. "Are you threatening me, son?"

Reznick stepped forward and grabbed Mulcahy by the throat, pressing hard against the carotid artery. "Listen, you fat fuck, this is how it's going to work. You are going to give us access now, or you won't be able to swallow for a month." He squeezed tight for a couple of seconds and Mulcahy flushed a dark red, teeth clenched with pain. "Am I making myself clear?"

Mulcahy struggled and gasped for breath.

Reznick held tight, until he slowly released his grip. "So, I'll ask again. Can we see the fingerprint guy?"

Mulcahy gulped in air as he held his throat before nodding furiously.

"Is that a yes?"

"He's in his office," Mulcahy croaked. "By the water cooler."

Reznick turned and looked at Chisholm, who was nodding his head. "Thank you so much for your help, Mr Mulcahy."

It was a long walk down tiled corridors.

Chisholm spoke first. "That was out of line."

"He was out of line."

"That's not how I operate, Reznick. Do you understand?"

"Absolutely."

"Are we clear?"

"It won't happen again."

Reznick was wired. They took a right down a long corridor until they reached a cubby-hole office by a water cooler. The door was open, and sitting at a desk was a baby-faced dark-haired kid wearing a navy suit, white shirt, pale blue tie and shiny black shoes. He looked twenty-five, if that.

Chisholm approached the open door. "Are you the fingerprint guy?"

"Sir, Special Agent Lee Horowitz," he said. "I'm from the

Bureau but assigned to Port Mortuary."

The young man sprang out of his chair and offered his hand. Chisholm shook his hand and smiled at the kid. "You mind if we come in and take a seat, son?"

Horowitz flushed crimson and pointed to the chair opposite his desk. "Please, but I only have two chairs."

Chisholm sat down as Reznick stood and leaned beside the door, arms crossed.

Horowitz sat down. "I'm sorry, I believe I've been a bit presumptuous contacting you guys about identification of the two gunshot victims from New York."

Chisholm said, "We've smoothed it over with the director. OK, you called us, Horowitz. You said there were developments. We're all ears, son."

Horowitz took a deep breath. "I had started preliminary work on the hands, photographing them, checking the fingerprints, before we got the dead Marines in from Afghanistan. That became a priority."

"So, let me get this straight. You had started work, but then this had to be stopped until after the autopsies and identification of the Marines?"

"Absolutely."

Chisholm nodded but said nothing.

"It was only a few minutes I spent on both the two bodies from New York, but I saw similarities on the thumbs and forefingers of both victims."

"What kind of similarities?"

Horowitz turned his laptop around and tapped a couple of keys. Huge color close-ups of a male index finger appeared on the monitor. "Look really close; you see it?"

Reznick saw a wafer-thin gelatin-like sliver covering the small area where a fingerprint would be taken. "Shit."

"Indeed. I've still to do the analysis, but as a preliminary assessment, I would say that this is the residue from an attempt to thwart fingerprint detection technology. It might be glycerine, but it might be a glycerine/gelatin hybrid."

Chisholm stared at the image. "So, how does this help us identify them, Horowitz?"

"Sir, in my opinion, this is the residue from a highly sophisticated attempt to fool a biometric fingerprint scanner."

Chisholm nodded. "And?"

Horowitz looked up at Reznick and Chisholm. "Low-end optical fingerprint scanners can often be fooled with a simple image, but nowadays the scanners check for electrical current and blood flow. But there are numerous examples of how the characteristics of gelatin are similar to a human finger and can fool high-end scanners."

Reznick stared at the image and shook his head. "The clear gelatin allows the scanner to read a false fingerprint."

Horowitz nodded. "Precisely."

Chisholm picked up a pen and pointed to the gelatin residue on the photo. "What about liveness detection technology?"

"This type of thing can spoof most of what we have at US airports. That's the reality."

"How the fuck have we not sorted this out?"

Horowitz shrugged. "Take your pick. Design, cost, political will. As it stands, research is ongoing to find a balance between price, user-friendliness and security of the system. But the bottom line is the system is heavily flawed. And determined and sophisticated terrorists can circumvent fingerprint technology used in airports across America."

Chisholm rubbed his eyes and stared at the image. "OK, so what've we got? We've got an attempt by these two individuals to conceal their identities, right?"

Horowitz nodded.

"Next question. Who are these people? What about their true fingerprints?"

Horowitz grinned. "Thought you were going to ask me

about that." He tapped the laptop keyboard and two side-by-side fingerprints were on the screen.

Chisholm said, "What are we looking at?"

"Digitally enhanced fingerprints showing what we believe the full fingerprints would show, if the minute sliver of gelatin on the fingers was erased."

Chisholm bit his lower lip. "Hang on, so the fingerprints we're looking at were scanned and signs of the gelatin residue were removed, right?"

"Right. With a 0.04 percent degree of doubt, these are the real fingerprints of the man and woman with gunshot wounds."

"So you're 99.96 percent certain that these are accurate fingerprints on the screen. But there has been an attempt in the past to conceal their true identity; am I keeping up with you?" Horowitz nodded. "You got it, sir. And guess what else?"

"What?"

"We got a match. I contacted a source at the Russian Foreign Intelligence Service, and they said they had an exact match with our computer-generated fingerprint. That's why I wanted to speak face to face."

"Have they given the identities of these two individuals?"

"Not yet. They're waiting to get proper clearance to release that information. But they did tell me two things."

"What?" Chisholm said, grinding his teeth.

"Both the man and woman were Spetsnaz at one time."

Reznick's blood ran cold. "Russian special forces..."

"The thing is they aren't just Russian."

"I'm sorry, you're not making sense."

The fingerprint kid blushed.

"So what the hell are they?" Chisholm said.

Horowitz cleared his throat self-consciously. "Sir, they're also Chechens. Brother and sister. Islamists."

THIRTY-THREE

Three hours later, the full IDs of the two Chechens were on big screens in a conference room back in McLean. The talk was of another Boston-style bombing.

Chisholm stood, hands on hips, chewing some gum. He glanced round at the two sullen pictures up on the screens. "We got a major problem on our hands and it's coming at us from all directions. This is Anatoly Umarov and his sister, Kristina. Is this the one Kendrick knew?"

A deathly hush.

"We don't know at this stage." He cleared his throat. "Leave that aside just now. Anatoly is the one to focus on. He is the cousin of Caucasian insurgent leader Dimitri Umarov and one of his inner circle. And we believe he would have been acting on direct orders."

General Black stared at the picture, eyes hooded.

"The Umarovs are notorious. They are part of a radical jihadist movement that the State Department has classified as a threat to the United States." He pointed at the photo of Anatoly Umarov. "This guy, along with his cousin, reactivated a dormant Chechen suicide battalion, Riyadus-Salikhin. They are guerrilla fighters. They are linked to suicide bombings on Moscow's subway that killed forty people, the bombing of a luxury train that killed twenty-eight and an attack that nearly killed the president of Ingushetia. He is wanted by

Russia for kidnapping, homicide and treason. And his cousin is the self-proclaimed Emir of the Russian North Caucasus, an unrecognized Islamic state known as the Caucasus Emirate."

General Black leaned back in his seat. "This changes everything." He looked across the room at Chisholm. "This is clearly an Islamist operation, right?"

"The problem is, General, we do not have a clear, definitive assessment."

Black said, "What do you mean? This is clear as day."

Chisholm sighed. "I think it is imperative that we keep an open mind. We've got to question assumptions. But yes, also see different perspectives. We do not understand what the purpose of this mission was. Are they part of a cell? Are those two Chechens the cell? Is there something bigger going on behind the scenes? The analysis, as it stands, is not conclusive by any means, and we're still trying to see how Kendrick fits into the picture."

General Black pointed to a senior FBI counterintelligence specialist, Miles Griffin. "How does Kendrick fit into this? And please, Miles, spare me any management-speak. I've had my fill of it."

Griffin took off his glasses and leaned his elbows on the conference table. "We're looking at this from multiple angles. Motivation, behavior, counterterrorism, threat analysis, source intelligence, and we're pulling in CIA and Homeland Security know-how, and, as Sam says, we just don't get it. The cutouts are there. Jamal Ali visited Pakistan four times since he got out of jail. His sister is most likely the cutout, as Reznick alluded to from the outset. The intriguing aspect to all this is, and we keep coming back to this, the role of Kendrick. How does he fit into this structure?"

Black's face reddened. "What the hell are you talking about? What structure? Are you saying he is part of this Islamist cell?"

"Not at all. Let's leave aside Kendrick for a second. The latest analysis I've seen, within the last hour, does show that there is an escalating risk of terrorist operation in the US in the coming days. Timescale? Unclear."

The color seemed to drain from the General's face. "What?"

"Timescale is pointing to a terrorist attack, almost certainly Islamist in nature. But we're only forty-eight hours from the anniversary of 9/11. That's flashing us red lights big time."

Black nodded. "So all this – taking out O'Grady, the intern Lieber's disappearance, Meyerstein taken out, not to mention putting the squeeze on Froch?"

"The majority view from my analysis is that this group or cell, whoever they are, are making sure their guy gets a clean run at this. At all costs. But Kendrick is causing us all a real headache. Who the hell is he? No one knows."

Chisholm said, "We need to pull him in. Right now."

Black grimaced. "On what grounds? We have nothing. If we jump on Kendrick, we don't know if there is a plan B, C or even D. Not to mention the network would still be in place, on the ground, in America. I say the sound strategy would be to watch and wait."

Chisholm sat down in his seat and shook his head. "With respect, sir, I don't concur. My concern is that all these signals are going to get lost in the noise from the data that's pouring in."

Black glared across at Chisholm. "I don't give a rat's ass if you concur, Sam, because, where I stand, no one is able to give me a straightforward assessment."

Chisholm sighed. "This is not an exact science. We all know that. As it stands, the range of probability from analysis across the intelligence spectrum suggests that the possibility of a terrorist attack could be as low as sixty percent. But that extends right up to some analysts who are giving an eighty-nine percent probability, which can be translated into saying that there is a significant probability that an attack is imminent. Everyone believes Kendrick fits into this. But they're not sure how."

Black's face was like stone. "I'm finding it hard to get my head around the fact that Kendrick could be an Islamist. We have no concrete proof. Why the hell would an upper-middle-class white American head down this route?"

Reznick said, "Neither did a lawyer in Marin County whose son went to fight with the Taliban. A middle-class kid from a beautiful background in California. John Walker Lindh. Remember him? His father described him as a 'sweet kid'. I interrogated him after the prison uprising near Mazar-e Sharif. It happens. Good kids go bad. He wasn't a bad kid intrinsically. He was naïve. He wanted to learn about Islam. He developed fluency in Arabic. And then he got radicalized. He took up arms against America. So it happens. He went to Pakistan and joined a radical Islamic group in the North-West Frontier Province."

The rest of those around the table listened intently.

Reznick said, "The possibility must exist that something has happened to Kendrick. Did he convert, and was he then radicalized?"

Black said, "There is no proof of that."

"The possibility exists. And think about it. What phenomenal cover. White middle-class American, covertly protected by white Chechens. Easy for all to blend in, right? We all have the picture in our head of the Middle Eastern-looking guys with beards, toting machine guns or semiautomatics. Well, I've got news for you: the two Chechens in the morgue may just be the tip of the iceberg. These Islamists are willing to lay down their lives to avoid giving themselves up." He pointed at the screens. "Anatoly Umarov shot his sister and then shot himself to avoid us getting them alive. Fake fingerprints. That may point to a highly sophisticated operation. They may also be well funded. I'm telling you, we've got a major problem on our hands."

Chisholm said, "Froch was set up and has confessed that he was being blackmailed. This may point to a foreign government. Russia? We don't think so, but we can't rule them out. But we've got to focus on the possibility that the Chechens may be proxies for a Middle Eastern power. Syria? Iran? We just don't know. There might also be a parallel operation going on; the possibilities are endless."

Black said, "Let's focus on what we do know. Tell me more about these Umarovs."

Chisholm sat down and flicked through his papers. "The Umarovs deny that the Chechen separatist movement is linked to al Qaeda or any jihadist groups, and claim they only want independence from Russia. But Umarov's cousin as recently as 2011 expressed solidarity in an intercepted cell phone conversation with 'brothers in Afghanistan, Iraq, Somalia and Palestine'. Interestingly, his cousin has publicly attacked America, Russia, the United Kingdom and Israel for oppressing Muslims. He believes in Sharia law. And he is implicated in the Beslan siege."

Reznick said, "Here's something else to consider. We were identifying an Iranian Shia connection from early days. But I think we can say that if Chechens are involved this is far more likely to be a Sunni Islamist threat."

General Black said, "Wahhabis, like al Qaeda, is that what you're saying?"

"I'm not an analyst, but that has got to be a possibility. But I think you have to remember that bin Laden wasn't a Wahhabist. Most Islamic extremists followed the ideology of Sayyid Qutb, not Wahhabism."

An FBI intelligence expert was nodding. "That's a very good point indeed and easy to overlook. Wealthy Saudis and the Saudi government are the paymasters for Muslim Brotherhood chapters and hardline Islamists. And they're pulling the strings in Syria with their jihadist links."

Black's eyes were hooded.

Reznick said, "What about a foreign government pulling the strings?"

Chisholm stared back at him but said nothing.

"You know how it works, guys. A government doesn't want to leave their fingerprints on an operation. But I don't think we can rule out the Iranians. The Chechens are nice cover for them. Look at Bosnia way back in the 1990s. The Iranians were involved in supplying the Bosnian Muslims with large numbers of multiple rocket launchers and huge caches of ammunition. This included 107mm and 122mm rockets. All made in Iran. The Iranian Revolutionary Guard was very active on the ground in Bosnia, and the CIA estimated that around four hundred had been detached for future terrorist operations."

Black said, "Chechens being used as proxies?"

Reznick sighed. "The problem with all this conjecture is that we still can't pin down how Kendrick is involved. The doctor that likes to do good. The doctor that likes to row. The doctor that saves lives. The doctor whose ex-girlfriend is in a psychiatric unit accusing him of drugging her, and another girlfriend who is missing. Wouldn't that bother you if a girl you knew was missing?"

Black said, "But wasn't Caroline Lieber the one who was obsessed with him?"

Chisholm pinched the bridge of his nose. "Something is not right. Something is just not clicking into place."

Black said, "Is it possible that we need to start looking elsewhere?"

Reznick said, "Perhaps. But perhaps we still need to connect the dots with this guy. If what some of us are saying is correct, that Kendrick may be an Islamic convert, when did this happen? His ex-girlfriend didn't mention any Muslim sympathies or ties."

Black said, "Look, he's under surveillance 24/7."

Chisholm said, "I really think we need to bring him in."

Black said, "And say what? Are you in the middle of a terrorist operation, doc? I mean, come on."

Chisholm stared at Black. "We don't have to be so obvious. We could say that we are in the middle of an ongoing investigation and ask if he could help us. Ask him to fill in the blanks of his past. If he can't, why not?"

A few nods round the table.

General Black said, "Look, it's September eighth. We're watching him. His new cell phone is being tracked. We've got all the agencies working on this..."

Just then, there was a sharp knock at the door. Everyone turned around as the door opened.

Walking in, ashen-faced, head held high, was FBI Assistant Director Martha Meyerstein.

THIRTY-FOUR

It took a few awkward moments. General Black stood up first and led a long and generous round of applause as Meyerstein made her way to the table. "Christ almighty, good to have you back," he said.

Meyerstein's face was drawn. She looked gaunt. Her carefully applied makeup could not hide the dark circles around her eyes and the pallor of her skin. She looked fragile, almost vulnerable. She took the seat next to Black and reached for a glass of water, her hand betraying a slight shake. She looked at those around the table and smiled. "You don't get rid of me that easy, guys."

Some forced laughter before a palpable sense of relief swept through the room.

Chisholm shook her hand and sat down. "Great to have you back, Martha. Are you up for this already?"

Meyerstein cleared her throat. "I'm here. I'm not my usual hundred and ten percent. But I'll manage. OK, so where the hell are we?"

A five-minute overview briefing followed, outlining the latest theories on the two Chechens and the blackmailing of Froch.

Meyerstein listened intently but remained silent.

General Black said, "This Chechen link, in light of what happened to you and with what happened in Boston still fresh in all our memories, has to make us wonder if there are others. I for one don't believe these two are acting alone."

Meyerstein nodded. "Look, I'm coming at this cold. I need to get up to speed. And quick. I'm going to take the next couple of hours to read the briefings, updates and threat assessments we've got."

General Black looked around the table. "And when Assistant Director Meyerstein returns, she will be leading the investigation. Are we all clear on that?"

Murmurs of approval around the table.

Meyerstein smiled. "Before I disappear for a couple of hours, what's the latest on Kendrick?"

Chisholm said, "We're still missing part of his history. Something's not adding up. Roy's guys are busting a gut on this. They'll get it."

Meyerstein's gaze went around the rest of the room. "But when? Look, this guy Kendrick, something's wrong. I can't put my finger on it. Let's get some answers. And damned quick."

A few nods around the table. "OK, meeting adjourned. Let's meet up in four hours' time. Let's get to it." A shuffling of papers and everyone began to drift out of the room.

Meyerstein approached Reznick and took him aside. "Hey, I believe I owe you one. Thank you." She held his gaze for a moment and smiled. "I mean it."

Reznick felt all eyes on him. He was uncomfortable and shrugged off her gratitude. "Forget it. All part of the service."

Meyerstein gave a tired smile. She sighed long and hard. "I need to speak to you and Sam in private. Couple of things I'd like to run past you. But not here."

Chisholm and Reznick followed her out of the building and into the back of a waiting car. Meyerstein sat up front. They were driven in silence all the way to the FBI HQ in Washington, each lost in their own thoughts. Reznick sensed something was up. She knew something. But what?

She stared ahead, occasionally glancing at her Blackberry when its red light flashed, indicating she had a message.

The more he thought of it, the more he realized the investigation was in deep trouble. Was she going to tell them that she was no longer leading the investigation? Was that it?

The car pulled up at the security guard before being waved through. They took the elevator to the seventh floor of the Hoover Building and headed along a corridor to an electronic door. Meyerstein punched in a four-digit code and they went on through. Down a corridor flanked by the offices of the most senior FBI agents, until they reached Meyerstein's. Her name and rank were etched in silver on the glass door.

Meyerstein led them inside, where a young agent wearing a sharp suit and tightly knotted tie was standing by a window, waiting for them.

Meyerstein shut the door behind her. "Take a seat."

Reznick and Chisholm did as they were told. The young agent remained standing.

Meyerstein sat down in her seat and leaned forward. "This is Larry McNair; before you ask, he's new. He's an FBI counterespionage expert, electronic surveillance, all that stuff."

Reznick nodded and McNair smiled back.

"I've been doing a lot of thinking since I got out of the hospital. It's given me time to reflect on the investigation and how it has developed, or not, as the case may be. And I started thinking about how I'd gotten involved. It was right that I was assigned to head this, missing State Department official and all that. But then I started thinking about the special access program. What was the rationale behind that? I didn't give it much thought earlier. I just assumed the rationale was sound. Why wouldn't it be, right?"

Chisholm said, "It makes sense."

Meyerstein said, "Remember, Jon, we got the last number O'Grady called – Caroline Lieber – and I asked you and Roy to chase this down, which you did, and this led us to Kendrick.

But initially, I kept that information from the main grouping for a time. The main members of the special access program."

Reznick said, "Why was that?"

"I've thought of that. And you know what? I don't have the answer. A hunch, perhaps. Maybe just my cautious nature."

Neither Reznick nor Chisholm said anything.

Meyerstein continued, "This is difficult to explain. But I've felt that... I've felt that we're being second-guessed every step of the way. Something isn't right... I was attacked, drugged and left for dead in a goddamn State Department bathroom. I mean, how was that possible?"

Chisholm said, "Froch. He was compromised."

Meyerstein smiled. "Yes. But I believe there's someone else not connected to Froch who is playing us."

Chisholm ran a hand through his hair. "Whoa! What are you saying?"

Meyerstein said, "I don't know. But yesterday, I sent a secure message to McNair, who visited me in the hospital."

Reznick and Chisholm looked across at McNair, who stood looking slightly embarrassed.

"I asked McNair to help me out."

Chisholm shrugged. "In what way?"

"I wanted to make sure that none of the rooms and offices we had were being bugged."

Reznick sat back in his seat and shook his head. "You kidding me, right?"

Meyerstein shook her head. "You know what McNair found out? My office, which was allocated to me within the Department of Intelligence, and yours, Sam, along with the conference room we meet in, are all bugged."

Chisholm said, "Bullshit. Those offices will be routinely swept for bugs."

Meyerstein said, "This is no bullshit, Sam. McNair? Do you want to jump in here?"

McNair blew out his cheeks. "Absolutely. The listening devices are in the walls. Don't know how long they've been there. But it's a sophisticated job."

Meyerstein said, "And that's why, gentlemen, I brought you here. Someone is keeping tabs on what we're doing and why."

The revelation had come clear out of the blue. Reznick's mind was racing. The more he thought of it, the more he was wondering if there was anyone around the special access program he could trust.

Chisholm stared at McNair. "Let me get this straight, son. Every office used by those working out of the Department of Intelligence assigned to the special access program was compromised; is that really what you're saying?"

McNair flushed red. "It doesn't end there. We also found anomalies on the phone lines used by the team. Again, I've done the tests, and all came back with the same results. Someone is listening in on your work."

Chisholm's eyes became hooded. "Who we talking about?"

McNair said nothing and looked at Meyerstein.

Meyerstein leaned back in her seat. "Sam, this bug doesn't emit radio waves. That's how high-end this operation is. We would have to drill through the walls of my office at the Department of Intelligence to retrieve the bug to identify it. That in turn would presumably defeat the purpose, as we would have alerted those listening in that we were aware of them."

Reznick looked at McNair. "You say everyone? And that definitely includes General Black's office?"

McNair covered his mouth with his hand and cleared his throat. "The tests were conclusive. Two bugs in the walls of his office. Covert listening devices."

Reznick said, "I think we've got to assume that it wasn't bugged when it was built. It must've been recent."

McNair nodded. "Absolutely. A sweep of the building would have been done. Here's how it works. The traditional audio bug emits radio waves that can be picked up by a standard radio-frequency bug detection. But more sophisticated bugs switch frequencies. So what you need is technology that picks up the electronic noise from the device's circuitry. But these are only found if you are conducting comprehensive sweeps of the office and if they are emitting radio frequencies. Interestingly, the last time these were carried out was seven weeks ago."

Reznick leaned forward, hands clasped. "Fuck."

"This is something on a highly sophisticated level. Virtually undetectable with routine anti-bugging equipment."

Chisholm sighed, eyes closed.

McNair continued. "As Assistant Director Meyerstein said, these devices don't emit radio waves. For example, instead of transmitting conversations, bugs may record the conversation within the room. And the people that planted them can retrieve the devices as and when they like." He paused for a moment.

Meyerstein said, "Go on, McNair."

McNair said, "We've got military-grade equipment that can look for magnetic fields, or electrical noise given out by computerized technology in digital tape recorders, but most offices have photocopiers and computers, so the background noise is very difficult to deal with. But what we did was sweep the rooms using thermal cameras, and we detected the residual heat of a bug or power supply concealed in the walls. Simply put, the devices located hot spots where the bugs were."

Reznick said, "And you are certain that within these walls are these bugs that don't emit radio waves?"

"In my opinion, one hundred percent conclusive."

"Covert ops, no question." He turned to Reznick. "Where would you start in figuring out where these recording bugs came from and how they carried out the placement?"

Reznick sighed. "Tough one. OK, first, we can't rule out that these have been a permanent feature within the Office of the Director of Intelligence since the place was built. But I think it's a helluva lot more likely that they'd have been inserted by a two-man, maybe three-man team, one night, under the cover of maintenance. I trained CIA guys in just such work. The whole place could be done, the plasterboard walls pulled off and drilled back into place with bugs, a lick of paint. But to answer your question, where this came from, you need to head back to the start of this investigation. The special access program, I mean."

Meyerstein shifted in her seat. "It began when I got a call."

Reznick said, "A call, that's it? From whom?"

"A three-star general in the Pentagon; I'm not at liberty to divulge. He just told me that a special access program was up and running, and I had been tasked to head up the investigation with General Black."

Reznick smiled. "So this is from the Pentagon. Christ, that doesn't narrow it down much."

Meyerstein said, "Yeah, would they do the bug work themselves?"

Reznick said, "Specialists. CIA, perhaps?"

Chisholm said, "The question arises: what is the purpose of the bugs? Surely this was just finding O'Grady and a possible emerging security threat. But bugging the offices? I mean, what the hell is this?"

Reznick looked at Meyerstein. "The sophistication of the bugging perhaps narrows it down."

Meyerstein said, "Go on."

"Way I see it, the only people who have access to this facility and access to the technology is an American government agency. Intelligence, defense, clandestine, who knows?"

Meyerstein said nothing.

"Here's something else to consider. What do we really know about General Black?"

Meyerstein shrugged. "What do you mean?"

"I mean, who the hell is he?"

"He works out of the Pentagon. That is all I know."

Reznick looked at Meyerstein. "The way I see it, the people who requested the bugging of the special access program offices and the phones wouldn't have expected them to be found."

Meyerstein nodded. "Obviously, yes."

"They are assuming that we don't know that they are listening in. So, I reckon we've got three options. Option number one: go straight to General Black and tell him what we know. The response? Who the hell knows? Option two: keep quiet and find out who is behind this. Problem is, this is very time-consuming and moves the focus away from possible security threats. Option three: keep quiet and concentrate on the investigation."

Meyerstein looked at McNair for a few moments. "I am instructing you, Special Agent McNair, not to reveal what you know to anyone. We'll deal with this. Do you understand?"

McNair nodded. "Yes, ma'am."

"Head back to the Office of the Director of Intelligence and get back to work. You understand?"

"Absolutely."

McNair left the room, shutting the door quietly behind him.

Reznick let out a long sigh. "The whole thing is getting under my skin," he said.

Meyerstein said, "Me too. Sam, where would you go from here?"

Chisholm said, "My feeling is that we should be up-front. We have nothing to hide. We speak to General Black in private, letting not only him know but in the process those that are listening in."

"Jon, what about you? What do you think we should do?"

Reznick said, "I thought it interesting that in the meeting, Sam, you said that you thought we should bring Kendrick in. I would have taken what you had to say very seriously. But Black flat-out disagreed." He looked at Meyerstein. "What would you do if you were in Black's shoes?"

"I'd haul in Kendrick. He has questions to answer. Bringing

in Kendrick would alert those within any cell that we're on to them. However, I still think we should pull him in."

Reznick smiled. "So, you both agree that Kendrick should be brought in. I agree. I also think Black's option of wait-and-see is a risky strategy."

Meyerstein said, "So, how do we move forward with regard to the bugging of the offices? Do we speak directly to General Black?"

Chisholm said, "Absolutely."

Reznick sighed long and hard. "I'd go one step further. I'd say this should be raised with everyone else round the table. Put it right up front."

Meyerstein shook her head. "That would be like I'd ambushed him. I think it better to keep it restricted. But I'll speak to him myself. Face to face."

Reznick shrugged. "Whatever works for you. There is another aspect that should be considered. I agree you need to bring it to Black's attention, but for another reason. And it's this. He would either sit on that information and do nothing, or would pass on the information of the bugging to someone higher up within the Pentagon."

Meyerstein picked up a pen and began playing with it for a few moments. "And how would we ascertain if that information has been passed on and to whom?"

"Track his calls and emails and messages. Electronic surveillance."

Chisholm said, "Are you fucking crazy, Reznick?"

Reznick shook his head.

Meyerstein said, "Are you seriously saying we should consider this?"

"Your investigation has been compromised, perhaps from day one. You need to get to the bottom of this. And General Black may provide the answer."

THIRTY-FIVE

When they returned to the Office of the Director of National Intelligence in McLean, an exhausted Meyerstein went straight into the meeting with General Black and the other members of the special access program. Her train of thought was interrupted with flashbacks to the face of the woman who had carried out the attack in the State Department restroom. Knots of anxiety washed over her as she shuffled her papers. She took a few moments to compose herself, knowing all eyes were on her.

She had begun to think of broaching the subject of the bugging with Black while she listened to three senior intelligence experts – from the FBI, National Counterterrorism Center and Homeland Security – around the table confirming a real and growing threat with New York as the target city. She wondered how Black would react. Was she making the right call?

Her problem was that, although there was a convergence of views among the intelligence agencies warning of an impending yet unspecified threat, no one could agree what the target was and who would be carrying out the attack. The discussions became heated, not surprisingly. Black listened intently, scribbling on his notepad, as the debates raged.

The President's national security advisor said, "I've got to let you guys know that the President is increasingly concerned that we have not established the exact nature of the threat. I mean, what is actually going on?"

Chisholm spoke up. "Like we've said again and again, there are numerous strands. The kidnapping; the attempted murder of Meyerstein; Froch; McGovern; Jamal; Akhtar, who has decided to plead the Fifth; Chechens and, of course, let's not forget Kendrick."

"So why the hell aren't we bringing him in?"

General Black sidestepped the question. "My main concern is that the Chechens are the proxies for Iran or Syria, Sam."

A red light started flashing on the phone in front of Chisholm before he could answer. He picked it up, eyes hooded. "When? Keep with him?" He put down the phone. "Surveillance teams are saying Kendrick is now on the move. He just jumped into a cab on the East Side. We have three separate teams – one on a motorbike and two in cars – tracking his every move."

Black cut short the meeting. "OK, let's focus on Kendrick's movements and we'll reconvene in an hour."

Meyerstein said, "Jon, I want you back in New York with Sam and his guys until this is over. I think we're all agreed that's the endgame target. You OK with that?"

"What's the brief?"

"I want you on the ground as we continue the surveillance on Kendrick."

Reznick nodded. "You got it." He joined the rest of the team shuffling out of the room.

Meyerstein got up and leaned over Black. "You mind if I have five minutes of your time, General? Something important."

Five minutes later, they were in Black's huge corner office. He sat down behind his desk and leaned back in his seat.

Meyerstein sat down and stared across at Black. He sat, twiddling his thumbs, his gaze locked on to hers. She sensed malevolence within him just waiting to explode. He was keeping it in check. But only just.

He forced a smile. "You sure you're OK to be back working so soon after what happened?"

"I'm fine; thanks for asking. Still trying to get my head around it."

"I've got to say, Martha, what happened has shocked everyone. Truly shocking."

"General, this has been a difficult investigation from the start; I don't have to tell you that."

Black nodded sagely, steepling his fingers.

"You see, there's a couple of things I want to talk about. And I thought it best to talk to you in private on these matters."

"I'm glad you feel comfortable doing that."

"General, I'm not going to beat around the bush. The whole thing is far more complex than we'd first envisaged. A simple kidnapping, or so it appeared, but peel back the layers and we have Islamists, Chechens, the honey trap on Froch, what happened to me, Kendrick... It's all over the place."

Black cleared his throat. "I don't disagree with any of that. It's been hard. On you more than anyone."

Meyerstein sighed. "How is it possible for Froch's activities to go undetected? I just don't get it. And how the hell can a Chechen woman get access to a secure State Department office in Midtown Manhattan at the same time I was meeting Froch? Only a handful of people knew. We're none the wiser if Froch was directly implicated in that."

Black shifted in his seat. "Those are very good points. How indeed is that possible?"

His gaze seemed to linger too long. "What I'm getting at is that this special access program has been compromised. Do you want to know how much it's been compromised?"

Black put up his hands as if to silence her. "Martha, I understand you're upset and angry at what happened to you..."

"You're damn right I'm upset and angry. I've got a right to be. But this is not about me. It's about the investigation. And it got me thinking."

"Got you thinking about what?"

"It got me thinking about who exactly I can trust. And you know what I found?"

"What?"

"The only person I can really trust is Reznick."

Black shifted in his seat. "I'm sorry; I don't follow. None of what you're saying makes any sense."

Meyerstein took a few moments to compose herself before she said what she really wanted to say. "I brought in an expert, General." She outlined for Black what she had already told her team.

Black's face flushed dark red. "Are you out of your mind, Martha?"

It wasn't the response she had expected. She felt her cheeks flush. "Don't ever talk to me like that, General. I'm not one of your raw recruits at the Pentagon you can push around. Do you understand me?"

Black shook his head. "Now listen here, Meyerstein, I don't care if you're an assistant director of the FBI; you've crossed a red line."

"No, General, I've not crossed the red line. Someone else has. The very people who are bugging these offices and listening in on our conversation right now."

Black leaned forward, eyes black. "OK, let's for now leave aside that I wasn't made aware that you had sanctioned an electronic sweep of these offices. Now, are you absolutely sure there are devices there?"

"We are. No radio signals. Someone would need access and technical know-how."

Black sighed and shook his head. "I think it's important that we don't sidetrack ourselves with questions as to who was responsible for this and who ordered it at this stage, but focus on the investigation, and once it is concluded we can get to the bottom of that."

"You kicking it into the long grass, is that it? Are you refusing to raise this with your superiors at the Pentagon?"

"No, I'm not. While you are conducting the investigation, I will relay these findings to the White House directly and will authorize a full surveillance sweep with immediate effect. Are you OK with that?"

Meyerstein nodded. "Yes, sir."

"When I have some news, you'll be the first to know. Now, if it's all right with you, I've got around six hours' worth of analysis from five intelligence agencies to get through with regard to this emerging Islamic threat. I think we're done, don't you?"

Half an hour later, Meyerstein was on a Gulfstream heading for New York with Reznick and Chisholm three rows back, deep in conversation. She perused the latest analysis but her thoughts inevitably drifted to the bugging and Black's response to it.

The more she thought of it, the more she realized his response was unsettling. He seemed angrier that she'd carried out a sweep than at discovering the offices were being bugged.

She pushed those thoughts aside as she began to focus again on the myriad strands of the frustrating and complex investigation.

Why hadn't Stamper filled in the blanks on Kendrick's overseas work? Stamper was meticulous and wouldn't leave any stone unturned. He would get to the bottom of it. She knew that.

Reznick sat down beside her and handed her a hot black coffee. "Drink it; you look like you need it."

Meyerstein smiled. "Yeah, I guess so."

Reznick looked at the papers covering the table in front of them. "You're snowed under."

She sipped some of the piping hot coffee. "Tell me about it."

"I take it your meeting with General Black didn't go too well."

Meyerstein sighed before she relayed their exchange.

"So, where do you go from here?" he said.

"I feel very conflicted. The investigation is paramount. Distractions are not good. But bugging the intelligence offices? Who did this? Why? How long have the bugs been there? Is this connected to the special access program? Have they been in place for years? The problem is, Jon, these questions are going to be almost impossible to find answers to." She sighed. "What would you do?"

"I've told you what I would do. I would find out what General Black is up to and work it back from there."

"I need a judge to sign a warrant."

"Then get him to sign it."

"Might be a bit tricky, considering it's an unacknowledged special access program. Its very existence wouldn't be acknowledged, so that would be a catch-22."

"Then be more creative. Put him under surveillance without authorization?"

Meyerstein closed her eyes. "I don't know. Where does that end?"

"It ends when you learn who authorized the bugging. Listen to me; you see, all this smoke and mirrors, Froch, the murder of a diplomat, a missing intern, Islamists – I'm telling you, this is not a cell-like operation by one terrorist group. There's something else at work."

"What are you getting at?"

"Nothing is what it seems."

"Jon, you're getting pretty obtuse, if you don't mind me saying."

"Sometimes, just sometimes, the story you see is not the whole story. It's not even the real story."

"What the hell is this, Jon, some philosophical discussion?"

"Maybe."

Meyerstein's phone on her armrest rang and she picked it up. She listened intently, nodding a couple of times. "You kidding me?" She closed her eyes. "Superb work, Roy. Send it over to me. Right now." She ended the call.

Reznick said, "Development?"

Meyerstein pressed a button on her laptop and scrolled down the messages in her inbox. "You could say that." She came to one from Roy Stamper and double-clicked the attachment.

A grainy color picture showing bearded, battle-hardened Islamists wearing army fatigues. Reznick stared at the image, focusing on each and every man. Then Meyerstein took a pencil and pointed to a beautiful brown-eyed woman. "Kristina Umarov, the Chechen shot dead by her brother."

Reznick saw it was her immediately. "Jesus."

"That's not all." She pointed with the pencil at a ruggedly good-looking, bearded Caucasian guy in the middle. "Take a closer look."

Reznick leaned forward and stared at the picture, long and hard. The cold, blue eyes. Handsome face. Mid-twenties, perhaps. "Son of a bitch."

Meyerstein looked at the picture long and hard. "Dr Adam Kendrick just outside Grozny, Chechnya, sometime in the 1990s."

THIRTY-SIX

It took a few moments for Reznick to get his head round it. He stared at the image for some time. The same piercing blue eyes he'd seen in the photos in Kendrick's DC home. "How the hell did we get this?"

Meyerstein sipped her coffee. "Russian security services raided the homes of Chechen leaders and their associates as well as relatives of the Umarovs in the last forty-eight hours. We'd circulated an image of Kendrick a few days ago. And they found this in an old FSB filing cabinet, Kristina Umarov in the same photo as Adam Kendrick. One of my team, Special Agent Brian Martin, has gone over it ten thousand times with the latest facial recognition software. It's a perfect match for both. One hundred percent."

"What was his cover?"

"Russians think he slipped into the country while working for an American medical charity which is now defunct, American Medical Aid across Frontiers."

"Never heard of them."

"Neither have I. But in the time he said he was working for the Red Cross in Somalia, he was with them."

Reznick stared at the image. "Adam Kendrick. Who the hell is this guy?"

Meyerstein nodded. "I know. It's all pointing to Kendrick. But... I don't know."

Reznick looked out of the windows as the plane descended through the clouds and emerged into perfect blue skies as they began their approach to New York. His mind was racing. "We definitely have to bring him in."

A shudder from turbulence. Meyerstein said, "No. I want you to shadow him. I think there's a bigger picture here and we use Kendrick to get to it. But we keep tight on him to make sure he doesn't cause trouble."

Reznick sighed but said nothing.

"The problem is there's nothing in Kendrick's past to suggest Islamic links."

"Unless he's been converted abroad. Over time, become sympathetic, and ultimately radicalized."

"That's a journey and a half."

"As I've said, it's the same journey John Walker Lindh made. American Taliban, remember?"

"The problem is, with Lindh, everyone knew he had become a convert to Islam, a precursor to radicalization. With Kendrick, we still seem to be missing something."

Reznick nodded. "What about Stamper and his team?"

"They're digging further into Kendrick's past to come up with something. Stamper is convinced we don't have the full picture."

Reznick said, "No question about it. But in the meantime, the question about what to do with Kendrick."

"We stick with him real tight."

She looked across the aisle as Chisholm scrolled through emails on his Blackberry. "Sam." She cocked her head toward the seat at the opposite end of the table.

Chisholm sat down and sighed.

Meyerstein turned her laptop around. "Dr Adam Kendrick with some Chechen friends."

He looked at the pictures long and hard for a long time. "How did we get our hands on this?"

"As I just told Jon, Russian security services uncovered it at the home of a Chechen during a raid."

Chisholm said, "Martha, we need to bring him in."

"No. We shadow him. See who or what's behind this."

"Martha, you and I both know we need to get that bastard Kendrick out of sight and find out what he's all about."

"No. Let's hold fire and keep close tabs on him."

Chisholm said, "This doesn't sit right with me at all. Why the hell are you doing what Black tells you? You're leading this goddamn thing. It's bullshit."

"He has the veto as the chair of the program."

"It's bullshit. Don't let him tie our hands behind our backs, for chrissakes."

Meyerstein said, "The picture changes everything, Sam. We'll keep this to ourselves. See where Kendrick takes us."

"What do you mean, keep it to ourselves?"

"I don't want Black to know about this development."

"Why the hell not, Martha?"

"When I met with him earlier, he said he'd get on to the White House about the bugging of the offices. McNair is monitoring Black's phones. The only call he's made is to an unlisted number at the Pentagon."

Chisholm crushed an empty Styrofoam coffee cup and threw it on the floor. "This is getting crazier by the second."

Meyerstein sighed. "I know it's hard to contemplate..."

Chisholm said, "The bugging of the offices, Black, and now the photo of Kendrick with some Islamists. Nothing makes any sense."

"OK, here's what I want. Jon mentioned earlier about putting Black under surveillance."

"You can't be serious."

Meyerstein shook her head. "No. I want to do some digging on him. What's he up to? Who is he really working for? I want to know everything about him."

Chisholm showed his palms. "Whoa... are you serious?"

"Have you got a problem with that?"

"Yeah, very much. I think that's crossing countless lines."

"I'm not asking you to put him under surveillance. I want to know more about him. Simple."

Chisholm went quiet for a few moments before he spoke. "You want me to dig down into where he fits into this?"

"You have contacts all over, Sam. I want you to reach out to them. Discreetly, mind."

"This is risky. I'm telling you, Martha, if this gets out, someone's gonna get burned."

"I'm well aware of that. But you know what? Under the circumstances, I'm going to take my chances. I need to know what is really going on. Is there a separate agenda?"

"What do you mean by a separate agenda?"

"Let's see what you get for me, Sam."

Chisholm looked at Reznick for a few moments then let his gaze lower to the floor. "This is a the-end-justifies-the-means kind of thing isn't it?"

Reznick said, "It is what it is."

Chisholm let out a long sigh. "OK, leave it with me."

Meyerstein leaned forward and put her hand on Chisholm's arm. "Thanks, Sam."

The phone on her armrest rang again. "Meyerstein." She nodded. "Are you sure?" A beat. "Shit. Keep on it. We'll be landing in less than five minutes."

She ended the call. "That was surveillance on Kendrick. He's been dropped off in Queens and he's walking."

Reznick shrugged. "Walking? Walking where?"

Meyerstein sighed. "In the direction of Flushing Meadows. US Open tennis."

"What?"

"We've got him covered. He'll get a priority search."

"That's irrelevant. There could be some others inside. How the hell have we missed this?"

"The focus was on 9/11 commemorations."

Meyerstein felt a headache coming on, drilling deep into her head. "Look, we're landing at LaGuardia. Virtually on top of Flushing Meadows. We'll be there in fifteen minutes. I want you inside with the red team under Phil Gritz."

"And what do you want me to do?"

"You watch and wait. If he makes a move, you shoot to kill."

THIRTY-SEVEN

A few minutes later, the plane descended and landed at LaGuardia. Reznick was picked up by Gritz and his red team – all in jeans, T-shirts, cargo pants and sneakers – in an SUV and they headed to the stadium. Crowds surged all around the tennis complex. They pulled up half a mile from the stadium and stepped out into the broiling midafternoon sun.

Gritz put on his shades and a Panama hat as Reznick felt the sweat run down his back. "Weapons concealed at all times; we will be waved through by their security, OK? We're going to be running facial recognition software through all cameras around the site to identify any potential people of interest. This is a big place. And it can get a bit rowdy. It is New York, after all. What're we talking about? We're talking about 22,547 seats and ninety luxury suites. So a lot of area to cover. But the main focus is Kendrick. We stick with him when he joins a line for a soda, when he goes for a shit, and we mix it up. We change position every twenty minutes, so three new positions in an hour. The action is all going to be on the main court. Like I said, it's a big place. But it'll give us good cover to use binoculars at will."

Reznick said, "Where's he going to be sitting?"

"We'll know that when he enters the ground in a few moments. But we're going to be all over the place. We've got a few guys who will be taking up position shortly in the nosebleed seats. Mingling. Eating dogs. Doing what Americans do, right? We'll also get people in the suites, which are directly behind courtside, used by the banks and other corporate guys and sponsors. We will be able to keep a close eye on Kendrick from there, too."

Reznick said, "We got any more intel on Kendrick?"

"Nothing."

"What about any more of his Islamic buddies showing up?"

Gritz rolled his eyes as he handed out grounds tickets to his team. "We don't know shit. We do know that we need to keep tight on him. This might turn out to be nothing."

Reznick pulled on the white Nike baseball cap and then the shades, putting the ticket in his back pocket. He was teamed up with a young FBI kid, Tom Blake, a muscular, preppy-looking kid. "OK, son, let's do it."

"You got it," the kid said, veins bulging in his neck as if he liked to work out.

They disappeared into the crowds headed for the stadium, the smell of sweat and cigarettes mixing with the sound of raucous laughter. A few minutes later, they were in a huge line at the South Gate, directly in front of the Unisphere, the giant steel globe marking the 1964-65 World Trade Fair at the site. Fifteen minutes later, they were ushered inside the stadium by the security director and into a crammed concourse.

Lines of people already queuing for bottles of cold Heineken, Grey Goose vodka, Mexican food, mojitos, burgers and everything in between. Throngs of people making their way to their seats. The incessant drone of loud voices, hyper New Yorkers bawling into cell phones, people braying about the shit visibility from their seats. It was an assault on the senses. Lobster-red-faced corporate types wearing button-downs and pleated khakis, nouveau riche guys flashing their gold watches, a boozed-up morbidly obese guy wearing a Yankees hat dragging his overweight kids around, uptown

Manhattan women wearing designer summer dresses and carrying expensive handbags, the smell of liquor and cooking filling the air. Moet & Chandon hospitality signs fluttering in the light late-summer breeze.

Reznick and the kid headed up an escalator. His earpiece buzzed into life. "Jon, Kendrick has just gone through the gates. He's headed for the expensive courtside seats where you'll be sitting."

"Where exactly?"

"You will be situated behind the baseline on the south side of the stadium. You will be handed a courtside ticket from an usher. He's a Fed. Big black guy, Special Agent David Jackson. Can't miss him."

"OK, got that," he said as they made their way through the concourse as the crowds headed toward their seats for the semifinal match.

They stepped out from beneath the stadium and into the broiling sun. Reznick squinted. The Arthur Ashe stadium towered high, the promenade seats mostly empty. But in his area it was a lot busier.

A huge black usher stepped forward. "Tickets, guys," he said, slipping the tickets into their hands. He flashed them a smile. "Enjoy the game, guys."

Reznick nodded and they headed down to their seats. The kid was about ten yards from Reznick. He sat down as Reznick headed farther down the steps to his seat and saw the row. He squeezed past a chic-dressed black woman and her impeccably attired partner, who was wearing a sky-blue suit and Ray-Bans, speaking into a phone. He sat down on his seat at the end of the row, eight seats from the front. "Jon," Gritz said into his earpiece, "three down from you; you got a fix?" He scanned the row and saw Kendrick wearing brown tortoiseshell shades, a US Open Panama hat, white polo shirt and khakis, talking into a cell phone. "Great stuff, yeah."

"The section to your right; can you see Special Agent Blake?"

Reznick turned round and saw the kid, Blake, wearing a black Adidas baseball cap, pretending to read the New York Times. "Got him."

"OK, take it in turns. If he gets up, you follow him, Jon. Then alternate that with Blake. We've got plenty of cover beside the restrooms, agents working on the burger vans and even the Heineken stands."

"Nice."

Gritz gave a throaty laugh. "We're keeping a nice overview of that area, Jon, and I'm watching you on a monitor. We're all set up."

Roars from the restless, noisy and boiling crowd as people stood up all around when one of the players won a set. "Keep me posted."

The crowd whooped and hollered and high-fived and eventually sat down as the players took a two-minute break.

Reznick turned round and stole a glance at Blake, who was pretending to be on the phone. He wondered what the plan was. Was Kendrick planning to carry out a terrorist attack here live on TV? Was there going to be someone else involved?

He looked over towards Kendrick and saw he was still on the phone. That had been ten minutes.

The more he thought of it, the more uneasy he felt. It was a risky strategy to allow Kendrick free rein. But as he sat in the middle of a broiling tennis arena in New York, the anniversary of 9/11 a couple of days away, he did see the logic of letting the operation continue, if indeed it was an operation. Was this a reconnaissance? Predetermined? The problem was that no one knew a thing. All they had was coincidence, cutouts and a grainy picture taken in Chechnya. Did it all add up?

Did it, hell.

Slowly, the sun dipped behind the huge stands. His shirt was sticking to his back. He drank some cold water from a bottle.

It felt good. He poured some down his neck, which felt great.

Kendrick eventually ended the call and put the phone into his pants pocket. He lifted a pair of binoculars and focused on the action for a minute or two, despite having no need for them, as they were sitting so close. He pointed the binoculars higher toward the nosebleed seats diagonally opposite.

The earpiece buzzed into life. "You see what he's doing, Jon?"

"Yup."

"You see the game fine?"

"Great line of sight. Perfect view of both players. Unless you're nearly blind, no need for binoculars. No one around here has them. Anything or anyone of note in that area?"

"It's nearly empty."

Reznick stood up as a fat guy squeezed past. "Unless he's just curious."

"I don't like it."

"I guess we've got to just sit tight."

The earpiece went quiet as the crowd cheered another point.

Reznick's shades allowed him to scan anything he wanted. He caught sight of a roaming Heineken vendor with a portable keg in a backpack, dispensing beers.

His earpiece crackled into life. "Don't even think about it, guys," Gritz said. "Might be tempting. But let's focus."

Reznick smiled as more shouts, clapping and stamping came from those around at a winning point. The smell of hot dogs from a couple of huge white kids sitting with their plump mother, sporting a diamond-encrusted Cartier watch.

The waiting went on amid a hubbub of noise as the smell of fries wafted across the courtside seats. The place was like a zoo.

Half an hour later, Kendrick got up from his seat and headed up the stairs toward an exit.

Gritz's voice on the earpiece. "Blake, you take this."

Blake waited a couple of moments before he headed out into the concourse.

Gritz's voice. "Yeah, we got him." A long pause. "Blake's on his tail. He's on the escalators and is now entering the Aces restaurant on the club level between gates three and four."

Over the next half an hour, as Reznick sat amid the hubbub, he got updates from Blake and Gritz on Kendrick. Kendrick was eating alone. He drank chilled sparkling water with a slice of lemon, ate some sushi and then had some frozen strawberry yogurt. He paid the bill with an American Express.

A full forty-five minutes after Kendrick had left, he returned to his seat. He was immediately on the phone.

Gritz's voice. "He must be using a new, untraceable phone. Fuck!"

Reznick nodded and saw one of the players fluff a shot and groan and scream out loud. He felt like doing the same.

The noise levels cranked up a notch as the stadium began to fill up, the floodlights on and the action on the court hotting up. The sun was now down and the stadium was in shadow, but the humidity was high.

Reznick swigged some more water as the interminable match dragged on.

The voice of Gritz in his earpiece. "Jon, stretch your legs for ten minutes. Blake's got it covered."

"I'm looking at the back of the guy's head. Where are you?"

"Suite 110 northeast of where you are, but behind courtside seats. Watching you and Blake right now. You wanna move?"

"Yup. I can't see shit."

"Get yourself freshened up, and one of my guys, Special Agent Curtis Montgomery, will wait for you outside the bathroom and bring you along, make sure there are no accreditation problems with the US Open security guys."

"Crew-cut guy?"

"That's him."

"OK, I'll see him in a few minutes. Get someone to cover my spot."

"Leave that to me, Jon."

Reznick went to the bathroom and splashed some cold water on his face. He bought himself a large Coke from a hot dog concession stand and guzzled it down. The caffeine fix and sugar rush felt good. More alert. Then he spotted Montgomery, who cocked his head, and they headed to the suite where Gritz had set up base.

A quick knock by Montgomery and they went in.

Gritz was standing at the far end of the suite, staring through binoculars, as was his sidekick. He turned round.

"Any movement?" Reznick said.

Gritz offered his binoculars. "Take a look for yourself."

Reznick sat down and scanned the crowds where he'd sat. He brought the spectators into focus.

"You got it?"

A moment later, Reznick got a fix on Kendrick. "Yup." He sipped a large cup of water and placed it down between his feet. He took off his sunglasses and wiped the lenses with his T-shirt, then put them back on. He focused on Kendrick's face for a few moments. "What the hell you up to?"

The sky darkened further, tinges of red peeking through the gloom. Floodlights bathing the stadium as the evening wore on. The game seemed to go on forever. The crowd got louder. More boisterous. The place was jammed.

Grunts from the courts as the players toweled the sweat off between points.

Kendrick got up and took the steps to the exit, disappearing from sight.

Reznick's throat felt parched and he swigged some more water from a bottle. "Where's he going?"

A moment later, a voice in his ear. "We're on it. He's into the bathroom again; I got him."

Ten minutes later, Kendrick was back in his seat. The voice in his ear said, "OK, guys, probably nothing, but Kendrick just put in some contact lenses in the bathroom. This doesn't tally with his medical file. Twenty-twenty vision, by all accounts."

Reznick said, "Interesting."

The voice said, "Yup, we also didn't see him take any old lenses out, although this might point to him wearing prescription sunglasses."

Reznick looked at Gritz who was shrugging. "OK, copy that."

Gritz stared through his binoculars. "That's an anomaly."

Reznick nodded. He watched as Kendrick slid his shades into his shirt pocket. "Maybe."

Gritz groaned. "What the hell is he all about? What is he up to?"

"What's the latest intelligence on Kendrick?"

"No change. They're scratching their heads over this one. What is he up to? Where's the cutout? What's the point?" A long sigh and he cleared his throat. "OK, please be aware it's a full house. And that'll mean long lines for the restrooms and bars and just about everywhere else. The whole place is really jammed tight."

Reznick knew that, even with electronic surveillance and the dozens of Feds round the stadium, the crowds would make it trickier to keep tabs on Kendrick. Time dragged as the watch-and-wait continued.

Half an hour later, Kendrick got up from his seat again and headed up the stairs to the nearest exit.

Gritz said, "He's on the move, people. Guy's got ants in his pants. Montgomery, you're on this."

Montgomery's voice. "Got him." A long pause. "He's picking up a coffee. Heading back to seat."

A few minutes later, Kendrick returned. He sat down, sipped some coffee and proceeded to watch the tennis. He blew on the coffee and inspected the side of the Styrofoam cup.

Reznick stared through the binoculars, focusing on the cup. "White Styrofoam cup. Why is he still inspecting it?" He was transfixed, watching Kendrick examine the cup. Then he put it down, between his feet, beside a cup of water.

Reznick watched as Kendrick opened his eyes wide for a few moments as if his lenses were hurting. Maybe a bit of grit or dirt in his eye. But then again, maybe it wasn't grit. What if he wasn't used to wearing lenses?

He focused in on Kendrick's face with the powerful field glasses. Clean-shaven skin, glistening with sweat, chiseled jaw and steely gaze. "Green eyes."

Gritz said, "What?"

"He doesn't have green eyes."

"You sure?" Gritz punched in some keys on a laptop and pulled up the medical records. "Yep, color of his eyes is blue."

Reznick looked through the glasses for the umpteenth time. "I'm looking just now and see hazel-green eyes. You tell me what you see."

Gritz said, "What the fuck? Green eyes. Who the hell are you, Adam Kendrick?"

Reznick sensed something else was afoot. "We're onto something. People's eyes don't change color."

Gritz said, "Unless he is wearing colored lenses."

Reznick said, "The question is why? Why the change in eye color?"

"Jon, I'm not a fucking ophthalmologist."

"Neither am I. Run it by your analysts. Put it into the system."

Gritz nodded. He punched a number into his cell and relayed the change of eye color and the contact lenses. Almost immediately, one of Gritz's team responded. "Keep checking that." He ended the call.

Reznick's mind flashed to the image of Kendrick inspecting the foam cup. "Something's going down."

Gritz shrugged. "What?"

"I think Kendrick's just been given a hidden message, written on the cup."

THIRTY-EIGHT

Kendrick stared again at the words scrawled in ultraviolet pale blue writing, invisible to the naked eye, but clear as day through the specially tinted contact lenses. The noise of the crowd he could barely hear as he reread the short message for the umpteenth time to ensure he wasn't getting it wrong. The message said simply:

Treat yourself to a hot dog and Coke. Then wait. Then proceed to East 81st Street Hostel... this is your base camp.

His heart began to pound hard and his mind raced. The adrenaline was beginning to flow, his true intentions hidden from all in sight. He looked around and his heart sank. The American public in all their gory glory, unaware of the man sitting among them. His true intentions. Some waddling down the steep concrete stairs, carrying mountains of junk food and watching a sport they didn't understand or play. Pampered, morbidly obese, chugging back beer, wine, burgers and whatever shit they could stuff down their throats.

The Land of the Free of his childhood had become the Land of the Living Dead. A nation of fuckwits, halfwits and dimwits. People who worked their guts out so they could consume junk food and die premature, horrible deaths. A nation that had long ago given up the ghost.

He was not one of them. He hadn't given up the ghost.

Kendrick was part of a new breed. He had his orders. This was the moment he had waited for.

He took in a deep breath and dropped the cup onto the ground and kicked it away from his seat amid the rest of the trash lying around his feet.

Kendrick clapped a winner down the line and jumped to his feet alongside everyone else. He felt like an automaton. A robot. Preprogrammed. He was following orders. To the letter. He left his seat and bought a hot dog smothered in onions and mustard and a small Coke from a vendor. Just like they wanted him to. He knew they wanted him to blend in. It was mission-critical. They knew he despised junk food. But that was a small price to pay.

His heightened metabolism would burn off the calories almost as soon as it was ingested. He finished the dog, wiped his mouth clean with the napkin and washed it down with his sugary drink. He got up and chucked the paper and cup in a trash can at the end of the row.

Kendrick sat down again and wondered if this is what it was like to be high. His thoughts turned to the next step. The carefully planned exit from the stadium. Then his journey to the base camp.

The more he thought of it, the more he realized he was on the verge of greatness. But as he'd been reminded time and time again, patience and a clear mind were all that mattered.

And from there, he knew how it would all end. He could almost see it play out in his mind's eye.

Kendrick's mind flashed back to the sniper shot that killed the man called O'Grady. The man who had jeopardized the mission, they said. He remembered the struggle with the ropes. But he also remembered the surge of excitement he felt. They had set him a challenge. And it had been carried out. To the letter.

Kendrick's gaze wandered round the stadium under the full glare of the floodlights. One of America's great sporting spectacles. Little did they know how tonight would end in the smartest part of Manhattan.

THIRTY-NINE

In a secure conference room in the FBI's New York field office in Lower Manhattan, Martha Meyerstein was standing and staring, hands on hips, at a huge screen beaming back real-time pictures showing Kendrick at Flushing Meadows. Watching with her were half a dozen strategic intelligence analysts assigned to the special access program, trying to establish what threat lay over the horizon.

She felt her mind wandering ever so slightly, thoughts flashing back to the attack on her. The woman's face. She felt fragile after being rendered unconscious by the fentanyl. Her vision was blurring occasionally, but she didn't want to alarm those around her. She wished Sam Chisholm and Roy Stamper were with her. She always found it useful to listen to other theories and ideas coming from those she trusted closely, to get a full appraisal of any given situation.

What she wouldn't give for them to be here now.

But Chisholm was convinced he had a lead and had left to meet with a "high-level source", as he called it, near Battery Park. She hoped he wasn't on a wild-goose chase, as she could have used his input at this stage. Meanwhile, Roy Stamper was working out of Liberty Crossing at McLean, running down leads on Kendrick.

Her gaze fixed on the pictures from Flushing Meadows. Kendrick was sipping a Coke, clapping occasionally, looking slightly distracted. She shook her head. "I don't know, guys. Has a message been passed to him?" She sighed. "Maybe. But why such an elaborate setup to pass on a message?"

Special Agent Angie Gifford, a counterterrorism intelligence analyst brought in from FBI HQ, was glued to a MacBook Pro showing instant intelligence messages and traffic being fed through from the team's base in McLean. "Ma'am, the only thing everyone is agreed on is that something is afoot. And Kendrick is a central component of this. The photographic evidence of Kendrick in Chechnya with these Islamists is pretty compelling, though."

"Compelling is not conclusive."

"Absolutely, ma'am."

Meyerstein closed her eyes for a moment, feeling a headache coming on. She tasted a bitter chemical aftertaste in her mouth and wondered if it was traces of the fentanyl. "There are so many strands, but nothing is pulling them together into a cohesive whole. We just have fragments. What we really need are all the pieces of the jigsaw to put together to give us the picture."

Gifford looked up at the screen and grimaced. "He's just sitting there. No obvious contacts. And not even cell phone conversations."

"Forty-eight hours to the anniversary of 9/11."

A few minutes later, Meyerstein went through to the windowless room adjacent to the main hub of activity and shut the door ahead of a videoconference with General Black and other senior members of the special access program team back in McLean, as she prepared to give them an update.

Black said, "Martha, we're watching events in real time too. We are in touch with the White House almost continuously, and still we don't seem to have this nailed down."

Meyerstein felt her blood pressure hike up a notch and her cheeks flush. "General Black, the strategic analysis is unequivocal. There appear to be elements in place for a possible attack, no question. We don't know where and who but are of the view Kendrick is involved, and we need to know who he is communicating with. We have surveillance in place. We're doing everything we can."

"And yet, two days before the 9/11 anniversary, we are still no further forward in establishing what network is in place, if any, who is involved and what the target is. Frankly, it beggars belief. Is this going to be a repeat of the Boston bombings?"

"Sir, I don't think we can wait any longer. I say we bring Kendrick in right now. That's also the view of Sam Chisholm. I think it is important to..."

Black slammed the palm of his hand hard down on the table. Papers scattered everywhere. "May I remind you that..."

A national security advisor put up his hand. "Sorry to butt in, General, but from what we know, and revelations about this picture of Kendrick in Chechnya..."

"We don't know how authentic that is. Christ, it came via the Russian security services. Are we really to believe what those people say?"

The national security expert shook his head. "General, I know Russia very well. I was stationed there for the best part of a decade. I know how they think and operate. And I must now concur with Assistant Director Meyerstein and Sam Chisholm: we need to bring this guy in now. We can't afford any fuckups. It might be tenuous, but we cannot take the slightest risk with national security."

"What about the network? How are we going to find out who's involved?"

Meyerstein interrupted. "General, I appreciate your candor, and your rationale can't be faulted, but this is a fast-moving situation and we all believe this is a real and credible threat."

Black's face darkened.

"Sir, with respect, I would ask that we apprehend Kendrick right this instant."

Black stared straight at her from the screen before he looked at those around the table in McLean. "Show of hands: who thinks we should pull this guy in?"

Everyone's hands went up, apart from Black.

"OK," he said, "here's where I'm at. What we don't want to do is create a panic or alert others that he is being taken in. Remember this match is being shown live, around the world. So, it's best we apprehend him as he leaves."

"But sir, as long as he remains in place, there is going to be uncertainty. Far better to just get him out of there right now."

"As I said, apprehend him when he leaves the stadium. Am I making myself clear?"

Meyerstein sighed. "That's fine, sir."

Black stared through the screen, eyes piercing. "Let's keep a lid on this. Keep us updated."

The screen went blank.

Meyerstein felt her anger mount over the coming minutes. She wanted to move on Kendrick now. She got up and went through to the main hub in the open-plan living room: laptops, printers, telephone wires and the smell of coffee. She began to pace the floor of the conference room when the phone on the oval table rang. The caller ID showed it was from Sam Chisholm's cell phone. "Talk to me, Sam."

"I got something you need to see."

"What is it, Sam? I'm kinda busy."

"Face to face. I have some crucial information."

Meyerstein wondered why he wouldn't just tell her what he knew. "Sam, where exactly are you?"

"I'm not far. Battery Parking Garage; you know it?"

"Sure. Not far."

"I'm on the fifth level. I need to talk. Right now."

"Sam, I'm real busy. Come in and we'll talk here if it's that important."

"No." His tone was strident. Not like him. "A source of mine... he wants to speak to you face to face. He has some documents."

"Documents? What sort of documents?"

A long sigh came down the line. "Martha, they concern... they concern General Black."

Meyerstein sighed. She knew Gritz, Reznick and the dozens of agents in and around Flushing Meadows had Kendrick's every move monitored. "OK. Give me twenty minutes."

It should have been a short drive down Broadway but evening traffic had snarled up.

"Goddamn, what is this?"

The driver shook his head and pointed farther down the street. "Looks like a bad one." She craned her neck and saw a cyclist had been knocked down, surrounded by paramedics. She considered walking the mile or so on foot, but within a few seconds they were on the move, and the driver somehow managed to weave around the traffic accident. They skirted the periphery of the World Trade Center site, right down Liberty Street, and then hung a left down Greenwich Street.

The red neon sign of the parking garage up ahead.

"Up to the fifth level," she said to the driver.

"Sure thing, ma'am."

A few moments later, they arrived on the fifth. It was jammed with cars in the dimly-lit concrete catacomb. She got out of the vehicle, her FBI minders never more than a yard away. "Where the hell is he?"

She looked around. "He definitely said he was on the fifth." Damn, she'd forgotten to ask what car to look out for.

Meyerstein took out her phone and punched in his number. It rang out. No sound of it anywhere. "What the hell? He definitely said the fifth?"

A couple of her men fanned out across the fifth level.

Meyerstein stood and scanned every vehicle. The click of the FBI agents' shoes echoed around the garage. Up ahead at the far corner of the garage, she spotted a black Lincoln. She thought she saw two people inside. She headed straight for it, past the other agents. As she got closer, her stomach tightened and her heart rate quickened.

Bad thoughts seeped into her mind. Alarm bells were ringing. Why the sudden call from Chisholm? Why the urgency? Why face to face?

She strode on towards the Lincoln. Ten yards away, she stopped dead in her tracks. The smell of cordite hung heavy in the air. Then she saw it.

Specks of blood splatter across the inside of the driver's window. She felt her insides move as she stepped closer. Time seemed to slow down. Then stop.

Gray brain tissue and dark blood sprayed all across the side and back window. Inside, Sam Chisholm, eyes open but no life in them. His face frozen in shock, as if he knew in that split second what fate awaited him. One bullet hole in the forehead, the back of his head splattered across the passenger window and beige leather seats. Another man, not known to Meyerstein, two shots drilled into the right temple, double-tap execution-style. Blood congealed around the entry wounds, sinews, tiny fragments of bone and brain matter on the man's ashen face.

She recoiled with horror.

The news about the double murder spread like wildfire through the FBI. Meyerstein had been back to the nearby Manhattan office, where she had fielded more than a dozen calls from everyone from Langley to the Department of Homeland Security, and from the national security advisor to the Office of the Director of Intelligence. But the one person who did not speak to her was General Black.

She began to focus her thoughts. The NSA had pulled up the call from Sam Chisholm and the verdict was clear. The call was genuine. It was made from his FBI cell phone. Video analysis from within the parking garage showed him arriving with an elderly man.

It took the FBI exactly fifteen seconds to formally identify the man as Marcus Belling, a retired rear admiral who had worked out of the Pentagon since the 1960s until he retired in 1986.

The more she thought back to the call from Chisholm, the more it was clear he had something on General Black. A connection, perhaps. Information about his Pentagon past. Belling would have worked with or come across Black at some time at the Pentagon during the height of the Cold War. Vietnam. Laos.

The shock and the adrenaline were still coursing through her veins, and they propelled her on. She hooked up a secure video link to Roy Stamper and they talked.

"Martha, I'm so sorry about Sam. I know you knew him well. I mean... I don't know what to say."

Meyerstein was determined to be all business. She cleared her throat. "Sam's deputy, Special Agent Jamieson, is leading the counterterrorism team on this. But I need to speak to General Black right now."

Stamper grimaced. "Might be a problem. He's not here, Martha."

"What do you mean, he's not here? I was just speaking to him a little while ago."

"I mean, he's been out of the office the last thirty minutes or so."

"Shit."

"I've tried his cell but there's no reply. I was just about to trace his phone via the GPS."

"Do it now."

Stamper punched in a few keys on his laptop in front of him, eyes locked on to the info. "We've got him near us. Gated community in McLean."

"That's where he lives."

"He's back home now? That doesn't make sense."

"None of it makes sense."

"You want me to go and speak to him?"

"No, you focus on your own work. We've got Kendrick. Leave the general to me. I want to speak to him myself. Face to face."

"Be careful, Martha."

She was driven to LaGuardia and caught an evening flight to Reagan International. Her mind raced throughout the one-hour flight. She popped a couple of Advil with a glass of water. She knew deep down something was amiss. Had been from the get-go. When the flight touched down in DC, it was late and dark.

She picked up her car from the near-deserted economy parking lot and drove across to West McLean. Fifteen minutes into her journey, her phone rang.

"Meyerstein," she said, focusing on the GPS.

"Martha, it's Roy. I got something. It's all beginning to take shape. But not in a good way."

"Tell me we've still got Kendrick in our sights."

"We're fine with that. We got him covered."

"So, what is it?"

"Firstly, Black's a member of the Trilateral Commission. Did you know that?"

Meyerstein was aware of the organization set up by Rockefeller in the early 1970s. It included powerful banking, corporate, political and military interests. "I didn't know that."

"He's not on any public list, but he has attended the last dozen or so meetings. I have it on good authority that he is a very influential member of the Commission."

"What else?"

"Here's the kicker. Our computer guys, along with the NSA, have accessed heavily encrypted DoD files, including redacted secret files, relating to General Robert Black."

Meyerstein was getting butterflies in her stomach. "I'm listening."

"We believe Sam Chisholm had access to the same files."

"And?"

"Black was on the periphery of a cabal at the Pentagon that was at the center of setting up an unauthorized plan to try to replicate Operation Northwoods.

Meyerstein's blood ran cold. She'd read all about the operation. He was referring to an infamous and highly secretive false flag operation planned within the American military during the Cold War to carry out apparent terrorist attacks on the US, hoping to blame the Cubans.

"Goes way back to the early 1960s, the plan, apparently."

"Cuban missile crisis era, right?"

"Precisely, Martha. I'm just checking this as it comes in, so you'll have to bear with me."

Meyerstein's mind was racing ahead. "Just to be clear, we're talking about the same Operation Northwoods? The one way back in the time of the Kennedy administration?"

"How do you know this?"

"I read about it. It was a series of false flag proposals, put forward by the American military, but rejected by the Kennedy administration."

"I'm just reading this stuff for the first time. This is nuts."

"The plan was drawn up by the CIA and would have entailed using CIA operatives to carry out terrorist attacks on US soil but blame it on the Cubans, allowing America to declare war on Castro."

Silence down the line.

"So the question is now: is what we're dealing with Kendrick a false flag? Americans bombing or shooting Americans?"

Stamper said nothing.

"What else? I need to know more about Black's part in this."

"Black was a young officer at the time but, along with others of the same political outlook prevalent at the time, he became aligned with a hawkish grouping. This group was led by General Lyman Lemnitzer, chairman of the joint chiefs of staff way back in the 1960s, but his plan to launch bombings in the Miami area and in Washington was thrown out by Robert McNamara."

Meyerstein felt her heart beat faster, her mind going into overdrive as she got closer to Black's home.

"I've got more. Black wanted to recast the Northwoods plan once in the 1980s. This was based on the original blueprint of the work of Brigadier General William Craig, Black's mentor, and other right-wing patriots, as they saw themselves. Lemnitzer and Craig thought Kennedy was a no-win president. They thought he was soft on Castro. Black was trained by Craig."

The oncoming headlights made Meyerstein wince. "Craig?"

"Yeah. Black was mentored by William Craig, the architect of the original Operation Northwoods. And Black in turn proposed an Operation Northwoods–style plan, including bombings, shootings and plane crashes, to blame on the Iranians and galvanize public support for bombing Tehran to dust in 1981. Black's plans were codenamed Operation Dustbowl. That's what they wanted to turn Iran to. Dust."

"Are you serious?"

"It was how part of the senior military was thinking at the time. Black was on the periphery of the original Operation Northwoods. And then he revived the plan in the early 1980s, hoping to blame a spate of bombings and killings on the Iranian regime."

"How does this relate to Belling?"

"Apparently, Belling got wind of the 1981 blueprints that Black had circulated as a secret briefing paper. Belling worked out of the Pentagon, but, ironically, it was Belling who was edged out towards retirement. Black had numerous backers, both militarily and politically, no doubt through his Trilateral Commission contacts, although the plans were never acted on and were finally scrapped after the Iran-Contra scandal broke."

Meyerstein's brain was racing ahead of her as the lights of the oncoming cars raced by. "So, how did Sam Chisholm find out about this?"

"Chisholm had an old Pentagon source, a friend of Chisholm's late father. Both were in the army. And he pointed him in the direction of Belling. Said Belling had something on Black, or words to that effect."

Meyerstein's mind was in overdrive. Scenarios ran through her head at breakneck speed. "Roy, I want you to relay this information directly to the President's National Security Council."

"They already know."

"Good. OK, this kind of puts a different spin on the analysis pointing to Islamists, right?"

"Counterintelligence and counterterrorism are still working on this information. They are up to speed with this information about Black. But I'm awaiting the latest from them. Expect an update within the hour."

"Is that everything?"

"Not quite."

"Not quite? You got something else?"

"Yeah, on Black. Martha, it's true General Black works out of the Pentagon and has since the 1980s. But we're drilling down. He is not reporting to anyone within the Department of Defense. I have that on good authority from three separate people."

"What are you talking about?"

"Martha, he's CIA. Always has been."

"Since when?"

"Since forever. Vietnam, Korea, Laos: he's been on the ground each and every time. You name it. He's been there. And then some."

"It's all pointing one way, Roy."

Stamper said nothing.

"This whole thing has the look and feel of an Islamist operation, but if there are elements within the military, or the CIA, or the government, who want to use that as a pretext for their devices? What if this is Black's false flag? What if this is his Operation Northwoods?"

A long sigh. "Martha, what is really going on?"

"That's what we need to find out."

"The Islamist prints are all over this. Right through New York. Jamal Ali. The mosque. Chechens."

"But what if that was what they wanted us to see? What if that was the reality they wanted to create for us all?"

"Indeed."

Meyerstein spotted a sign for McLean. "Where does the good doctor fit into this? Is he the patsy?"

"I'm looking straight at him on my monitor. Sitting as cool as a cucumber under the floodlights, eating an ice cream, watching goddamn tennis."

"There is more to Kendrick than meets the eye. We're still missing something on him."

"Martha, I have twenty-five people who are solely working on Kendrick. They're going through everything."

"Well, you know what, Roy? They damn well better get something soon. We need to fill in the blanks. Do you hear me?"

"They're working their butts off."

"Triple the team working on Kendrick's past. I need something. We are missing something."

"Martha, we're operating at the outer edges here..."

"I'm sick of excuses, Roy. I want answers. Make it happen. You have my authority to draft as many agents as you need.

We need a breakthrough."

"I hear you."

Meyerstein sighed and wished she hadn't snapped at Stamper, who she knew would be working every angle. "OK, for the guys at the stadium, Roy, the instructions for Gritz and Reznick and all the others: they stick to that bastard like glue. And as soon as he leaves we hustle him away, got it?"

"That's all in place. We should've done this days ago."

The GPS voice announced that she was approaching McLean. "Roy, it's time to deliver. We're fast running out of time."

FORTY

Meyerstein ended the call and headed along dark tree-lined streets straddled by 1940s Cape Cod–style homes, and past newer, grander properties. Tidy. Affluent. Conservative. And rather beautiful.

She pulled up outside an older Cape Cod partially shielded by huge oaks. She switched off the engine and saw lights on inside, curtains drawn. She contemplated the location. McLean. A Beltway city in Northern Virginia. Upscale, safe, orderly. Best known for two things: Tysons Corner, a leading shopping hub on the East Coast, and the home of the CIA on the outskirts of the city.

She'd been to the new headquarters building, renamed the George Bush Center for Intelligence. Irony was never one of the strong suits of the CIA. But as she sat outside Black's home, she realized a picture was slowly beginning to emerge.

A picture not of a military man at the Pentagon but of the CIA, now an executive arm of government, reporting to the director of national intelligence.

Only now, at the eleventh hour, was she was beginning to connect the dots in her head.

As she drove on, she thought of the East Village mosque used by Akhtar, who had taken the Fifth. Was that the façade in case the real plot was uncovered? Was there even an Islamist plot?

Her mind tracked back to the numerous confidential reports she'd read about the true nature of the Islamic threat to the US and how it had really emerged. It was American policy during the Soviet rule in Afghanistan to use mosques to recruit those who would fight the Russians. Geopolitics. She knew about Camp Peary, also known as "The Farm," where the CIA trained young Arab nationals from countries like Egypt and Jordan, along with young Afghans, who were taught strategic sabotage skills. And so the blowback went on. And on.

The jihad that the US had created and fostered and nurtured was engulfing large parts of the Middle East, before those same jihadists turned their gaze on America. Bin Laden himself was linked to a jihad refugee center in Brooklyn.

But her investigation was now not about jihadists. They were going to be the patsies, while the true nature of the emerging threat would lie undiscovered.

The more she thought about it, the more she felt a terrible emptiness within her. Was this her country? Was this her government? Was this how it had always been?

She turned into a deathly quiet tree-lined street and saw the house. Floodlit garden, shielded by massive trees and hedgerows. Lights on in upstairs windows. She walked up to the front door and knocked three times.

Her heart was beating fast as she waited. Inside, footsteps. The door opened. A small gray-haired woman wearing an orange blouse and long skirt answered the door.

Meyerstein flashed her ID. "Sorry to bother you, ma'am; I'm looking to speak to General Black."

The woman stared at Meyerstein. "This is most irregular, is it not?"

"Indeed it is, Mrs Black."

"Do you mind me asking what this is about?"

"I'm sorry; that's not possible."

She sighed. "I see."

"This is not about me. This is about your husband. Now, are you going to invite me into your house or do I have to go and get a warrant from a judge?"

Mrs Black's eyes bored into Meyerstein for what seemed like an eternity. Eventually, she opened the door wide. "There will no need for that. My husband is in his study."

Meyerstein followed her down a long carpeted hallway.

"If you must know, my husband began to feel unwell and had to return home. The doctor has just left."

"I'm sorry; I didn't realize."

"No, I don't suppose you did."

Mrs Black escorted Meyerstein to the study at the far end of the house. She knocked on the door.

"Come in, Esther."

Esther Black opened the door. "Darling, sorry to trouble you again; Assistant Director Meyerstein has popped in to see you."

General Black looked up from a pile of papers on his huge teak desk, two lamps on, and stared at Meyerstein. He was wearing a pale blue button-down shirt, chinos and dark brown loafers. A desk phone and a cell phone sat neatly beside each other. Wooden blinds drawn. Two leather sofas. Black-and-white pictures of the general with various presidents over the years on the walls. "I see. Well, you better show her in."

Meyerstein stepped into the room.

His wife looked across to her husband. "Can I get you a coffee or tea, darling?"

Black shook his head. "I'm fine, thank you."

"Assistant Director? Coffee or tea?"

Meyerstein smiled. "No, thanks. I'm good."

Mrs Black shut the door behind her.

General Black pointed at one of the sofas. "Take a load off."

She sat down and cleared her throat. "I've been trying to contact you, General. Have you heard what happened to Sam Chisholm?"

Black's eyes were hooded. He sighed. "Indeed I have. Appalling. In all my years..."

"I've got some questions for you, if you don't mind. They're starting to build up."

"I'm sorry; I don't follow. I thought this was about Chisholm."

Meyerstein felt his gaze on her and she instinctively shifted on the sofa. "Sir, I have grave concerns. And I feel the need to ask you some questions, once again, face to face."

"Well, here we are."

"My first question, General, is: why wasn't I told that you had taken ill? You are chairing this special access program which I'm leading."

He sighed. "I apologize. I should have made you aware of that. My doctor advised me to get the hell out of my office." Black leaned back in his leather seat and sighed again. He was playing it cool. Aloof. "Forget me. What about Chisholm? How the hell did that happen? I heard you found him. Meeting up with some source."

Meyerstein nodded, images of Chisholm's blood-spattered face seared into her mind.

"What was the meeting about?"

Meyerstein went quiet for a few moments. She wondered how much she should reveal. "I got a call from Chisholm saying a source of his wanted to speak face to face with me. A source that used to work at the Pentagon."

Black nodded. "I've listened to the call. And I know who the source was."

The news was a surprise to Meyerstein. She wondered who had passed on that information. Was it someone within her team? Outside the team? "You've listened to the call?"

A thin smile cracked his face as if he enjoyed toying with her. "Marcus Belling was in the car with Chisholm. We went back a long, long way. Hell of a nice guy, but he was... how can I put it, more cerebral than practical."

Meyerstein averted her gaze for a moment. "He had documents. Documents about you, General. Did you know that?"

Black said nothing.

"Do you have any idea why Marcus Belling would want to speak to Chisholm urgently about you? What sort of documents do you think he was talking about?"

Black's steely gaze fixed on her. "Marcus Belling was a good man. But he was naïve."

"Naïve? In what way?"

"He believed that this great country of ours always had to play by the rules."

"And you don't believe that?"

Black let out a long sigh. "Meyerstein, you should know better than anyone that, sometimes, you've got to break the rules to get the results. You turned a blind eye to the rules when you tracked down that government scientist, Luntz, didn't you?"

Meyerstein felt her face flush. She was tempted to rise to the bait. But she focused on the questions at hand. "You seem to know a lot about me, General. I've been finding out some information about you. And it makes for interesting reading."

Black said nothing.

"Why didn't you tell me you worked for the CIA?"

"I didn't think it was relevant."

"Isn't it? We have the documents, General. The documents that Belling knew about for all these years. The plans you drew up. Top secret plans. Black flag operations across the US. Plans to kill Americans. Bombings. Shootings. Plans to galvanize public opinion against Iran. Plans that would have allowed the military to launch a full-scale war against Iran. The same kind of plans that were hatched in the 1960s to try to start a war with Cuba. Then it was called Operation Northwoods. But you had drawn up plans for Operation Dustbowl. And now we have the latest plans that we're seeing playing out in real time in New York. You wanna talk about that, General?"

Black pinched the bridge of his nose and smiled. "Do you know anything of military strategy? Do you understand the first thing about what it takes to protect the cherished freedoms we have at our disposal?"

"I know what this great country of ours stands for."

"Meyerstein, you're a very competent FBI assistant director. But you've got a helluva lot to learn when it comes to knowing how to keep our country safe. We need to fight each and every day across all parts of the world, each and every goddamn day, just to make sure we can live as free people."

"According to whose rules, exactly, General?"

Black said nothing.

"Do you believe in democracy, General?"

His gaze wandered round the room for a few moments as if considering the nuances of the argument. "Up to a point."

Meyerstein shifted on the sofa. "And what point is that, General?"

"The point where the people lead us over a cliff. Politicians, for example. Sometimes, the average American doesn't realize what the hell is happening in Washington. We have to be aware of all threats which politicians are either too scared to confront or too afraid to reveal to the American people."

"What threats? Real or imagined?"

"Don't denigrate what people like me do, Meyerstein. We make tough calls, day in, day out. Every goddamn day, every goddamn night. Unseen. Unappreciated. We do the dirty work that is necessary so we can all sleep at night. You need men like me to do what's necessary."

"Sir, I'm going to ask you straight."

Black stared long and hard at her. "Fire away."

Meyerstein felt a knot of tension in her stomach. "And I expect a straight answer."

Black nodded.

"Is a false flag operation underway? Is Kendrick spearheading this operation? Is that what this is all about?"

Black closed his eyes for a moment and smiled. He sighed as he allowed a silence to open up. "There are forces at work, both within the borders of this great country, and outside, whose job is to look after the interests of America."

Meyerstein felt her blood pressure rise up a notch. "The interests of America? And what exactly do you deem to be in the interests of America?"

"We need friendly governments who understand freedom. We need governments who make sure that the insidious presence of communism, in all its guises, is crushed. We need governments to understand the ever-present threat of radical Islam. They don't want to convert us. They want to crush us. That threat has never been so real. It's never gone away."

Meyerstein said nothing, as it was clear he was on a roll.

"What do you think the Crusades were all about? It was pacifying them. That's what we're doing each and every day across the globe. We need to be strong. They want to wipe Christianity and America off the map."

"Who's they?"

"You know full well, Meyerstein. We also need to remind people, from time to time, that there are venal regimes that will stop at nothing to wipe us off this earth. It is an ongoing battle. And sometimes, things get messy."

"Is that right? Is that what this is, General, a black flag operation to galvanize a new wave of public support for this war against Islam?"

Black said nothing.

"You're not above the law, General."

"The law? Gimme a break. The law is an ass. We all know that. People like me ensure that our way of life is preserved. And along the way, there have to be casualties."

Meyerstein paused for a few moments. "American casualties OK, general?"

"You don't see the big picture, Meyerstein."

"I find your earlier reply to my original question interesting, General."

"In what way?"

"You didn't answer a straightforward question as to whether you were aware that there was a black flag operation underway in the USA. What I got was a rationale for black flag operations."

Black leaned back in his seat and sighed. "Sometimes, Meyerstein, it's better not to see the full picture. If the public really knew what was done in their name, they would descend on Washington in their millions and burn it down to the ground."

"Let's get back to what's going on right now. And I'm going to ask you a second and final time, General... is there a black flag or false flag operation, either authorized or unauthorized, underway in America?"

"Meyerstein, I don't see where this line of questioning is leading us."

"Could you answer the question?"

"What are you really wanting me to say?"

"Tell me the truth."

"Meyerstein, you have no idea what the truth is. No idea at all, hidden away in your ivory tower in the goddamn Hoover building, not seeing what is really going on."

"Are there others involved? Because, if there are, we will find them, and they will be hunted down, no matter who they are."

"There is no black flag operation."

"You know what? I don't believe you." Meyerstein pulled out her phone and punched in Stamper's number, which was on her speed dial. "Roy, you at Liberty Crossing?"

"That's right."

"Send round a full team to the home of Lieutenant General Robert J Black, including FBI forensics and computer specialists. How long before you can be here?"

"I'm sorry?"

"You heard me, Roy. How long?"

"Eh... A matter of minutes."

"Get to it."

Meyerstein ended the call and looked across at Black. His face was ashen. "This is not going to be pleasant for any of us, including your wife."

He leaned forward. "What the hell do you think you're doing?"

"We're taking you in, sir. You've got a lot of questions to answer."

"Are you serious?"

"Deadly."

His eyes were glassy. He opened his mouth for a moment as if at a loss for words. "Have you lost your mind?" He shrugged. "I mean... we're on the same side, aren't we?"

"I don't know; are we?"

Black got to his feet and stood up. Clearing his throat, he sighed. "You have no idea who you're dealing with."

Meyerstein said nothing.

He stood staring at her, his lined face beaded with sweat and jawline set as if in granite. His eyes bored into hers. She didn't flinch. She stared right back at him. She had learned from her father the importance of eye contact. Not being afraid. The sound of an old grandfather clock was all she heard.

"Sir, you're going to be taken from here and interviewed at length."

"Can I pick up some things?" He was breathing harder.

"No. Nothing."

"What about Esther?"

"What about her?"

"What will I say?"

"Tell her what you like."

Black bowed his head for a moment, as if weighed down by events. He looked up at Meyerstein. "I need to go to the bathroom. Do you mind if I freshen up?"

Meyerstein looked at her watch. "Five minutes."

Black stood for a few moments, gaze fixed on her. Then he breathed out long and hard before he went into the bathroom. The sound of the door locking. The sound of running water. Then a long silence.

She closed her eyes. She was mentally exhausted. Her mind began to race. And then she sensed something was terribly wrong. Her heart began to pound. She jumped from the sofa and ran toward the bathroom door. A single shot rang out.

FORTY-ONE

The shocking news of General Black's suicide, amid growing suspicions that a false flag operation may be underway, was still sinking in as Reznick, Gritz and the other Feds watched Kendrick from the FBI control hub within Flushing Meadows.

It was a worrying sequence of events, intelligence still being pieced together.

Gritz was staring through the binoculars, cell phone pressed to his ear. "Fucker is still just sitting there."

Reznick was handed a cell phone by one of Gritz's men.

"Assistant Director Meyerstein wants a word," he said gruffly.

Reznick took the phone and sighed. "You OK?"

"What do you think?"

Reznick said nothing.

"Look, I'm just about to land in LaGuardia. I need to be on the ground." She sighed. "So, what do you make of this?"

Reznick could hear the anxiety in her voice. The doubt. The fear. "You did the right thing by speaking to him. The whole thing has suddenly become clearer. Here's how it is. The Islamic threat is their cover. But the real and present threat comes from Kendrick and those who are behind this; Black is only the tip of the iceberg. And that's why we need to haul Kendrick's ass in right now. A false flag is being set up. And it's underway."

Meyerstein went quiet for a few moments, her mind processing a morass of facts, analysis and data. Her senses were switched on, knowing that something was going to go down. But no one knew what exactly. "Have you read Stamper's analysis about false flags?"

"Yup. I know all about false flags. I know people that wrote the CIA manual on it."

"Which brings us back to General Black. He was CIA. No one told me."

"That's the way they operate. Need to know. If you're not one of them, you don't need to know shit."

"Jon, if this is a false flag, what do I need to know? This is an inside job, hidden within the Islamist threat, right?"

"Meyerstein, firstly, you need to know that it will go deeper than Black. He can't be the only one. You need the military, Pentagon, CIA and NSA axis to make this work. But it might be wider than that."

"Jesus... why would anyone want to make this work? I mean, killing Americans?"

"You don't know the half of it."

"The suicide of Black is a game changer. The probability of an attack scenario from a false flag operation is now being described as highly likely, according to counterterrorism. And they believe Adam Kendrick will deliver... but, crucially, he is not an Islamist."

Reznick picked up the binoculars and stared through the glass at Kendrick eating a hot dog. "Not for one minute. He's an all-American guy. At least on the surface... the photo in Chechnya is vital. I still think we need to find out more about his time there."

Meyerstein sighed. "I see that you flagged up the color of his eyes. What's that all about?"

"The colored contact lens is a very elaborate ruse. Sometimes used by high-end card sharks. They can read cards marked with ultraviolet pens, invisible to the naked eye. But in this case it may, I stress may, enable Kendrick to read hidden messages. The added attraction of that is that it helps them stay clear of electronic chatter."

Meyerstein went quiet for a few moments.

"What are you thinking?"

"I'm thinking I want him out of there now before the crowds all disappear at the same time. That'll make it tricky to keep an eye on him."

"Absolutely."

"But I don't want to draw attention to us taking him away. I'm thinking... I'm thinking we should wait till he next goes to the bathroom and take him then."

"Sounds good. I'll pass on to Gritz and his guys."

"Jon, I'm due to land in fifteen minutes. But all you need to know is that Kendrick doesn't leave our sight."

Reznick stared through the binoculars as Kendrick dabbed the corner of his mouth with a napkin after eating a hot dog. The roar of the crowd outside the box made Reznick wince. "Got you."

Meyerstein said, "There are a lot of questions. The intern is still missing."

"Consider her dead."

A long silence opened up before she spoke. "We don't know that for sure, Jon."

"Trust me. She's out the way. What about Jamal's sister?"

Meyerstein sighed. "Chantelle McGovern? Still under surveillance. But we think she's been radicalized by her dead brother. And Akhtar is part of the same East Village grouping... the question is, were these guys planning a terrorist campaign? No evidence as yet."

"And we return to my point. They are brilliant cover for the main event. Kendrick leaves this trace and we pick up the morsels they are feeding us. It's real cute. Someone wanted us to get the Islamic connection if we latched on to Kendrick. But we're being played. Have been since day one."

Meyerstein said, "Kendrick I still do not get, despite the Chechen link."

"The Chechens and the East Village Islamists are the cover. They're the backdrop. But Kendrick is the key. Has been since the get-go."

"Stamper's still working on piecing together Kendrick's past."

"He needs to get his finger out. Why is this taking so long?"

"Jon, I've got two other lights flashing. I need to take these calls."

"Speak again soon."

Reznick ended the call and relayed the message to Gritz, who in turn fed the information to the rest of his team.

A few minutes later, Kendrick got up from his seat and headed up the stairs from his courtside seat.

Reznick held his lapel microphone, "Stick to him like glue, you hear?"

Gritz pressed the binoculars almost up to the glass. "That's affirmative. Tail him. We don't lose this guy."

A few moments later, an FBI agent's voice. "Joined a line for the bathroom."

Reznick was handed a bottle of water by a young Fed and he chugged it back in one shot. He stared at the monitors in the suite showing the lines and the half dozen agents milling around on the periphery. Scores of people in and out of the bathroom every couple of minutes, dozens more milling around. He looked across at Gritz. "Who's going to take him and when?"

"Special Agents Atkins and McKiernan. Both ex-college wrestling champs. Trust me, he ain't goin' nowhere."

The flow of people in and out of the bathroom. The seconds became minutes.

Reznick adjusted his headset. "That's nearly five fucking minutes he's been in there; get in there and pull him out."

Gritz nodded. "Yeah, that's a go. Repeat, get him out of there. Don't care if he's goin' for a dump. Get him out, right now."

The two Feds barged through the line and a few spilled beers, shouting and pushing until three other Feds flashed badges and the boozed-up tennis clowns backed off.

A few moments later, the voice of Special Agent Hassiter crackled into life. "We got a problem."

Gritz clenched his teeth. "What do you mean?"

"He's gone. He must've slipped out."

Gritz pointed to his right-hand man. "Run the surveillance cameras again from the moment he went in. Shit! Shit! Bullshit! You believe this?"

Reznick headed for the door of the box, earpiece in. "Get the facial recognition guys to scan all the faces leaving the bathroom. He's changed his outfit and given us the slip. I think he left before the match finished."

"Fuck!"

Reznick negotiated a series of teeming corridors, people mingling, chatting and hanging around, before he was swept along and fought past a crowd of people out of the stadium and into the sticky night air with dozens of Feds.

Gritz's voice. "We need to seal off the perimeter. He's not in his seat. There's no one there. The fucker is on the move!"

Reznick stared off into the distance. Hundreds of people were streaming away early from the match and heading for the train back to town. "He'll have gone. Check the cameras in and around the stadium. We need to pick up the scent quick before it's too late."

Gritz said, "What a mess."

Reznick's blood was boiling. "Let's quit whining and find the bastard."

He barged past the crowds and headed instinctively in the direction of a ramp that led to the adjacent subway stop.

Gritz's voice in his earpiece. "Jon, there's a 7 train about to leave! Get yourself onto the northside platform. The Citi Field side."

Reznick was there in seconds but saw the magenta diamond shape with the number 7 on the side pulling away as he got on the platform. "Fuck."

"We're checking the cameras on board."

"You've ID'd him?"

"Not sure."

"Fuck. What is he wearing?"

"We have footage of him heading up the ramp... Yup, three minutes ago, wearing glasses, khaki trousers, sneakers and black T-shirt, knapsack thing on his back. You're right, Jon; the fucker has changed."

Reznick said, "The 7 train. That heads directly to Manhattan?"

"Goddamn super express. Three stops before Manhattan."

"How long till Manhattan?"

"Stops at a couple of shitholes in Queens. Thirty, maybe thirty-five minutes. Times Square, end of the line."

"You need to stop the train?"

"We're already trying to do that. No one seems to have the fucking authority."

"What about boarding at one of the Queens stations?"

"Hold on, Jon; I got something. There are cameras on the train and we're scanning all the passengers. Hold on..." The waiting seemed to take forever. "Shit. He didn't get on the train. Target is not on the train. I repeat, target is definitely not on the train."

"So where the hell is he?"

Reznick looked over and saw the huge silhouette of the Mets' new stadium, Citi Field, in the distance.

"The fucker's out there somewhere. He's still in Queens."

FORTY-TWO

Meyerstein's plane was just about to land when the phone on her armrest rang.

"Martha, it's Roy. I just heard about Black. Are you OK?"

"I'm fine. What about Kendrick? What's the latest on him?"

"They're scouring Queens within a three-mile radius of the stadium."

"Shit."

"Indeed. Look, we've got something on Kendrick. And it ties it all together."

"What've you got? Spill it real quick."

"Martha, we've been searching every goddamn database we have access to on this guy for days. And each and every time, it's come back clean. Clean-living doc, overseas medical work. You know the drill."

"Yeah, come on, Roy."

"We got a lead. Kendrick's real background. And it makes sense. It all makes sense."

"Roy, could you please cut to the chase?"

"The photo which was passed to us by the Russians, and which we've verified, shows Kendrick in Chechnya alongside this Kristina woman. We've been negotiating through a back channel with them, and they opened up their own secret files on Americans in Chechnya."

"So how does Kendrick fit into this?"

"The CIA was, in effect, the operational commander for operations in Chechnya. The Chechens were our proxies. Special Forces including SEALs were involved. And I was given the name of a former SEAL in Chechnya who knew Kendrick very well indeed."

"You kidding me, right?"

"Nope. Apparently Kendrick saved this SEAL's life."

"When?"

"When he was with Adam Kendrick in Chechnya."

"I'm sorry, how does this guy know Kendrick?"

"Dr Adam Kendrick was Captain Adam Kendrick, assigned to Special Forces operations as a lead medic. But he was funded through college by the CIA."

"You're kidding me?"

"No, Martha. There is no record of it at all in official files. Incredibly high IQ, 148. Fast-tracked. Took a shake-and-bake month-long army course. Operated in a support capacity. But that's not all. He's a crack shot, sniper, super fit and is classic SEAL material."

Her mind was struggling to take it all in. "Slow down, are you saying..."

"The guy I spoke to said his fitness levels were remarkable and he fit their profile. He didn't shoot his mouth off. He blended in. Analytical thinker. Problem solver. Very value-oriented, patriotic, so much so that he put service above self. But he was as cold as they come."

"Kendrick is CIA?"

"Yes, he is. The guy said that Kendrick was afforded great cover when he entered war zones as an NGO medic. But he was feeding back information all the time from field hospitals, contacts he had established, enabling the CIA to build up a picture of things on the ground, without any fingerprints."

"Shit."

"There's more. The man in charge of recruiting Kendrick way back in the 1980s was..."

"Black."

"Got it in one try. General Robert Black."

"Christ... how didn't we know about this?"

"Who the hell knows? One final thing. And this is where it gets really, really unsettling."

"Oh great."

"Firstly, Kendrick was adopted by a childless couple in DC."

"Yeah, I think I read that. So?"

"Just bear with me. His natural parents died when he was a baby. Car crash. He was adopted by an older couple in DC. They died when he was at college. His adopted mother was called Alice Kendrick. His adopted father was Peter Kendrick."

"Roy, I read that. So?"

"We started digging further back. There were incomplete records and that's what's taken us so long. It's been a nightmare trying to piece it together. But we've got it. And we've connected the dots. It hasn't been easy, let me tell you. Do you know who Peter Kendrick's second cousin was?"

"Roy, you wanna quit playing games and tell me?"

"The second cousin was a woman named... Esther Beveridge."

"And?"

"When she married, she became Esther Black."

Meyerstein's blood ran cold. "The general's wife."

"We've triple and quadruple-checked this and gone over and cross-checked the records, both paper and computer, incomplete records held by the Children's Bureau and numerous other agencies. Robert Black saw the boy had a high IQ. But he also saw the kid was manipulative, superficial, charming and unable to relate to others. And he referred him to a CIA psychologist. The boy was deemed to be a 'highly intelligent psychopath.' But this has all been hidden away, out of sight.

"The records show that the boy was a bed wetter until well into his teens and was often setting off fires in the community where they lived. Esther Black asked her husband to see if he could help with the boy. And it was from there the connection between Black and Kendrick was formed, unseen all these years."

Meyerstein was struggling to take it all in. "You think Kendrick's primed to carry out an attack?"

"He's the one. I'm sure of it."

FORTY-THREE

Half an hour later, Reznick's mood was darkening as he sat buckled up in the back of a speeding SUV with four Feds as they headed across the 59th Street Bridge into Manhattan. Through the metal and steel struts and beams, he saw the Midtown skyline, smokestacks, the Empire State, lights.

Gritz was sitting in the passenger seat. He turned and looked at Reznick. "How the fuck did we allow this to happen? He might still be in Queens, for all we know."

Reznick said nothing, not wanting to engage in conversation. His mind was still racing, thinking about the information contained within Stamper's report on Black.

Gritz scanned his iPad to read the latest update. He shook his head. "We don't even know if he's in Manhattan."

Reznick's nerves were twitching. "That's where he'll be headed. Manhattan is the epicenter of all things New York. To the rest of the world, Manhattan is New York."

Gritz said, "This false flag is bullshit. Are we seriously to believe that Black would have authorized such actions? Are you kidding me? This is goddamn treason."

"You need to read Roy Stamper's report. It's all there about Black. He's CIA. He was responsible for drawing up a false flag plan in the 1980s based on Operation Northwoods, and Kendrick is the triggerman."

"He's a goddamn doctor."

"Yeah, a CIA doctor and a trained sniper."

"It doesn't make sense."

"That's the whole point. You need to keep up, Gritz."

Gritz shook his head. "The whole thing is a crock of shit."

"It makes sense in their world. The end justifies the means. Doesn't matter who gets hurt."

"O'Grady. Froch. Chisholm. How does he fit into this?"

"It's all about shutting down those who pose a threat to the operation. The attempt on Meyerstein's life. And let's not forget the intern is still missing. Almost certainly dead."

Gritz shook his head. "I've been with the FBI for the best part of twenty years, and I've never seen anything like this."

Gritz's cell rang. He answered on the first ring. He nodded. "Get this information out to the other teams now. I want the remaining teams in Queens to head into Manhattan." He ended the call. "Kendrick popped into the East 81st Street Hostel ten minutes ago, and CCTV images show him leaving three minutes ago, backpack slung over his shoulder. Step on it, Jimmy."

The car sped over the bridge and into midtown Manhattan as the traffic slowed to a crawl.

Reznick said, "We staked him out there before."

Gritz screwed up his face. "What?"

"Yeah, we staked him out. He also worked a hostel, homeless shelter in the East Village and a soup kitchen."

"So why the hell is he going back there now?"

Reznick stared out of the window. Yellow cabs crawled by, neon-lit delis, and pedestrians and tourists shuffling around on the sidewalks. Skyscrapers towering all around, nearly blocking out the inky black sky. "I think we're reaching the endgame."

"Tonight? No one is saying anything is going to go down tonight."

"I'm saying it."

"You got to be kidding me."

"It's tonight."

"Let's focus on what we do know. He's on the move in the Upper East Side. He's on foot. Let's assume he's within twenty blocks of the hostel by the time we arrive."

Reznick's mind was racing. "Why is he returning to that hostel? Unless... Unless he's returning for a pickup."

"A pickup? Of what?"

"Final instructions? A weapons stash, perhaps? The hostel must have cameras..."

Gritz's phone rang and he held up his hand as if to silence Reznick. "You're in the hostel? Good, we need to know where he went, who he talked with, and if he picked up anything. You know the drill. ETA perhaps three minutes for us." He ended the call. "FBI SWAT is all over it."

Reznick said, "First thought that comes to mind is: what crowded, enclosed areas are there within walking distance?"

"Hundreds. Bars, restaurants, outdoor cafes. And then there's Central Park. Fuck."

"Are there any VIP functions around this area tonight?"

Gritz said, "Are you kidding? There are functions and openings and new bars and restaurants and A-listers all over the East Side, 365 nights a year."

"OK, that narrows it down."

"Jon, we are working on an assessment which is really an assumption that Kendrick is going to carry out an attack. We just don't know that."

"It's gonna be around here. Very close."

"We're flooding the place. We're combing each and every street in the Upper East Side."

"What if he goes to ground?"

"Where?"

"What about the Lenox Hill doctor he stayed with? He's within the radius."

"Outer edges. But I can't see him heading back there."

"Worth getting a team there, just in case."

"Jon, we haven't got any information to storm in there... It doesn't work like that."

"So, how does it work?"

"Well, you need legal authorization for a search."

"Then get it. Kendrick is the number one suspect in the city, he's a terrorist risk, he's on the loose, and he's stayed there before. You want me to go on?"

Gritz flushed red as he punched a number into his cell. "I want the go-ahead to get into the townhouse of William Rhodes, medical director of Lenox Hill Hospital. Lives on East 63rd Street." He nodded. "Let me know when it comes through." He turned to face Reznick. "Would he be dumb enough to go there?"

"We can't just rely on trawling round every street."

The radio crackled into life. "We got a fix from a camera on what we believe to be our guy. Just spotted heading south. East 73rd Street is the latest fix."

Gritz clenched his fist. "Yes! Ten blocks away. We have cars five blocks from there. They're one minute away."

Reznick's senses were switched on. "You need some of your guys on the ground to grab him."

Gritz nodded. "We're closing in on foot and by car. We're gonna get him."

The car screeched through a red light and across Fifth Avenue.

Gritz looked at the driver. "You wanna get us killed, Jimmy?"

"I wanna get us there, sir."

"In one piece would be nice."

Two minutes later, they were crawling along the tree-lined row houses of affluent East 73rd Street. Scanning the sidewalks.

Gritz peered ahead. "He can't be far from here."

The radio crackled into life again. "He's crossing Madison and heading west along East 74th Street. He's moving fast. We think the park."

A few moments later, they turned onto East 74th Street and the traffic was gridlocked.

Reznick opened the door.

Gritz said, "Where the hell are you going?"

"He's mobile; I'm going mobile."

"We have teams working this, Jon."

"I got this."

Reznick slammed the door shut, ran down Madison and turned west down East 74th Street. Past stately town houses, fancy cars, past the Caravaggio restaurant.

Gritz's voice in his earpiece. "Where the hell is he, people?"

A long pause. "He just seems to have vanished. I lost him on Madison. He was moving fast."

Gritz's voice. "He's dropped off the radar. Last sighting just about where you are, Jon, heading west. Team Red, head north along Fifth. Jon, head south along Fifth."

Reznick ran across Fifth, nearly getting killed by a screeching cab. His heart was pounding, sweat dripping off his face in the muggy night air. "So where the fuck is he?"

Gritz's voice. "Terrace Drive. Camera just picked him up. He's heading into the park."

Reznick said, "I'm on it." He turned right into the road leading through the park and stopped, scanning the sidewalks. Joggers, tourists, rollerbladers and skateboarders practicing tricks. "Terrace Drive is a big goddamn road."

Gritz said, "All teams converge on Terrace Drive from Fifth Avenue. Target is mobile..."

Reznick continued along Terrace Drive. "This takes us straight to the West Side."

Gritz sighed. "Come on, someone... gimme a break on this. Speak to me."

Less than a minute later, Reznick was heading past Strawberry Fields and a few Lennon fans lighting candles, and out into Central Park West. In the distance, he saw the spectral figure running across the street, partially obscured by tree foliage. The silhouette matched the physique he had witnessed.

The figure stopped about fifty yards away.

Reznick stopped running and stared long and hard at the man. He saw immediately that the man was dressed almost identically to Kendrick. But this man wasn't him.

The guy was twenty pounds heavier and nearly ten years older, albeit the same height.

Reznick watched as a woman jumped out of a cab and embraced the man. "Christ almighty... Someone has fucked up. This ain't our guy, Gritz."

A long pause. "Reznick, what was that?"

"It ain't him. I just got a good look. It is not the target. I repeat, not the target. He is hugging some woman and they're laughing and joking, and this is not him. I'm at Central Park West and 72nd."

Gritz sighed and a long silence opened up. "Shit... Facial recognition has confirmed that this is not our guy. Not our fucking guy. Fuck! Fuck! Fuck!"

A few moments later, Reznick was picked up by a Fed unit in an SUV and they headed to the hostel on East 81st.

Gritz was outside the hostel leaning against a Suburban, cell phone pressed to his ear. "Well, tell him we got it wrong. Next time, I'm going to kick his ass." He ended the call and stared at Reznick. "We lost him. We fucking lost him. How did this happen? How the fuck did this happen? First the bastard slips away, and then we follow some poor chump through the park."

Reznick was handed a bottle of water and took a large gulp. It felt good. "So, what now?"

"We establish where he was, the last known confirmed sighting."

"So, where is he?"

Gritz shook his head. "We know he was here thirty minutes ago. We have people focusing on what we do know. We have people scanning surveillance cameras across the Upper East Side and agents out all over the place."

"So why the hell isn't he showing up?" Reznick snapped, struggling to contain his fury.

Reznick and Gritz were interrupted by one of the FBI SWAT team. "Kendrick left here with a bag. He went to a bathroom inside, saying he had to pick up some personal belongings, and returned a few minutes later. It looks like the ceiling tiles were lifted, and whatever was stashed there was retrieved. But we don't know what."

Reznick's pulse quickened. "He's picked up his cache. He's going for his target."

Gritz's cell phone rang. "Yup." He nodded and began to frown. "Yeah, but I thought he was at the Plaza tonight? So, what changed? We have him as staying at the goddamn Plaza." He let out a long sigh. "OK, OK, relax, I hear you. OK, that's real close to us. But the hotel will be on lockdown. Staff vetted. Let me know if you need us." He ended the call.

Reznick shrugged. "Who you talking about?"

Gritz said nothing for a few moments.

"Gritz, talk to me; who are we talking about?"

Gritz cleared his throat. "The President, his wife and his family are staying two blocks from here tonight. The Surrey Hotel. Secret Service has the hotel secured. It's on lockdown."

Reznick's mind was racing. "What was all that about the Plaza?"

"Secret Service is a law unto itself. Short-notice change from the Plaza to the Surrey. No questions asked."

Reznick ran his hand through his hair, matted in sweat. His mind flashed to the images in his head of Kendrick photographing the high floors of the Plaza. "Shit."

"What is it?"

"When I was tailing Kendrick, he took pictures of the Plaza. I think he was intelligence gathering. Perhaps checking line of sight. What if it's the President who's the target? And Kendrick is here now to take out the President at the Surrey?"

Gritz went quiet for a few moments before he looked at his watch. "Two blocks from here; he will arrive in twenty-three minutes."

"Gritz, listen to me. This shit is gonna go down. And it's gonna go down tonight at the Surrey."

Gritz said nothing.

"So, what exactly is on his schedule tonight at the Surrey?"

"Only one thing. A private meeting with a handpicked group of 9/11 families, survivors and first responders. There will be no press or media of any sort. No advance notice. A White House photographer will take some pictures and footage, which will be released to the media tomorrow morning when the President has left the hotel for the 9/11 commemorations. Trust me, the whole street will be shut off so no one can get near when he arrives or leaves. There is no chance of anyone, let alone Kendrick, getting close to him."

"Let's assume that's correct. Then it just leaves one option, doesn't it?"

"Sniper?"

Reznick nodded.

"This is Manhattan. You're surrounded by towers and skyscrapers everywhere."

"Let's get over there, see for ourselves."

"Reznick, it'll be crawling with Secret Service. They don't like people stepping on their toes."

"Yeah, well, that's just too bad."

FORTY-FOUR

Reznick and Gritz were reluctantly allowed through the cordon on Madison and stood outside the Surrey on East 76th Street. It was nestled less than a block from Central Park. Secret Service guys in dark suits checked through last-minute schedules. But Meyerstein was already there and talking to the head of operations.

Reznick walked over to her as she ended the conversation. "We need to talk." The Secret Service guy took that as his cue and moved away to join the rest of his team.

Meyerstein said, "What the hell happened, Jon?"

Reznick said, "He got away; that's what happened."

Gritz blew out his cheeks, hands on hips. "I take full responsibility for this, ma'am. We screwed up."

Meyerstein put up her hand to stop him. "I don't want to hear any sob stories. We need to find him. And quick."

Reznick pointed across the street. "All these areas directly opposite and the blocks leading to the park have been checked and secured?"

She nodded. "Locked down. Nobody can get in or out. And each and every occupant or deli owner has been vetted by the Secret Service."

Reznick turned and looked away from the park toward Madison. Towering over the intersection was a huge monolithic building with an art gallery at street level. "What's that over there?"

"That... That is the Carlyle. Big-time, big-bucks hotel."

"You see what I see?"

Meyerstein said, "Line of sight?"

"Precisely."

"Yeah, but that would be a red flag. Secret Service would spot anything moving within a block of here. They've got people on roofs and inside that very building. Sniper teams watching everything. Besides, the place will have been swept room by room."

"If it were me, that would be my top choice."

Meyerstein turned again and looked across at the windows of the Carlyle and the huge monolithic tower.

Gritz intervened. "Reznick... the hotel's been swept. You're fixated on tonight. The internet chatter we intercepted is telling us something is planned for tomorrow. It's symbolic, if nothing else."

Reznick stared up at the towering windows looking down on one of the busiest intersections on the East Side, AC units outside each room. "When people tell me a building has been swept, you know what I think?"

Meyerstein said nothing as Gritz shrugged.

"You can never be certain. And that means you check again. I say we go in."

"Reznick... it's secure." Gritz sighed and looked at his watch. "Eight minutes." He closed his eyes for a moment. "You think he might be hiding there? The Carlyle is loaded with cameras and agents in and outside the hotel. No chance. We would've picked it up, and that's leaving aside multiple sweeps."

"Listen, I don't think you understand who and what you're dealing with. There is a possibility that the President could be a target. It could be tonight. We can all see there are plans in place... and these people will not be denied."

Meyerstein looked at her watch, pulled out her cell phone and punched in a number. "Jenny, it's Assistant Director

Meyerstein. Jenny, I want to know when last there was a sweep of the Carlyle building. In fact, send me the building plans." A long pause as if the woman on the other end of the line was checking information. "Area confirmed as secured an hour ago. OK. Thanks." She ended the call and turned to Reznick just as her iPad mini beeped. "Here are the plans." The three of them crowded around the table to see. "One hundred and eighty-eight rooms and fifty-one residences, 35 stories high. Look at this. The building is actually two separate buildings."

Reznick said, "I don't follow."

Meyerstein pointed to the front elevation on the tablet. "Look here. The hotel is basically the tower on the south of the frontage. The building closest to us, which we think of as the Carlyle, is in fact a seventeen-story apartment house with a separate entrance, a service door, at 50 East 77th Street. There is also a basement garage entrance on East 76th Street."

Reznick looked up at the tower, windows high up, hundreds of feet above Madison. His gaze wandered to the apartments, carved out of pristine limestone. "Separate entrance. Interesting."

"Here's another interesting point. There is a tunnel system which connects the two properties, subbasement if you like."

"You kidding me, right?"

Meyerstein shook her head. "Nope. Look at the plans."

Reznick studied the drawings showing the internal structure, memorizing the layout of the building.

Meyerstein said, "OK, Jon, let's assume you're right, that he has somehow managed to evade surveillance systems. Kendrick, where would he be?"

"Hiding until the coast is clear. He's gone in through the service door and is positioning himself with a clear line of sight."

Meyerstein looked at Reznick.

"Do you really think he's in there?"

"If I were him, that's exactly where I'd choose."

They strode across Madison and along East 77th. Black canopy showing the entrance to the apartment complex.

Meyerstein said, "Carlyle House."

Reznick sighed. "No Secret Service presence, only an elderly doorman and two local cops."

Gritz looked at his watch. "Six minutes. It'll be secure. You can count on it."

Reznick said nothing.

Gritz said, "Look, these are the private apartments of rich and very powerful people. It's not the sort of place you can go in and kick in doors."

Reznick said, "I don't give a shit who they are."

Gritz's face was like thunder. "Look, this ain't gonna happen. Secret Service is calling the shots."

"Listen to me. They need to be checked over one more time."

Meyerstein held up her hand to silence the argument. "Will you two knock it off?" She punched a number into her cell. "Director Steel, Martha Meyerstein, Assistant Director FBI. I'm standing across the street from your guys outside a side entrance of an apartment block, adjacent to the Carlyle. Something I need to run by you." She nodded. "Sir, we have a guy on the run in this area. Now, the President is due to turn up at any moment. I know the building has just been swept but I want to put one of my teams in for a final look." She closed her eyes for a few moments as she listened to Steel. "Sir, I understand."

Meyerstein ended the call and turned to Reznick and Gritz. "They have five two-man counter-sniper teams on rooftops all around here to make sure there is no possibility of a lone nut. Satisfied?"

Reznick said, "I hear what you're saying. But let's do this one more time. Just on the off chance."

"On the off chance of what? Look, they've swept the location. It's fine."

Reznick said, "The line of sight from a few of the Madison Avenue–facing apartments is perfect for a sniper. Let's be a hundred percent that he hasn't gotten in."

Gritz sighed. "The Secret Service has this under control. Now, if it's all right with you..."

Reznick said, "I think we should do one more sweep, room by room, on the Madison side."

"With respect, Reznick, I don't. It's been done; the Secret Service is very, very thorough."

Meyerstein's cell phone rang, interrupting the discussion. "Hi, Roy; look, can it wait?" She grimaced. "OK, what've you got?" She nodded and listened as Stamper spoke for nearly a minute. "OK, we're on the ground." She ended the call.

Reznick said, "What was that?"

Meyerstein ran a hand through her hair. "FBI's computer team is saying that for ninety seconds a thirty-five-yard radius of surveillance cameras on the Upper East Side went down. It's like a corridor from 81st Street."

Reznick shook his head. "Jamming. Shit, this is what I was worried about. Does the Secret Service know about this?"

"They do now. You wanna know where they've pinpointed as the fulcrum of the last signal?"

"The Carlyle?"

Meyerstein's eyes were hooded. "More precisely, where we are standing."

Reznick felt his blood rate hike up. "We need to get in there."

"Roy also has the Secret Service sweep logs. There's a major problem."

A blaring siren in the distance, and Meyerstein winced.

Reznick said, "Tell me."

"The sweep was signed off personally by Director Steel."

Gritz shook his head. "What? Why would he oversee that? Hang on..."

Meyerstein lifted her hand as if to silence him. "When the sweep was being carried out, Director Steel was briefing his team in the Secret Service's New York field office in downtown Brooklyn."

Reznick screwed up his face. "Are we sure he signed off on it?"

"Roy's seen the documentation. It's got his digital signature on it."

Reznick felt ill at ease. He couldn't abide endless discussions. He was used to action and getting the job done. "Kendrick's in there. I know it. This was to go down at the Plaza. But something's changed. He's in there now. Waiting."

A blaring siren in the distance, honking of horns.

Reznick said, "Who can order a change of venue for the President?"

Meyerstein stared at him for a moment. "Director Steel has the authority. He can make that happen."

Reznick said, "Kendrick and Black couldn't have been acting alone. I don't buy that."

Meyerstein nodded. "I agree."

Gritz's eyes widened in disbelief. "Are you serious?"

Reznick said, "Listen to me. The whole special access program was set up when O'Grady began to get too close. I believe he suspected something wasn't right about Kendrick and tried to contact that intern. It's not plausible that the State Department didn't know what O'Grady knew. And so he was gotten rid of and Black put in charge of a secret investigation to try to keep things quiet and steer the operation clear of Kendrick."

Meyerstein sighed and nodded.

"And that's why when you and Chisholm were closing in, you were targeted."

Meyerstein gave a thin smile. "Thanks for reminding me."

"This is a cabal. A cabal within the highest echelons of the American military and the CIA. And who knows the President's schedule better? Who is allowed to change it at no notice? This cabal includes Steel. Black has form in this area."

Both Meyerstein and Gritz went quiet for a few moments as they digested what he had said.

Reznick spoke first. "We've got to go in. Right now. No fucking around."

"Jon, we have no authorization at this stage."

"There's no time for that. We need to get in and find this bastard. Fast."

Meyerstein said, "OK, let's assume we get in there. How do we do a sweep of a locked-down hotel? Do we evacuate first?"

Reznick felt the adrenaline begin to pump around his body. "No. Low key, room to room. I know this stuff."

"What about SWAT?"

"Definitely not. That is not what you need in these circumstances. We don't want to alert him that we're in the hotel."

Meyerstein said nothing.

"We'd start out with hotel rooms with line of sight to the Surrey."

Gritz began to shake his head. "This is nuts. I can't believe what I'm hearing. None of this makes sense. Besides, you need authorization."

Meyerstein stared at him, stony faced, a haunted look in her eyes. "Leave that to me." She turned to Reznick. "So, what are you waiting for? You're on."

Reznick turned and headed for the side entrance.

FORTY-FIVE

A sense of foreboding washed over Meyerstein as she watched Reznick disappear into the hotel. She knew she had to deploy Reznick in such a matter. It was the right thing to do. But still, she was beset by doubts plaguing her like a recurring bad dream.

Meyerstein pulled out her cell and punched in the secure direct office number of FBI director Bill O'Donoghue. He picked up after the third ring.

"Martha, what the hell is going on? How did we let Kendrick slip? The last update I saw was that Kendrick was watching goddamn tennis. I've just gotten out of a meeting, and I hear Kendrick has dropped off our radar and General Black has shot himself."

"I know; it's a mess."

"You're not kidding." He sighed. "You on the ground?"

"Yes, sir. New York. Sir, we want to gain access to an apartment building adjacent to the Carlyle Hotel."

"Why? You think Kendrick's in there?"

"Absolutely. It's also a line of sight to the President's hotel."

"But the Secret Service..."

"Sir, I've spoken to Director Steel, and he said the area had been secured."

"And I don't doubt that."

"Sir, surveillance cameras were jammed in a route around the Upper East Side earlier; GPS pinpoints the entrance to the Carlyle apartment building as the last spot where the signal was probably received. Bottom line? I don't believe the area is secure."

O'Donoghue let out a long sigh. "We lost Kendrick. And now you're saying you don't trust the Secret Service to secure an area?"

"Yes, sir." Meyerstein sighed as more sirens blared in the distance. She raised her voice. "Sir, the analysis my team has is that a false flag operation is underway. CIA fingerprints."

A long silence opened up between them as if the director was considering his response. "This is a bit of a leap, Meyerstein. I don't know—"

"You know the up-to-date picture, sir. There is the connection between Black and Kendrick. Black also has form on false flag operations. And that's what Chisholm's source at the Pentagon told him. And that's why they were taken out. I also believe O'Grady was on to them."

O'Donoghue sighed. "I agree with your analysis."

"Sir, we want to do a final sweep of the Carlyle apartment complex. We don't have much time."

"The Secret Service leads on this, Martha; you know that. They don't like people encroaching on their turf."

"I've talked to Director Steel. He doesn't want to know."

O'Donoghue went quiet for a few moments. "The Secret Service is very good at what it does."

"I don't doubt that, sir. But I'm requesting that you use your influence. We need to get in there and do a sweep. I need you to cover for me, sir."

O'Donoghue said nothing, as if contemplating his options.

"Sir, I need you to make this happen. We're going to do this low key. But we're running out of time."

A long pause. "I've heard enough. Leave this to me."

The line went dead.

Out of the corner of her eye, Meyerstein saw a huge, imposing figure approach. She turned to face a man wearing an impeccable dark suit, white shirt and maroon tie, shiny black shoes, surrounded by five colleagues.

Meyerstein recognized the face immediately. "Bryan," she said as she shook his hand. "I wondered when I'd bump into you."

Bryan Simon was the special agent in charge of the Secret Service in New York, working out of Brooklyn. His handshake was firm. "We seem to be at cross purposes here, Martha. This is Secret Service business."

"Are you aware of what's happening, Bryan? Have you seen the updates?"

"I see all updates, Martha."

"I'm talking updates in the last ten, fifteen minutes." Meyerstein quickly ran over the background to Kendrick and Black's connection, Black's suicide and the false flag intelligence analysis.

"Look, Martha, my first concern is the immediate vicinity and that it has been secured."

"Do you know who by?"

"Yeah, it was one of my guys, Jimmy Lorenti."

"Where is Jimmy just now?"

Special Agent Simon shrugged. "He's in the Surrey, as we speak; why?"

"You're saying he did the sweep of the Carlyle apartments?"

"Yes. He was the one who I scheduled to do it. He knows the drill. He's the best I've got."

Meyerstein pulled out her phone and turned the screen towards him, showing the sweep logs. "What does that say, Bryan?"

His eyes scanned the screen. "I don't understand..."

"According to this, Director Steel signed off on the sweep of the apartments. Yet we know he wasn't on site at that time. Bryan, are your guys up to speed with regards to Kendrick?"

Simon flushed as he stared at the screen. "We were informed of Kendrick by our Protective Intelligence and Assessment Division in DC. We are aware of your concerns."

"Bryan, why has the director signed off on this? He wasn't even on site. Have you ever heard of such a thing?"

Simon shook his head but said nothing. The radio he was holding crackled into life. "Bryan, I need to see you right now, thanks. Couple of issues to be clarified." It was the voice of the director.

Meyerstein said, "What are you going to do, Bryan?"

"Martha, I'll ask about this. Trust me, I didn't know anything about this. Leave this to me."

The minutes dragged and still no call back from O'Donoghue. She turned and looked at Gritz. "ETA for the motorcade."

"Two minutes."

Meyerstein looked across Madison and saw the throng of Secret Service men, police manning the cordon tape. Her gaze was drawn to a black canopy – almost certainly bulletproof – being pulled out, securing the entrance to the Surrey.

Her cell phone rang. The caller ID showed it was O'Donoghue.

"Martha, I've just spoken to Director Steel. I explained our concerns in depth..."

"And?"

"He reminded me in no uncertain terms that they were the lead on this. I agreed but said we had very particular concerns for the President's safety."

Meyerstein closed her eyes and wished he'd get to the point. "What did he say?"

"He listened and we talked, and he agreed that there can be a fresh sweep of the whole apartment complex, just as soon as the President is safely inside his hotel."

"Got that, sir."

Meyerstein ended the call. She had what she wanted. She was now counting on Reznick. He had to deliver.

FORTY-SIX

Reznick strode through the glistening black marble art-deco lobby of the Carlyle – adorned with lavish oil paintings, huge mirrors and beautiful murals – and past the smiling concierges, well-heeled guests and a Secret Service agent talking into his cell as he headed towards the elevators.

A white-gloved porter smiled at him. "Evening, sir; which floor?"

Reznick hadn't envisaged company. "Thirty, please."

The porter punched in the number and the doors shut and the elevator ascended. "Which suite are you staying in, sir?"

"3001," he lied.

The porter screwed up his face. "Oh... I thought that wasn't in use until tomorrow at the earliest. Hollywood regular of ours is booked in for that. But I was sure it was empty."

Reznick said, "I'm just staying the night. What's your name?"

"I'm Joe. Joe Morriso. I know all our guests. Pleased to meet you, Mr...?"

The elevator stopped suddenly at thirty and the doors opened.

"I'm Donald Simpson."

"Well, Mr Simpson, I hope you enjoy your stay at the Carlyle."

Reznick nodded. "Thank you."

He was glad to get out of the confines of the elevator and down to business. He headed down the corridor and saw the stairwell doors.

Reznick pushed them open and climbed the dimly-lit wrought iron stairwell toward the thirty-first floor. His rubber-soled Rockports squeaked as he bounded up the highly polished stone floors. His mind was focused.

His earpiece crackled. "Hold it, Jon," the FBI techie said, "we got some movement on thirty-one."

Reznick pressed himself up tight against the stairwell wall.

A few moments later. "OK, chambermaid with security guy waiting for elevator. Yup, doors opened and they're in. Three, two, one. And, we're all clear on thirty-one."

Reznick said, "Thanks."

He pushed through the doors and turned right for room 3103.

Reznick swiped the card and cracked the door. No sign of life. He shut the door and pulled the penlight from a back pocket. He pointed it around the lounge. It was a plush tower suite with views of Manhattan through the huge windows. The penlight strafed the rest of the room. Grand piano in the corner. Monogrammed cushions with the letter C in a fancy typeface. He crouched down and pressed his ear to the carpeted floor. Muffled chatter in a downstairs room.

He scoured the rest of the suite, bathroom and bedroom, closets, under beds. Nothing. Just a fresh scent of pine and cleaning polish in the air. He headed back into the lounge, switched off the penlight and crawled across the carpet toward the windows.

The terrace was empty.

Reznick got up and headed towards the door, pressing his ear against the wood. No sounds in the corridor, only the vibration from someone walking in the room above.

Low humming as if from a nearby air-conditioning unit. He whispered into his lapel, "How's it looking on thirty-one?"

"You're clear."

Reznick quietly opened the door and pulled it shut. He looked straight ahead and headed down the corridor, through the doors and up the stairwell to the thirty-second floor.

"Good work, Jon. Three more. Next stop is 3203. How you feeling?"

"I'll tell you when I find this son of a bitch."

Reznick stopped at the doors to the thirty-second floor, cameras strafing his movements. "I'm about to enter the thirty-second floor," he whispered. "Are we clear?"

A long pause. "Hold on."

Reznick stood and waited for a reply. He needed to move. What was taking so long?

A long sigh. "Finally clear, Jon. Go on."

Reznick headed through the doors and saw room 3203. He swiped the card and opened the door.

The suite was cloaked in semidarkness, only the glow of the moon from the Manhattan sky giving any light. Sofas, ornate antique tables, the smell of beeswax polish. He took out his penlight and flashed it round the room. Modern art on the wall. He headed through a door and down a hall to a small bedroom.

Creaking floors from above, the sound of voices. Loud TV. Game show playing.

Reznick headed through into a bathroom, fluffy monogrammed towels and a hint of eucalyptus in the air. He checked in wardrobes, under the bed, in closets, but found nothing.

He went back to the living room and opened the doors that led to the terrace. A warm breeze blew in, billowing the lace curtains, the lights of the city as far as the eye could see.

Reznick carefully shut and locked the terrace doors and headed out of the suite. He pressed his ear to the door. The vibration from the nearby elevator. He opened the door.

Then he felt cold metal pressed hard against his neck.

FORTY-SEVEN

Meyerstein was pacing the sidewalk, wondering how Reznick was getting on, when her cell rang.

"Martha, it's Bryan Simon."

Meyerstein sighed. "Bryan, what's going happening on your side?"

"I just wanted to keep you in the loop."

"I'm listening."

He sighed. "Martha, I've just spoken to Jimmy Lorenti..." The traffic noise was drowning out his words.

"Sorry Bryan, what did you say?"

"Martha, he didn't carry out the sweep."

The traffic noise of blaring horns wasn't helping. "Bryan, can you clarify? It sounded to me like you said that Lorenti didn't make the sweep."

"That's what I said."

"OK, so if he didn't do the sweep, who the hell did?"

"Look, don't bust my balls over this. Martha, I've got to be up front. I didn't know anything about this; it was a..." The sound of radios crackling down the line, as if from Secret Service colleagues nearby. "Martha, the team who did the sweep was headed up by Charles Higgins, Assistant Special Agent in Charge of the Office of Protective Operations. He is responsible for daily security operations and strategic planning to support the Presidential Protection Division. And he reports to the chief of staff, Director Steel."

Meyerstein's mind was racing. "On whose orders?"

Simon said nothing.

"Bryan, help me out here."

"Look, I can't say any more."

"Come on, Bryan. Did Jimmy not inform you?"

Simon sighed long and hard before he cleared his throat. "All I know is that Higgins spoke to him face to face and told him that the sweep had been done and I had been informed."

"He said that? But that wasn't the case, was it?"

Simon said nothing. His silence told Meyerstein all she had to know. The Secret Service had changed a predetermined sweep.

"Bryan, we go back a long way, right?"

A long sigh. "Sure."

"Look, I know the Secret Service has ways of doing things. Tried and tested. Safety first. Why did it change things in this case?"

"Can I be honest? I really don't know. Look, the motorcade will be here any minute."

The line went dead.

Meyerstein's blood ran cold as the area went into full lockdown ahead of the motorcade. She thought of the threat they were facing and wondered if she had made the right call. Even amid the din of distant sirens and agents talking loudly into cell phones, her doubts and lingering fears returned.

She moved her team into a nearby high-tech FBI mobile command vehicle – which had just arrived – for a pre-sweep briefing. The tension was palpable.

Meyerstein made a beeline for an FBI techie with headphones on, monitoring the Carlyle's security cameras. She tapped him on the shoulder and the young agent pulled off his headphones. "What's the latest?"

"Don't know; we seem to have lost his connection."

Meyerstein said, "Goddamn. Gimme a break."

"Reznick asked for a list of empty rooms on the Madison Avenue side of the Carlyle from the eighteenth floor up."

Meyerstein saw Reznick's logic. It made sense for Kendrick to hide out in an empty room with line of sight. It would enable him not to be disturbed if he was in radio communication with a handler, receiving instructions. "I want his connection back up and running. Fast! Do you hear me?"

The kid just nodded. "I'm on it."

Meyerstein turned to face the assembled, heavily armed Feds. She thought of Reznick, perhaps prowling the corridors of the upper floor, going from empty room to empty room. The not knowing what exactly was going on and why the connection had been broken was unbearable.

She glanced at her watch, radios crackling in the background, monitors switched on to the same feed as the surveillance cameras inside the hotel and the apartments they were about to search.

Meyerstein said, "I make it that we have a minute until the President arrives and is escorted inside the Surrey. Special Agent Gritz is in charge of search operations on the ground, I'll be coordinating with the technical and computer agents here in the mobile command vehicle."

Matthew Suarez, director of security at the Carlyle, said, "Ma'am, I've got to say we have no indication that there has been any breach of security. Our cameras have detected no one who shouldn't be here. Each and every guest and resident we know very well. Besides, we've been in lockdown for hours."

"Mr Suarez, firstly, I appreciate your cooperation. The surveillance cameras within the Carlyle and within a thirty-five-yard radius of where we believe Kendrick was situated blacked out, probably because of jamming. It lasted no more than ninety seconds. But we have to assume the worst."

Suarez flushed a deep crimson. "I can assure you that..."

Meyerstein put up her hand to silence him. "Look, we're going in. We have the authority."

Suarez nodded his head, suitably chastised.

"OK, while we believe he will be higher up, we can't take anything for granted. Therefore, ground floor to seventeen, what are we talking?"

Suarez said, "It's mixed. Some private apartments, some owned by the hotel."

"What about above seventeen?"

"That's the tower. It's ninety percent plus hotel."

"OK, what about access to each and every apartment and room?"

"Each agent has a Carlyle uniform and a master card."

Meyerstein turned to the search team and held up a glossy printout of Kendrick. "The same photo was circulated to each and every member of the team. We're behind the curve on this and have been from the get-go. I want to make this clear. He is very dangerous. He's Special Forces–trained. A crack shot. Ferociously fit. We also now know he's undergone specialist training at the Farm."

Gritz said, "What kind of specialist training?"

Meyerstein said, "You name it, they do it. Map reading, communications, standard-issue Special Forces training, light to heavy weapons, machine guns and automatic weapons. Military forces from around the world train there. Counterinsurgency. And let's not forget PSYOP. Survival. Infiltration. Interestingly, parts of PSYOP are black flag operations. The psychological impact being so profound that it changes public perceptions. Oh, and I nearly forgot, they teach you how to kill with your bare hands."

Gritz shook his head. "Jesus Christ. So we've got a Special Forces–trained sniper. Shouldn't we consider evacuating the hotel?"

Meyerstein shook her head. "There would be panic, and in that panic God knows what could happen. Surprise is the best tool we've got."

Gritz said, "OK, so if we're not evacuating surely this is a job for the FBI SWAT teams?"

Meyerstein shook her head. "That wouldn't work, either. It would get messy. We can't afford to have residents and guests fleeing from the hotel. We need to go in quiet. Slow. Methodical. He'll be armed and dangerous. That's why we've sent Reznick in ahead of you guys."

Gritz scratched the back of his head and sighed. "OK, let's do this."

Meyerstein said, "The first seventeen floors to Andy and the red team. The tower, eighteen and above: the blue team with Special Agent Gritz."

Gritz nodded, eyes hooded.

"Room by room, nice and easy, knock on the door, smile on the face, and say 'we're Carlyle management, checking that the air is working properly, as we've had a couple of complaints from guests.'"

An FBI techie, watching the cameras on the motorcade route from his monitor, said, "Cadillac One two blocks away."

Meyerstein and the team glanced across. Her attention switched to the monitor checking outside the Surrey as the first outrider appeared and the Secret Service crowded round the entrance like a protective shield. A few moments later, the Beast, as the President's limousine was called within Secret Service circles, swept into view. Her throat felt dry and her stomach knotted. A huge Secret Service agent got out and opened the rear door of the huge Presidential Cadillac. A female agent did the same on the opposite side of the vehicle as a cordon of agents filtered around the car.

A few moments' delay and the President got out and headed toward the canopy as his wife and kids were ushered inside, out of sight. They were visible for barely five seconds as a huge entourage followed them into the hotel. Time seemed to stop.

Meyerstein let out a long sigh. "OK, the President is inside." She turned to face her team. "That's our cue. We need to do this right." She pointed at Special Agent Andy Hayman. "Andy, you're former SWAT, right?"

Hayman nodded. "Yes, ma'am."

"You're in sole charge of the red team, ground level up to seventeen."

Hayman nodded.

"You guys go in first. I'm going to brief the blue team."

Hayman and his team left.

Meyerstein glanced again at the monitors, but this time inside the Carlyle. "Gritz, you are leading the team on the higher floors. The tower. Look out for Reznick. That's where he'll be. The last we heard, he was on thirty-two."

Meyerstein turned to the director of security, Suarez. "Now, your deputy, he's assigned to the red team?"

Suarez nodded. "He is."

"Then you will be assigned to Special Agent Gritz's blue team. Floor by floor, eighteen and up. You know the residents intimately, the floor plans, and you know the place inside out, right?"

"Absolutely."

"OK, I want you to knock on each and every door. They will know your face. They will trust you. What I need from you, though, is people you don't know, don't recognize, or anything which appears untoward."

"Leave it to me."

Meyerstein looked at Gritz. "This'll take time. But I don't mind how long it takes. What I do mind is that we get this guy."

Gritz said, "You want him brought in?"

"I want him out of there, dead or alive."

FORTY-EIGHT

Reznick's hands were raised and the gun pressed to the side of his neck. He felt the man's warm breath on his face.

"Are you lost, Mr Simpson? This isn't your room, is it?"

Reznick said nothing.

"Who are you, sir?"

Reznick waited for a few moments. He counted down in his head. Three, two, one. He swiped his arm back as if swatting a fly and grabbed the gun, redirecting the weapon away from his body. Then he elbowed the guy with a ferocious jolt to the side of the neck. The guy collapsed in a heap as if hit by a sniper.

He took the man's gun and tucked it into his waistband. He swiped the card for the empty room and dragged the unconscious man inside to the bathroom.

Reznick tore up some Egyptian cotton sheets and tied the man to the toilet, mouth bound and hands behind his back. He rifled through the man's inside pockets and pulled out an ID. He scanned it. Secret Service. Jeff Renoz.

Shit.

He tapped his earpiece and whispered, "Why no heads-up?"

"Cameras have all gone down, Jon."

"Shit."

"The search is focusing on occupied rooms. You're checking the handful of empty ones."

Reznick nodded. "Got that." He relayed what had happened.

A long sigh. "OK, got that, Jon."

"I'm heading to the next level."

"You gotta be careful. The Secret Service guy you bumped into must've been part of their presidential protection detail. They've got a suite on the thirty-third."

"Which one?"

"3305, which has perfect line of sight, apparently."

"I've still got 3301 and 3303."

"Both empty. And both owned by a Hong Kong businessman when he's in New York on business."

"Kendrick must be in one of them."

"Take care, Jon."

A few moments later, just as he was about to leave the suite, his earpiece buzzed again.

"Jon." The voice of Meyerstein was soft, almost a whisper. "Where are you?"

"Thirty-second. Nothing so far. What about the others?"

"Negative. Look, the red and blue teams are going room to room. There's only the floor above the one you're on. Those are duplexes, on two levels. So they reach the top, the thirty-fourth, although entry is only from the thirty-third."

Reznick said, "Copy that."

"If he's anywhere, he'll be there."

"What about the stairwells and elevators?"

"Cameras are down. Still trying to get them up again... Hang on."

A long silence opened up.

Reznick said, "You still there?"

"Hold on, Jon. Just been messaged by Secret Agent Bryan Simon."

"I'm listening."

"Jon, hold on; we're just checking this. Something about the President's itinerary." The silence lasted for nearly a minute. Eventually, she came on the line again. "I don't believe this."

"What is it?"

A long sigh. "Jon, we've got a problem."

"Yeah, no kidding."

"No. Another problem. In exactly seventeen minutes, the President is meeting the families of 9/11 victims."

"How's that a problem? He's out of sight."

"Negative. The reception is on the rooftop terrace at the Surrey."

"No fucking way."

A long sigh. "It's all been arranged. There's going to be a string quartet playing... No one knows about it. The details are not out there."

"Well, someone knows about it. And I'll bet that someone is Adam Kendrick and the people directing this operation."

Meyerstein said nothing.

"Look, while we have Kendrick on the loose, surely it would be safest for the President to be kept away from prying eyes? It's a no-brainer.

"I know, Jon, but this is out of my hands. I spoke with Steel but he brushed aside my concerns. Jon, I feel sick. I think this is when it's going to happen."

"No question, this operation is a green light. I bet Kendrick has been hunkered down up there since he got in, right under the noses of the Secret Service snipers."

"Jon, there are seven rooms on the thirty-third. We've got to find this guy. No ifs, ands or buts. You must get this guy at any cost."

"On it."

Reznick headed up the stairwell to the thirty-third floor. The final floor to sweep. There were only two suites to check. He whispered into his lapel, "I'm about to enter the thirty-third. Contact the counter-sniper team and let them know I'm on their floor."

"Gimme a minute."

Less than a minute later, Meyerstein's voice was back in the earpiece. "The message has been passed on."

Reznick responded. "I'm going in."

He crouched down and cracked the doors to the thirty-third. No sign of life down the narrow corridor.

Reznick pushed open the doors and got to his feet. He headed down the corridor. He got to the first empty suite and pressed his ear to the door. A faint sound of water in an old lead pipe, maybe underneath the floor. He swiped the card and cracked the door and peered into the darkness of the huge suite. Then he crawled inside and shut the door quietly behind him.

He didn't move as he got his bearings.

Slow is smooth, smooth is fast. The military mantra he still used.

Reznick took his penlight from his jacket and strafed the room. Piano in the corner, antique walnut furnishings, just like the other empty suites. But his senses were cranked to the max.

He felt something. He didn't know what.

He reached for his Beretta and took it from the belt strapped to his chest. He felt his finger on the cold trigger. His heart was beating hard. Senses were all switched on as he began to scour the three-bedroom suite. He headed up the duplex's stairs, the lights of the city below, partially lighting the room. The glass doors to the balcony were open and the curtains were billowing in the summer breeze.

Reznick slowly approached the open door and shone the penlight. As the curtain blew out, he noticed black boots sticking out from below. He crouched down and slowly approached. The curtains billowed again and he saw the crumpled bodies of two counter-snipers with a bullet to the forehead each.

Suddenly, a figure emerged from the shadows to Reznick's right. He dived to the floor and shot twice at the figure's head.

A flash of light from the gun and a muffled phut sound from the silenced 9mm. The figure crashed to the floor facefirst through a glass coffee table. He wasn't moving.

Reznick moved closer. He was in the kill zone. He turned the body over and stared at the bloody face. It wasn't Kendrick.

His earpiece crackled into life. "What the hell is going on?" Meyerstein shouted in his ear.

"I've just taken out a trigger man. It means Kendrick isn't alone. But it also means Kendrick is still on the loose."

A few seconds later, Meyerstein's voice on the earpiece. "Jon, we've lost radio contact with the counter-sniper team. The line of sight from terraces and balconies on that floor to the President is wide open. You have to act now!"

Reznick said, "I'm heading straight there now."

"Jon, the President is on the roof terrace now. I can see him on our monitor. There are scores of people around him. There's a Plexi shield that's been erected all around the roof terrace..."

"That won't stop Kendrick!" Reznick hissed.

Reznick knew that someone like Kendrick would have access to military-grade bullets that could tear through the best Plexiglas. He bounded down the stairs of the darkened duplex, opened the door and crouched down as he headed along the corridor to room 3304.

He pressed himself to the corridor wall as he moved closer. He swiped the card and pushed open the door, knowing he was a sitting duck. He crouched down low and shut the door as quietly as he could, a soft metallic clicking sound. He thought of the suite layout he'd just seen a few moments earlier.

The smell of cordite. Sweat. The faint sound of traffic outside seeping into the room.

Eyes adjusted. Too slowly.

It was happening. Here and now.

Reznick kept low and crawled through the living room, past a table. Breathing hard, the sound of his heart beating the only noise. He knew he couldn't afford one false move. He had to get this right. His gut reaction was to storm through the suite. But that wasn't the smart way.

Slow is smooth, smooth is fast.

He pulled himself up and stayed in the crouched position as he headed for the duplex's stairs. His eyes were still adjusting.

He took the first step. A second. And the rest in a matter of seconds.

Reznick got down low again and crawled through the upper living room, past a table.

From his right, the sound of traffic. The French windows to the balcony were open the same as in the last suite.

He made his way through the darkened upper lounge, banging into a table leg. He winced at the pain. Drapes billowed from the open windows at the far side of the room.

He was within six yards.

Then he saw something. Crouched at the far end of the huge terrace. A spectral figure in black. A night vision telescope on tripod. The figure seemed oblivious to Reznick closing in. He was peering through the night vision scope and adjusting the eyepiece. Reznick saw the green LED indicating that the scope was on.

The man's head turned, and he stared at Reznick.

Reznick was already in the zone. He didn't hesitate for one second. He pointed the handgun and pulled the trigger. Nothing. He pulled it again. Nothing. An empty click.

His 9mm had jammed.

Fuck.

The world seemed to slow down.

Reznick's brain switched gears. He rolled over until he was flat on his stomach again. The man stood up but Reznick had already pulled out the Secret Service agent's Belgian-made FN Five-seven handgun out of the back of his waistband. He aimed the handgun for the second time and squeezed twice.

Two shots rang out.

A flash of light exploded, temporarily illuminating the room, a sharp recoil and a deafening noise.

The masked figure stumbled back as if in slow motion before he collapsed in a heap on the balcony. Writhing in agony, he knocked over the rifle and tripod.

Reznick scrambled to his feet and jumped hard on the man's chest, ripping off his mask. Staring back at him, eyes blazing, was Adam Kendrick. Fine-boned, strong jawline. He gripped his face and squeezed tight on his jawbones. "Who else?"

Kendrick's eyes were open wide and he grinned up at Reznick.

Reznick smashed his fist into Kendrick's nose. The sound of a bone cracking and blood spurted onto his face. "Who sent you?"

Kendrick stared up, bleeding, face impassive. His eyes began to roll around in his head. Then he slipped away.

FORTY-NINE

The moments that followed were a blizzard of activity. Secret Service agents sporting semiautomatic weapons and a fully armed FBI SWAT team stormed in, tied the unconscious man's hands behind his back with zip ties and dragged him out to the waiting paramedics. The rest of the Feds conducted a thorough sweep around the apartment and the one opposite. They found the two dead counter-snipers, bound, gagged and shot in the head. They were already cold.

Reznick relayed the information to Meyerstein.

"Goddamn."

Reznick felt numb as he was hustled out and crammed into the elevator with three Secret Service guys. No words were spoken as they descended to the lobby.

When the doors opened, Meyerstein was waiting, cell phone pressed to her ear. She held up a finger to indicate she didn't want to be disturbed. "Yeah, it's over; we got him. Being transferred as we speak to a safe facility. Speak to you later."

Meyerstein was expressionless. She cocked her head in the direction of the mobile command center. "Very well done." Then she smiled.

Reznick said nothing.

"You OK?"

"I'm OK."

Meyerstein sighed and looked at him. Tears were now welling up in her eyes but she managed to maintain her composure. "We lost some... We lost some good men along the way."

Reznick had never seen her like that before. He had to look away for a moment. "It happens. We move on."

Meyerstein dabbed at her eyes. He could see how empty she was. He realized better than anyone the empty feeling. Despite taking down the bad guys, the crushing loss of the good guys whose families would have to live without them was too much to bear.

When Reznick got back to the command center, there were a few pats on the back and "good work, big guy" muttered by some of the tech guys. But the overriding mood amongst the Feds was down.

Kendrick shouldn't have given them the slip out at Flushing Meadows. And how did Kendrick's accomplice, yet to be identified but believed to be a Chechen, get into the hotel? He wondered if he was a sleeper and had evaded security with a fake passport.

Reznick gulped down a small bottle of water and was given a black coffee in a Styrofoam cup. He took a big gulp and enjoyed the caffeine hit. He looked across at the monitors, most showing inside the upper floors of the Carlyle where he'd just been. "Who's on the thirty-third and thirty-fourth floors right now?"

Meyerstein sat down beside him. "Gritz and his guys have got it covered. Forensics, too. It's not a nice scene."

Reznick nodded, head bowed.

"How you feeling?"

"Glad we got him. Sorry you lost some of your guys."

"We all know there are sacrifices along the way. They're not the first and won't be the last."

Reznick closed his eyes for a moment and let out a long sigh. "Damn."

"Jon, it could've been worse."

"I know."

"A lot worse."

"Where's the President?"

"He's just been discreetly taken inside. No one is any the wiser."

"What about the media?"

"What about them?"

"They must have got wind of something with all the SWAT guys around?"

"There's a media blackout. So that will work in our favor."

"Or the people behind this... maybe it will work in their favor, too."

Meyerstein gave a wry smile. "Indeed."

Reznick looked across at the monitors. "So, where they taking him?"

"Military facility. He'll be flown to Andrews Air Force Base."

Reznick nodded and gulped the rest of his coffee. His mind flashed to the moment when the SWAT team stormed in and hustled out the injured Kendrick.

"Roy Stamper is monitoring–"

Her cell rang, interrupting her conversation, and she rolled her eyes. "Never a goddamn break." She pressed the green button to receive the call. "Yeah, Meyerstein." She frowned. "What the hell are you talking about?"

Reznick looked her way.

"SWAT has him. Andy's in charge, right?" A long silence. She closed her eyes for a moment. "That doesn't make any kind of sense, Roy. I watched them go in myself. Shit! I'm going to switch to radio." She ended the call and one of the techs that was wearing headphones handed her a two-way radio. "Talk to me, Roy."

The voice of Roy Stamper, working from the special access program's offices in McLean, crackled into life.

"Martha, the SWAT guys were diverted to Midtown with authorized FBI codes."

Meyerstein stepped out of the command center and paced up and down the sidewalk, sirens in the distance. Milling about, unmasked SWAT guys looking wired. She had the radio pressed tight to her ear when Reznick joined her. He could see and hear something was wrong. "I'm standing right beside them. So, who's got him?"

Stamper said "They took him away in a dark blue SUV."

Reznick interrupted, feeling his anger rise. "There's been a switch, hasn't there?"

Meyerstein stared at him and nodded. "Roy, which direction."

"I'm pulling up the footage. OK, they headed down East 76th Street."

Meyerstein ended the radio link and looked at Reznick. "You're right; there's been a switch. We need to track them down before this crew disappears with Kendrick."

Meyerstein turned to the SWAT guys around her. "I need four of you to go with Reznick."

Reznick said, "We don't have time for this."

He ran out onto the street and saw a passing motorcyclist slow down at the lights. He pulled his gun and jumped in front of the guy, who braked hard on the Ducati.

The guy flicked up his visor. "What the fuck?" he screamed.

Reznick hauled the poor guy off his bike, climbed on, adjusted his earpiece before he gave the engine a few revs, and sped away.

His earpiece crackled into life with Stamper's voice. "Reznick, got a sighting of vehicle. Clarification, it is in fact a black Nissan SUV and is heading down Park Avenue."

Reznick's body was flowing with adrenaline as he began the pursuit through the Manhattan night. He hung a right and headed down Park Avenue, weaving in and out of the traffic, past red lights, screeching traffic, narrowly avoiding being flattened by a couple of trucks. The smell of car fumes and the sound of blaring horns, and neon lights as he took a left.

"Jon, we're tracking your signal." He sped past a Capital One bank on his right.

"Where the hell are they?" he shouted.

"Jon, you're heading down East 59th Street. We think they might be heading back to Queens."

"Copy that."

Reznick was getting buffeted in the wind at high speed when he caught sight of the car as it sped towards the lower level of the Queensboro Bridge. "Fifty yards behind! I got this."

The getaway car was doing eighty at least, other drivers pulling over before they were rammed.

"They're on a rampage!" Reznick shouted into his lapel microphone. "We need support."

The sound of a chopper approaching above the bridge.

Reznick revved hard, weaved through the traffic and raced across the bridge, the East River below. "NYPD is on this too, Reznick. East 25th, heading onto Queens Boulevard. Ease up."

Were they serious? Ease up? Bullshit.

Reznick kept his head down as they headed deeper into Queens. Speeding down the Long Island Expressway at ninety-plus, keeping the SUV in his sights. The wind buffeting his face and body, he held on tight as the high-powered bike threatened to send him crashing off the road.

He accelerated hard and caught sight of Kendrick's silhouetted face in the back seat, two huge guys on either side of him, and a driver.

Reznick reached for his gun with his left hand as he drove the bike with his right. Suddenly, a rear passenger window came down and a handgun appeared.

He braked hard as the SUV tore ahead of him, leaving him in its wake.

"You OK, Reznick?" Stamper shouted.

"I'm on it."

Reznick felt the adrenaline surge through his body. He screwed up his eyes as he went through gears. He caught sight of them as he saw a sign for Grand Central Parkway.

The Nissan took a hard right; a Buick cut in on his lane and he screeched to a near halt as the SUV with Kendrick disappeared into the distance.

"What the fuck you doing?" Reznick shouted at the wide-eyed driver of the Buick as he sped away, tires screeching as the rubber tried to get traction.

The lights of the chopper were on the pursued car. His mind was racing. Where were they headed?

The rushing wind was nearly taking away his breath. Grit in his eyes.

"Goddamn!"

He saw a sign for JFK. Farther and farther away from Manhattan. The lights of the chopper guiding him.

Suddenly, from the getaway car up ahead, the sound of a rifle shot. Above him, the helicopter veered out of control.

Reznick felt his focus tighten, blocking out everything that wasn't in his sights. He was in the zone again. It wasn't long before he was on the Van Wyck Expressway heading south. He spotted the black Nissan veering wildly across the road. "He's in my sights again," he said. "I'm gaining."

"Jon, the NYPD and the FBI are not far behind."

Reznick couldn't see shit apart from the black Nissan and the glare from oncoming headlights. It was a bleak stretch of road. He felt his stomach knotting tight.

"Jon, you are now on the Nassau Expressway and you're heading for Rockaway Boulevard."

Up ahead, Reznick could see the Nissan veering in and out of the slower cars as if on a slalom course.

Reznick checked his speedometer, which was showing 108mph. "They're doing a hundred and ten, easy!" he shouted into the microphone, unable to know if his voice would be heard in the wind.

"We hear you, Jon. Be careful, I repeat, be careful. This is a dangerous stretch of road. Brookeville Boulevard. It's known as Snake Road. Hang back if need be."

Reznick smelled salt water on his face as he stormed onto Rockaway Boulevard. He was starting to make a mental calculation. He was now within yards of the Nissan, which was careering wildly, round a narrow bend and then another. He was aware they were close to water. Salt marshes.

Suddenly, the barrel of a rifle was smashed through a rear window and pointed straight at him. He swerved and a shot rang out. The bullet ricocheted off the chrome on his bike.

It has to be now.

He pulled out his gun and with his right hand controlled the bike at full speed. A quick switch to his firing hand. And he took aim and fired three shots at the Nissan's rear left tire. The tire exploded, sparks flying as the rubber was chewed up at high speed.

He crouched down low on the bike's gas tank, fearing another bullet.

The Nissan flipped violently through the air and off the road, disappearing into the darkness and crashing into the water.

Reznick screeched to a halt and ditched the bike. He sprinted across the road toward the water, gun in hand. The smell of gasoline wafting across the dark salt marshes. The light from the moon showed that the car was maybe thirty yards out and nearly totally submerged in water, twisted onto its side. He waded into the dark water, chest deep. But still, the car was maybe ten yards away from him.

A car pulled up behind him and three Feds ran towards him.

"The car is in the water!"

A split second later, police sirens and lights from a chopper swooping in low.

He turned and faced them. "They're all in the car. No one got out. We need to get them out."

The cop waded in and pulled Reznick back to shore. "Stay back, sir."

Reznick watched as the cops formed themselves into a chain and, using the lights of their cars for illumination, waded into the water and searched in and around the waters for nearly a quarter of an hour.

The minutes ticked by. Fire crews pulled up. Slowly, they began to drag out the bodies, trapped underwater in the locked car.

Three bodies were taken from the water and laid out, side by side. Three men, and Kendrick wasn't any of them.

Reznick said, "There's one more. There's one missing."

One of the cops turned round, shaking his head. "There's no one else, buddy."

"I'm telling you, there is one more! I saw three in the back, one driving. There's four!"

"He ain't here."

Slowly, it began to dawn on Reznick. Kendrick had escaped.

"Goddamn, there's one more guy."

But as the minutes passed by, no other body was found.

EPILOGUE

When the pale orange dawn peeked over the horizon, NYPD underwater divers were scouring the marshy waters on the periphery of JFK as they searched for any other bodies. Reznick had changed into fresh clothes and was in an FBI operations truck with Meyerstein.

She stared out of the window. "How the hell could he have gotten away?"

Reznick said nothing.

"The only goddamned one."

Reznick shook his head. "The others were his cover. He had the training to survive virtually anything, even with gunshot wounds. We know that."

"Shit."

Reznick felt the exhaustion wash over him. "Means he's still out there. You reckon the airport was where they were headed?"

Meyerstein nodded. "The FBI has impounded a private jet registered in the Caymans to, get this... a Chechen warlord."

Reznick shook his head. "Classic false flag. How convenient."

Meyerstein said nothing.

"This was a false flag from the get-go."

She sighed. "I've said enough."

Reznick stared at her and saw the anger in her eyes. "So, what now?"

"People need to know what really happened. I don't believe for a minute that General Black and Kendrick were the only ones involved. This goes way deeper."

A silence opened up between them for a few moments. Reznick spoke first. "What a mess."

Meyerstein nodded. "There's going to be a Senate Intelligence hearing. It'll be a closed session. You will be asked to appear."

Reznick sighed. "We were played. From the outset."

"The talk on Fox is of an Islamist plot. Same with CNN. The CIA and the Pentagon."

Reznick sighed. "Like I said, this is more than Black and Kendrick."

Meyerstein stared at him, eyes dead.

"Let's go for a walk."

They headed outside and walked along the Jamaica Bay shoreline, the sound of planes landing nearby at JFK, birds in flight, the Manhattan skyline in the distance.

Reznick said, "You know what's really going to happen, don't you? Are you prepared for what awaits you?"

Meyerstein shrugged. "What are you talking about?"

"Here's how it's going to work. If you put your head above the parapet, you're going to be made out as a loose cannon. Oddball. They're going to isolate you. And then the media will be fed stories about you."

Meyerstein ran a hand through her hair. "Listen..."

"Meyerstein, I'm going to spell this out for you. There are two ways to destroy a person."

"What do you mean?"

"You can either put a bullet through their head, or there's something more elegant. You neutralize that person by dredging up their private life. Make you out to be an unfit mother. They'll leak stories about you having a breakdown not that long ago. Having affairs. Being unpatriotic. That's always the killer."

"Jon, that's not going to happen..."

"Isn't it? Listen to me, that's what awaits you if you speak out. That's what awaits me if I speak out. This goes way beyond General Black. This is worse than Operation Northwoods. This made it off the planning boards at the CIA. Soon, in a matter of days, there will be foreign intelligence agencies friendly to the US pointing the finger at whatever regime we don't like. That's how it works. That's how it's always worked."

Meyerstein knew he was right. "My father was a lawyer. A very good lawyer. And he always stressed to me that there were two kinds of people in the world. Those that bent with the wind. And those that stood firm."

"And where do you stand?"

She turned and smiled. "I've spent a lifetime in people's faces. I'm not about to turn the other cheek now, Jon."

Reznick nodded. "We understand what went on. It's important America learns from this. We need to root out this cancer. But bear in mind they're going to try to bury you first."

Meyerstein's throat tightened. "Well, they better bring a mighty big shovel. Because I'm ready for them." For a few moments, her gaze lingered on the sparkling waters before she looked up at a vapor trail from a huge plane leaving JFK. "What about you?"

Reznick looked at her. She seemed vulnerable and alone. "What about me?"

"How are you going to deal with this?"

"The way I always have. I tell them straight. They don't like it, that's their business. I'm going to stand beside you and tell it like it is. Like I said before, I don't do walking away."

Meyerstein looked at him long and hard. She smiled and her face softened. "You saw this earlier than anyone. You did not yield."

"Never."

"Why is that, Jon?"

"It's in the blood. It's the way I am. It's the way my mother was. It's the way my father was. We do not yield."

"Amen to that."

They stood together and stared out over the water as a new day dawned.

ACKNOWLEDGMENTS

I would like to thank the follow people:

Many thanks to my editor, Bryon Quertermous, and everyone at Exhibit A Books for all their hard work, enthusiasm, and belief in the Jon Reznick books. Also, thanks to Sam Copeland in London.

Special mention has to go to the FBI's Angela D Bell and Jonathan B Zeitlin in the Bureau's Washington DC headquarters, who assisted my numerous queries with impeccable professionalism.

I would also like to thank my family and friends for all their support and encouragement. But most of all to my wife, Susan, who read over an early draft of *Hard Kill*, offering terrific advice with good grace and infinite patience.

ABOUT THE AUTHOR

JB Turner has been a journalist whose articles have appeared in UK newspapers including the *Daily Mail*, the *Daily Telegraph*, the *Scotsman*, the *Daily Express* and the *Herald*. He worked as a freelance journalist for several years before he began work on his first novel. JB Turner is married and has two young children

jbturnerauthor.com
twitter.com/jbturnerauthor

"I just added Farrell and Kearns to my
short-list of favourite characters."
Matt Hilton, bestselling author of the
Joe Hunter series

Author of
WOUNDED
PREY

SEAN
LYNCH

THE
FOURTH
MOTIVE

A Farrell and Kearns thriller